Thom Racina's riveting novels

Never Forget

"Racina . . . has a deft ear for dialogue."
—*Publishers Weekly*

"[*Never Forget*] succeeds admirably . . . a novel that will not be forgotten by readers."
—*Midwest Book Review*

The Madman's Diary

"Fast-paced momentum . . . crisp dialogue and quirky characters."   —*Publishers Weekly*

"Takes off at a rapid clip and never eases off the throttle. *The Madman's Diary* is an exciting thriller with an unexpected ending that begs for a sequel."
—BookBrowser

Secret Weekend

"*Secret Weekend* starts as a breezy read that quickly turns into a pulse-pounding suspense thriller. . . . Thom Racina has written an exciting winner."
—*Midwest Book Review*

continued . . .

Hidden Agenda

"A fast-paced thriller . . . a smart, up-to-date read."
—*The San Francisco Examiner*

"Colorful . . . fiendish . . . good entertainment . . . could be a heck of a movie." —*Publishers Weekly*

"A timely story . . . filled with recognizable people."
—*Library Journal*

"A wild romp through my news terrain . . . I had a great time with it!" —Kelly Lange, NBC news anchor and author of *Trophy Wife*

"*Hidden Agenda* is a thrilling and savvy ride through the worlds of broadcasting, politics, and religion. Real names make it feel chillingly nonfictional, and the ending is a triumph of integrity over hypocrisy. It's unique, and I was spellbound."

—Sally Sussman, head writer, *Days of Our Lives*

"The power of television news taken to its logical extreme. Thom Racina's ingenious story gives the reader a peek into the media's well-hidden backstage." —Bill O'Reilly, anchorman, Fox News, author of *Those Who Trespass*

"One of the great what-if? stories of the last five years. Racina has done it again, kept me awake for twenty-four hours straight."

—Bill Hersey, writer/producer PBS, NBC

"Great read, wonderful characters and plot, boffo finish. . . . I loved this book."

—Bob Healy, The Music Network

Snow Angel

"Chilling suspense."   —Judith Gould

"Fast-moving. . . . Racina spins a highly cinematic tale set against dramatic backdrops . . . a memorable villain who generates considerable suspense."

—*Publishers Weekly*

"A chilling cliff-hanger chase."   —*Booklist*

"A tale of obsessive love run nastily amok."

—*Kirkus Reviews*

"Powerful, compelling . . . a highly charged thriller with a surprise ending."   —*Tulsa World*

Also by Thom Racina

Snow Angel
Hidden Agenda
Secret Weekend
The Madman's Diary
Never Forget

DEADLY GAMES

Thom Racina

For
Amelia
& Ian —
Play the
game!

Thom R

A SIGNET BOOK

SIGNET
Published by New American Library, a division of
Penguin Group (USA) Inc., 375 Hudson Street,
New York, New York 10014, U.S.A.
Penguin Books Ltd, 80 Strand,
London WC2R 0RL, England
Penguin Books Australia Ltd, 250 Camberwell Road,
Camberwell, Victoria 3124, Australia
Penguin Books Canada Ltd, 10 Alcorn Avenue,
Toronto, Ontario, Canada M4V 3B2
Penguin Books (N.Z.) Ltd, Cnr Rosedale and Airborne Roads,
Albany, Auckland 1310, New Zealand

Penguin Books Ltd, Registered Offices:
80 Strand, London WC2R 0RL, England

First published by Signet, an imprint of New American Library,
a division of Penguin Group (USA) Inc.

First Printing, December 2003
10 9 8 7 6 5 4 3 2 1

PUBLISHER'S NOTE
This is a work of fiction. Names, characters, places, and incidents either are
the product of the author's imagination or are used fictitiously, and any
resemblance to actual persons, living or dead, business establishments,
events, or locales is entirely coincidental.

For Laurence Ling,
who said the magic words
one night at dinner at the Haunted Ink Bottle

My deepest gratitude to: my editor at NAL, Genny Ostertag, who shaped the manuscript into the book it is today; Kara Welsh, Claire Zion, Leslie Gelbman, and dear Rebecca Crowley (all that enthusiasm!) at NAL; Jane Dystel, the best agent in the business (even though I drive her crazy) and the gang at Dystel & Goderich Literary Management; Alicia Maris for making my mug look better in pictures than in real life; my second family in Wilton, Connecticut, for your creative support (and all those good meals); Connie Roderick, for plowing through the unedited pages and bringing Laurence into my life; Karen and Marty Kurzer for getting the ball rolling; Robin and Rosie and all the kids at Celebrity Books in Palm Springs for their endless enthusiasm (and that swell birthday cake), let's do the street fair forever; Jim from Michigan, my Palm Springs VillageFest cheerleader; Kelly Lange, my talented (and gorgeous) partner in crime; Friday Endings, for being so good to me; and Mark Larson, for illuminating evils that lurk beneath the surface (writers learn from these things) and for instigating "the chip" idea way back when—its success is the definition of poetic justice.

Prologue

Kirkwood, Missouri

Loretta Seianas couldn't eat. She maneuvered the slice of roast beef from one side of her plate to the other, then rearranged the mashed potatoes. She could manage only a sip of her iced tea, and picked at one of the Pillsbury Crescent rolls. When her father urged her to put some food into her mouth, her mother told him to let her be. "She's nervous. Confirmation is very important to these kids."

Having been raised in a strict Roman Catholic home, the sacrament of confirmation promised to renew her faith at a time—the problematic teenage years—when it surely would be tested. Since her first day in school, Loretta had been instructed by nuns, priests, and Catholic lay teachers to be guided by the Church. Today was a day she—and her parents—had looked forward to for a very long time.

After lunch, she put on the simple white dress she and her mother had picked out for the ceremony. Her mother fussed with her hair, adding a sprig of lilies of the valley. It complemented the dress well and appeared almost fairylike in her auburn curls. Loretta, her mother was sure, would be the most beautiful of God's soldiers that afternoon.

"Time to go, girls," her father called. As he went to the garage to back out the freshly washed station wagon for the trip to Our Lady Queen of Angels, Loretta brushed her teeth one more time and sprayed a mist of Bonne Bell cologne onto her budding bosom. Then she lifted the corner of her mattress with one hand while the other reached far under it. Feeling the gun that she had taken from her father's army footlocker in the basement, she pulled it from its hiding place. Eyeing it impassively, she unhooked the safety and slid it into the small white shoulder bag she and her mother had picked out to accessorize the dress. Then, smiling and eager, she joined her parents in the car.

At the church, the congregation was buzzing. It wasn't often a cardinal came to Queen of Angels. No prince of the Church had visited Kirkwood for twenty-four years, the pastor had excitedly reminded the gathered faithful the previous Sunday. That Cardinal Eric Meeks had chosen to visit this small parish was proof that this shepherd "reached all the flock." Today he would confirm thirty-three congregants. Loretta Seianas would be number twenty-two.

As the moment approached, Loretta's father moved to the front of the center aisle to capture every moment on digital video. Her mother proudly beamed as she gazed at her little angel watching the cardinal bestow the sacrament on the girl beside her. To either side of him, two attending priests, the monsignor and the assistant pastor she'd known since grade school, paid no attention to Loretta. Their concentration was on the cardinal and the girl he was confirming. Thus, no one saw Loretta reach into her little white purse, except her mother, who thought she was reaching for a tissue.

When the three men moved into place in front of Loretta, she made eye contact first with the pastor, the old monsignor. He smiled and nodded happily. Her father got a close-up. Then she looked up at the assistant pastor, the younger, athletic man with whom she played baseball on Saturdays and chatted at the recent dance in the school gym. When her eyes focused on the cardinal, she withdrew her right hand from her bag. She brought the gun up quickly in her clenched fingers and shot the man through the white vestments covering his chest.

At the sound, everyone thought, *What was that?* As Cardinal Meeks' body froze—for what seemed forever, as if in slow motion on Loretta's father's camera—she got off another shot into the monsignor's heart. She would have shot the assistant pastor as well if a fast-thinking altar boy hadn't lunged for her. Horrified screams began to echo off the walls of the church.

Loretta was knocked to the marble floor. Before anyone could grab her, she drew the pistol up under her chin. Just as the altar boy threw himself on her, she pulled the trigger a final time, sending the bullet up through the roof of her mouth, blowing a hole out the top of her head. The final image on her father's video—he was paralyzed, not believing what he was seeing, not even realizing he was still taping—was of his daughter lying there, her white dress stained with the blood of three people.

Loretta Seianas was twelve years old.

Chapter One

The ugly secret came out on their honeymoon.

Until that moment it was everything a new bride could hope it would be. They were staying at the Villa del Sol, an elegant resort in the enchanting Mexican coastal town of Zihuatanejo. Tyler and Quinn made love under the stars on the beach, went diving with a group of kids from California who couldn't believe they were spending the day with the "Game King," as one of them called Tyler, and drank more margaritas than they ever dreamed they could consume. One evening, after a delicious dinner of grilled fresh red snapper, they walked hand in hand along the beach. Finally, they sat together in the sand, looking at the moon over the water. Tyler ran his hand through Quinn's auburn hair and said, "The moonlight makes your eyes look greener. And more beautiful than ever." He was rewarded with a passionate kiss.

As Quinn pulled back, she gazed at her new husband. On one level, he was the slick embodiment of success, and yet he also seemed casually hip and mischievous. He had a goofy grin—like a kid, almost lopsided—that set off his near-perfect features. His hair was curly and brown, graying just slightly at the temples, his ears were large, his chin firm, his lips full. As they'd dated, she guessed he was the kind of guy who probably had to shave twice a day. She was now going to find out. This was for keeps.

They talked about where they were going to live. "The New York place will easily accommodate both of us," Tyler said, "even the three of us, if Joanie comes up for Christmas break." Quinn's daughter was in her first year of college in Williamsburg. "But what should we do about D.C.? It's crazy for us to keep two places there. I'll sell the house if you'd rather hold on to the Virginia condo."

"I think I like the house better," Quinn said.

"Really?"

"There's only a few things I can't live without, and they'll fit in your house perfectly," she explained. "I've never been wedded to things. They don't have much meaning for me. It's what's inside that you take with you. Furniture you can leave behind."

She took a deep breath and curled up again in his arms. "You know, I feared I would never find love again."

"At least you had it once before," he replied, taking her hand. He bent forward and kissed her lips lightly. "I didn't know what it was like until I met you."

She gave him a teasing smile. "Waited thirty-six years for me, huh?"

He smiled right back. "Don't remind me."

A piercing voice cut through the magic. *"Oh, there they are!"*

Quinn and Tyler both turned to see where the voice had come from. An overweight woman wearing a floppy Mexican sombrero was dragging a younger man toward them from the patio above. "Oh, dear," Quinn said.

"Who the hell are they?" Tyler wondered.

"I think people from dinner."

As the couple came closer, the woman gleefully sang, "It's them! I told you, Ben, I told you it was them." She stopped before them. "You're the famous Tyler Bryant, aren't you? From Zzzyx." She pronounced it "Zizz-zix."

"Zee-zix is the way to say it," Tyler corrected her.

"Just what I said." The woman was bubbling. "And Quinn Roberts!"

Quinn corrected her. "Quinn Roberts Bryant, as of a few days ago."

"I'm Honey Kandora, and this is my son, Ben. He's addicted to Practice Run."

The megapopular computer game had swept the market since the day it was introduced almost three years earlier.

"Incredibly cool game," Ben piped up, "but I can't seem to get to be a Front Runner."

"I sometimes wonder if I could," Tyler said, smiling.

"Man," Ben said, "you created it. What do you mean?"

"It's easier to create it than play it." Tyler reached up to shake the teenager's hand. "Howdy."

"Hi."

The mother crouched down on her knees in the sand. "We were sitting there at dinner and I kept saying to Stanley—that's my husband, he went to bed— I said, 'Stanley, that's Tyler Bryant and his new bride over there. I'm sure of it. I read about them in *People* last week.' Getting married in Costco was wild."

Tyler said, "Probably didn't hurt their business any."

Quinn explained, "It's where we met."

Ben added, "So I said, 'Ma, wait a minute, we can't follow them down to the beach and interrupt them. They're on their honeymoon. They came here to get away from people like us.'"

Quinn was diplomatic. "Yes, we did, but it's really nice of you to wish us well."

Honey pulled an autograph book from her bag. "Well, congratulations, and best wishes for a long and happy life together. Will you both sign?"

As they did, the woman told Quinn, "I read about the wonderful work you do. God bless you."

"Thank you."

Ben said, "Hey, Mr. Bryant, when's the new version being released?"

"Not till next Easter," Tyler told him. "Still working the bugs out."

The teenager pointed at him, smiling. "I'll be first in line."

Tyler put his arm around Quinn in a signal that it was time for the fans to leave them alone. They took the hint. "See you at breakfast," the woman called as they departed.

"We're eating in the room tomorrow morning," Tyler whispered to Quinn as he pulled her tight.

"Lunch and dinner too," she added, and then felt his lips drown out any more words she might have been planning to add.

But they were not yet alone. "Oh, Tyler," Honey called back to them, "Stanley and I were wondering at dinner. Did your poor brother ever get out of jail?"

Quinn stiffened. Brother? Jail? She pulled out of his arms.

"No," he said to the woman, "he's still there."

"Hey, Mom," the boy said with a gentle nudge, "I think maybe we should let these people enjoy their evening." He waved to Tyler. "Great meeting you, man. I mean, whoa."

When the two disappeared, the romantic mood was destroyed. Quinn looked at him questioningly. Tyler got up and walked down to the water's edge. He kicked at the sand a bit, shrugged, and then strolled to some boulders being spattered by the light surf. He sat on one and waited.

Finally, her feeling of betrayal giving way to curiosity, Quinn walked up behind him. Sensing her presence, without taking his eyes from the moon over the water, Tyler said, "His name is Drew."

"You never mentioned any brother." Quinn's voice was caught in her throat. "In all this time, from the day we met, you never told me you had a brother."

"Half brother, actually. Different fathers."

"And he's in jail?"

He sounded ashamed. "Drew is in a federal penitentiary."

The word startled her. "Penitentiary? Prison?" That explained why he wanted to keep the embarrassment of a half brother a secret. She found herself almost relieved.

"My old man died when I was seven," he went on. "Three years later, Drew was born. He's ten years younger than I am, so we were never very close. I mean, we really didn't grow up like brothers."

She sat on the next rock over, brought her legs up, and clasped her ankles. "So what happened?"

"We are alike in one way: He's a computer geek. A genius, but the kind who can't put on the same color socks in the morning, you know?"

"He had a job?"

Tyler nodded. "Software company near Seattle. He headed out there and joined up with some other freaks like him. The next thing I heard, he'd been arrested for hacking."

"Hacking?"

"Into the Pentagon."

She turned to him. "That's why the woman read about him?"

Tyler nodded. "I did everything I could to help him, pulled strings, but there was nothing I could do. It was a serious crime." He kicked an incoming wave, sending up a light spray. "Damn, the kid is brilliant. He could have used that talent for something positive."

"He could have worked with you."

Tyler nodded sadly. "His trial started early in September 2001, and we thought we had a good defense, but then came 9/11 and he was cooked. He got twenty years."

"My God."

"Even Kevin Mitnick, the greatest hacker of all

time, only got five. Drew became a scapegoat." He turned to her, looked into her eyes. "You see why I don't talk about it?"

She understood. It was his only brother. She knew that Tyler had stopped speaking to his mother, who was an alcoholic, years before. His father was dead. Drew was his only family, and he was behind bars. She was upset that he had not shared the story with her before, but she could now feel how deeply this loss pained him, and she suddenly realized how important her love was to him. "Do you see Drew at all?"

He shook his head. "He won't have anything to do with me."

"Why?"

"He believes I could have done more to get him off the charges, or maybe have his sentence reduced."

"How long has he been in prison?"

"Well, with the jail time before the trial, over three years now."

She blinked, trying to remember the case. "You had different fathers. What is his last name?"

"Concardi."

It rang a vague bell. "Somewhere in the cobweb-ridden recesses of my mind, I think I recall hearing something about it."

"It was big news, but it got lost in the fallout of 9/11. When he was first arrested, I wasn't quite as successful as I am now. But if you go on-line and look up the *New York Times* articles about the case, you'll see it. '*Up-and-coming video game czar*,' I think they called me."

"Did Brandon know him?" Brandon DiForio was

Tyler's closest friend. He had flown in from Kansas City for the wedding.

"No."

"Didn't you grow up together?"

"Brandon was my college bud."

She blinked. "I thought he said something about when you were kids."

Tyler looked uncomfortable. "Yeah, we were kids when we went to college."

She laughed, thinking, *Let it be.* But it felt uncomfortable for her too.

"I don't have any lifelong relationships like you have with Susan." He had met her dearest friend and business partner, Susan Horgan, at the wedding as well, and was charmed by her and her husband, Patrick. "I envy you." He looked wistful. "We went camping together one summer when Brandon and I were in college, before Drew went out to Seattle. Just the three guys." He laughed. "Drew was a disaster. He couldn't catch a fish, couldn't tie down a pole. It was a riot. He just kept worrying his laptop batteries were going to die." He shook his head. "I miss him, though. I wish we had been able to get closer growing up. Then maybe life might have taken a different road."

That struck a strong chord with her. "I always say I wish I had done this or that with my mom and dad, or that I had told them that." Her parents had been killed by a drunk driver on a Maryland highway one Sunday afternoon. "All these regrets."

He seemed to understand. "You feel completely abandoned, totally alone."

"In a way, you were. I was too. My husband left

me. My parents died. Your dad did the same, you lost your mom to booze, your brother to prison. It's a wonder you're still standing."

"You got me walking again," he said softly.

She put her arm around him. Having been an only child, she had desperately wanted a brother or sister. She wished she'd been able to give Joanie a brother or sister. What must it feel like, she wondered, to have that gift and then lose him to prison? She couldn't imagine how she would cope with that.

But enough gloom. They were on their honeymoon, after all. She took his hand and pulled him off the rock. They walked up the beach, back toward the resort. "Hey," she said, "I forgot to tell you. I got an E-mail message from Susan at the office earlier. Sony just started selling a new Vaio desktop model, so we get two thousand of their old computers. They're destined for South America. Wanna fill them with games?"

He smiled again. "You never quit, do you?" She'd been hounding him for years to donate his games to put in the computers of the foundation she headed, the Foundation for Education. They gave away computers to kids all over the globe.

"Games make a computer so much less daunting to a third world child who has never used one before. When they can have fun with it, when they can enter a fantasy world, they won't be afraid to use it for learning."

"Honey, Zzzyx is yours as well now. You can decide how many copies you want and just call Ronnie yourself."

"Ronnie?"

"Veronica Ashton. My assistant."

Quinn had met her at the wedding. "Just didn't equate Ronnie with Veronica." She didn't tell him she found the woman cold and distant. "Is Practice Run available in Spanish?"

He pulled her into his arms. "Hell, yes. Chinese, Japanese, French—you name it. That way the world will be chomping at the bit for number five. And we, my darling, make another fortune."

They had reached the sweeping patio off the beautiful dining room of the resort. She glanced around at the place, the lush romantic setting that his wealth had provided, and said, "Since I've never made a fortune in my life, I won't argue with that."

They had met at the Arlington, Virginia, Costco, of all places. While her daughter, Joan, was perusing the music CDs, Quinn picked up Kelly Lange's newest Maxi Poole mystery and pushed her cart over to the vast games table. They were all there: The Sims, The Matrix, Counter-Strike. Quinn knew them well. She had managed to package some of them—Ultima Online, Medal of Honor, and Collapse!—in the computers that the foundation gave away. But at the top of the heap was Practice Run. Quinn wanted it. Badly. For it was the only computer game that she knew of that actually encouraged kids to read. She'd worked tirelessly to convince the jerk who had created it to donate copies so she could include them on the free computers. No go. She figured he was just too cheap.

She turned the box over. It looked enticing. A blend of RPG, Role Playing Games, and ISG, Intelligent Strategy Games, it was the perfect challenge for skill and concentration. Her own teenage daughter had bought one of the first editions. What Quinn liked about it was that once a player reached a certain level, he or she had to read long text passages to be able to go on to the next level. And you had to retain what you read, you had to remember the clues, because it became pertinent in the challenge of the upcoming strategy. If you didn't recall what you read, you were slammed back to beginner status and had to start all over again. It forced kids to read with comprehension. *Not a bad marketing ploy,* Quinn thought with a degree of irony, *aimed directly at parents, who had the deep pockets.* It was the most expensive game of its kind.

"I'd hold out for the new version if I were you," a voice said. "Practice Run V will be out next Easter."

She blinked, looked around. Had the voice been directed toward her?

"It's gonna rock."

Her eyes found him. The man who was indeed speaking to her. Tyler Bryant himself. The creator of the game, with a strong jaw and an earring in his right lobe. Standing on the other side of the vast table, facing her. He had recognized her. "Well, I'll be," she said.

She wanted to smile, but she didn't dare. She didn't like him, she had to remind herself. She'd never met him in person, but knew his face from countless TV appearances, newspapers, and on the Net. And she'd spoken to him on the phone each time he turned her down. She indicated the box in her hand. "Checking up on sales?"

He smiled. "Actually, shopping for mundane

stuff." He pointed to the megapackage of toilet paper in his cart.

She had the same in hers, and she couldn't help but smile.

"You live around here?"

He shook his head. "New York, mainly, but since our plant is in Rockville, I have a house in D.C. as well. This is the closest Costco."

Quinn's daughter walked up clutching three CDs and a huge box of Corn Flakes. "Hi."

"Hi," he said. "I'm Tyler Bryant."

She blinked. "Oh, cool! I'm Joan Roberts. I love Practice Run. I play it all the time."

"A girl after my interactive heart." He flashed his big green eyes and pulled on the lobe that held the earring.

"You're great," the girl bubbled.

Quinn rolled her eyes. "Generous too. He's sold about a hundred million copies of his games and still won't donate any to kids whose parents can't afford to buy them."

"Never say never," Tyler warned.

Quinn laughed. "Oh, like there's hope?"

He winked. "Things could change now that we know one another. Let's have a drink together some time."

She was incredulous. "A drink? *Us?*"

"Mom," Joanie urged softly, "say yes."

"Some other time," Quinn replied to Tyler, and pushed their cart away.

"Mom," Joanie said, "why'd you say no? He's cute."

"He's an arrogant creep. Come on, we're out of laundry soap."

That was before he started on his concerted campaign to change her mind.

They returned to D.C. from their honeymoon one day earlier than planned to be interviewed for a piece in *Barron's*, posing for photos with a beaming Joanie. The girl loved having the famous Tyler Bryant as her stepfather. She was also glad they were putting their apartment on the market because Fifteenth Street, where Tyler's house was, was so much more youthful, alive, and colorful. Everyone Joanie's age lived in the District—if they could afford it. She only hoped they'd make the move before she had to go back to William and Mary for her second semester.

Tyler owned a three-story row house in the middle of a block that had been built for the working class who served the rich mansions around nearby Dupont Circle. The top floor was taken up by a sumptuous master suite, comfortable guest room, and bath. The middle floor featured a living room filled with antiques and a book-lined library. The lower floor had an intimate but charming dining room and a sleek, stainless steel kitchen–cum–family room with a wall of French doors opening onto a two-level stone patio and a garden shaded by six delicate ginkgo trees. It was the opposite of what Quinn pictured a video game king living in.

The next afternoon, while Tyler was working at his manufacturing plant in Rockville, Maryland, Quinn and Joan packed up the kitchen stuff they had decided to take with them, sharing a pizza from

Coppi's, a place around the corner, when they took a break. They'd been wrapping dishes in sheets of that morning's *Washington Post*, and as they ate, Joanie stopped at an article that caught her eye. "Mom, look at this."

Quinn scanned a story about a Baltimore teenager who had inexplicably set fire to a Methodist church after running over and killing the pastor with the family car in the church parking lot. The girl, Mary Doyle, who had been an honor student, the article said, sat catatonic amidst the flames leaping into the sky, immolating herself before the firemen could rescue her and the police could take her into custody. The pastor of the church had been a good family friend, her parents asserted, their daughter had never been in trouble before, and they were unwilling to believe that the charges against her were valid. "Even though it was our Buick that killed the reverend, we firmly believe our little girl was not driving it," they commented.

But an eyewitness said he saw the girl deliberately aim the car at the man as he returned from walking the parish mascot, a dog named Luke, who wasn't hurt. The witness also said that as he called the police from his cell phone, he saw the girl take a can of gasoline from the trunk of the car and pour it on the doors of the church, and on her clothes, and then set herself on fire. Police were investigating.

"It sounds like that other case a few months back," Joanie said.

"The girl who shot the cardinal?" Quinn said.

"Yeah, it's weird," Joanie said, wrapping the paper around a dinner plate.

After driving to the Fifteenth Street house, they started to unpack the dishes they'd wrapped. "I really like this house," Joanie said. "It's comfortable."

Quinn agreed. "He brought me here for a drink the night of the symposium. I thought the same thing."

Joan giggled. "To think you almost turned that down."

Quinn smiled. "Fate is unpredictable sometimes." The night after meeting in Costco, she was surprised to find that Tyler was one of the participants in a symposium on education that she was moderating at the Folger Shakespeare Library theater. In front of hundreds of people, he challenged Bill Gates and Carly Fiorina to donate more hardware and software than they'd ever done before, matching them with copies of Practice Run. When it was over, an astonished Quinn went over to thank him. "You owe me a drink, lady," he'd said, winking.

"Were you attracted to him from the start, Mom? Come on, tell the truth."

"I don't know, maybe. I was so overwhelmed that he'd suddenly become so generous that I probably was on a cloud. I mean, he donated twenty thousand copies of the game."

"You didn't come home that night."

Quinn turned purple. "Will you please not remind me."

"Oh, I thought it was cool. I liked him from the start!" Joanie was about to stack some of the dishes in a cabinet, but stopped. "Mom, there's stuff in here."

When Quinn saw that several of the kitchen cabinets were filled with filing boxes, she recalled Tyler saying he planned to take them to his apartment in New York. "Just put them in a big carton and I'll deal with it later," he had told his wife. So they cleared out the cabinets and Joanie began to refill them with dishes and glassware.

Quinn went upstairs to rearrange the closets in the master bedroom. She left untouched the one filled with Tyler's clothes—she'd never seen such a mix of Prada and Gap. The other one, which was to be hers, resembled a storage shed, she discovered to her dismay. She pulled a vacuum cleaner from it and properly stowed it in the broom closet off the kitchen. Files that looked important she took down to the library and set on his big desk. When she lifted out several pairs of shoes that she wasn't sure he still wanted—some Docs and old, worn sneakers—she found a flat tin canister under them. As she lifted it with one hand, it slipped from her grasp and hit the floor, causing the lid to pop off. Inside were several photographs.

She bent down to take a closer look. There was Tyler at about age ten, standing proudly next to a crib holding a crying baby. Tyler again at about seventeen—God, he was cute!—with a seven-year-old watching him with what looked like adoring eyes. Drew Concardi, the secret brother, she guessed. An oversized shot captured the two boys together at a miniature golf course. There were several of Drew alone, hair getting longer and longer as he got older, one of him hunched over a keyboard, looking completely unaware that his photo was being taken. Another in a basketball uniform that looked like it was going to fall off his skinny body.

Under the photos was a newspaper article about his sentencing. Quinn read it, fascinated. It brought back some of the details of the case, underlying the enormity of what he'd done. Under that were other clippings, but these were recent. Peering at them more closely, Quinn was shocked by their subject matter. They covered the teenager murders she and Joanie had just been talking about at lunch.

She found the same *Washington Post* story that they'd read: Mary Doyle in Baltimore, setting a church on fire. One covered the girl who shot Cardinal Meeks. Another featured the murder of a Congregational minister by a teen named Christina Proctor, while visiting Nova Scotia. She, like the others, had killed herself.

She remembered the odd conversation she and Tyler had had about where to get married. "Not in a church," he had said firmly.

"But I'm Catholic," Quinn explained.

"I don't care. You won't get me into a church. Any church. Ever."

Quinn was surprised. It was the one issue they hadn't discussed. Oh, she'd told him she had been born and raised Catholic and that her faith meant a lot to her. It had gotten her through the loss of her parents in a car crash. He'd said he was "nothing." And that was that.

"Why do you have such an aversion to churches?"

He gave her a look as if she didn't understand.

She didn't. "Tyler, it's the way I was brought up. I won't feel married unless it's blessed by the Church. You don't need to convert. You don't need to do anything. It's common now that non-Catholics—"

"You don't get it."

His sharp voice stunned her. She blinked. "Get what?"

"Religion is the biggest scourge ever to be inflicted on this planet."

Shocked, she stared at him. She could see he meant it. "What?"

"Most atrocities since the beginning of time have been committed in the name of God."

She thought through his assertion. "Well, that isn't really true."

"I said most."

There were certainly enough examples in history. The Crusades. The Inquisition. Muslims and Hindus slaughtering one another. More recently, the Protestants and Catholics in Ireland. Peaceful Bali being bombed by Islamic extremists. She saw his point. "I understand what you mean. But you can't condemn all religion because of that."

"I'm an atheist."

She smiled, trying to joke a little. "Hey, we don't have to tell the priest that."

A mask of pain and anger descended over Tyler's face. "You still don't understand."

She was clueless. "Understand what?"

His body tensed. "Don't ever expect me to set foot in a church, anywhere. Ever."

Thinking back on that conversation, Quinn wondered why in the world Tyler had collected these news articles. Had they interested him because of his revulsion for religion? That was the only possible explanation that she could come up with. Sure, that was it. He didn't approve of such behavior, but he probably related to it with his atheistic stance that religion was the root of evil. That *had* to be it.

But that didn't answer one more question. Why had he hidden the news clippings and photos in a storage closet in his bedroom?

New York City

Herman Goldstein, studying hard and long in the yeshiva, came to adore one favorite teacher, Abraham Nussbaum. The old man enthralled all the boys who studied under him.

Herman had described the rabbi to his parents as "a man of peace, a man of God, and very cool." But a practical man as well, as the rabbi himself pointed out many times. "I have to go now," the old man would joke to the boys after a lesson, "not to pray but to buy gifts for my wife so she'll feed me brisket tonight without kvetching so much about her day."

So Herman Goldstein was thrilled when Rabbi Abraham Nussbaum entered his uncle's shop on Forty-seventh Street. "Rebbe!" the boy exclaimed.

The old, bearded man blinked through thick glasses. "Hermie?"

"Yes, rabbi."

"What are you doing here?"

The boy wiped his hands—he'd been polishing gold—and offered his hand in a manly gesture. "This is my uncle's shop, sir. May I welcome you?"

"I thought you worked in a sausage shop," the rabbi said.

"That's my brother."

"Yes, well."

The enthusiastic boy called through the curtain into the back room. "Uncle! Uncle, come!"

A middle-aged man sporting a white beard like the rabbi's appeared. "A customer? Let Shelly handle it."

"Sheldon went to lunch. Uncle, I want you to meet Rabbi Nussbaum. He is the great teacher I have told you about."

"Ah, yes, of course," the uncle said. "Shalom."

"It's an honor to have you in our shop, sir," the boy said.

"You are, maybe, checking up on him, rabbi?" the uncle asked. "He's not doing his homework?"

The rabbi pulled on his beard. "I'm looking for a bracelet. For the right price, of course."

"A deal you can stay in Brooklyn for," the uncle said. "Quality you find here."

"Then show me quality at a good price for my darling Goldie."

The uncle showed him several bracelets at different price points. They dickered, the uncle showed him some more, they argued, the rabbi threatened to go across the street, the uncle spit on the floor to emphasize that the owners of the shop across the street were crooks, and when they finally decided on a nice gold one, the uncle warned the rabbi that he was robbing him blind and he'd have to stay open late for three weeks to make up for the loss, but the rabbi knew he was making a nice profit.

The boy brought some tea from the back room, but the rabbi declined. He wanted to catch a train before rush hour. He ventured into Manhattan as little as possible these days. "This is most certainly not," the rabbi stated emphatically, "as some of our people once thought, the promised land."

"I'll walk you to the subway," Herman suddenly said.

"You'll what?" the uncle exclaimed.

"No need, no need," the old man said. "Just have to be careful no robbers see me come out of here carrying this box."

"I'll go with you," the boy again suggested. "I'll guard you."

The uncle looked the boy up and down. He weighed a hundred pounds and stood less than five feet tall. "Some guard."

But the boy, in his hero worship of his teacher, prevailed. "Just go on home yourself, Herman," the uncle said. "Sheldon and I will close up today."

On the way to the subway, the rabbi asked the boy what he wanted to do when he grew up. "Other than wanting to be, God forbid, a rabbi."

"I want to live in Israel. I want to join the military there."

"Yes, yes, everybody has to. I have family serving right now. It's a good thing, an honorable thing." He shook his head. "But so dangerous now."

On Lexington Avenue, the rabbi stopped at the subway stairs to buy the afternoon paper and to say good-bye to the boy. "But I'm on the same train," the boy explained.

"Of course."

They swiped their Metrocards at the same moment. While they waited for the Brooklyn-bound train, the rabbi asked how he liked working for his uncle. "He's a nice man. He cheats people with a smile."

The boy saw the look on the rabbi's face. "You got a good deal."

The rabbi muttered, "Sometimes I wonder if she's worth it." He scratched his beard. "Don't marry, boy. I know that is heresy, but you might be happier in the long run. Give your life to the Torah. Have a girl-friend. But don't marry."

The boy peered out over the edge of the plat-form—something his father had always warned him against doing. When he saw the big bold headlight coming up the track, he stepped back, grasping the old man's hand. "The train is coming, Rabbi."

"So it is, so it is," the rabbi answered. He turned to face the tracks, clutching his worn black briefcase to his side. As the train approached, slowing down, the rabbi felt the boy suddenly clutch his other hand tightly. He thought perhaps the power of the train, the noise, the energy, scared the boy. But then he re-alized that Herman had grasped his hand so tightly because he wanted to guide the rabbi. But not onto the train.

As a throng of astonished people looked on help-lessly, the boy yanked the old man into the path of the oncoming train. They fell onto the tracks only seconds before the first car mangled them. Moments after the impact, you could not tell that anything had happened, except for the splash of blood that had flown up to hit a woman's skirt as the first car sped by.

Herman Goldstein was thirteen years old.

Chapter Two

Tyler couldn't get back to D.C. for a week, and Quinn found it impossible to leave work to go to New York. She called him several times from her office on Capitol Hill, and he dialed her between meetings and, after he got home, late at night. Zzzyx Games was involved in a distribution deal with Middle Eastern countries, and the negotiations had become protracted. His longtime assistant, Veronica Ashton, had worked on the deal for a very long time, but she could not close it. They wanted the right of censorship, which Tyler was refusing to give them. He himself had to step in, trying his best to assure all parties that his games would not offend their religious beliefs. They had long been popular in the more secular Israel—some hard-line Islamists called Practice Run "a Zionist plot"—and the teasers were available to any kid with a computer and a connection to Game Spot anywhere in the world. In fact, that's what had prompted the deal in the first place. Thousands of Middle Eastern kids now wanted to buy Tyler's games because they had played the on-line versions on the computers of proliferating Internet cafés.

The following Saturday, Quinn flew to New York at last. She and Tyler hated the fact that this separation had lasted almost as long as their marriage, and made up for it by making love passionately on the living room floor, under an expanse of glass that looked out over Central Park. His penthouse was atop the new AOL Time Warner building on Columbus Circle. The apartment was the epitome of a successful computer programmer's having made it big: glossy bamboo floors under walls boasting a Picasso, a Caillebotte, two Warhols, and a de Kooning, priceless Asian antiques blended with sleek granite and leather, and all the newest, cutting-edge media equipment. On Joanie's first visit at New Year's, just before she went back to college, she said she could spend the rest of her life in the place in front of the big HDTV screen with a remote in her hand, choosing from seemingly every DVD ever made and the coolest video games one could imagine—many of them prototypes for future games that hadn't even been announced.

As the sun set over New Jersey, Tyler and Quinn sat together on the leather sofa, still naked, sipping wine. As the stars appeared, the lights of Manhattan began to glimmer beneath them. When they decided they'd better eat or else turn into complete lushes, they dressed and walked to Peter's, a popular dining spot a few blocks up Broadway, where they ran into Quinn's old friends, media wiz Judy Katz and her husband, Howard. The foursome had a wonderful meal, and then caught a late movie down at the Lin-

coln Plaza Cinemas. On the way back to the penthouse, they prowled the huge Borders bookstore in
the AOL building. It was not until they were snug-
gled in bed that Quinn asked Tyler about the clippings.

She was right, he said. He had been fascinated by
the first one, the story of the girl in Missouri who had
shot a cardinal in cold blood, then had taken her own
life. It was hatred for religion taken to the extreme.
What really caught Tyler's interest, though, was that
more murders followed. Was there some kind of
backlash against religion? Were kids turning on the
teachings of their parents? He just found it curious.

She did too.

He shared another killing with her, one she hadn't
yet heard about. He'd found it on the Net earlier that
day. It had happened last night, in Wisconsin. He
showed her the printout he'd pulled from his HP
shortly before she'd arrived. It was about the Martin-
son family, who'd all died on a highway at the hands
of their teenage son, Billy. From the report she was
reading, it seemed his father had forced religion
down his throat. Nothing the boy had ever said or
done while he was alive indicated that he was dis-
pleased with his strict religious upbringing. Only
after his death did authorities find a notebook filled
with antireligious sentiments, the most lethal of
which were directed at his father.

"Even so," Tyler said, "it's not a reason to take a
life."

She shrugged. "People do crazy-ass things these
days."

"Speaking of crazy-ass things," he whispered into

her ear as he moved on top of her, "I think I wanna do it again."

On Monday morning, the doorman called Tyler to tell him that Veronica, who had been ensconced in New York all week at the W Hotel, was down front in the car. They were going to their final meeting with the representatives from the Middle East. He kissed Quinn good-bye and hurried out. She poured herself a second cup of black coffee and decided to check her E-mail. His laptop was sitting there, open, on the black granite counter. Rather than walk down the hall to his office and use the desktop as she usually did, she just tapped the touch pad and the laptop screen illuminated. She opened the program, typed in her password, and her mail appeared. The first one she read was from her daughter.

HEY, MOM, QUESTION: A BOY I LIKE ASKED ME OUT. I DON'T KNOW WHAT TO WEAR. IT'S A CONCERT. ONLY SEEN HIM IN T'S AND JEANS AND TENNIES. BUT PEOPLE DRESS FOR CONCERTS HERE. I DON'T WANNA LOOK STUPID, YOU KNOW? WHAT DO I WEAR? HELP! XX J

Quinn replied:

HEY, DAUGHTER: JUST ASK HIM WHAT HE'S WEARING. XX MOM

Quinn answered several letters relating to work, one from her uncle Stephen Earls in Hong Kong. His lover, Boon, was having some kind of minor foot surgery and would be laid up a week. What recent movies did Quinn recommend they rent to keep him from getting bored? She typed up a list, and then sent an E-greeting card to Boon, wishing his big toe a speedy recovery.

When she tapped the touch pad to send the note, however, her other hand accidentally clicked on the button below it. With the left click button engaging at the same moment as the touch pad, the computer misread the signal, and suddenly the screen flashed, went black, and then a document appeared, wavering at first and then becoming steady.

Quinn shrank back. Tyler would be upset if she screwed up something that had to do with his work. Indeed, what was now on the screen looked like an outline, or notes, for a game. Curious, she started reading it. She quickly became fascinated, for it sounded delightful. But as she scrolled down the screen, a chill came over her. What first read as a virtual-reality game set in an ancient cathedral— chasing a bad monk through the various dank chapels and naves—turned into a kind of mad manifesto about religion and eradicating religious leaders. An outlined sentence, in a kind of window, set off from the rest of the text, said:

TO CREATE AN ARMY OF TEENS TO REJECT THE VERY IDEA OF GOD AND RELIGION, THIS IS THE MISSION.

Her skin began to crawl. She scrolled down the page.

THE OBJECTIVE IS TO SLOWLY ERADICATE THE NOTION
OF GOD FROM EVERYDAY LIFE. AS THE PROGRAMMING
TAKES EFFECT, SEVERAL OUTSTANDING CANDIDATES
WILL BE CHOSEN TO CARRY OUT DEATH MISSIONS
AGAINST RELIGIOUS LEADERS, CULMINATING WITH—

"What are you doing?"

She almost jumped out of her skin. It seemed to
boom in her ears, even though he had spoken in a
normal tone of voice. Tyler had appeared right behind her.

She froze. The sound of surprise—of being
caught—was stifled in her throat. All she could do
was look up and say, "You're back."

"I left a file I should have put in my briefcase."

"I was checking my E-mail. Something went
wonky."

"You're using my work laptop."

She nodded. "I didn't think you'd mind. I didn't
bring mine."

"You always use the desktop in the office."

He was right. She did. "I just thought it would be
easier checking my mail here."

"How'd you find *this?*" He pointed to the screen.

"Like I said, something went wonky. I was trying
to send an E-mail reply. The screen blinked and this
is what appeared."

He looked as if he didn't believe her.

"Tyler, I wasn't prying. I wouldn't do that." She
sounded hurt that he would think such a thing.

He peered at the screen. Paused a moment. Then
he let out a hearty laugh. "You think it's real, don't
you?"

"What?"

He howled. "Oh, that's rich. You were believing it!"

She tried to smile. "Tell me this is not a game you are considering doing."

"It's a game, I guess, but a pretty twisted one." He proceeded to dig through papers piled up on the end of the long counter. "Very Thomas Becket, you know? Murder in the cathedral. I think someone sent it to me because they knew my stance against religion. I would have been tarred and feathered if I'd ever tried to develop it. Anyhow, it's too Dungeons and Dragons for my taste."

"Someone sent this to you?"

He nodded. "Anonymously. Called it a proposal."

"Didn't it worry you?"

He shrugged, starting to search another pile for the document he'd returned for. "Not really. Thought it was kind of silly."

The newspaper articles of all the recent murders came to her. "It could be dangerous."

He found the file he'd returned for, slid it into his briefcase. "Listen, I'm late now. Gotta go." He bent forward and kissed her on the cheek, then moved his hands to the keyboard. In a few strokes, the offending document disappeared from the screen. "I'll tell you all about it at dinner." He closed his laptop, picked it up, and clutched it under his arm. "What's that restaurant you told me about, the one you love so much?"

"Vice Versa. Fifty-first between Eighth and Ninth."

"See you at eight, okay? And doll up. I hope we'll have a deal to celebrate."

And with that he was gone.

But her unsettled feeling was not.

Late that afternoon, at a table at Vice Versa, they raised champagne glasses to toast the deal he'd finally secured.

Quinn had arrived early to have a drink with the owners, Daniele and Franco, who had become her friends soon after they opened four years before. They dished, laughed, and caught up, telling Quinn how thrilled they were that she was now happily married. They were pleased to meet Tyler when he arrived, and everyone knew from his grin that he had aced the big deal Quinn had told them about. Franco ordered up the best champagne for the celebration, and Daniele seated them at the best table in the house.

It had taken all day, Tyler explained to Quinn, but he'd finally calmed the fears that the new edition of Practice Run contained anything objectionable to Arab sensibilities. He felt the whole thing was a joke, though. "I mean, look, the games are as Western as anything out there. They reflect Western values. But hell, if they put their blessing on them, am I going to argue?"

"It's all hypocrisy," she agreed. "They want to make money too."

"I think that's the thing I hate most about organized religion. The hypocrisy."

That reminded her of what she'd discovered on

his laptop earlier. "That proposal I came across today really was disturbing," she said.

"Yup. Well, it appealed to me at first, but you're right."

"You know what's strange? A game about killing religious leaders sounds like the clippings you saved."

He nodded. "That's why I kept them." He smiled as he scratched his temple. "I must say, on a certain visceral level it had some appeal."

"To an atheist like you, maybe."

"To lots of people, I'm sure. I mean, it's all fantasy, taking our aggressions out on those figures of authority who promise they are helping us, only, in time, we learn they actually were trying to ruin us."

"Tyler."

"Okay, okay. I won't go off, I promise."

"After this anonymous person sent you that proposal, what did you do?"

"I thought about it," he said honestly. "You know Medal of Honor?"

"Sure. It's an old game, but still very popular."

"It's popular because kids get to blow away the enemy after landing on the beach in Normandy."

"German soldiers," she reminded him. "Not priests and rabbis."

"What's the difference?" he said over his champagne. "They're still the enemy."

"You really believe that?"

"Yes," he said forcefully. "Religious leaders pose the biggest threat to mankind because they fill young people with hate."

She tried to reason with him. "Sometimes, yes. But I think religion is mainly about love."

He gave her an incredulous look. "You think the towel-heads who flew the planes into the Twin Towers did it for love? You think that girl went berserk in Missouri and killed a cardinal because of love? No, it was fear, hate, intolerance for other faiths. Faith itself is an outmoded notion best left for textbooks, attached to the Rose Kennedys of history."

She shook her head. "You're talking to a Catholic who believes in the goodness of the human heart, and feels love for others, no matter what their beliefs. God is a universal notion. All religions that worship a higher being—whether you call him Lord or Buddha or Allah or Prophet—are unified in praying to the same spirit."

"There is no such thing as Buddha or Allah. It's a notion concocted to manipulate armies, to conquer nations, to keep people in line, and to make money. Mainly to make money. I mean, look at the Vatican!"

She was shocked at his outburst. "How were you raised? What religion?"

"None. You know that. That's why we didn't marry in your church. I was brought up atheist, the way the world should be. Organized religion is simply big business, out to—"

"Tyler, stop, please. I don't want to continue this. Not tonight, not when we're celebrating."

He softened. "I'm sorry. I climb the soapbox too easily sometimes." He reached over and touched her hand. "I love you."

"Hey, Miss Roberts. Sorry, I mean Mrs. Bryant."

Quinn looked up to see her favorite waiter. "Peter,

hi. It's Quinn, you know that. And this is my husband, Tyler."

Peter shook Tyler's hand. "Congratulations, a little late. Can I pour you more champagne?" Once he did, he took their order. "Back with some bread in a minute."

"Tyler," Quinn asked, "after you received that sick idea for a game, didn't it worry you when you read that something like it was really happening?"

He blinked. "How do you mean?"

"The clippings. I mean, kids have killed religious leaders."

He shrugged. "Yeah, actually, I did my good deed. I checked it out with my tech people."

"And?"

"They said it was nonsense."

She gave it some thought. "You know Susan Horgan, my partner?"

"Of course I do."

"You met her husband, Patrick, at the wedding."

"Sure."

"He's an FBI agent, remember?"

He nodded. "So?"

"He deals in computer crime. He helped Kenneth McGuire put Kevin Mitnick in jail."

"Really."

"I want to tell Patrick about this and see if he thinks there's a connection."

Tyler shook his head. "That's silly. I told you, I think it's a coincidence."

"What is there to lose?"

"I guess you're right." He took Quinn's hand across the table again. "Still love me?"

"Of course. Why would you doubt that?"

"The look on your face."

He was wrong. She did love him. It was trusting him that she wasn't sure about. Because somewhere inside her, warning bells were ringing.

Chapter Three

Quinn tried to laugh at herself on the train back to D.C. the next day. What had she been thinking? Why was she being so suspicious? Some lunatic had anonymously sent Tyler a frightening manifesto that seemed to match what a few teenagers in various parts of the country had recently done. These deaths of religious leaders were random and repetitive, she was aware of that. But what if they were not? What if they connected somehow to the nut who had sent Tyler the game proposal?

What bothered her most was the instinctive distrust she was feeling. By the time the Acela reached Union Station, she was even more convinced that there could be something more to it. And by the time she reached the Foundation for Education office, only five minutes away by cab, she promised herself she would talk to the FBI about it. There was no harm in getting a second opinion.

"I'm sorry I'm late," she told Susan as she entered. "Missed the early train."

Susan hugged her. "Too much amour last night?"

she asked, pushing her glasses down to peer over them. Then she sighed. "I remember what it was like to feel so newly in love. Glorious. Mad. Incredible."

"I thought you still feel that way," Quinn said soberly.

"One kid and fifteen years of marriage later, it diminishes." Susan couldn't hold back a mischievous grin. "But only somewhat." Indeed, she and Patrick were still very happy. They were both on their second marriages, the one that was meant to be. James, their thirteen-year-old son, was the delight of their lives. They had a warm, charming, rambling house in what had once been the countryside in McLean, near Dulles Airport, the perfect spot to raise a young boy and yet be convenient enough to both parents' work. Susan and Patrick had honored Quinn and Tyler by being bridesmaid and groomsman at their wedding, along with Joanie, who had proudly served her mom as maid of honor, and Tyler's college buddy, Brandon DiForio.

"Not much is happening today," Susan told Quinn. "The only call we had was Cairo. They got the shipment."

"Great."

"There's a letter coming from Mubarak himself, thanking you."

"Thanking *us*."

"You made it happen." Susan wiped her glasses with a tissue. "They might want you to go to Egypt for a function at the new library in Alexandria."

Quinn said, "Oh, I'd love to see it." Then she went to her office.

A few minutes later, Susan popped her head in as

Quinn was going over the mail. "So what did the newlyweds do in New York?" She paused for effect. "Beyond the obvious."

"I took Tyler to Vice Versa, where we were treated like royalty. We celebrated Tyler closing the deal for distribution—speaking of Egypt—in the Middle East."

Susan shook her head. "Practice Run is like Starbucks. Today Seattle, tomorrow the world. I sometimes wonder, will the commonwealth of coffee eventually collapse like the Roman Empire?"

"What do you have against Starbucks?"

Susan shrugged. "I'm a Peets gal."

"Speaking of Starbucks . . ." Quinn lifted the mug on her desk.

Susan got the coffee thermos and filled it. "Peets Mocha Java," she proudly said. "My weekend was blissful. Patrick and I got to sleep late, read the Sunday paper in bed, work in the garden."

"Where was the kid?"

"James had a sleepover on Friday, and the same kind of thing in a tent on Saturday."

"Tent?"

Susan rolled her eyes. "In the woods in Maryland. I don't want to ask."

"My idea of camping is a Marriott with room service."

"I'll tell you one thing: Patrick and I acted like we were on our honeymoon all weekend. I mean, the kid's away, parents will play."

Quinn shook her head. "You two are something else."

Susan went back to her desk and brought Quinn

some paperwork to look over. "My husband the G-man just got an interesting case. Internet identity theft. Lots of money involved, apparently."

"It's amazing how vulnerable we all are now."

"Patrick says it's virtually impossible to protect yourself if some hacker wants to get at your stats." Susan started back to the outer office. "Bank accounts, stocks, private E-mails—they can access them all," she called over her shoulder.

That reminded Quinn of the thought she'd had earlier. "You know, all the way back on the train I thought about something I want to check out with Patrick. There seems to be a series of unrelated killings of religious leaders—"

Susan put her head back in. She looked startled.

"What?" Quinn asked, reading her face.

"Did you see this morning's papers?"

Quinn shook her head.

"You didn't read the *Times* on the train?"

"I worked."

"Coming right up."

Susan returned in a few moments and placed the *Washington Post* on her desk. Susan stood back, facing her with folded arms. The headline startled Quinn. TOMMY CALDWELL—SUICIDE BOMBER? "Another one," Susan said.

Quinn gasped. She skimmed the story. Tommy Caldwell, a preacher famous for being only sixteen years old, had been scheduled to give a sermon at Orange County's Crystal Cathedral. When he was presented to the overflowing congregation, he'd hugged Bernadette Zawadski, the first female pastor of the church. In the process, he'd detonated a plastic explosive that had killed them both and four choir members standing nearby.

Susan said, "Isn't it awful? It was deliberate too."

Stunned, Quinn read the article thoroughly. Tommy Caldwell had been billed as "Generation Z's Billy Graham." He'd been "called," he had claimed, by a mystical force one night while drinking Corona with buddies out in the California desert. Just last week Caldwell had appeared on *Live with Regis & Kelly*, demonstrating real star appeal. Why would he do such an inexplicable thing?

Quinn felt herself overcome by a wave of fear. But fear of what? She tried to think it through. Teenagers were killing religious leaders. The murders appeared to be random, using various methods in various parts of the country, over the past six months. But could there be a pattern? Was it part of some kind of plot? If so, who was behind it, and why? It sounded like the game proposal that had been sent to Tyler.

She called him. "Have you heard the news?"

"You mean about California? Yes."

"What do you think?"

"It's terrible," Tyler replied.

"Just like the others."

"Yes. I'm watching CNN."

"Any mention of a plot?" she asked. "Any connection to the other incidents we were talking about?"

"Quinn, I think we're overreaching."

"Ty, we can't be the only people putting this together!"

"But there must be nothing concrete connecting the incidents or authorities would be doing something about it."

"I'm going to talk to Patrick about it. The guy whose manifesto you read could be behind this."

"Honey, do what you want, but you know the Federal Bureau of Investigation is nothing more than a collection of lazy bureaucrats who approve visas for terrorists."

"Patrick Horgan is no such thing."

"Have it your way." He took a breath. Then he calmly asked, "Honey, why is this becoming so important to you?"

"I don't know. It's just that there have been so many of them."

"I think you hate that I agree with the underlying premise."

"Tyler, don't tell me you believe these people deserved to die."

"I didn't say that. Nothing like that."

"Patrick is part of the FBI computer fraud division. If that game—"

"Quinn, it was only a proposal. There *is* no game like the one you read about on my laptop."

She knew he was right. "Do you want to come with me when I talk to Patrick?"

"No, I'm just too busy up here."

"I'll let you know what I find out, then."

There was a long pause. Then he said, "Okay. Listen, I gotta go, work to do. Bye, darling." He hung up.

Susan had been standing there, listening. "What was that all about?"

"When can I talk to Patrick?"

"Patrick? My hot Irish stud?"

"Patrick Horgan the FBI agent, not Patrick Horgan the hot lover."

"Come for dinner tonight."

"I'll bring the wine."

The Horgan house rose on a lush Virginia hillside, nestled into a winter forest of naked birch and evergreens. Snow covered the expanse of lawn surrounding the house and barn, which Susan and Patrick had long ago turned into a marvelous space with offices for each of them, two guest rooms, bath, and a comfortable reading area. The barn was lined with thousands of books. Federal agent by day, Patrick Horgan was by night a writer who had turned out three brilliant but somewhat inaccessible tomes on James Joyce, his hero. Susan had been a television producer and writer in New York for years before she met Patrick, and her Emmy for one of the daytime dramas she had penned acted as a quirky doorstop. Computers seemed to be everywhere—on Patrick's desk, on Susan's in the barn loft, and two in the main house in the den off the kitchen that James used as his lair.

After dinner, while James and a friend played the latest version of Practice Run in the den, Quinn laid out her worries. Patrick and Susan were both fascinated. They'd heard of some of the other incidents—sure, everyone had—but they would never have thought to connect them. A bombing of a church in Santa Ana didn't have any association with the shooting of a cardinal in St. Louis. And none of those incidents connected in any tangible way to a traffic accident in Milwaukee where a teenager had driven his family into a truck in a rainstorm, killing them all only minutes after his father had flown home from New York with the good news that a religious house there had agreed to publish his book.

"Isn't it suspicious?" Quinn asked. "Yes, it could just be coincidence. But on the other hand, maybe it's a plot of some sort to turn people against religion."

Patrick raised his eyebrows. Susan looked quizzical.

"To turn them against God," Quinn said with less conviction.

"That's ludicrous," Patrick said. "I mean, first of all, it's impossible."

Susan said, "I could see, perhaps, that some cult might brainwash their kids into becoming killers for the devil or some such thing, but this is all over the nation. How would someone get these kids to do this?"

Quinn told them about what she had read. "It was a proposal for a game whose whole point seemed to be the murder of religious leaders and the eradication of God in our lives."

Susan blinked. Patrick looked intrigued. "You talked to Tyler about it?" he asked.

"Tyler's no fan of organized religion, God knows. But he was upset by the game too."

"Did Tyler learn who it came from?"

Quinn shook her head. "I don't think so. He said it was anonymous, couldn't be traced."

"Everything can be traced," Patrick reminded her.

Susan said, "It sounds like this could be some kind of cult movement or something."

James Horgan dashed in, with his buddy Sam following closely on his heels. "Hey, Auntie Quinn, any chance, with me being your godchild and all, that I can get a Front Runner password?"

"Not fair," Sam warned. "You gotta be good. You gotta play Tyler for it. And you suck at this game."

"I do not," James snapped. "Practice Run is really difficult. Message boards are full of protests. Kids all over the world want to be Front Runners."

Patrick was in the dark. "What's that do for you, exactly?"

Quinn laughed. "I'm not sure I know myself."

Susan said, "You're married to the guy and you don't know how it works?"

"I haven't played many video games," Quinn admitted.

"You gotta get to the highest level in competition," James explained quickly. "Then if you win, you go on to play Tyler Bryant one on one. It's like the ultimate. If you win playing against him, you're called a Front Runner. You get a password no one else has, and you're a Front Runner for life."

"And Tyler creates a game just for you," Sam added. "One no one else will ever have."

Quinn smiled. She'd had no idea. "Really?" It intrigued her. She wondered how many games Tyler really created.

"Yeah," Sam said energetically. "It's like no one else will ever have that version—it's made for you and your interests and stuff. My pal Bobby almost got there, but lost out at the final run. Man, he almost had it!"

"I'm close," James asserted.

"No, you're not," Sam said with a scowl. "He's putting you guys on."

James tried to put his hand over his friend's mouth, but Sam pulled away, laughing.

"He's lousy at the game, and he wants to get a password from you so he can impress Kelly."

Susan and Patrick looked at one another. "Who's Kelly?"

James turned beet red and stomped off, seething with embarrassment. Sam shrugged and followed.

Patrick had a wry smile on his face. "Girls are starting to look good to them."

"Thank God," Susan said. "Maybe it'll get him away from that screen." She stood up and went to the liquor cabinet. "It's fascinating that these murders are all connected by an antireligious sentiment."

Patrick rubbed his chin. "Interesting concept, indeed. I, for one, don't believe in coincidence, but I don't know if this is in my area. Just because someone sent Tyler a game proposal doesn't put this under the heading of computer crime."

Quinn blinked her lashes as if to tease him. "You might know people in other divisions who could help?"

Patrick laughed. "I'll call Mike tomorrow. Mike Furnari, my sometimes partner. See what he thinks. And I'd like to see that proposal you found. I assume Tyler still has it?"

Quinn shrugged. "I would think so."

"Irish whiskey, anyone?" Susan offered.

Patrick looked up to see his wife holding a bottle of Powers. "Open the Middleton," he suggested.

"Bottle we bought on the last trip, in West Cork," Susan explained. "Quinn?"

Quinn declined. "I hear you're working on an identity theft case."

Patrick didn't seem thrilled about it. "Some cowboy in Montana stole the identity of a Boston investment banker and nearly cleaned him out. A fourteen-year-old."

Susan blanched. "You *sure* James and Sam are playing Practice Run right now?"

Patrick made a comical shrug. "Could be robbing Fort Knox." Then he chuckled. "Actually, I rather wish they would."

"Or copping secrets from the Pentagon," Susan joked.

"Tyler's brother did that very thing," Quinn said. "Patrick, did you work on that case? Drew Concardi?"

Patrick looked shocked. "That's Tyler's brother? Drew Concardi?" Then he began to nod his head. "Yes, I do remember that, of course."

Quinn said, "I had the very same reaction."

Susan took her lips off her glass. "But I thought you told me Tyler didn't have any family."

Quinn admitted that he had lied to her. "But he had his reasons."

Susan looked concerned. "Reasons?"

"Guilt, for not being able to help him more. Shame, probably. And certainly embarrassment."

Patrick said, "I had nothing to do with that case. I was working antiterrorism at that time." He took a slug of the whiskey. "But Mike did."

"Oh, yes," Susan said, energetically, "talk to Mike about it."

"Mike Furnari?" Quinn asked.

Patrick explained, "He works out of Manhattan. He was on the Concardi case from the start, I believe." He sank back in his chair, shaking his head. "Drew Concardi is Tyler Bryant's little brother. Imagine that."

"James, bedtime. Sam, go home," Susan called. Two groans from the den followed. "You have five minutes to wind up the game. Sam, Patrick will drive you."

"If I can figure out how to start the damned thing."

Quinn turned to him. "What?"

"Actually, I have an appointment tomorrow to learn my new car."

Quinn laughed. "Learn it?"

Susan rolled her eyes. "You think he's kidding?"

Patrick told her, "It takes a whole day in school. BMW created the absolute ultimate driving machine in the new 745i. It's also, unfortunately, the most technically frustrating vehicle on the road. They call it iDrive, but I'd be happy to dub it uDrive and let a chauffeur give it a go."

Susan said cuttingly, "It's bad enough we couldn't afford the car, now you want a driver?"

Quinn smiled. "Funny, you being Irish and all. I would think you'd want a Mini."

"I'm too tall and too old," Patrick answered. "Isn't it amazing? I work on computer crime, and I can't for the world figure out the computer in the car. Totally mystifying."

Quinn smiled. "It's probably very different."

"Navigation," Patrick quipped. "Never one of my strong suits."

Susan quipped, "Old age is creeping up."

"Darling, I'm only sixty-four."

Susan giggled. "And we can hear that voice beckoning from over the hill . . ."

With envy, Quinn watched them kiss. The Horgans were her role models. She wanted her marriage to Tyler to be just like this, and as long-lasting.

They heard game sounds coming from the den again. Susan shrugged. Patrick said, "James taught me Practice Run. It took me a while to get the hang of it, but when I did, it was smashing. I understand why it's such a phenomenon."

"Kids cut classes for it," Susan said with a degree of incredulity. "In my day, we only skipped school for Luke and Laura's wedding."

Patrick rose to his feet when Sam came into the room in his parka. "I'll talk to Mike in the morning and we'll see what we come up with."

"Thanks, Patrick," Quinn said, getting up to give him a hug. "And," she added, "happy new car."

The next day, Patrick called Quinn to ask if she could come down to the FBI headquarters in Quantico. Quinn told him when she would be free, and they set a time. "Hey, Quinn," Patrick said just before they hung up, "do you happen to have any copies of Practice Run that are Tyler's own?"

She was curious why he was asking. "What do you mean?"

"A copy or two that Tyler might have at home—copies not bought in a store."

"I guess so. Sure."

"Grab a couple. See you this afternoon."

When Quinn walked into Patrick's office in the Quantico headquarters, she was greeted by Mike Furnari. "I'm sorry," he said, "but Patrick is stuck in a meeting. He'll join us as soon as he can."

"It's good to meet you. Patrick said if anyone could figure this out, it would be you."

Mike winked. "He lies." The athletic, energetic, good-looking man rose from the desk. He straightened his tie slightly, making himself more presentable, but he looked like the kind of guy who was forever uncomfortable in a suit. Indeed, his jacket hung on the back of his chair. He took Quinn's hand. "Kind of a thrill to meet you. Heard a lot about you."

"And my husband?"

Mike Furnari laughed. "He's a legend."

She opened her briefcase and set two Practice Run jewel cases on his desk. "Patrick asked for these." Then she realized that piled behind him were ten or fifteen boxes of the game. She looked shocked.

He smiled knowingly. "Thanks."

"But?"

He spent the next forty minutes telling her what he and Patrick had hypothesized. "We think that you are right, that the game proposal you read"—he held up a copy they'd printed out—"really was the basis for a kind of program that could brainwash teens into becoming killers for some demented cause."

"My God," she whispered.

He went on to say that they had no reason to believe that the killings were connected to Practice Run, but it was a place to start. One way it could be done, he said, was subliminal imaging. "It's called steganography, and it's like invisible ink. Like reading between the lines."

"Patrick mentioned it, but I didn't really understand."

Mike explained, "It's a way to conceal a coded message inside an innocuous-looking photo, document, or other bit of media."

"Like a game?"

Mike nodded. "Like a game. After 9/11, people were worried that those tapes of bin Laden coming out of Afghanistan were really coded directions to zealous Al Qaeda cells. If his followers had been programmed somehow, brainwashed or hypnotized, they could see what we see but have a different reaction."

"How so?"

"Like if he played with his beard or took off his turban and scratched his head, we might think he's just got lice in his hair. The cells, however, would understand the movement as a direction to, perhaps, go out and blow up a bridge."

Quinn was intrigued. "Patrick explained to me that with encryption you know a message is being sent. With steganography, the message can be hidden inside any of the millions of images in the game?"

"It's like subliminal advertising," Mike told her. "Like when they flashed popcorn on the screen in movie theaters while you were watching Tom Cruise. You were never aware of it, but your subconscious picked it up and made you hungry. So you went out to buy some."

"Which is why it's against the law now."

"The reason we wanted you to bring a few more copies, different copies from the ones you might buy in a store, was to see if we could find any differences."

Quinn stiffened. "You think Practice Run is the common denominator in the killings?"

"We have no idea," Mike said in a calm voice. "We only figure that since this manifesto was sent to Tyler, the guy who sent it might have infected copies of his game with a subliminal program—like a virus."

"I can't believe it." She looked out the window at the barren trees. "Do you think this is possible?"

He loosened his tie at the neck. "My first instinct was to write this whole thing off as far-fetched. I mean, the game is seldom played on computers. Only recently have processors gotten fast enough to compete with video game players. It's iffy that his game is corrupted."

She fidgeted. "My God, my company puts computers into educational centers for kids all over the globe. Tyler's game is now on all of them. If someone *has* corrupted copies of Practice Run to do such a thing, we're both responsible."

"Not at all," Patrick said, walking in behind her. He reached out and touched her shoulder. "You can't be responsible for what you don't know." He gave Mike a little wave.

"How'd it go?"

"Usual horse shit," Patrick assured him.

"Have you tested copies of the game?" Quinn asked.

Mike pointed to the stack of Practice Run boxes. "Sure have. Nothing."

"But you really think this is possible?" Quinn asked.

Mike squirmed a bit. "Well, sure, anything's possible. I've seen hackers do the impossible, clearing out entire banks in a matter of hours. So yes, it's possible." He took a slug of water from a bottle he lifted from the floor.

Patrick added, "Every law enforcement official in this country is aware of these killings, but no one can find an explanation that fits."

Mike said, "A kind of hypnotism would fit." He opened one of the boxes and pulled out the discs. "It's kind of a cool theory, you know?" He realized she might take that the wrong way, so he said, "I mean, it appeals to me on an intellectual level."

Patrick added, "It's brilliant. That's what makes it so frightening."

Mike flipped open the plastic case and studied the CD. "We'll put this one through the wash."

Quinn didn't know if she should be thrilled or upset. "Yes."

"Your husband must be very concerned about this," Mike offered.

"Well," Quinn honestly replied, "he isn't convinced that this whole thing is related to the game plan he was sent. It's my paranoia that has pushed this. I've kept my suspicions to myself because, well, frankly, this game is his life, and if it were being used to do such things, it would just destroy him."

"Not to mention ruin his career," Patrick said.

Mike put the disc back into the case as Patrick said, "Rest easy, Quinn. Tell Tyler what we are thinking. Ask him to call me—we'd like to talk to him directly. As Mike said, we'll have a team go over this, under this, inside this. If there's anything on here other than code for a game, we'll find it."

Quinn changed the subject. "Mike, Patrick told me you worked Drew Concardi's case."

"I was the one holdout," Mike said, nodding. "I didn't agree."

"Didn't agree with what?"

"I didn't agree that he did it. Or, rather, that he did it alone." He realized he was being too forthright. An agent wasn't supposed to say these things; he was supposed to support the company line. "Just my opinion, of course."

"You mean, he might have been framed?" She caught the flash of agreement rush across his face and then disappear.

"Hey, he was tried, found guilty, it's over. It doesn't matter what I think now."

"He plea-bargained," she reminded him.

"Yes, pleading guilty."

"No contest. There's a difference."

"Mrs. Bryant—"

"Quinn."

"Quinn. Let's just say this: I don't agree that the government proved beyond a reasonable doubt that he was the one who did it. There was stuff that was ruled inadmissable in court. I think the kid got shafted, and he was either too loyal or too dumb to let us know who his partner or the real perp was. I mean, it would have taken a mastermind."

"Mastermind? So you believe he did hack into the Pentagon? The charge wasn't false?"

He looked stuck. "It was done, all right. It happened. I just don't know if it was him."

He looked at his watch. "Time for racquetball."

She smiled. "You didn't seem like the desk type."

Patrick laughed. "That's the understatement of the year."

Mike unbuttoned the top of his shirt. "Under these clothes I wear a tank top and running shorts. I live for my lunch break. Love staying in shape."

He certainly did accomplish it, she thought. And then blushed, feeling ridiculous.

Mike said good-bye, grabbed his car keys, and rushed out. Quinn stood up and turned to Patrick. "I can't wait to tell Tyler what he said about Drew. He'll be thrilled. Maybe there's still a chance."

Patrick nodded. And then picked up the Practice Run box Mike had been holding. "Ask Tyler if he's ever suspected that some copies of the game got altered or were infected with a virus."

She nodded. "I'd just like to know that Tyler isn't being used and that you guys can stop whoever is doing this."

"It's all still a theory," he reminded her.

"What are you going to do next?"

He smiled. "For starters, I'm going to see if we can find out if all the kids in these clippings played Practice Run."

The beltway traffic was hideous, and by the time Quinn got home that evening, she found a note from

Tyler saying he was going back to the offices in Rockville because a new evening shift of tech support hires needed his cheerleading. He told her not to wait up for him. She was disappointed, for she wanted to share the news she'd gotten at Quantico. As she walked into the library, she saw his laptop sitting on his desk. It seemed radioactive with temptation. Perhaps she could learn if he had ever worried about a virus in Practice Run.

Almost an hour passed before she finally located, buried deep in extensions in his hard drive, a folder that contained documents called Practice Run Plan, Front Runners, First Attempts, Future Upgrades. None of them would open, and though she attempted to read the files through other programs on the computer, none would work. She even tried re-creating a glitch like the one that had brought up the manifesto the first time, tapping the touch pad at the same time as clicking, to no avail. All she got were error messages and, twice, freeze-ups. Well, she deserved it, she figured. What she was doing was just plain wrong.

But she did find one curious thing. In the computer's recycle bin, she located a previously deleted file. It was a copy of a *New York Times* article titled POPE, AT ECUMENICAL MEETING, DENOUNCES VIOLENCE IN RELIGION'S NAME. She read it with interest, a piece about the Pope calling together Muslims, Christians, and Jews to affirm his belief that "whoever uses religion to foment violence contradicts religion's deepest and truest inspiration." The article stated that a principal motive for the Pope's convening the gathering was the claim by the Islamic fundamentalists who carried out the 2001 attacks on the United States that they had acted in God's name.

Quinn closed the article, left it in the recycle bin, and shut down Tyler's computer.

Late in the night, Tyler slipped into bed with her. She woke up when he kissed her cheek. "Oh, hi."

"Hi."

"What time is it?"

"Three. Whipped the new support group into shape."

"Mmmm."

He pressed his naked body against her night-gown. "When we first went to bed together," he murmured, "you wore nothing."

She blinked. "That's because you stripped everything off me."

"Ah, yes, but then you never wore anything again."

"That's what honeymoons are for."

He brought his right hand up to gently cup her left breast. "But lately you've started acting like a nun."

"Ty, it's too late for a religious discussion."

He kissed her again, this time on the lips. "The only religion I want to worship is you." He pulled the covers down with the same hand, moving atop her.

In the moonlight, she could see the outline of his firm, masculine frame. He'd kept in shape in his personal gym in the New York apartment. He looked like a young man. He was sexual and sensual, knowing very well how to please a woman.

They made love and it was good, but Quinn's head was still caught up with what had happened that day. When they were done, he rolled over and said, "Man, if all else fails, we can make porn tapes and peddle them on the street. We're hot." He took a deep breath and looked like he was ready to drift off to sleep.

Abstractedly, almost to herself, she said, "I went to Quantico today."

"What?" His eyes flickered toward hers.

"I met with Patrick and his colleague Mike Furnari. Mike worked on your brother's case."

Tyler sat straight up, wide awake. "I know. I remember the name."

"He doesn't think Drew was guilty."

Tyler nodded. "He was the only one, unfortunately."

She was disappointed. "So you knew this."

He nodded. "And it doesn't help."

"Well, that's not all they told me."

"Yes?"

She told him everything. "I took a copy of Practice Run to Quantico because Patrick asked me to. He and Mike suspect that a computer program has prompted those kids who have killed religious leaders, and because that game proposal was sent to you, they are starting with Practice Run."

He looked stunned. "Starting what?"

"Decoding it. Seeing if there is some kind of virus embedded in copies of it."

He looked like someone had hit him with a cement block. "Why would they think that?"

"Well, they might be wrong—in fact, they probably are wrong—but won't it be better knowing it's not your game? That it's not in my computers? I mean, we just gave the library in Alexandria five hundred of them. Wouldn't you just die if some kid turned into a killer because of one of those laptops?"

He nodded, but almost in slow motion. "It certainly would hurt Zzzyx." Then he shook his head. "Quinn, this is crazy."

She took his hand. "I know, I know, but something connects these acts, and Patrick wants to investigate."

"These two gumshoes think *my* game is making kids kill priests and ministers?"

"Only some copies, some corrupted editions. If it's true, they can find them and stop them and learn who did this to you."

"If someone did what to me?" He laughed. "No, it's too wild, too weird. Practice Run can't be doing this. We have the best quality control in the business. It's just nonsense."

"Calm down."

"I'm sorry, but if something like this got out—just the suspicion, just a rumor—it could destroy Zzzyx."

She crawled up to him and hugged him. "Honey, it's better to know. I was very impressed with Mike, and I know Patrick so well. He's very thorough. If there is anything for you to worry about, he'll find it, and he'll tell us."

Tyler slid down next to her.

She pulled the covers over both of them. "My Lord, it's almost four," she said, noticing the time.

"Do you have to say that so often?"

"What?"

"'My Lord' or 'My God'."

"It's just a figure of speech."

"One I hate."

"Come on Ty, ease up."

He suddenly jumped out of bed and walked over to the antique Asian wedding cabinet. As he rummaged inside, she asked what he was doing. "Finding an Ambien."

"Give me one too," she said. "It's been that kind of day. My brain won't shut down." He took his in the bathroom, then brought her one with a glass of water. When he crawled back in bed with her, she kissed him on the cheek. "I didn't want to upset you. I thought you'd be grateful that these guys are doing this."

"They just had better not let word of their theory get out."

She nodded. "But wouldn't that be better than not stopping the killers at all?"

He didn't answer, but only turned over.

The call answered on the fourth ring with a sleepy, "Yeah?"

"It's me. Throw some water on your face and listen up. There's trouble. I won't explain now, but I want you here tomorrow, catch an early flight."

"This serious?" the man's voice croaked.

"Extremely." The man who had placed the call ended it and pressed another speed-dial number. A voice picked up almost immediately. "You're up at this hour?"

"You know I'm addicted to Internet porn."

"This is no joke."

"You think I'm joking?"

"Listen up good. Keep your eyes on Mike Furnari."

"Mike Furnari?" the man said with surprise. "What the hell are we worried about Mike Furnari for?"

The reply sounded deadly. "Because I fear he could unravel the whole thing."

Cairo, Egypt

The Muhammad 'Ali Mosque at the Citadel had long been the most prominent in Cairo. For more than 150 years it had dominated the skyline, making it almost the symbol of the city. One of Cairo's most visited tourist attractions, it remained a working mosque where thousands of worshipers prayed. This evening it was filled to capacity because Abu Abdella, the fiery sheik, was returning home after a journey through the Middle East. For years he had preached the most radical form of Islam. He had supported bin Laden and Al Qaeda, relentlessly calling for all of Holy Islam to rise up in jihad against America and the West. His violent message appealed especially to teenagers.

Young men had appeared in droves tonight. Abdella, even though he was in his thirties, was perceived by kids as "cool." Why? He scandalously refused to completely disavow Western-style music, as other clerics had. He told young men whose beards were just starting to grow that stubble counted as far as the Qu'ran was concerned. They loved not having to let their beards get long and look old. He drew them in, commanding respect from those kids who were torn by the division between the secular West and the restrictive, religious East. Once he even appeared in jeans and a tee. But he always admitted that he sinned, reminding his followers that God forgives. The Cool Cleric, as the international *Newsweek* called him, was derided by the hard-liners but worshiped by the young. He insidiously cloaked hatred in a hip package. Proof that his message was insidious—and dangerous—was the presence of his private army, strong, armed men surrounding the mosque, protecting him.

His sermon tonight was peppered with jokes—unheard of in most mosques—and stories of teenagers he'd met in Jordan, the Emirates, Saudi Arabia, and Syria who sounded just like these kids. "This is not a point in one's life where you should contain natural impulses or feelings. But you must dedicate this exploration—even with the sins that may accompany it—to Allah. Did your own fathers never taste wine? Did your mothers never once feel desire while looking at handsome boys in the bazaar? This is human! This is natural! We stray, but we find our way back to Islam. For Islam is, more than anything, a natural way to live God's law."

"Your interpretation is heresy!" a pubescent boy suddenly shouted. "You blaspheme."

"I say what I feel, from my own experience," Abdella shouted back happily. "I admit I'm a sinner. And I know I'm forgiven, for that is what Islam teaches. But the infidels, they cannot be forgiven, for they want all Muslims dead. Like the Jews who kill our Palestinian brothers every day, they want us eradicated."

The harangue went on for almost four hours. Abu

Abdella was a charismatic figure, and one that was hard to figure out, which is what gave him his immense appeal. He polarized youth, generating discussion within families that went on for weeks, raising his fame a notch higher every time he spoke. Tomorrow, he was going to rile them as a guest speaker at Cairo University.

But he would never make it.

Shortly after the mosque closed, on the terrace looking out over the vast city, under the stars, Abdella continued his conversation with a group of students who had refused to let him go. There were twelve of them, one of whom was the boy who had called him a blasphemer. The boy was seething, which was not lost on Abdella's small army of bodyguards. They kept careful watch over him.

Their eyes should have instead been focused on the slender youth who came up to Abdella to say good night, thank him, and kiss his hand. The boy, who later would be identified as Ismael Krani, a shepherd's son from Giza, reached into his tunic as he bent forward, withdrawing a razor-sharp knife with which, in one fast, practiced movement as he arose, he slashed Abdella's throat. Though attacked by the bodyguards and eventually beaten to death, the boy never once stopped smiling.

Ismael Krani was fifteen years old.

Chapter Four

"Patrick? It's Quinn. I'm in New York. Did you hear?"

"About Cairo?" Patrick Horgan said.

"He was fifteen! It's the same pattern."

"Don't jump to conclusions, Quinn. They grab boys off the streets at ten there. With nothing to live for except roaming the streets, it's no wonder these kids are brainwashed into dedicating their lives to Allah."

"Obviously this kid didn't want to do that."

"That's my point. Some rebel."

"But the game!"

"Quinn, just because it fits into a pattern doesn't mean it has to fit into *that* pattern."

Susan grabbed the phone from her husband. "We're in the car. Wait, Patrick will put it on speaker."

Quinn waited for what seemed forever. She heard them arguing in the background. Susan finally said, "He can't seem to get iDrive to do it. He's having a terrible time getting a handle on this thing. He got a 745i, but a 747 would have been easier to pilot."

Quinn said, "Susie, I feel so responsible. When we

donated the computers to the library in Alexandria, there was thunderous applause. It seemed the environment was positive."

Susan said, "But, Quinn, that was too recent for this kid to have been led to do it by a corrupted version of the game."

"I hope so."

Susan asked, "You coming back tonight, as planned?"

"Yes."

"Switch to Dulles. I'll get you. You'll come to our place for dinner."

"Great. Susie, put Patrick on again, okay?"

"Yes, honey, see you soon. Here . . ."

A moment later, Patrick said, "Yes, Quinn."

"Have you found out anything yet?"

He hesitated. "Nothing substantial. There's nothing on the discs we can see. If code is buried in there, it's too sophisticated for the Bureau to find."

"Wonderful."

"Tyler might have more success himself in trying to uncover a virus. He promised to have some people in his development department do that."

"You've talked to him?" That news surprised Quinn.

"He called me yesterday. We had coffee together."

"I didn't know."

"He seemed fascinated by my car, and seemed rather grateful for what Mike and I were doing. He was most congenial and helpful."

"I haven't spoken to him." She could hardly bear to ask the next question. "So, does it look less likely it's his game that's doing it? Tyler says if word got out it could ruin him."

"Truth is, Quinn, we're just not sure. And it's too early to tell about the boy from Egypt, whether he ever played it or not."

"This is the first time a kid has killed a Muslim leader. The others have been Christians and Catholics, a Jew. Maybe it doesn't connect to the others. Maybe it was simple retaliation against an Islamic fundamentalist."

"You know, this whole thing about religion, the Christians were no better," Patrick reminded her. "Wholesale slaughter of the infidels, men, women, children—it was common practice if you didn't believe. It goes back to the eighteenth century, when this country was founded mainly on the freedom from the old notion that there was one true religion and everyone who didn't agree should die."

"We teach tolerance."

"Teenagers are a pretty intolerant group, remember."

Quinn said, "This morning I got an E-mail from an official in China, petitioning us for computers for a new school in Shanghai. I thought to myself, this is probably safe. After all, communist China is still a relatively godless place."

"See you tonight. For now, sit tight."

"Easy for you to say in that luxurious car," Quinn said with a smile.

In the Zzzyx Games world headquarters building in Rockville, Maryland, Veronica Ashton set down a box of still-warm Krispy Kremes. "Anything else? Espresso? Coffee?"

"Vodka," Brandon DiForio joked. "Helps my jet lag."

Tyler grinned. "Make us some espresso, Ronnie."

She went to his expensive Italian machine sitting on the sleek marble slab under the window. "Coming right up."

Brandon dug into the doughnuts. "Boy, these are good."

Tyler looked at his only close friend. "You know, some people's greatest fear is going blind, some fear losing their kids before they themselves die. Yours should be diabetes."

"Funny man." Brandon bit into his second glazed. "So what did you make me come all this way for?"

"I want to first know how the new version is coming."

"It's got its bugs. But you know that."

"I'll work them out as soon as you're ready for me to take over," Tyler said. "But remember, it has to be out on Easter. We're advertising it already."

Brandon put his feet up on the conference table and sipped his coffee. "The problem is making it do everything you want it to."

Tyler gave Veronica a glance. She didn't seem to be listening. "This is the only chance."

"No, it's not," Brandon protested. "We could do it in steps, as we planned long ago."

"Not any longer." The espresso machine hissed with steam. "By the way," Tyler continued, "we're being investigated by the FBI."

Brandon's doughnut stopped halfway to his

mouth. "What?" Brandon put his feet back on the floor, and stiffened in his chair. "Why?"

Tyler watched his secretary. "Some nonsense Quinn is paranoid about."

Veronica brought over the first cup. Brandon took it, but set it down. "That subliminal program stuff?"

Tyler nodded as he waited for Ronnie to bring him his demitasse.

"Who's on the case? You know a lot of people over there."

"A guy named Patrick Horgan." He smiled as Ronnie handed him his cup.

Brandon shook his head. "Never heard of him."

"You met him. At the wedding. Susan the bridesmaid's husband."

"Oh yeah. Tall guy. Older."

"He works in the computer crime division."

"Ah."

"With our old pal Mike Furnari."

Brandon gave a nod of recognition. "Well, well, just like the old days."

"In a way, yes. The whole thing with Drew."

Veronica opened Tyler's stainless steel bar refrigerator and gave them each a curl of lemon rind.

Brandon said, "Mike's good. We both know that." He looked uncomfortable about the secretary standing nearby, cleaning the coffee machine. "What's coming down?"

Tyler explained. "I saw Horgan myself. His hunch is someone might have put a virus on certain Practice Run CDs."

Brandon laughed. "Oh, really."

"They think some copies are corrupted."

"Happens all the time," Brandon said smiling, now reaching for his coffee, relaxing a bit. "I just hope it doesn't slow us down. Your friend in the Bureau, he could certainly keep you posted on this, maybe even step in."

"I've already spoken with him."

Brandon looked satisfied. "So what do you want me to do?"

"Nothing. You're so disconnected from me and Zzzyx that I doubt they'd bother you. You just keep focused on the new version."

Brandon blinked, looking uncomfortable because Veronica was still hovering. "Man, when you first told me about this . . . this crazy idea Quinn has, it sounded like there was gonna be blood in every church, synagogue, mosque, and revival tent in the world."

Tyler grinned. "And what's wrong with that?" Then he looked serious, and turned to Veronica. "Give us a moment," he asked her.

"I'm just cleaning up," she protested. "You can trust me."

"Of course, Ronnie. But we need a few minutes in private. Hold the calls."

"What if it's your wife?"

"Nobody," Tyler ordered.

Veronica put down her sponge as Brandon said, "Can we push the date a little past Easter?"

"No way," Tyler warned.

"Candy has taken over the radio show, to give me time to finish. I'm pushing myself, but I do need to sleep sometime."

"What for?"

"Screw you, buddy." Brandon finished his coffee.

Veronica smiled at them both and left the room. At her desk, she looked back in through the huge glass panel that served as one wall of Tyler's office. She saw them huddled, deep in discussion now. She wished Tyler had let her stay. To prove her loyalty. To show him her allegiance. To demonstrate how much she cared.

She saw them look concerned, then burst into laughter. Tyler got up, rubbed the earlobe holding his silver hoop, a sure sign, Ronnie knew, that he felt nervous. He paced as he spoke, and then slapped Brandon on the shoulder. Then, suddenly, Tyler seemed to remember something and she picked up her desk phone before it even buzzed. "Yes?"

"Ronnie, check my calendar. Am I playing a winner one on one tonight?"

Veronica already knew the answer. "At nine."

When the office door finally opened and the men emerged, Brandon said, "Listen, I came all this way. You gonna buy me dinner at least? We should celebrate."

"Celebrate what?" Tyler asked.

"Drew's birthday."

An icy look glazed over Tyler Bryant's face. "Well, sure," he said coldly, "we'll have a cake and blow out candles too."

Veronica added, "He's been there three years now." Her poker face did not conceal a grin.

"And counting," Brandon chuckled, grinning as well. "You should be a good brother, Ty, and give him a call."

"I already sent a card."

*   *   *

Think of you often. Love from your only brother, Tyler.

As rage surged from deep within him, Drew Concardi grabbed the card and envelope with both hands and tore them to pieces, again and again and again, until the floor was littered with confetti. The guard who had passed him the envelope came back to his cell door. "Pick that shit up."

"Fuck yourself," Drew muttered, and sat on his bunk. He put his head down in his hands, not aware of the cell door being unlocked, not hearing the shuffling feet that went with it. He was, however, aware of the whack the guard gave him on top of his head.

"Pick it up, I said," the guard again ordered him. "Who the hell do you think you are?"

Drew's head rose just enough to see that he was staring at the man's crotch. He saw the zipper at nose level, the big belt buckle smack in front of his forehead, holding the gut right at hairline level. Without warning, Drew slammed his head forward. His skull cracked into the man's privates. The guard doubled forward in excruciating pain, and then vomited. It spattered all over the inmate, who was on top of the guard in seconds, flinging him to the cement floor, slamming him against the cell bars, pulling his hair like a ferocious cat going after the keeper who had tormented him for years. In seconds, two other guards and an orderly ran into the cell, holding Drew down so the nurse could stick a needle into his right arm.

When the warden got there, the inmate was quiet but seething. "He got too close to me," was all he said when he saw the woman standing above him.

The warden looked exasperated. "I'm going to have to put you in solitary again."

"Tell him to shove his birthday cards up his ass." Drew stared directly up at the blinding fluorescent lights in the infirmary ceiling.

"Why do you hate your brother so deeply?" she asked.

Drew Concardi closed his eyes and smiled. "It would take too long to explain."

Patrick Horgan slid the disc in his computer and took another stab at Practice Run. He'd been playing the game as often as he could now that he was working on a case that involved it. He wasn't sure why, but it had occurred to him that one way to find a clue to what was going on might be by playing the game, not just looking at the underlying code that created it. Patrick had worked on steganography when Osama bin Laden issued his tapes after the September 2001 attacks. He had studied them for secret messages to Al Qaeda followers around the world. Perhaps something in Practice Run was hiding, as it were, in plain sight.

"Dad, you're too old to play this," James said, throwing his backpack down when he returned from school. "It's for kids."

"I'm a kid at heart," he corrected his son, "but I wouldn't mind a kid's help here."

James did his best. Patrick was already at level four, but they were getting harder. Reading and retaining what he read from the text passages was easy. The hard part was the coordination of brain and fingers to anticipate where the enemy was going to come from. James watched for ten minutes, pronounced his father hopeless, and reluctantly provided him with a set of cheats to help him.

"What are these?" Patrick asked.

"You get them on Web sites," James explained. "It's a way of jumping ahead."

"Cheating."

"Yeah. That's what they're called. Cheats."

Patrick shook his head. "Cliff's Notes for video games. Amazing."

Also amazing that it worked. Patrick advanced fast. When Susan said she was leaving to fetch Quinn at Dulles Airport, her guys were so involved in the game that they didn't even hear her say good-bye. "How far am I from being a Front Runner?" Patrick asked James.

"Miles."

"Huh? What do you mean by that?"

"Months."

"James, I'm doing quite well here, considering I'm an old fart."

James giggled. "You're okay, Dad. But to get to be a Front Runner, that takes skill. You can't use cheats to really advance through a level. The cheats just show you how to use the different weapons."

"So what good is that?"

"Once you know, then you can beat the level."

Patrick hunkered down. He hadn't become a computer expert for nothing.

The Horgan men were still at it when Susan and Quinn showed up. "Off!" Susan shouted as she walked by the den. It was a word she often used to threaten James with.

"Did you hear something?" James asked his father.

"Not a sound." Patrick was up to level five already, blazing along.

"I said *off!*"

This time they obeyed.

As Patrick walked into the kitchen, Quinn handed him a beer. "Tyler's joining us," she told him. "He called when I got off the plane and said he'd drive out so you two didn't have to take me into D.C."

Patrick looked apprehensive.

Quinn picked up on it. "Patrick, what is it? Do you know something you don't want Tyler to know?"

He shook his head. "On the contrary, I want to find out if he's learned anything we should know. Oh, that reminds me."

He put in a call to Mike in New York, but he couldn't be reached. Patrick left a message, and when he hung up, Susan said, "Ah, perfect timing. Potatoes are crisp, so dinner's ready, and I think I saw headlights drive in."

Tyler hurried into the dining room just as they were sitting down. "You getting to love the new wheels yet, Patrick?" he asked about the 745i parked in the garage.

"Damn," Patrick muttered, "I forgot to put the door down again."

"The car is supposed to do it," Susan reminded him.

"Right," Patrick amswered. As he got up and hurried to the entry hall to push the button to close the garage door, he called back to Tyler, "It's really a fabulous concept. All my life I have been driving cars.

Now they drive you." When he got back to the dining room, Quinn handed him the salad bowl. "After three classes and much wringing of hands, I know just to let it do its thing."

"Yeah," Susan said with a laugh, dishing out the beef stew to everyone except for James, who ate no meat, only fish. "The GPS really does guide you. It tells you when to turn right, when to turn left, when to brake, when to stop, right into the driveway. Pretty amazing."

"Cool stereo," James added. Then he said, "Hey, Tyler. My dad wants to become a Front Runner."

Tyler looked at Patrick over a forkful of salad he was about to put into his mouth. "You?"

"I'm too young, huh?" Patrick joked.

"Way too young," Tyler said with a laugh. Then he got serious. "I've had the best tech people go over dozens of discs. We put them through every conceivable test. Took them apart to see if the code had been tampered with. Zilch."

Patrick nodded. "Same for us."

"So it's not Practice Run," Tyler said, waiting for Patrick to chime in in agreement.

"Actually, I'm not so sure about that," Patrick said instead. "I'm just now checking on the boy in Egypt, but I've gone over all the ones who came before him. I uncovered two more incidents that may or may not connect—but I think they do. In Ireland, a nun was drowned by a girl named Kathleen Murphy, who killed herself, and a boy in France—Philippe Minogue—put a knife through a priest at a playground."

"Did he die as well?"

Patrick nodded. "Slashed his throat."

Quinn shivered. "Why do you think they are connected?"

Patrick looked right at Tyler. "They all played Practice Run."

Tyler pushed his plate away, disturbed, and Quinn put her hand on his shoulder. "But can you be sure they're killing nuns and priests *because* of the game? I mean, come on. These kids might all be taking the same drug or whatever."

Patrick shrugged. "We don't know for sure. Although Mike is working on finding out that answer. But now he's stuck with this grand jury thing."

James wanted to know what they were talking about. "I don't get it. The game has lots of killing in it. Why are you all upset about some murders? They're not real."

Susan said crisply, "You're done with your fish. You can be excused."

That piqued James' curiosity even more. "You guys talking about the priests in the cathedral?"

"What?" Patrick asked.

"He's talking about the highest level," Tyler explained. "To become a Front Runner, you choose a playing arena, like a space station in a new galaxy or a bizarre haunted house."

James eagerly added, "I'd pick the battlefield or that really cool armada on the high seas!"

"Another choice is a dark medieval cathedral," Tyler admitted.

James said, "That's what my friend Chris Saleh likes."

Tyler nodded. "The visuals are great. Furtive, defrocked priests running around like ghouls. You can even get killed by a falling giant cross."

"Yeah, Chris says it's cool."

"Okay, kid," Susan said, eager to get him out of there, "one hour till bedtime."

James got up and ran back to his PlayStation 2 in the den.

When Tyler heard the familiar sounds of his video game, he mused, "Music to my ears."

Then he seemed to sink in his chair. "You're sure all the kids who killed had my game in common?"

Patrick nodded. "And several others, from what we could figure out. But Practice Run is apparently the only one they *all* played."

In his own defense, Tyler asked, "Didn't they also have many other things in common? Like using the same toothpaste? Hell, the world's a global village these days."

"Yes," Patrick said, putting his last chunk of roast beef in his mouth. "You're right. It could be any one of a number of things." He looked over at his wife. "Do we have any coffee?"

"Coming right up," Susan said, as she and Quinn stood up to clear the plates.

"I have a question," Patrick said to Tyler. "About your winner's circle."

"Front Runners."

"Right. Is that the same game that's on the discs?"

Tyler nodded. "The highest level of play is part of the package. The player already has the game that determines Front Runner status. But if they get to FR level, then I create a new one just for them."

As Susan brought coffee and a platter of cookies to

the table in the dining room, a vehicle rolled past the Horgan driveway, without its headlights on. The big black Suburban with government plates pulled over and parked a hundred feet up the road, hidden in the trees. A muscular man dressed in black got out and swiftly made his way to the house. Stopping for a second to peer in the dining room window, where the group was enjoying themselves around the table, he moved on to his objective.

The house was divided into three parts. One consisted of the original building, a small farmhouse, which comprised the kitchen, dining room, den, and upstairs bedrooms. A second portion, a huge living room and an enlarged entryway built of pine, had been added on, and attached to that was the barn and the garage. If people were in the dining room, they could not hear anything going on in the barn or the garage.

The man pressed a plastic transmitter to the Horgan garage door keypad. In seconds it read the code and the door rose. Inside the garage was parked a blue VW Passat wagon and the sleek silver BMW 745i. The man felt inside his leather jacket for the chip. When he located it, he bent down and pressed it under the BMW's front wheel well, where the magnet attached to it snapped into place. He left as stealthily as he had arrived, closing the door behind him. He stopped at Tyler's Escalade, parked off to the side in the driveway. Reaching into his pocket, he withdrew a small piece of paper with a red 25 on it and slid it under the driver's windshield wiper.

And disappeared before the people in the dining room had even finished dessert.

* * *

It was pouring by the time Quinn and Tyler got into his SUV to leave the Horgan house. When Tyler turned the windshield wipers on as he was backing out of the driveway, Quinn noticed something under the wiper. "What's that?"

Tyler saw the paper and shrugged, "Looks like a valet stub. Odd. I didn't valet park today." It blew off as they merged onto Route 66.

"What do you really think, Ty?" she asked farther down the road.

Tyler peered into the falling rain ahead. "I really think it's something else. I think the fact that all these crazy teenagers played the game is just coincidence. I hope they find what's doing it. But I also hope they leave me alone."

"Could something like that really work?"

"The technology is there," he said. "You can brainwash someone with the right program. The mind becomes susceptible. It's hypnotism, really, and that's been around for a very long time."

She put her hand on his thigh. "Terrible rain."

"In January, no less. What happened to snow?"

"Watch out. You'll get what you wish for. I'll take rain any day."

When they got home to Fifteenth Street, they were surprised to see a Domino's delivery man knocking at the door. Quinn hopped out before Tyler found a parking place—her car was in the garage out back, which only held one vehicle. She called to the guy that he had the wrong house. To her surprise, the front door opened and she saw her daughter accept the pizza and pay the man. "Joanie!" she called, and hurried toward her. "What are you doing here?"

"Mom!"

When they got inside, Joanie told them what had happened. Her best friend and roommate at William and Mary, a girl from Germany named Stephanie Korodi, had just learned that her mother had been diagnosed with breast cancer. Since it was Friday afternoon when she got the call, Joanie proposed that they fly up and spend the weekend in D.C. She wanted Stephanie, who was already sleeping in the guest room, to feel the love and support of her family.

"Who's the pizza for?" Tyler asked, dripping at the front door.

Joan smiled. "Me."

Quinn and Tyler each had a piece with her, sitting in the family room, catching up. Joanie said that Stephanie had never been to Washington, and she thought it would be great if she showed her all the sights on Saturday and Sunday, to distract her from worrying about her mother. The prognosis was good, she told them. "Besides," Quinn reminded her, "medicine has come a long way. Cancer can be beat today."

"Are Stephanie's mother and father together?" Tyler asked.

"Yes. He travels a lot—some kind of engineer. He's American. That's why Steph goes to school here. But their home is in Hamburg." Joanie sipped the beer Tyler had opened for her. "So, how are you guys? What's new?"

They looked at one another and burst out laughing.

"What?" Joanie demanded.

"Let's just say your mom and I have had a trying few weeks, okay?" Tyler said.

Joan looked stricken. "You don't look like you're having problems."

Quinn took Tyler's hand on the sofa. "Not relationship problems. Work problems."

"Oh," Joan said, looking relieved. "You gave me a scare."

Tyler winked. "We're going to be together forever." He kissed Quinn and got up. "And now I'll leave you two to gossip about me. At least, I hope. I'm off to bed."

"'Night, darling," Quinn said.

"'Night, Dad."

Tyler turned and smiled at her, touched. She'd never called him that before.

When he was gone, mother and daughter continued talking, catching up, sharing some gossip, along with a little bit of Joanie's prying as to what had been going wrong at work. Quinn didn't want to get into the whole Practice Run problem, but she didn't want to keep things from her either. "You know how we worried about those teenagers who seemingly went crazy and killed ministers and such?"

"Yeah."

"It has to do with that. We—Tyler and me and Patrick—"

"Uncle Patrick is in on this? That's heavy-duty."

Quinn nodded. "That's where we were tonight.

We fear that these kids were somehow programmed to do it through their game devices or computers."

"You're kidding."

"Wish I were." Quinn gave her some of the details, but it was getting late and she needed some sleep. "It's going to be okay. At least for Tyler."

"Good." Joan yawned. "I got up at six this morning. I have an early class on Fridays. I should go to bed too."

"I'll turn out the lights and be up in a minute," Quinn said, moving behind the island to wrap the last few pieces of cheese and pepperoni.

"Hey, Mom," Joan said on the bottom step of the staircase.

"Yes?"

"You okay?"

"Sure. Why?"

"Dunno. Something. You don't seem like yourself."

"I'm fine, honey," Quinn said. "Honest."

Patrick Horgan gave up about the time Quinn was brushing her teeth. He had sat staring at the computer screen long after James and even Susan had gone to bed. He went over his notes, over the theories and the thoughts he'd written down, over the names of the assailants, the places where the killings had taken place, all the details he had about the killers and the victims, and yet he could find no link other than the fact that all of them at one time or another had played Practice Run. But that in itself wasn't enough. Which meant he was missing something. And it wasn't their toothpaste.

When he finally crawled into bed and turned out the light, Susan instinctively moved closer to him. He wrapped an arm around her, pulling her to him, kissing her on the forehead even though he knew she would not remember. He lay awake for a long time, Practice Run running around inside his head. He started to drift off finally. And then the answer came to him. He bolted upright so fast that he almost jerked Susan awake. Making sure he didn't disturb her more, he slipped out of the bed, put on his robe, and hurried across the creaky hall floorboards to James' room.

"James," he said softly, gently shaking his son. "James, it's Dad. Wake up. Come on, just for a minute."

James was thirteen. And it was not easy to wake a thirteen-year-old boy.

"James," Patrick said, this time shaking him so hard the bed rattled. "Son, wake up!"

"What?" James sounded sleepy and annoyed.

"James, tell me something. Practice Run. The Front Runners."

"What?" The boy was just about to turn over and slide back into dreamland, but Patrick wouldn't let him. "Daaaaad . . ."

"James, there must be a Web site for everyone in that winner's circle. The Front Runners."

"Of course there is."

"Give it to me."

"Now?"

"Yes, now. Just tell me."

James Horgan spelled out the Web site's address. And Patrick let him go back to sleep.

*   *   *

At six in the morning, Susan Horgan got James up, then went downstairs to put on the coffee. She found that Patrick had never been to sleep. "What are you doing?"

In his bathrobe, hunkered over his computer in the barn, he was completely dismayed. "I thought I had it figured out. I thought maybe it was only the Front Runners who were our killers."

She folded her arms. "Sounds a little easy."

He turned off the machine. "Yes, well, way too easy. I found all the names on the Web site James told me to go to. All the kids who have gotten into that winner's group."

"And?"

He looked glum. "There are two hundred and forty of them."

"Well, that's not surprising. How many million copies of the game are out there?"

"Trouble is, not one of the names matches any of the killers."

"Which exonerates Practice Run."

He could not answer because a bolt of lightning flashed so bright they thought the barn had been hit. The subsequent thunder rocked them. James ran in in his pajamas. "Did you guys hear that?"

They looked at each other as if to say, *Are we deaf?*

Quinn was with Joan and Stephanie in the National Gallery that afternoon when her cell phone rang. It was Patrick. He said urgently, "Quinn, I suddenly thought of something. It just came to me. I know I'm right. I have to see you."

"I'm with Joanie and her girlfriend, and we—"

He cut her off. "Quinn, I was up all night. I'm so tired I can barely see. I'm in the car right now, just leaving Quantico. Can you get away to meet me? At least for an hour? I went to the Web site for Front Runners this morning, thought I crapped out, but then I realized what I hadn't considered before."

She felt as charged as he sounded. "What if I came to the house tonight?"

"Yes. No, it's Susan's book club night. The book bitches gather over their cauldron to dissect Danielle Steel and down copious amounts of wine. How about a drink in Arlington or Alexandria?"

"Patrick, wait, hold on." She heard Joan tell her that she and Stephanie wanted to have dinner with some friends in Adams Morgan. "It turns out I'm free," she said into the phone. "And Arlington's a good idea because the apartment on Crystal Drive is under contract, so I need to drop off my old keys and gate passes and such." She thought about a place. "You're a meat and potatoes man. How about Ruth's Chris, down the street from my old place?"

"Fine. I have an errand in Georgetown first. Eight o'clock all right with you?"

"I'll see you there."

Quinn said, "Patrick," but then stopped herself, not wanting to continue with the rest of her question.

"What?" She heard loud music suddenly. "Damn. I tried to turn the wipers faster and I got Debussy blasting. So what were you about to say?"

She turned away from Joan. "Should I tell Tyler?"

His answer was the answer she feared. "No."

He hung up and then listened to the computerized

woman's voice direct him: "Turn left at the next light. Proceed left from there . . ." He stopped at the light and pulled off his glasses, wiping them with his shirt. Damn, he couldn't see a blasted thing. The rain was impenetrable. Thank God, he thought, for the girl hiding in the dashboard of the car. "Turn left here," she repeated, and he did.

The man sat at the console for a moment, debating the importance of the conversation he'd just heard. He decided it was worth putting through a warning call. It was answered on the first ring. "Yes?"

"Hey, something's happened."

"What?" the other man snapped.

"He just called from the car, wants to meet with Quinn. He sounds like he's learned something substantial."

"Impossible. He's an idiot."

"He put Kevin Mitnick behind bars."

"I'm aware of his greatest hits," the low voice barked.

"I'm only relating what I just heard."

There was no response from the other end.

"Hey, you there?"

"Do it," the man ordered.

"You sure?"

"Do it. We can't take any chances."

"Stop at the next light," the voice from the dashboard instructed Patrick. He didn't realize he was *at* the next stoplight until the voice said, "Stop now. The light is red." He wiped his brow and reached under his glasses to rub his eyes. The fan blowing cool air from the dash was keeping the windows from fogging up the way his old Honda had done, but it was drying his corneas. Lightning turned everything a milky white for a moment. Then thunder cracked loudly nearby. Rain pelted the car as he eased off the gas.

At the next corner, everything seemed to be a sea of color. He saw a swirl, through the water, of red, green, flashing yellow, fluorescent in store windows, blue flashing lights of federal cop cars, but they blended together in a mushy rainbow. His rain-sensing wipers were sensing the water, all right; he felt they were going to scrape arroyos into the glass because they were working so furiously. "Proceed ten feet and turn right," the voice ordered, "onto the Roosevelt Bridge."

Patrick obeyed.

But the minute he did, he knew something was very wrong. Had he not heard her correctly, or had the girl hiding in the dash goofed? He heard a scraping sound outside the car, then the sound of horns, then another crash. He hit the brakes. But they did not work. He seemed, astonishingly enough, to be accelerating.

That's when panic choked him. He was driving the world's safest automobile with technology that could pretty much save anyone from anything, and the brakes didn't hold. He was speeding up. No, he was spinning! It wasn't that the brakes weren't engaging, they were grabbing too tightly for the wet surface. Was he already on the metal grate of the bridge? Is that why he was sliding? Why did he seem to be moving faster? Where was the traction control? Why wasn't it working?

"Accelerate. Accelerate." The voice sounded just as mechanical, but somehow tense, somehow scared—or was it his imagination?

Defying the instruction, he tried pumping the brakes the way he did in the snow. The car careened through something, some barrier. Of the ten air bags in the automobile, only one deployed, on the passenger side. The windshield wipers stopped dead, right where they were sweeping.

He suddenly had the sensation that a bright light was sailing past his head. He whipped his neck to the left, realizing immediately that it wasn't a light that was moving: it was him. He twisted his head so fiercely to the right, to the opposite side of the car, that his glasses flew from his face. It was at that moment he realized that he was airborne.

The splash came as the front end struck the dark, swirling water, and the car pitched forward so that it landed top first in the Potomac. Patrick, upside down, trying desperately to keep his senses about him, reached for the door handle. It was locked. All the doors were supposed to open in the case of a crash, but instead they had frozen shut. He knew what happened. He must have plowed through barricades set up to provide warnings that the bridge was still under construction. Patrick knew that it had been closed the better part of the year. What had he been thinking—that it had suddenly reopened?

His thoughts quickly moved to the problem at hand. The car was sinking, deeper and deeper into the cold black water, and he was still upside down—

the seat belt tensioners had worked and they were holding him. He desperately felt for the seat belt latch, found it, pushed it, and he was freed from the constraint. But the driver's door would not budge.

In desperation, he opened the window. It would only go down partway. Icy water poured in, battering him. Patrick sucked for the last bits of oxygen left in the chamber and took them into his lungs.

He held it as long as he could. He tried to force his way out through the cracked window, but became stuck. At last he let out the breath that his lungs had clung to, and mouthed two words that no one would ever hear. "Susan. James."

And then everything went black.

Chapter Five

Quinn knew the manager at Ruth's Chris because she had often eaten there when she lived nearby. She told him she needed a very private table, so he put her upstairs in a small, comfy room overlooking the river. The rain continued to pour, coming down in dark, heavy sheets. The Potomac, what she could see of it through the rain-splattered windows, was black and forbidding tonight. There was only a squiggly outline of the Washington Monument in the foggy, floodlit background. She sipped her martini slowly, nervous about what Patrick was going to tell her.

She waited until eight thirty, then dialed his cell phone, which did not transmit the call. Thinking that perhaps he was having trouble with the technological miracle he was driving, she waited another fifteen minutes. Then she started to worry in earnest. She called Susan, interrupting her spiel about the book her club was discussing, alarming her, which she didn't mean to do. The rain worried them both, because Patrick was not the world's best driver. "But he's in the world's best car," Quinn reminded her. Susan said something must have come up.

At nine fifteen, Quinn left the restaurant after eating only a salad. Afraid to call from the moving car in the wet streets, she dialed Susan again while the valet was bringing it around. The book club gals had departed, James had just come home—drenched, Susan said—from a birthday party at Sam's house. Quinn decided to go there. On the way, she called Tyler. He said he would join them, and arrived an hour after Quinn did. "Susan, it's going to be okay," he promised, hugging her as he entered. They put on the teakettle and sat around the fireplace and waited. For what seemed like forever.

The call didn't come until almost midnight, after Susan had repeatedly contacted the police. By then she was completely beside herself. When the phone rang, she was certain it was going to be Patrick telling her, laughingly, a mad caper story explaining everything. Instead, a police officer informed her that there had been an accident. Someone had glimpsed Patrick's distinctive license plate—*FinWake*—as the car crashed through the barrier and called it in.

Tyler drove them in his Escalade to the Roosevelt Bridge, where the cop said Patrick's car had gone into the water. The span had been under construction for months and would not be finished for several more. The bridge was being reinforced, and the center roadway was missing while construction proceeded. Patrick had inexplicably driven over the orange cones, mowing down a warning sign with blinking yellow flashers, and straight through a barricade with more flashing lights on it, right off the edge of the roadway into the water. *My God*, Quinn thought. She had been standing looking out at the river from the restaurant while Patrick was floating in it.

"He could be alive!" Susan shouted to the cops and detectives gathered there. "He could have gotten out, swum for shore."

"Yes," the spokesman said, "we have divers going down in a few minutes. We have men searching the banks, also in boats. There is every chance that he made it out of the vehicle. Was he a good swimmer?"

James, who had refused to stay home, shouted, "He is the *best* swimmer."

The cop managed a grim smile. "That's good, kid. That's good."

They stood vigil for hours under umbrellas in the rain, watching the boats, the rescue workers, the divers, find nothing. Finally, at nearly six in the morning, just as Tyler suggested they go get coffee and some food at a nearby restaurant that had just opened for breakfast, word came that they'd located the car. "What about my husband?" Susan cried.

The spokesman shrugged. "Too dark to see down there. They're bringing it up in a little while. We got a boat on the way."

"He's not in there," Susan said, clutching her son to her. "Patrick's not in that car."

But he was. When the crane on the barge lifted the car from the depths, they saw that it was now a beautiful, silver, $76,000 coffin. Once the water had drained from the windows and crevices, they could make out the outline of a man trapped in the partially open window. "Oh," Susan cried, her knees giving way, "no . . ."

"Mom!" James shouted, turning away, clinging to her body with all his might.

"I don't believe it," Tyler whispered, looking stunned.

Quinn couldn't say a thing. Disbelief choked her. Grief flooded her being. But another emotion ran rampant at the same time. When she looked over to see Tyler comforting Susan and James, she was gripped with fear like she'd never known.

Though born in Ireland, Patrick Horgan had come to America as a boy, become a citizen, and proudly served his country in the Vietnam War. Thus, he was buried in Arlington National Cemetery. When Susan accepted the folded flag that had adorned his coffin, she closed her eyes and said an old Irish prayer that Patrick had loved. She and James spent a private moment kneeling at the coffin, then hugged everyone who'd come, inviting them to the house.

"Quinn, it's Tuesday, a workday," Tyler said right after Susan and James had left for home. "I have to get out to Rockville. I've got another one on one with a potential Front Runner."

She understood. "I'm going to spend the night at Susan's."

He nodded. "That's good. She needs all the help we can give her."

Quinn let him kiss her on the cheek, and then nodded and watched him drive away. As she walked toward the line of cars starting to leave the cemetery, a man's voice asked if she needed a ride to the Horgan house. She turned to see Mike Furnari standing there. "Oh, Mike, hello."

He looked devastated. "He was the best partner I ever had. I mean, he was so much more than an agent I worked with."

"I know all too well," she assured him. "My daughter thought of him as her uncle."

He shook his head. "I didn't take it all as seriously as Patrick did, you know?"

"What?"

"The thing he was working on."

She blinked. "What do you mean?"

"Practice Run."

She felt the breath pulled from her. "You think his death has something to do with that?"

He looked her straight in the eye. "Don't you?"

At the Horgan house in McLean, Susan explained to the gathered friends and family what the police investigation had uncovered. Patrick had been relying on his new car to get him to Arlington in the rain, following the directions that the navigational system gave him. The system had prompted him to turn right onto Roosevelt Bridge, despite the signs, cones, and barricade.

"He must not have been aware of it in the rain," a cousin offered. "Visibility was zero."

"You might have a lawsuit against BMW," a neighbor said.

"That's no consolation," Susan snapped. "Still," she told them, "the car's 'key' is actually a computer chip that collects all the information on its operation. You can take the key fob into the dealer, shove it into their computer, and diagnose what's wrong, all without the car."

James said, "Like a black box after an airplane crash."

"Kinda," Susan agreed. "They said the nav system must not have registered that the bridge was out, even though it was supposed to. BMW claims the bridge closure was in the system, and it was impossible that the car would have given him directions to travel that route."

Quinn and Mike Furnari shared a look. Then she pulled him aside, all the way to the barn. "Okay, Mike, level with me. What was Patrick going to tell me that night?"

He hadn't a clue. "Just before I went in to testify before a grand jury in Manhattan, he called me from headquarters to tell me that he had spent the night trying to prove what he'd thought had been a brilliant theory, but that he'd not been able to accomplish that."

She said, "He mentioned going to the Front Runners Web site."

Mike nodded. "Later, he left a message at my office that sounded excited, saying he had come up with another thought, something about the Front Runners, that he was going to check out with you. But I don't know what it was."

"So neither of us do."

He nodded. "But his computer is right here." Mike walked over to it and turned it on.

He started to go through a case of CDs set up near it.

Susan walked in after a while, looking utterly drained.

"You going to be all right?" Quinn asked.

Susan nodded. "I need to go up to James. He's cried himself to sleep every night since it happened. My mom is helping him get ready for bed."

"I'm glad Jane is here to help," Quinn told her.

As Susan passed them, she slipped Quinn a key.

"What's this for?"

"His filing cabinet. Mike knows which one."

Mike was so intent on sliding the CDs in and out of the computer, he hadn't heard them.

"What he was going to tell you has to be in there," Susan assured her.

"He didn't give you *any* idea?" She had thought that if Patrick had any evidence to show her, it would turn up in the car, but only the BMW's thick owner's manual had been found. He had apparently been planning to tell her what he had figured out, not show her hard evidence.

Susan shook her head and left.

Quinn handed Mike the key to Patrick's filing cabinet. "Maybe you'll find something in there."

"Good," Mike said, "because there's certainly nothing on these."

"What?"

"They're blank."

"Erased?"

He shrugged. "Could be. Seems like an awful lot of blank CDs, though."

Quinn looked as concerned as he did.

Mike, who knew where Patrick's secret filing cabinet was located, moved his desk and rolled up the

Persian rug underneath it. Hidden in the floor of the barn, the safe was approved by the FBI. Mike inserted the key into the lock and the door opened easily. When he looked inside, he said, "Someone's been here before us."

Quinn was startled. "How do you know?"

Mike shrugged, pointing. "It's empty."

Quinn was shocked. "Are you sure there was ever anything in it?"

"I know this safe. And I knew Patrick. He kept everything he deemed important in there. I've never seen it empty in my life."

"But Susan hasn't left the house since that night," Quinn reminded him. "The only people here have been me, Susie's mother, Jane, and a few of James' friends."

"Quinn," Mike said gravely, "I don't want you to be upset by what I'm about to suggest, but I have to ask it. What about Tyler? Was he here?"

Quinn and Mike were drinking coffee at midnight in the Horgan kitchen when Susan came down the stairs. "What are you two doing?"

"We're trying to guess why Patrick was so eager to see Quinn last Saturday night."

Susan didn't understand. "The safe didn't tell you anything? His computer files?"

"Someone beat us to it," Mike explained. He told her that sometime since the accident, someone had made their way into the Horgan house, erased all of Patrick's computer discs relating to the investigation, and cleared out the hard files.

She grabbed a coffee mug for herself. Quinn poured. "I don't believe it," Susan said. "How?"

"Hey," Mike reminded her, "Patrick and I ran into roadblocks several times on other cases." Susan winced. Mike realized he'd chosen the wrong word. "I'm sorry."

Susan nodded, realizing she was being naive. She watched Quinn pour some creamer into her mug and then cut her off with her hand. She suddenly blurted out what they had all been thinking but no one had yet voiced. "If it is Practice Run, if somehow these kids become killers because of that game, then we know who really killed Patrick."

Quinn was considering the exact same thing, but could not fathom it. "No, it can't be. Mike and I were talking about it. Someone sent Tyler a game proposal. Someone is using him."

"Quinn, come on," Susan said. "You meet him, he sweeps you off your feet, you suddenly have a handsome man who loves you, a father for your girl, someone in the same business as you are—it's what everyone wants. But you don't really know him. You didn't even know he had a brother."

"There were reasons he didn't tell me about Drew."

"Sure, and those reasons make your heart cave in for him. The poor guy! You feel sorry for him and understand why he hates God. Then you find this game plan, this manifesto. He says it's some nut, something he didn't do. But kids are killing priests and rabbis and reverends. Nothing connects them, nothing at all but one common denominator: Practice Run."

"I know, I know," Quinn said, her nerves jangled. She got up and paced around the room. "But how could he do it? I mean, how could a video game turn all these kids into killers?"

"You already know the answer to that, Quinn," Mike reminded her.

Susan rolled her coffee mug between her hands. "But why do only some of them act out and actually kill?"

Mike said, "Patrick thought it was the kids who had made it to the Front Runner levels. But there are too many of them."

Susan said, "It's like the elite tier of a frequent flyer program."

Quinn shrugged. "But you just don't suddenly go berserk and kill. You need madness, outrage, mental illness, a misguided sense that what you are doing is right. Don't those elements have to be there? Don't you have to somehow justify murder in your own mind?"

"Like the Islamic terrorists," Susan added.

Mike said, "Yes, exactly. Someone who kills in the name of the better good, which is another way of saying in the name of God." He bit his lip. "Or you could be brainwashed or programmed to become an innocent assassin."

There was a long silence.

Mike finally broke it by saying, "Listen, the truth is there's something more that Patrick theorized that he didn't get to share with us. He was stopped. His records taken. If Practice Run is making these kids kill, then it was Tyler who broke in here and stole Patrick's notes—"

Susan gripped Quinn's hand, for they both knew what was coming next.

"And that means for sure it was Tyler who killed him."

Chapter Six

Back at work the next day, Susan tried hard to put on a brave front, but it was clear she was in agony. Quinn told her to take time off, to be good to herself, but Susan insisted that working would be better than staying home, where grief might overwhelm her. Always precise and organized, she filled every extra minute of the work day with filing, reorganizing folders, something to keep her mind occupied. Quinn was proud of her, for she was doing a remarkable job of dealing with her loss. Then, suddenly, when Quinn was walking out of her office, she found Susan weeping with the phone still in her hand.

"Susie, it's okay," Quinn said, setting the phone back in the cradle, pulling her up and into her arms. "It's going to hit you again and again. Let it out. Don't fight it. Be miserable, be devastated, it's the only way to work through it." Then Quinn added softly, "I went through it when I lost my parents."

"It was BMW on the phone," Susan told her as she tried to stop crying. "They completed their investigation into why the navigational system in Patrick's car malfunctioned. They want to see me."

"I'd love to go with you."

"I think I could use some support."

At the BMW dealership where Patrick had bought the car, a humorless German official from BMW's Montvale, New Jersey, headquarters who had examined the car's computer explained what they had found. "The computer in your husband's 7 Series was working correctly. Indeed, the navigation system had picked up the bridge closure, and it was in the car's program. But it had been overridden."

"Overridden?" Quinn asked.

The man said, "Tampered with. It instructed the driver to take the bridge, into the river. Someone was actually directing this action, feeding it into the computer at the time of the incident."

Susan was shocked. "Someone was guiding him?"

"Like remote control?" Quinn added.

The man nodded. "The brakes, traction control, automatic unlocking of the doors, the air bags—all bags but one—were overridden."

"How?" Quinn demanded.

The man pulled out a sealed plastic bag from the drawer and showed it to them. "This was under the right front fender, in proximity to the onboard computer."

Susan and Quinn stared at what looked like a hearing aid battery. "What is it?" Susan asked.

"A powerful high-tech transmitter."

"Oh, my God," Susan said, bringing her hand to her mouth.

"We are sending it to the FBI this afternoon." He raised his eyebrows knowingly. "To Mr. Furnari."

Susan exclaimed. "Who has that kind of technological know-how?"

"Certainly no one at BMW." He shrugged. "It would have to be a computer expert. A genius of some sort."

Quinn closed her eyes.

Quinn and Susan poured themselves some wine when they got back to McLean. "Patrick was a terrible driver," she asserted, "but I knew he wasn't that bad. I knew it had to be something more than being disoriented in the storm." She shook her head. "But I never quite expected what we heard."

Quinn shivered, squirming. Denial was getting the better of her. "But are we sure? Why are we so positive it's Tyler?"

"Because he hates religion. He hates God. Because the manifesto was in his computer. Because he had access to our house. Because he could design an override to the car."

"Someone could have hacked into Patrick's car computer the way they hacked into the game. Someone who might want to set him up, get back at him."

"Who? Name someone."

"I don't know." The word *hacked* spurred a thought. "His brother maybe."

"Why him?"

Quinn explained. "Well, he's in jail for computer crimes."

Susan offered a possibility. "Maybe it's Tyler's assistant, that Veronica gal," Susan said sourly. "I remember that cold bitch from the wedding."

"She's just a secretary. She's not smart enough."

"Right," Susan snapped, "just my point. Tyler is a genius."

"Susie—"

Susan cut her off. She didn't want to hear more denials. "You heard Himmler say only a computer expert could have done that. And to create some kind of genius game that brainwashes kids into becoming part of a future godless army, that takes genius. Sick genius, but genius nonetheless."

Quinn sat silent for a moment. She changed direction. "Maybe going to the authorities about this isn't the only way to stop it. Maybe we should find someone who can destroy the programming."

Susan tried to put her growing anger aside. Yet she could find no real enthusiasm. "Well, who?"

Quinn grasped at straws. "The brother. We just said he's a hacker. If he could hack into the game, he might be able to uncover what's in there."

"You said he's in prison."

"And I don't even know where," Quinn said, abruptly looking doubtful.

"It shouldn't be too hard to find out." Susan looked at Quinn, but suddenly turned away, tying the dish towel she was holding into knots.

"What is it?"

Goose bumps spread over Susan's arms. "You just won't face the fact that it's Tyler, will you?"

"I'm not sure."

Eye to eye, she said, "You're not sure? You paved the way. You started it."

Quinn was startled. "What?"

"You dragged Patrick into this. Now he's dead."

"What are you saying?" Quinn asked. She saw a look in her friend's eyes that she had never before witnessed.

"I'm saying," Susan shouted, "that you're in denial. I'm saying you will do anything to blame this on someone else to relieve your own guilt."

Quinn gasped. "My guilt?"

Susan was holding back tears. But her voice was cutting. "If you hadn't brought Tyler into our lives, my husband might still be alive!"

It hit Quinn like a slap in the face. An angry retort that she knew, as much as she hated it, to be true. *If* Tyler was behind it. She still wasn't positive. No, it wasn't her guilt that was rejecting the notion. It was her desire for irrefutable proof.

But her dearest friend in the world was in agony, and embittered. Could Quinn continue to be the one to comfort her? Or would this chasm begin to separate them forever? She wanted to take Susie's hand, put her arms around her, but thought better of it. Instead she just whispered, "Susie, I'm sorry. I'm so sorry."

Susan could not look at her.

Then, suddenly, the front door slammed. James was home. Susan's mother had picked him up after school and they'd spent a few hours together. Susan put her hand on his shoulder. "You hungry?"

He shook his head. "I ate at Gram's. Dad was gonna take me to the Y to swim with him tonight."

"I'll take you, darling."

He looked like he was about to cry. "I don't want it to be like this, Mom."

"I don't either. Believe me, James, if I could change any of it, I would."

He rubbed his eyes. "Mom, sell the Passat."

"What?" Susan blinked.

"Just sell that car. I won't ride in it anymore." And he walked out.

"I don't understand," Susan started to say.

Quinn stopped her. "I think I know. He won't ride in it because it's German," she explained.

"Oh, my God." Then Susan broke down in tears. Because she understood all too well.

Susan silently started making dinner, and Quinn pitched in to help. Susan did not tell her to get out of her kitchen. Quinn hoped that the earlier outburst had not injured Susan's love for her, but she would give her time to deal with her feelings. Yes, if Tyler was behind it, Quinn did feel guilty. She didn't blame Susan. Not one bit. In her shoes, she'd feel the exact same way.

And then they heard noises coming from the den. Quinn, who hadn't really heard the sounds of computer games since Joanie had played them in her room back at the Virginia condo, didn't immediately recognize them. But Susan did. She froze when the familiar squeals and shots and zapping sounds rocked the walls. She dropped the plate she was holding onto the tile floor. She flew out of the kitchen faster than Quinn could get off her stool. She seemed possessed.

When Quinn ran into the den, what she saw startled her. Susan, her mild-mannered friend and a tol-

erant mother, had snapped. She was standing next to
the desk, holding James' computer keyboard in both
hands, screaming, "You're never to play this game
again! You hear me? You understand me? Never!"

"Mom, no!" he called out, but it was too late. She
slammed the keyboard down onto the windowsill so
hard that several keys flew off. "Play the piano, not
games! Never again—never!" she shouted. Then, dis-
solving, realizing what she'd just done, she leaned
against the window and sobbed.

Quinn put her arm around James and guided him
out of the room.

For two days Quinn waited to hear from Mike
Furnari. She put in calls to him both at Quantico and
at his office in Manhattan. But she heard nothing.
Tyler was in New York, thankfully, so she did not
have to deal with pretending that everything was just
fine before she got some kind of confirmation from
Mike. But doing nothing drove her crazy. So she
picked up the phone and after a few calls learned that
Drew Concardi, Tyler Bryant's half brother, was in a
new federal prison, a minimum-security facility in
the middle of the Arizona desert. On the Internet, she
read the institution's quirky history. The IRS had con-
fiscated an unfinished resort, and rather than let it sit
empty (there had been no buyers), the government
decided to put it to use. She found out that the warden's name was Aggie Spivak, and that the phone
number was readily available.

But the moment she was about to call there, Susan
walked into her office with the news that the ship-

ment of computers destined for China had arrived. "Are we going to put the games on them?"

Quinn blinked. She hadn't even thought about that. "Yes. All but Practice Run."

"What if Tyler finds out?"

"I'll tell him it was an error, an oversight. I want to see the brother. He's in Arizona. Where am I flying to next? I know you booked something."

"Kansas City, day after tomorrow."

Quinn laughed at the ironic choice. "Yeah. I have to play the smiling wife of the world's great game guy, thanking the city for their commitment to education."

"You'll do fine. But you won't have time to go to Arizona. Joan has a break from school and is meeting you and Tyler in New York."

Quinn closed her eyes. "I forgot."

"Got to keep up appearances."

Quinn nodded. "Hey, how is James doing?"

"Okay. He understood that I went crazy. But I stand by my edict: No more Practice Run."

"He hasn't asked why?"

"Constantly. I refuse to answer. But I'm sure he's playing it at Sam's."

"Tyler's hard at work on the new version that arrives at Easter."

"God help us."

"I don't want to sound like Tyler," Quinn said, "but God's not going to have anything to do with it."

In Kansas City to give a speech on education, Mrs. Tyler Bryant, as everyone now called Quinn, noticed a familiar face in the crowd: Tyler's good friend Brandon DiForio. When Quinn came over to him, he introduced his pretty wife, Candy, and they immediately suggested they have a drink together in the hotel lounge.

Nestled in a quiet corner, Candy said she was sorry she had not made it to Quinn and Tyler's wedding. "I hear it was pretty cool."

Quinn joked, "A girlfriend of mine said thank God we did it in Costco because it's the only place you can witness nuptials and buy toilet paper, filet mignon, and laundry soap at the same time."

"A wedding after my own heart," Candy agreed.

"You should talk," Quinn said. "Tyler told me you two got married on Internet radio."

"It was wacky," Candy explained. "It was June, we wanted new listeners for our show, so it just fit."

Quinn turned to Brandon. "How did you and Tyler become such good friends?"

He smiled. "We were young and crazy. I think we liked each other's uncommon first names, you know? I mean Brandon and Tyler—it was a bond."

"He was close to you but not his half brother?"

He nodded and played with his tie. "His mom was always three sheets to the wind, so home wasn't a place he wanted to be. Oh, I think he wanted to be close to Drew, but the kid was such a loner. Plus the age difference. Ten years is huge."

"Why was Drew a loner?"

He looked blank, considered the question. "He never had social skills. He was more like a jock, but he wasn't really. He was just weird. I think he resented Tyler's pizazz."

"His whole life?"

Brandon smiled. "Tyler was always onstage. The ultimate overachiever."

"You think Drew resented his fame, then?"

"Ty overshadowed everybody," Brandon said. "I think maybe the hacking incident was Drew's way of proving himself smarter."

"Smarter?" Quinn laughed.

"It outdid his famous brother."

"Commit treason to get a headline bigger than bro's?"

Brandon shrugged. "Had it not been right after 9/11, I'm sure Tyler could have gotten Drew off with a lighter sentence."

"Why does he hate God so much?" Quinn suddenly asked.

"Drew?" Brandon asked, caught off guard.

"Tyler."

Brandon quickly recovered. "Lots of people don't believe in God."

"I don't," Candy interjected.

"I do," Quinn said, "but that's neither here nor there. I was just wondering why Tyler has such a deep-seated loathing for all things religious. You must have realized it back in your college days."

Brandon said, almost snarling, "Catholicism was shoved down my throat. But all those prayers didn't help keep my parents alive."

Candy explained that Brandon's father had been killed in a freak accident at work, when he was very young. In the very next year his mother had been diagnosed with pancreatic cancer. "He and his sister were raised by their grandmother, who was very devout."

Quinn wouldn't be sidetracked. "Were both Tyler's mother and father nonbelievers?"

"*Drunk* is the only word I'd ever apply to his mom," Brandon said. "I don't know about his father."

Quinn said, "You know, I always thought that someone turns atheist only after having been religious first. A reaction, you know?"

Brandon glanced at his wife, and she immediately looked at her watch. "It's that time, my dear."

They got up. Brandon asked, "Quinn, you still in town tomorrow night?"

Quinn nodded. "Meetings all day, flying out Thursday morning."

"Come for dinner."

Quinn manufactured a warm smile. "I'd love to."

At the DiForios' house, Quinn felt oddly uncomfortable. Although the home was decorated with taste, she kept noticing—in the living room magazine rack, on the den bookshelves, in the pile of reading material in the bathroom—literature about religion. There were old magazines, saved only, Quinn surmised later, because they had cover stories about God and religion. Most of the books on the shelf were books about religion through history, thick tomes on Islam and Christianity and the religious-right movement in the South.

At dinner, when the subject of Tyler's lack of faith came up again, Brandon said, "Maybe I'm to blame. I was so rabidly antireligion because of the way I lost my parents that maybe some of it rubbed off on Ty."

After dinner, a curious Quinn asked Candy to

show her the rest of the house. After a tour of the usual bedrooms and baths, she led Quinn down a breezeway to what looked like an editing studio in what had been the original garage. Quinn spied several computers and scanners, screens and reels, a control board and no windows. "What do you use this for?" she asked.

Smiling, though sounding slightly nervous, Candy replied, "The radio show. We work from home."

"Forgive me, I never asked," Quinn said. "It's a talk show, right?"

"Right."

"What about?"

"About religion mostly," Candy replied.

That left Quinn feeling chilled. But it certainly explained the reading material. When she was leaving, however, she saw something on the foyer wall that she had missed when she arrived: a wall-sized blowup of a poster advertising the first edition of Practice Run. Not even the egotistical Tyler had such an adornment on his New York apartment wall.

Quinn graciously said good-bye. Yet she walked out of the house certain that Tyler had kept another secret from her. Brandon DiForio was much more involved with his business than he had let on.

Quinn called the Dave Gallup Correctional Institute in Arizona and got Warden Aggie Spivak. Quinn identified herself as Andrew Concardi's sister-in-law and asked if she could visit him. The warden seemed surprised by Quinn's request. Drew would see no one, except perhaps his brother, who, she added in a disapproving tone, had been promising to visit ever since Drew had been incarcerated.

Quinn blinked. "I thought it was Drew who would not see Tyler."

"It's the opposite," the warden stated. "And I should know."

Quinn thought that was curious. Tyler had obviously lied. But she couldn't tell a stranger that. "Listen, I think I could help Drew understand why Tyler has never visited, and perhaps, in the long run, reunite the brothers."

"I'll relay the message to the prisoner," Aggie told her. "I'll call back and let you know."

Quinn gave her the number and hung up.

"Mom, what's wrong?" Joan Roberts had watched her mother pick at her fettuccine with veal ragout at Maria Pia for over forty minutes, eating hardly a bite. She had come up from school to spend a wonderful weekend in New York with her mom. But it wasn't turning out to be very wonderful. "Come on, what is it?"

Quinn shrugged. "Work. Pressures. Stuff."

"Is it your marriage?"

Quinn looked up at her daughter. "Why do you think that?"

"Hello? You're not yourself, Mom. Tyler said it too, last night at the play. You seem . . . worried. Distant. I picked up on it when I last saw you in D.C."

"I have a lot on my mind."

"Well, I came up to New York to have fun, and we're not." Joanie put her fork down and finished her Diet Coke. "I can be miserable just fine at school, you know."

Quinn reached across the table and touched her daughter's arm. "Honey, I have a problem right now, a big one, one I can't talk about."

Joanie froze. "You're not sick or something, are you?"

Quinn smiled and assured her she was perfectly well.

"That's good," the girl said, breathing easier. "Stephanie's mom has decided she's going to do chemo first, then surgery."

"That's often the procedure these days," Quinn said.

Joan threw her an accusatory gaze. Did she know that from firsthand experience?

"Hey, I'm fine. Honest."

They finished up and left the restaurant. As they were walking, Quinn asked how Joan was liking her second term. "Is it tougher than you imagined?"

The girl shrugged. "No. Yes. No."

"That's certainly clear."

Her daughter hesitated. "Mom, Stephanie is thinking of taking time off to go help her mom."

"That seems right."

Joanie paused again, a beat too long. "I've thought about going with her."

Quinn stopped walking. "When were you thinking of doing this?"

Joanie shrugged, "Soon, I guess. I don't know."

"You're dropping out?"

"No," Joan said defensively, "just a break."

"You'll lose all your credits for the semester."

"*You* did it," Joan reminded Quinn. "You took a year off to travel."

Quinn had done just that, and had always been glad she did. She had to admit that now. "There's something to be said for it, yes, but couldn't you take a break, say, after this year is finished?"

"Maybe. But I would feel better going with Stephanie."

They walked some more. This sudden decision was very mysterious. It was unlike her daughter. She wondered if something else was prompting it. She had to be careful how she asked. She would make it sound as if she were changing the subject. "So you still playing Practice Run?"

Joanie squealed. "I wish! Who has the time for games?"

That was exactly what Quinn wanted to hear. She pressed no further. As they started across the street, Joan took her mother's hand. "What?" Quinn asked, surprised by the gesture.

"I just want you to be okay," her daughter said. "Whatever it is. I want you to be okay, you and Tyler to be okay—"

"Hey, don't worry!" Quinn stopped and hugged her girl.

"Mom, when you first met Tyler, you were ecstatic. You had always said you never expected love to come around again. Now you don't seem so happy." Joanie waited for a reply, but Quinn didn't offer any. She turned her head and kissed her mother's cheek. "I love you, Mom. I love you a lot."

Quinn said, "I'll say a prayer for your friend's mom, honey." She held back the tears that she was hiding, for she knew that if she let them fall, she would spill everything to her daughter, and then there would be no turning back.

Augusta, Georgia

Willie finished his chores early. Knowing he had time before he needed to cook his mama dinner, he ran into the battered shack they called a house and started stripping in the kitchen. "Willie Chesterfield, what you doin'?" his mother called from her recliner in the parlor. "You not goin' back to school to waste time on that computer again, hear?"

"No, Mama. The computer lab is closed now. I've got band practice." Willie tossed his dirty, grass-stained shirt into the old Maytag. He found a clean one from the pile that he had fetched earlier from the line strung between the shack and the rickety shed out back. "We're practicing for the parade, Mama." He yanked off his filthy old jeans and stepped into the Wal-Mart cargo shorts he loved. "I'll be back in plenty of time for dinner."

"I told you, I ain't got no money for no uniform," his mother warned him.

"It's okay, Mama. Remember, we sold that candy? It raised money for the instruments and for the uniforms." He laced up his Nikes again, then looked in the faded mirror. He dipped his hand under the kitchen sink faucet and pressed his hair back off his forehead.

"Willie, child, I'm still feelin' poorly."

"What can I get you, Mama?"

"A little lemonade, baby."

"Sure, Mama." He looked up at the clock as he opened the refrigerator door. It wasn't very cold in there, but he wasn't about to tell her that. She'd be moaning and groaning about how everything was falling apart and she had no money and the welfare wasn't what it used to be and did you know that Gladys Washburn down the street got herself a new Whirlpool Gold, now how'd she manage that, she must be whoring again.

"Not a lot a ice, Willie."

"Right, Mama." He put two cubes in the glass and brought it out to her.

She was staring out the window. "Well, I'll be. Them again."

"Them who, Mama?" the boy asked.

"Them missionary fellas."

"Where?" He followed her gaze. Across the street, under Marie Johnston's magnolia tree, were two men in their twenties, dressed, in the sweltering heat, in dark suits, white shirts, and ties. "Them Baptists?" he asked.

"Mormons." She said it as if she were saying *cockroaches* or *snakes*. "They done been here before, child. They gonna save our souls. I told them, 'Children, my soul's been saved by Jesus way before you was born.'"

Willie smiled. "You think they'll come here?"

"Mormons, Willie. They don't give up easy."

"Oh."

She repositioned herself, all 310 pounds, in her recliner so that she could keep an eye on them out the window. "See, Marie Johnston's turning them away.

Shoo! Gotta be Northern boys, think Baptists need savin'."

"You okay, Mama?"

"Sure, child. Run along now. I'm gonna be getting hungry, and I don't know what I do if my little Willie ain't here to cook me those good pork chops."

Willie, who had consistently been at the top of his class in all the years he'd been in school, thought his mother sounded like the perfect stereotype Negro he'd seen on old old movies like *Gone with the Wind.* But to try to get her to change was pointless; things were what they were. "You just run along, child, and you toot that horn loud, you hear your mama?"

He didn't play a horn. He played a snare drum. But he didn't correct her. Because suddenly he had no intention of going to band practice. Instead, he stared at the closet where they kept the brooms, the broken stepladder, and the old paint cans, looking for the shotgun that his cousin Jimmy had given them when his dad had run off.

"Willie, what you doin' in there?"

"Nothing, Mama."

"I don't hear you leavin', boy." Then her attention shifted to the Mormons. "Oh, well, I told you. They comin' on here."

Willie opened the closet door.

They heard the footsteps—hard ones made by shoes with leather soles—on the creaking porch, and then a knock on the door. "Willie, you gonna get the door? Or you want your mama to scare these boys off?"

"You can get it, Mama. You know them."

"Okay. Lordy, I'm a-coming," she shouted, pulling

her bulk from the chair. "Yes, yes, yes, I know, youse in a hurry to get my soul, but my soul already been got." She walked into the little entrance area, where a dusty Christmas wreath still hung incongruously. They knocked again. She reached for the handle and pulled open the door.

Two blue-eyed, bright-faced young men stood there. "Howdy, ma'am," the younger one said.

"Afternoon," the blonder one said.

"You boys, when you gonna give up on me?" Mrs. Chesterfield said with a warm smile. "Go save that woman down the street, that Gladys Washburn. She got the devil in her."

"Mama?"

"Maybe you can take her back to Salt Lake City for some savin' and give me that nice new icebox she got with the devil's money." The woman let out a laugh.

"We're from Orem, ma'am," one of the missionaries said.

"Mama, move aside."

"What, child?"

As Mrs. Chesterfield turned to look at her son, the two boys saw what was standing behind her: a scrawny teenager holding a shotgun. The second the big woman stepped to her left, the gun blazed. The younger of the two missionaries was shot in the stomach, and doubled over into the house. The other turned to run, but a second blast stopped him in his tracks. Shot in the back, he died as he sprawled down the steps of the house.

Willie Chesterfield did not hear his mother's cries, or even realize that she had sunk to her knees in shock and grief. He didn't even know she was there anymore. He was in a kind of trance that had started the moment she had said the word *missionaries*. As he went out the back door and into the shed, Marie Johnston came running across the street barefoot, screaming, calling for help.

When the police found him fifteen minutes later, Willie was hanging from the only item he'd not yet put on when the missionaries came: a new belt that he'd gotten for his birthday, a cool one that matched the oxblood of his Sunday school Skechers shoes, and had been lying on top of the washing machine. Now it formed a noose, from which his limp body hung.

Willie Chesterfield was fifteen years old.

Chapter Seven

When the Georgia murders hit the news the next morning, Mike Furnari called Quinn. "Sit tight. Don't let your husband know anything's up. I've found something. I'm going to try to get to D.C. to see you tonight."

Quinn didn't have time to respond. He'd already hung up.

As she cooked dinner for Tyler that night, she did what Mike had instructed, tried her best to make Tyler feel that nothing was wrong. But she kept thinking about a boy who never had a chance, a boy named Willie Chesterfield. As with all the others, there seemed to be no motive, no clue as to what would cause such an aberration in a perfectly normal and smart kid, but she was sure of one fact. She knew that young Willie had been addicted to Practice Run.

She tried to keep her worries from Joanie when her daughter called later that evening. Joan reminded her that Parents' Weekend was two short days away, and she expected them both to come. There was no way that Quinn could tell Tyler not to come, so she pretended that she was looking forward to a wonderful weekend together as "a family." Joan also assured her she still hadn't decided what to do about school. Perhaps if they were right on campus, Quinn thought, she could talk her into staying the rest of the spring term.

Tyler and Quinn ate in the dining room, with a fire burning in the corner. His mind was on the Willie Chesterfield killing as well. "One thing I'm sure of," he told her, "is that when the new version of the game comes out, whatever corrupted copies that might be out there will be obsolete, because no one will be playing the old version."

What worried Quinn was what he was going to put on the new version.

In the middle of dinner, her cell phone rang in the kitchen. She knew it was Mike. She'd been carrying the phone around with her because she was waiting for his call. But when they'd sat down to eat, she had forgotten to bring it to the dining room. Because Tyler had gotten up to get seconds in the kitchen, he answered it. Quinn dashed into the kitchen on the third ring, about to tell him to let her get it, when Tyler handed her the phone, and said, "It's some guy named Michael."

She froze. Tyler saw her reaction and joked, "Secret boyfriend?" He waited for her to laugh.

She did not. She played nonchalant. "Oh, please," she muttered, "gimme a break."

He said, "From the look on your face, it might be true." He dished up his food and walked back into the dining room.

Into the phone, Quinn said, loud enough for Tyler

to hear, "Hello? So did you get the computers for me, or are we going to have to go another round?"

"Right," the voice said at the other end of the line, covering.

Quinn said, "Wait, I'll have to go upstairs to the study and check my calendar. Hold on." She walked through the dining room and up the stairs, muttering to Tyler, "I wish they'd leave me alone outside the office."

He nodded, and she couldn't tell if he believed her.

Upstairs, out of earshot, Quinn said, "Okay."

"You free tomorrow at noon?"

"Yes. Yes, of course," she said eagerly.

"You up for a walk?"

She wondered if she was hearing right. "A walk? Why?"

"Safer."

"I understand."

"Noon. Lady Bird park?"

"Fine." He hung up.

When she returned downstairs, she told Tyler, "Michael represents an Asian manufacturer we've not worked with before. Cheap laptops."

"Ah." He looked like he was pouting.

Then she laughed. "Oh, you're jealous."

"A little."

"That's silly, honey." She walked to him, kissed him on the cheek, and took his plate. "Now, I got some cheesecake this afternoon . . ."

Soon, they were sitting on the sofa where they had had their first kiss, eating cheesecake and drinking espresso. "I think," Tyler said apprehensively, "that I worried about the call from that guy because you've been so distant lately."

She knew she couldn't deny it. No matter how hard she'd tried to cover her fear that she had married a madman, it crept into every moment of their lives. So she thought of a convenient, and true, worry. "I'm concerned about Joan."

He was taken by surprise. "Something I don't know?"

She said, "She might quit school."

"What? She's dean's list material." He was truly concerned.

She was glad. Her change of subject had worked. "She wants to backpack around Europe."

"Now?"

"Yes. I told her to wait till the year's over, but I'm afraid she may not listen to me."

He seemed shocked. "Why?"

She shrugged. "Stephanie is considering going to Germany to help her mom through the cancer treatments and surgery. Joan wants to go with her."

"I see. That's very generous of her."

"I guess I've been on edge about it."

He put an arm around her. "Hey, it's her life."

She giggled. "But it's my money."

"Honey," he said, pulling her closer, "it's not the end of the world."

She feigned a smile. Then she let her head drop to his shoulder. She knew that would placate him for now. When they got up, she would determinedly do the dishes, telling him she had papers to go over and that he should go to bed, she'd catch up with him later. When he would be fast asleep. When he would not be awake or aware enough to want her.

It was living hell.

Mike Furnari took off his earmuffs when he saw Quinn drive into the parking lot off the George Washington Parkway. "Walk with me," he said, before she had even gotten all the way out of the car.

She did. "Did you find out what Patrick learned?"

"No. I'm not sure we'll ever know that. But I uncovered something on the discs."

She felt the icy air fill her lungs. "Which ones?"

"All of them."

She stopped. "Every disc you have?"

He nodded. And continued walking. "It's subliminal stuff, and I can't decode it yet. But I'll bet my career it's what we're after. I've got the best technicians on it, but it's brilliant, it's genius. And, so far, impossible to break into."

Brilliant, genius. Those words again. Tyler.

"Whoever created this didn't want anyone—certainly not law enforcement—finding out what is there." He led her over a bridge.

She realized they were heading along a path paralleling a parking lot for the Pentagon, which made her think about Drew. And the fact that the warden had not gotten back to her. She turned to Mike. "So you believe it now?"

He quickened his pace. "I was much more skeptical than Patrick was, I'll admit that. But yes, I do."

"But you can't stop it?"

"Stop it? We aren't even sure what it is."

"You know what it is!" she said loudly. "Another boy just killed because of it."

"I know what it is, yes. I believe you. But I can't stop it till we decipher exactly what is there and figure out how it does what it does and learn how to disarm it."

"How much time is that going to take?"

"No clue. But I think your husband should be told."

"No!" She realized she had shouted it.

Mike pulled out his water bottle from the holder around his hips. He leveled with her. "You and Patrick feared Tyler himself created this, didn't you?"

"Yes."

He took a drink and faced her, wiping the wet from his lips. "You must be in living hell right now."

She nodded. "I am."

He led her to a nearby bench. "Listen," he said, "at this point there's not much I can do. Oh, I could seize outstanding copies of the game, shut Zzzyx down for a while, but I don't even have probable cause. My superiors won't listen to gut instinct, only hard fact."

She looked distraught. "In the meantime, more people will die?"

"Tell me more. What else do you know? Anything that could help lead me somewhere."

She thought. "There's this guy. His name is Brandon DiForio. He's Tyler's college friend. He runs some kind of Internet radio station. He and his wife are rabid atheists. I was in their house. They had a big Practice Run poster on the wall. Books on religion. I'll bet anything that they have something to do with it. I think something's happening there."

He nodded. "Makes sense that he wouldn't create this out of the Zzzyx offices in Rockville."

"The DiForios live in Kansas City."

She expected him to look surprised that the possible base of operations was so far away, but his face registered nothing of the kind. His reaction was more like, *Ah, it's starting to fit now.*

"What is it?" she asked.

"Kansas City."

"Yes?"

"Drew Concardi." He drew up his legs and crossed them under him on the bench.

"What's Kansas City got to do with Drew?"

"That's where the hacking came from. His computer was traced to Kansas City."

"I didn't know that."

"He said his laptop had been stolen, that he'd never been in Kansas City, but American Airlines had a record of tickets that put him there on the days he broke through the firewall in the computers in that very building." He nodded over toward the hulking Pentagon.

"But that could have been set up," she said, remembering Mike's doubt about the case. "Someone could have bought those tickets and flown there pretending to be him."

"Someone who had taken his computer but managed to put it back in his apartment by the time we showed up," Mike agreed.

And Quinn knew who. "His brother." She shivered. "So we're right."

"Let's walk some more," Mike said, unfastening

his locked legs and jumping up. "Tell me everything else you know."

As they walked at a slow pace, Quinn told him her theory about Drew, that he might be able to help because she guessed that the real reason Drew was locked away was that he'd figured out just what they had come to learn. That Practice Run was Tyler's evil mind control that needed to be stopped.

"I want to see Drew," she told him. "I've already called the warden at the prison where he's serving his term. I'm waiting for her to get back to me."

"I'd like to talk to him myself," Mike said. "I think he'd remember me."

"You met during the investigation?"

He nodded. "Many times. Good kid. Kinda tough, kinda quirky."

As they neared the parking lot again, Mike reminded her to do just what she had been doing: to go about her business as if everything was normal, and to not let her husband get even a glimmer of the fact that she suspected him. Tyler had to be convinced that the FBI investigation had died with Patrick.

"I really fear for all those kids out there who are being brainwashed," she said.

"I fear for you," Mike replied.

"Me?"

He gave her a look as if she were completely dense. "Your life is in danger. Don't you realize that?"

Chapter Eight

Parents' Weekend at William and Mary was a festive affair. Tyler booked a room at a romantic bed and breakfast not far from the campus. Quinn, who at this point could barely stand the sight of her husband, much less his touch, tried something she had never in her life thought people really did: She said, "I have a headache."

Actually, she feigned car sickness as they neared Williamsburg. And although she perked up enough to have a hamburger with Joanie and Stephanie and three of their friends, when back in the room Quinn managed to put off Tyler's advances. It was a shame, she thought. The bed was a four-poster, the bedding satin and silk, the fireplace enchanting. She was with one of the most handsome men she'd ever known, a man women would line up to spend a night with in this setting. But she could not abide his touch.

In the morning, she went for a power walk with Joanie, the way they used to when they lived in Crystal City. Quinn didn't want to alarm her, but she needed to make sure she wasn't playing Practice

Run. After a half hour of light conversation, she brought up how excited everyone was about the new version coming out at Easter. Joanie astonished her by saying, "Great. But I don't play it anymore."

"You don't?"

"No time, Mom. This isn't an easy school, you know?"

Quinn stopped on top of a hill. She bent forward, resting her hands on her knees, breathing deeply, fearing that the next words Joanie was going to tell her were that she was quitting this school.

"Mom? Earth to Mom."

"What?" She snapped to reality. "I'm sorry, my mind wandered off." They both sipped some water. Quinn assumed Joan had decided to stay in school, and thus didn't bring up the subject.

"Why are you worried about me playing Dad's game?" Joan asked.

"Worried?"

"You said it once before too."

"Well, you were addicted to it once," Quinn said. "I can't believe you've been able to give it up."

"There are more important things now."

Relieved, Quinn stretched out some, shifting from leg to leg.

"Mom, don't tell Tyler, okay? I don't want him to be disappointed."

"It'll be our secret, honey," Quinn assured her.

Joanie dropped the bombshell at dinner. In a quaint little country restaurant that cost big-city prices, she announced, "I've dropped out."

Quinn dropped her fork. It clattered on her dinner plate.

Tyler put his hand on Quinn's. "That's what your mother has been fearing."

"I wanted to tell you earlier, Mom, but thought we should all be together for it."

"When?" Quinn asked her daughter.

"Today."

"You waited until Parents' Weekend to tell us?"

"We just decided. Stephanie told her dad this afternoon. I want you to meet him. He flew in from Hamburg."

Tyler said, "We can all be depressed together."

"No," Joanie tried to assure them, "this is good. Mom, Dad, listen. It's not just Steph and her family. I'm not happy here. And it's not the school. It's that I should have taken some time off in between high school and college. I've been in classes since I was, like, what? Three?"

"Four," Quinn corrected her.

"Right. It's time for a break."

Tyler looked concerned. "What are you going to do?"

A dreamy smile brightened her face. "See the world. Stephanie knows people in Paris, and I want to see Rome and Florence, maybe the Greek islands. We're just going to knock around and come back in time for school in the fall."

Quinn looked at Tyler, who shrugged helplessly. "I guess it's done, then," she said, dejected. "We obviously don't have any say in the discussion."

"Mom, just let me grow up."

Quinn nodded, trying to forget the fears and apprehension of the past month. "I imagine I'll have to." She picked up her fork, trying to erase the upset from her face. She speared a potato on her plate. "Just don't come home pregnant by some long-haired Romeo from Oslo who seduced you with poetry on the banks of the Tiber."

Joan laughed. And hugged her mother. "You're the greatest, Mom."

"Mrs. DiForio?"

"What are you selling?" Candy asked the man in her doorway. Her voice turned snide when she added, *"The Watchtower?"*

"My name's Mike Furnari. I'm an agent with the Federal Bureau of Investigation." Mike showed her his badge and ID. "I'd like to ask you and your husband some questions, if you don't mind."

The woman looked startled. "He's . . . Brandon is on the air."

Mike smiled. "I tuned in the other day. Interesting show. I don't mind waiting."

She pulled the door open wider and let him in. "What is this about?"

"We're conducting an investigation into a video game called Practice Run." He glanced at the huge poster on the wall and nodded. "I see I've come to the right place."

Candy backpedaled quickly, ushering him into the living room. "Would you like something to drink?"

"Sure. Got a soda?"

"Coming right up." She nearly fled the room.

When she left, Mike saw what Quinn had been talking about. There must have been two hundred books on religion. It fit, because their talk show was all about why it should be eradicated. "I understand," he said when the woman returned with a can of Pepsi, "that Brandon is an atheist because his parents died when he was very young."

She nodded. "No God would allow that sort of pain and suffering. But how do you know that?"

"Heard the show, heard him talking about it. How about you?"

"Me?"

"Why do you hate God?"

"Brandon showed me why the very concept of God is ludicrous."

Mike sipped his Pepsi. "There's a book I like. Called *Why Bad Things Happen to Good People*. You should read it."

"I have," she said, "Rabbi Kushner." She pointed to one of the books on the shelves. "It's crap."

"I think it's helpful putting bad things into perspective, like parents suffering with painful cancer, or an accident that suddenly kills a father in the prime of life. It shows us that man has free will. It isn't just up to God."

Brandon DiForio walked in. Surprised to see Mike, he asked, "Who are you?"

Mike told him.

"What do you want?"

"I investigate computer crime."

Candy made a joke of it. "I can assure you, our computers have committed no crimes."

"My friend and partner, Patrick Horgan," Mike continued, "was recently killed by someone with brilliant computer knowledge. I'm very interested in learning who was behind it."

A flicker of unease crossed Brandon's face. "But why come here?"

"That," Mike said, gesturing to the big poster of Practice Run. "We think that has something to do with it."

"So why don't you talk to Tyler?" Brandon asked.

"I plan to. And his wife as well. Do you work with him?"

Brandon shook his head. "He's my best friend. I stood up for him and Quinn. But I don't have any business connection with him."

"Just share an antipathy for God, huh?"

Brandon didn't look amused. "We share many interests."

"How well did you know his brother?"

"Drew? Not well at all. I'm Tyler's age."

"Was Drew ever here? In this house? On your computers?"

Brandon laughed. He was unsure whether to answer yes or no. "Why would he have been?"

"Are you investigating Tyler or Drew?" Candy asked with a hostile edge.

Mike saw that he was getting nowhere. "Mind if I look around?"

"Yes," Candy said, her hands on her hips. "I most certainly do mind."

"If you want to search the place," Brandon informed him, "you'll need a warrant."

Mike's eyes turned hard. "That can be arranged." He got to his feet and told them he'd be back with a warrant in his hand.

The moment he left, Brandon watched him walk to his car. Then he grabbed the phone. When the call was answered, he said, "We have trouble. Big trouble."

Five hours later, Mike Furnari returned to the Di-Forio house in pouring rain. Two Kansas City police officers accompanied him, one remaining in the car out front, the other going to the back door to cover it. Brandon DiForio, in his pajamas, opened the front door before Mike was able to knock. "Man of your word, huh, Mike?"

Mike held out the warrant, and Brandon took it, pulling the door open wider, encouraging the FBI agent to enter. From the foyer, Mike saw Candy, in a bathrobe, sitting on the sofa. "I'm sorry it's so late," Mike said, "but if you'll just show me where your studio is, we can hurry this along."

Candy said nothing. She stared at him with folded arms and a look of contempt on her face.

"Follow me," Brandon said, "it's back here."

Mike followed Brandon through the kitchen and down a breezeway that had once connected the house and garage, but now served as a kind of hallway to the studio. Because it was lined with windows on both sides, something caught Mike's eye as they approached the door to the studio. Outside the glass that looked out on the backyard, Mike glimpsed the front of a vehicle. All he saw was the windshield, the hood, and chrome front bumpers. But he knew it was a Chevy Suburban. The truck of choice for the U.S. government. Which made him go stiff.

"Well," Brandon said, holding open the door to the studio, "you wanna look in here or not?"

Mike swallowed. And told himself he was being paranoid. Lots of people chose black Suburbans. He could well imagine Brandon driving one. Hell, last he heard, his ex-wife drove a Lincoln Navigator. The FBI didn't have a lock on SUVs. He shook off the apprehension and walked into the studio.

He instantly felt the cold steel of a gun press into the back of his neck. "Hold it right there."

As his hands were bound behind him and his weapon taken from inside his jacket, he suddenly knew why Drew Concardi's crime had been traced to Kansas City. His mouth was gagged and a burlap bag placed over his head and tied around the neck. Now he also knew why the Bureau had never learned about Tyler's evil plan. And he knew what had happened to the policemen who had come to the house with them: the Bureau had flexed their muscle when Mike entered the house, and sent the good officers back to the station house.

As he was led by one man and shoved by the other in to the Suburban, he knew something else that he had never counted on: Tonight he was going to die.

He rode for what seemed like hours in the back seat of the Suburban, feeling the gun pressed to his head the entire time. He could only think of the reports he'd read about the *Wall Street Journal* reporter Daniel Pearl, who'd been kidnaped in Pakistan in much the same way, then driven a long way to disorient him.

After an hour, Mike could tell that the SUV had turned off pavement and was now using all four wheels to navigate a muddy road filled with potholes. The two men, whose faces he had never even glimpsed, never said a word. He doubted he'd have recognized them even if he had seen them. He wondered if they were even agents. Probably not.

The Suburban stopped abruptly. Mike heard the driver's door open first, then the passenger's door. It was raining hard. That's why he felt the mud under the tires. They pulled him out of the vehicle and shoved him. He fell, tripping over rocks or tree roots, he couldn't tell which, and then felt one of the men kick him in his side, ordering him back to his feet. He groaned as he stood up, for the pain seemed to paralyze him.

They made him walk for what seemed twenty minutes, but was probably half that. The problem was that they were going through heavy brush. Were they going to kill him in some remote place and leave him for the animals to eat? He cringed at the thought. And wracked his brain to think of what he could do, but he was helpless and he knew it. He prayed.

Suddenly, he heard water. Rushing water. It sounded like a small creek that was overflowing with runoff from the rain.

"Jesus, the mud," one of his captors suddenly said.

"Shit!" The other one sounded pissed off. "Careful."

"This is close enough," the first guy said.

"The orders said . . ."

A crack of thunder obliterated the rest of his sentence. As the noise rattled his teeth, Mike suddenly felt the earth under his feet giving way. He was sinking, sliding, as if falling into quicksand. The bank on which he was standing had collapsed. He was flailing in thick mud.

"Goddammit!" one of the voices shouted.

"Grab my arm, hold on," the other one ordered.

The order wasn't being given to Mike. He figured the second guy was trying to prevent the first one from ending up where he was, in what now felt like an ice bath. Cold water was swirling around him, twisting him, pulling him with its force. He could hear shouts from above, a panicked voice screaming, "There, he's there!"

"I can't see him!"

Mike held his breath and went down under the water. He knew the men were trying to find him. He didn't know if they had flashlights or not. But the lightning would certainly illuminate him. When he heard thunder, he could come up again—but would he hear it under water? His ears rang with the force of the current. He let himself go. And slammed into what he guessed was a tree fallen across the ravine.

Unable to breathe, he surfaced, gasping for breath, feeling mud in his throat because the gag tied around his mouth held his lips open. He sucked in air, choked, tried to pull in a breath, planning to go under again . . .

Shots rang out. He felt the first one blow through his shoulder, the pain hot and searing. The second bullet missed his neck by an inch, kicking up water as it struck the stream. But the third one, the third one hit him as a sharpshooter should: square in the chest.

And everything went black.

Chapter Nine

The phone rang Monday morning after Tyler had left for Rockville, just as Quinn was about to walk out the door to go to her office. She grabbed it, hoping it was Mike. Instead, an unfamiliar voice said, "Is this Quinn Bryant?"

"Yes. Who's this?"

"Agent David Dahbura, Federal Bureau of Investigation."

"Yes?"

"Mrs. Bryant, I'm calling to let you know that I've taken over the case that Agent Furnari was working on with you."

"What?" She was shocked.

"No cause for alarm, ma'am. It's just moved up the ladder a notch. I'm head of the Bureau's computer crime division."

"I'm glad to know you're taking this case seriously."

"It will elicit results faster, believe me."

"That's good." She felt apprehension, however. This was very abrupt. "But Mike—"

"Mike shared everything with me. Patrick did too, the afternoon of the day he died. It's now at the highest possible level in the agency, and we are on top of this, ma'am. We'll be in touch."

She was thoroughly confused. "Wait! What did Mike find out? He was going to see Brandon DiForio. He was going to—"

"Not to worry, ma'am. We know all about Kansas City, we are on top of that element too. We just want you to sit tight for now while we review everything that we've learned so far. You'll be hearing from me again very soon."

When he hung up, Quinn felt the same distrust creep into her bloodstream that had infected her the first time Tyler lied to her. She pressed her cell phone into action and called the FBI in Quantico. "Do you have an agent named David Da-boor-ah? I wouldn't know how to spell it."

"D-A-H-B-U-R-A, miss. Hold on, please."

At least I'm not paranoid, she thought. He's real. She'd read a beltway thriller once called *Hidden Agenda*, about putting a woman in the White House. In it, an FBI agent turns out not to have even existed. But now they were ringing a real phone. They were calling Dahbura's office. "Agent Dahbura." The same voice she'd just spoken to.

"It's Quinn Bryant. I just . . . was just checking to make sure this is on the level."

He chuckled. "Glad you did, ma'am. Agent Furnari said you were smart. If you'll excuse me now, however, I'm very busy. Good-bye."

"Bye." She hung up. She didn't like him. Too formal. Too tight. Mike had been a real person. But she didn't have to like the guy, she realized. She needed what he could accomplish.

So she waited.

And waited.

After hearing not a word for several days, she dialed Mike Furnari's direct number. He did not answer. It did not kick over to voice mail. She called back the regular FBI number, explaining she urgently needed to speak to Mike. This time she got his secretary. Quinn explained that she had been told that Mike had been taken off her case and that she wanted to thank him for what he'd done.

The girl said, "Well, I'm in the same boat. I want to thank him for the great birthday gift he sent my little boy, but no one knows where he is."

"What?"

"He just kind of disappeared."

Quinn could barely get the word out. "When?"

The girl seemed to realize she was letting out privileged information. Her voice became softer, as if she were trying to whisper. "It's been almost a week now that we've not heard from him. Ever since he went to Kansas City."

Quinn said nothing. Her tongue was frozen with fear.

"I'm probably not supposed to say all this. I just started a few months ago. Mike's a great guy. I'll tell him to call you when we do hear from him." She waited for Quinn to say something. "You still there?"

"Yes."

"Don't be alarmed. These are G-men, after all," the girl joked. "They do this kind of thing when they are on cases, in the field. Mike's just fine, I'm sure."

Quinn nodded, as if the girl could see her. Then she thought to ask something else. "Do you know Agent Dahbura?"

"David Dahbura? Sure. They're in the same department. In fact, Agent Dahbura has been trying to reach Mike as well. Must be top top secret."

Either that, Quinn thought, *or Tyler got to him first.* "Thank you," she managed to say, "I'm sure you're right. It's going to be fine."

Quinn felt panic setting in. She left several messages for Agent Dahbura, but none were returned. Finally, when she told his voice mail that she was going to call the *Washington Post* and tell them everything she knew, he called her back. He told her that he was a busy man, and reminded her that these things take time.

"What happened to Mike Furnari?" she blurted out.

He seemed solemn. "We don't know."

"He's still missing?"

"He seems to have vanished."

"Because of this case?" she asked.

"Don't jump to any conclusions, Mrs. Bryant. Michael was working on several cases that were far more dangerous than this one."

"More dangerous?" she cried. "Do you know how many people have died? Innocent priests and ministers, two missionaries who were no more than boys themselves. Innocent kids, kids like my very own daughter. Like your kids, David, if you have any."

"I do not."

"Well, you should. Then you'd understand my fear."

"Please, calm down. We are doing the best we can."

"Your best is not good enough," she shouted, and slammed the phone back into the cradle.

Susan heard her in the outer office and hurried in. "You okay?"

"I'm coming apart. I don't know what to do."

"I think I have good news. Line two is holding for you. It's that warden from the prison in Arizona. She said she needed to speak to you right away."

Quinn picked up the phone she had just nearly broken and punched the other button. "Yes, Warden?"

"Aggie Spivak here."

"Hi. I've been hoping you'd call."

"Sorry for the delay," the woman said, "but things back up. I'll get right to the point. It seems you and Drew have a mutual friend. An FBI agent, Mike Furnari?"

Quinn leaped to her feet. "Yes!" Susan watched the relief burst onto her face. "You've heard from him?"

"Yes."

"Oh, thank God. I was afraid . . . I don't know what I was thinking, just the worst, I guess."

"Calm yourself," the woman said in a soothing voice. "Mike explained how necessary it is for you to speak to Drew. He requested that you come out as soon as possible."

"I'm on the next plane," Quinn assured her. "Oh, Warden, thank you. You really made my day." She hung up and said to Susan, "Mike's okay. He's been in touch with her. She's going to let me talk to Tyler's brother. Book me a flight."

"When?"

"Tomorrow."

"What are you going to tell Tyler you're doing in Arizona?"

She thought about it. A name popped into her head. "Get Esther Dyson on the phone for me. She'll think I'm asking her to cover for an affair or something, but who cares? She is always throwing some kind of tech gathering—I'll just pretend I'm attending one."

"I only hope Tyler won't be suspicious."

"A risk I have to take." Quinn shrugged. "Don't you want to see him stopped?"

"No," Susan answered flatly. "I want to see him dead."

Chapter Ten

Quinn was struck by the sheer rugged beauty of the land that lay before her. Barren earth stretched forever in bizarre pink and mauve, shades she'd never imagined, sand shimmering in the blazing white sun as far as the eye could see. Rocks dotted the landscape everywhere, from pebbles glued to the melting asphalt to boulders the size of automobiles. She could feel the immense heat emanating from them even inside the air-conditioned rental car.

She'd been to Arizona only once before, for a few relaxing days in Scottsdale to participate in one of Esther Dyson's PC Forums, but that time she'd never left the hotel. She was supposed to be there now. At least that's the lie she had told Tyler. No one would suspect she'd come out to the desert for any other reason. You'd have to be mad—or desperate—to visit this inferno by choice.

She had to wonder why the federal government put a prison in the midst of such desolation. At least Alcatraz had ocean breezes and all that cool fog. Forget for a moment that the trek in this heat was hell on visitors. What about the poor bastards locked up in the prison? She guessed it made sense—try to escape, and after running only fifty yards you'd fry like an egg on a hot griddle.

She tried the radio. Out here? She laughed at herself for even considering the idea. Did she, whose name everyone connected to high-tech communications, really think this Chrysler was going to pick up a Phoenix FM station? She should have rented one with satellite radio. Oh, she could yank her Palm out of her bag and play some downloaded music, but in the end, she decided against it. Silence fit the desert vastness better anyway.

A glance in the rearview mirror showed her that she had bags under her eyes. She had been sleeping restlessly. She and Mike were the only people who could stop the spate of vicious murders. She *had* to stop them, for she was partly to blame. Practice Run. She winced thinking of the name and cursed the day she'd first set out to get it included on the computers her foundation gave away. She glanced at the folded *New York Times* on the passenger seat and shivered. Another murder. Another teenager.

Suddenly, a billboard advertising Sedona seemed to be reminding her that she had an alternative: She could simply drive to picturesque Sedona, buy some crystals, sit on one of those gorgeous red rocks for the afternoon, down a good bottle of chardonnay, and never go back. She'd often had fantasies of simply walking out of her life as she knew it. Whenever she traveled, she wondered what it would be like to actually live in one of those fabulous apartments overlooking Manila harbor, or perhaps in that ancient stone house on the barren Irish coast that Susan talked about so dreamily, and never show her face again. Just vanish.

She took the bottle of water that she'd propped in front of the biggest air-conditioning vent and placed it between her thighs. The perspiring plastic felt cool as she clenched her leg muscles so she could unscrew the cap. She drank three huge gulps and let some run down her chin. She was sweating, even though the temperature in the car had to be only in the high sixties. She wasn't even "gussied up," as her mom used to say; no silk skirt and clinging panty hose to make her perspire. She was wearing a white cotton tank top, linen shorts, and sandals. Tourist attire. But was it prison attire? Out here, in this scorching heat, she'd be surprised if the inmates didn't run around naked.

Almost an hour later, she saw a sign that read FEDERAL PENITENTIARY—DO NOT STOP FOR HITCHHIKERS. *Comforting*, she thought, but at least it meant she was near her destination. Another mile up the sticky asphalt highway, she took the right turn onto a smaller road where a tiny sign read DAVE GALLUP CORRECTIONAL INSTITUTE. She wondered if old Dave had been a lawman or a convict himself. She looked to see if anyone had seen her turn, which was ridiculous, for she'd been the only car on the two-lane highway for the past forty minutes. Her paranoia was getting to her.

It was windy—she could feel the car being buffeted about—and the road was winding. It led first up an incline to a kind of plateau that reminded her of a meringue pie, all white and brownish peaks and valleys. Then she found herself on terrain that looked like moon craters, a kind of hilly sanctuary of hot rock and brown craggy cactus. She wondered how they could even dream of incarcerating men in such a hideous place. It was like England of old, packing their criminals off to the colony of Australia when it was barren and uninhabited.

She followed a sharp curve around an enormous boulder and descended into what looked like a small, fertile oasis. Date palms swayed in the wind, whitish-leaved olive trees like those she remembered from Israel formed lush groves, and bushy dark green cypress stood at attention, in a perfect row, to provide a natural windbreak.

The front of the structure looked like a cross between the Phoenician and the Alamo. Then she remembered it had originally been built as a resort. Here? What were they thinking? It was so bizarre that she half expected to see golf carts and a Southwestern-motif McDonald's.

She approached the gatehouse, and a tanned, tough-looking man, dressed in a white shirt and badge and blue uniform pants, emerged into the blazing sun. That seemed right, at least. She pressed the driver's window button, and as it silently descended, the heat swooped in like the exhaust from a blast furnace.

"Can I help you?" His dark eyes peeked over his reflective silver sunglasses.

"I'm Quinn Roberts. I have an appointment with the warden." She took another slug of water while he grabbed a list from the gatehouse. She was surprised the paper didn't ignite from the heat.

"Says Quinn *Bryant*."

She hadn't even realized she'd not used her married name. *That* said something. "Roberts is my maiden name." Yes, just saying it made her feel safer. "I'm Quinn Roberts Bryant."

He still seemed suspicious, but he backed away. Inside the gatehouse, he pressed a button, and the gates opened with a loud buzz.

A shiver ran up Quinn's spine, despite the fact that it was now 110 degrees outside the car. "Can I go in?" she asked when the penetrating noise stopped.

He nodded. "First building on your right."

Inside the gates, the contradictions continued. The place was a cross between a Hyatt and Sing-Sing. The main edifice, where she aimed the car, obviously had been built as the resort's reception building. But beyond that were metal Quonset huts, nondescript long buildings all surrounded by high fences topped with razor wire. A group of inmates were working in a field of small palm trees—did they farm them here? She glimpsed a beat-up trailer that said INFIRMARY on it. And a swimming pool, which no doubt had been a carryover from the defunct resort. She parked in one of just three visitors' spots. When she got out of the car, she noticed the pavement was almost free of oil spots. This place had seen few visitors. It figured.

"Quinn Bryant?"

She turned on her heels. Coming from a bleak-looking building was a chunky woman of no-nonsense deportment, with short blond hair, dressed in the same white shirt and blue pants of the guard. "I'm Warden Aggie Spivak."

Quinn extended her hand. She noticed that the

warden's wrists, unlike the guard's, sported chunky plastic jewelry.

Aggie warmly took Quinn's hand and gave her an automatic once-over. "Oh, how I wish I could wear what you're wearing. Come on inside—it's warm today."

Warm?

Once inside, the warden got right to the point. "Drew Concardi doesn't want to see you. Or anyone. I'm only doing this for Mike Furnari."

"You know Mike personally?"

She shook her head. "When the FBI calls, I try to be accommodating. What do you want Drew to do for you?"

Quinn tried to be specific—and vague. "We need him to hack into a game that my husband created."

Aggie looked apprehensive. "I can't imagine he'd do anything for his brother. It was his famous brother who got him to plea bargain, assured him that doing so would get him probation only. He's very angry about that."

"Has Tyler never visited him?"

The warden seemed surprised. "You're asking me? You're married to the man."

"He doesn't talk about Drew."

Aggie nodded. "Another thing is that inmates don't have computers. And even if they did, his sentence forbids him from access to a computer or the Internet."

Quinn blinked. "I didn't know that."

"He was arrested for hacking. It was part of his sentence. So I don't know how he could do what you want him to do."

"Can I just visit him? There are other things I need to ask him as well."

Aggie looked at her as if she were clueless. "Do you know his history at all?"

"How do you mean? What he did? That it was just before 9/11?"

"That he tried to kill himself when he arrived here? And when that failed, he became so withdrawn that he refused to speak in anything but grunts for almost a year?"

"No. I didn't know."

"You know how many guards he's assaulted? How many other inmates he's taken a punch at?"

Quinn shook her head.

"Our shrink's said he's never seen so much rage bottled up in one person."

"He's been locked up almost three years now. Time hasn't dissipated his anger?"

The warden rested her elbows on her desk. "I believe your intentions are good, but I fear you made this trip for nothing."

"Why's that?"

"He's the most unpredictable prisoner we've ever had. A few weeks ago, he turned violent again. Head-butted a guard who brought him a birthday card from Tyler Bryant."

Quinn's eyes flashed. "Tyler sent him a card?"

Aggie nodded. "Took several men to hold him down after he assaulted the guy."

"How could that be? Drew Concardi's a skinny little weakling," Quinn said. "I've seen pictures."

Finally the warden showed a trace of a smile. "You seen any *recent* ones?" She answered her own question. "Of course not. Well, you have to do *something* in this place, and what he does is work out."

Quinn smiled in return, even as the warden became dour again. "I'll take my chances."

They crossed a dusty courtyard, then passed the trailer that Quinn had spied when she drove in. "Yeah, that's the infirmary," Aggie acknowledged. "He only got out of there yesterday."

Quinn looked over to the inmates working around the palm trees in the distance. "They farming them?"

"We make good money doing that."

"Who are most of your prisoners? I mean, what kind of crimes?"

"Word *Enron* mean anything to you?"

"White-collar," Quinn said, understanding.

Aggie pointed to one of the shabby Quonset huts. "That one's the new WorldCom headquarters. And that over there is the exercise area."

"I'll bet this is the only federal prison with a pool," Quinn said, sensing that she was right. It was big and blue, but it was surrounded by an ugly chain-link fence and more razor wire.

"Took some doing to get the Bureau of Prisons to let us fill it. But hell, it's hot here. It cools off the prisoners. Not to mention the staff. That keeps tempers down."

They approached the entrance to another Quonset hut. A guard nodded to the warden and unlocked the door for them. Inside, Quinn followed the warden down a long central corridor, and then Aggie ushered her into a small cubicle that looked like a cross between a cell and an examining room. There was another door at the far end, a metal table in the middle of the room with two chairs on opposite sides. Aggie gave a tap on the far door. "They'll bring him in here."

But another guard showed up alone. "I'm sorry, warden, but he's being impossible again."

Aggie groaned. "Now what?"

"He's out in the anteroom. I can't get him to come in here."

"What's he doing?" Aggie asked sternly.

The guard looked sheepish. "Exercises."

"Exercises?"

Quinn couldn't help but smile.

"What the hell . . ." Aggie stormed through the door, which the guard held for her, and stopped just past it. "Concardi, what are you doing?" She got no answer. "Concardi, I'm talking to you. You have a visitor."

Quinn took a step forward. She could see legs stretched out on the floor, strong, muscular, tanned legs wearing sneakers. And she heard his voice, a seething kind of growl in rhythm with the sit-ups he was doing. "You think it's like a drunk . . . who gets offered a shot of whiskey . . . after being sober for years . . . bang . . . he's automatically going to take it?" Quinn moved closer. She saw a shock of hair tied with a band around his forehead, rising and falling.

"Get up, Concardi," Aggie Spivak ordered sharply.

"Fuck the FBI. I don't want to be part of their experiment, don't want their charity," he shouted in rage. His words froze in his mouth as he saw who had just stepped into the anteroom.

"Hello, Drew," Quinn said evenly.

It took the young man a few moments to draw in his breath, to comprehend who his visitor was. And when he did, Drew Concardi said *"You."* simply, almost in a gasp. Quinn was shocked by what she saw. Drew was lying on his back on a sisal mat, his hands still clasped under his head, arms powerful, with biceps that looked like footballs. Indeed, this young man bore no resemblance to the skinny geek she'd seen in the photos of him as a boy. He was wearing a white tank top, just as she was, and green prison-issue gym shorts; his skin glistened with perspiration. His chin had a bandage on it, and one eye was swollen and black, but the rest of his flesh was a desert-roasted tan, with long brown hair falling from the headband, framing his face on the floor like some kind of halo from the dark side. He had the same full lips as Tyler had, the same prominent chin, eyes the color of dark turquoise, a high forehead with rich, thick eyebrows.

Drew sprang to his feet and scowled. "You," he said again, sounding amazed. "You of all people!" He laughed out loud. "So much for Mike Furnari, huh?"

"I'm working with Mike," Quinn told him.

Drew snickered derisively. "Gimme a break."

"Drew, I came because I—"

"Because *he* sent you, that's why. Just like he sent the birthday card. Or is he having a problem with the upgrade and needs lil' bro to save his ass?"

"Tyler has nothing to do with this," Quinn assured him.

"This my consolation prize? Toss baby brother a bone to take the edge off Ty's guilt?"

"For someone who, I'm told, spoke in grunts for a while," Quinn snapped, "you've become really rather eloquent."

"Don't patronize me," he warned.

Warden Spivak had had enough. "Drew, get your butt into the visitors' room."

The guard grabbed his arm, but Drew violently pulled away, pressing himself against the opposite wall.

"Drew, I understand your anger," Quinn said. "I just want to talk to you."

He almost spit. "You understand *nothing*, lady, nothing. You knew I'd never agree to see you, just like I wouldn't see *him* now, not even after all this time and his stupid cards and fucking Christmas baskets. Man, you really must think I'm retarded, don't you?"

At his raised voice, the guard came forward. "Let's keep it down, Concardi, or you're going back to your cell."

But Drew continued to shout. "Lady, get back on your high horse and ride out of here. Go back to New York or wherever the hell he's living now. You tell him thanks but no thanks, and remind him he's got a lot of balls sending you when he should have come himself, years ago."

"Tyler didn't send me!" Quinn shouted back. "He doesn't even know I'm here."

"Fuck him!" Drew shouted angrily. "And fuck you too!"

With a nod from the warden, the guard grabbed Drew's arm and shook him. "I told you, Concardi, the interview's over."

Drew let himself be taken away. "Get me away from her," he growled. "And tell her not to come back."

A pretty secretary ushered Agent David Dahbura into the Director's office in the vast FBI complex in Quantico. The older man watched with amusement as the girl's knees seemed to go weak as David brushed by her with a winning smile. When she left them alone, the Director said to David, "Why do women just seem to melt in your presence?"

"Because," David replied seriously, "I'm unattainable. They sense it."

"You're also full of shit."

David smiled. "That too."

"All right, what do you have for me?"

Agent Dahbura put on his most serious agency face. "You're not going to like it."

"I don't like most things I hear in this job."

David shook his head. "I'm still reeling from the shock."

"A state I have never seen you in."

"That partial fingerprint we lifted off the computer chip planted on Patrick Horgan's car belongs to Mike Furnari."

The Director's mouth dropped open.

"That's what I mean by shock."

"You can't be serious. Mike killed Patrick?"

"It's nuts. But it makes a twisted kind of sense. Mike has disappeared because he knew we'd be onto him. He's been the one behind this whole thing. Who better to cover up computer crime than the whiz kid of the computer crime division?"

The man behind the desk looked distraught. "But Patrick was his partner. They were close friends."

"I think he knew that Patrick was closing in. Mike got scared that he'd be found out, and thus disappeared without a trace."

The Director took issue with that. "There's no such thing as without a trace and you know it." He folded his arms. "Patrick and I started here on the same day. You know that?"

"No, sir."

"Good man. Very good man." He shook his head again. "Agent Furnari, Jesus." He looked Dahbura in the eye. "What about that game? Mike was behind the subliminal program? I mean, *is* there a subliminal program? What the hell do you guys know about it?"

"Not much more than we did when I first gave you the briefing. Mike knows what we don't. That's why I need to find him. I mean, with his expertise it's hard not to imagine him creating something so complex." He moved forward on his chair. "But in the meantime, I wouldn't worry. I don't think the contamination went beyond a few copies, a few kids."

"There have been deaths. *Are* they tied to it?"

"Possibly a few are. I'm on top of it." He stood up. "I'll keep you posted on my progress."

"Wait," the director said. "Mike told me he feared that the game king guy himself could be behind the programming."

"Tyler Bryant."

"Yes. What do you think?"

"I actually think Mike may have concocted that notion to throw us off his own scent."

*   *   *

It was almost three in the afternoon when Quinn left the warden's office with a regretful good-bye, having elicited the promise that Aggie Spivak would call if Drew reconsidered. Quinn had hoped that she would get through to him, but that was impossible.

Opening her car door was like unleashing the fires of hell; it was as if a furnace had exploded. She could barely touch the interior when she attempted to slide onto the hot, sticky seat. She half expected the steering wheel to glow red. The air was barely breathable. Now she knew why people put those cardboard reflectors across their windshields. She started the car, pushed the AC controls to the coldest and the fan to the highest settings, and hopped back out, hoping that if it ran for five minutes, it would start to cool down. Then she noticed something out of the corner of her eye.

Muscles.

She caught a fast glimpse of a muscular body walking inside the exercise-area fence. He had a towel slung over his shoulder. *No*, she thought, *it couldn't be him*. It probably was one of the guards taking a break, heading for the swimming pool.

But didn't Aggie say the inmates used it?

She jumped into the still hot car, drove to the end of the drive, and left it parked haphazardly half on the asphalt, half on the sand. She didn't even think about what she was doing. She hurried toward the exercise area and found herself facing the large pool.

There were no lounge chairs or lifeguards perched high above. Only one guard, the same guard who had led Drew back to his cell, sat, looking bored, on a bench at the shallow end. Next to the rim of the pool was a faded green towel, the one she'd seen over the guy's shoulder. And a pair of sneakers that looked like the ones Drew had worn. No one appeared to be in the blue water, but that's because he was under the surface, swimming with the precision of a shark. She hurried to the chain-link gate and faced the guard. "The warden told me to give it one more try."

He gave an unfriendly bark. "Good luck."

Drew swam the length of the pool twice without coming up for air, and when he did, in the middle of the long lane, he sucked it in without even opening his eyes, and went back under. When his fingertips hit the wall, he reversed direction, swimming to the other end again, where he surfaced, shooting up out of the water with a bolt. To find Quinn staring at him just a few feet away, crouched down, talking through the fence.

"You listen to me, and you listen to me good, you little prick!" she shouted.

He was so shocked he didn't say a word. He held on to the cement coping of the rim of the pool and looked at her in amazement.

"No one sent me, least of all Tyler. Tyler doesn't even know I'm here. I didn't even know *you* were here, didn't really know you *existed* until a month ago. I came on my own, and I'm risking my goddamned life to ask you to help me."

He pulled his long mane of wet hair back with one hand. "Help you what?" he spat.

"Destroy him."

He glared at her for the longest time. It was definitely not what he expected to hear. He dunked himself under the water, coming up again to shake the chlorine from his ears.

"I need your help, Drew," she called. "Please, just hear what I have to say. That's all I ask."

He didn't respond at first. Then, with his powerful arms, he lifted himself straight out of the water. He walked over to the fence until he was facing her. The guard rose from the bench, but Drew didn't get too close.

He was naked except for a pair of green gym shorts, and his wet body seemed to be covered in goose pimples. Quinn wondered if he was actually cold or if what she had said had shaken him.

"What kind of person are you?" he asked softly.

"What?"

"You're married to him. I thought you loved him."

"I did."

"I *do*," he asserted.

She nodded, expecting him to say that. "I know you love your brother, but also that you hate him. It's why you're so hurt that he hasn't done more to help you. But you won't love him anymore, not after I tell you what I know."

"What?"

"All this concern," she blurted out, "Tyler's cards, the Christmas baskets—like you said, it's all bullshit. It's to keep you from finding out."

He stiffened. "Finding out what?"

She took a deep breath. Here it was, the moment she'd feared. The moment when he would either believe her or reject her. "It's to keep you from finding out that your brother was the one who put you here in the first place."

Chapter Eleven

If Quinn had shocked him before, that didn't compare to the astonishment written large on his face now.

Quinn, now only inches away from the nearly naked, dripping wet inmate, held his attention. "I have to run to my car. I need my briefcase. I'll show you why Tyler framed you."

As Quinn rushed off, Drew grabbed the chain-link fence with both hands, rattling it, shouting after her. "What are you talking about? What do you mean?"

Behind him, the guard hurried to a wall phone. Drew continued to shout, rattling the fence. By the time Quinn returned from the rental car, two more guards were running over. From the main building, Warden Spivak came out. Yet as she drew close, she saw Quinn wasn't in any danger. "Calm down, Concardi," she warned.

"What did you mean, he put me here?" Drew shouted at Quinn. "You owe me an answer!"

Quinn turned to the warden. "He's agreed to talk to me. Can I continue?"

Aggie Spivak said, "This is highly unusual." Then she let out a sigh. "I must be getting soft in my old age. I'll give you fifteen minutes."

In the warden's office, Drew, still wet, wrapped only in a towel, told Quinn he needed an answer. "Why did you say those things?"

"Because I think Tyler manufactured the charges that got you arrested and ultimately sentenced to this place."

"You *think?*"

"No. I'm sure."

He did not believe her. "That's absurd. You're crazy."

"Am I? Think about it, Drew. Plea bargain? On those charges after 9/11? Come on. And after the sentence, who's your only hope? Tyler, with his connections. Telling you to trust him, trust his influence, he'll get you off one day. *Just a while longer, little bro.* Manipulation. But you believed. As I did."

"How so?"

"I trusted him. Until I had my first inkling."

"Inkling of what?"

She swallowed hard. "That something was wrong. That he might have married me for some bigger purpose."

Drew laughed derisively. "The infamous Costco wedding."

"My *wedding* should have been my first clue. Refusing to marry in a church." She leaned forward in earnest. "I met him and fell in love. It's that simple. I have a daughter. Her name is Joan, I call her Joanie, she's in college now—well, sort of. She liked Tyler even more than I did when we first met him. He was so charming, so believable, so seemingly honest in his feelings, that he swept me off my feet. But he's a fraud."

Drew winced and started to open up. "I wanted him to come. I prayed he'd come."

"He told me you wouldn't let him come."

"That's not true." His eyes flashed with hurt and with anger. "Why didn't he ever visit? Three years of promises. But those promises are all I have to live for. He's my brother! Who else is going to help me?"

"I am."

Drew just stared at her.

"He won't help you get out of here," Quinn reiterated. "You're a threat to his plan. I am too, but he doesn't know that as yet."

Drew looked flustered. "What plan?"

She shrugged. "The plan you also figured out."

"I don't know what you're talking about."

"You discovered what he was doing. Right?"

"I don't follow."

Neither did she. "Isn't that why he saw to it that you got locked up?"

Drew looked at her as if she were speaking Chinese. "I don't understand, lady."

"The game."

"Game?"

"Practice Run!"

"What about it?"

"You discovered what it does, right? It programs kids to reject religion. It's a form of mind control. He's out to create an army of teens to turn against religion and become a truly godless society."

His mouth dropped. "No," he gasped. "I don't know that."

She shook her head. "Where am I? The twilight zone? It's why he put you here. Mike Furnari and I both thought that had to be it."

Drew nodded. "Mike was the only one I thought was fair. I thought he believed me."

"He did," Quinn assured him. "He's going to come and talk to you himself. We agree that the only reason Tyler went through such elaborate steps to lock you away here on the palm tree farm—falsifying evidence, buying plane tickets in your name, stealing your computer to do the hacking from his friend's place in Kansas City—was because you had discovered what he was up to."

"Practice Run has an embedded program that is brainwashing the people who play it?"

She nodded.

"To reject God?"

"Yes. And, in some cases, the game actually propels kids to kill religious leaders."

He seemed stunned. "My game." His demeanor became very serious. "It's mine."

She blinked. "What did you say?"

He looked her in the eye. "I said, it's *my* game."

"What do you mean, your game?"

"Just that. Mine. Only the extra program wasn't designed to turn anyone against religion."

Now it was her turn to be stunned. "What?"

"It was supposed to influence a class of only about twenty kids to turn on their teacher."

"Now I'm lost."

"Quinn," he said almost proudly, "I'm the one

who created the extra program for Practice Run. It was mine, not Tyler's."

She had never been so astonished in her life.

The young man thought fast. "And if what you are saying is true, if Ty really did put me in here, then he did it because he wanted me far away from a computer, because I would be the only person who might suspect what was really going on."

"You were the brains behind the brilliant Tyler Bryant?" She was flabbergasted.

"I actually developed the game for him in the first place."

She was amazed. *"You're* Zzzyx. Not him."

He laughed derisively. "I gave him that name too. I saw it on a road sign on the way to Vegas once. It's a canyon or town or something, I think."

"You, the computer whiz, creating games since you were a kid." She felt the pieces fitting.

He nodded. "Started when I was twelve."

"What did you say about a class?"

"I was pissed off at a college professor. A real asshole. I wanted to turn the whole class on this hypocrite. Nothing harmful, just get everybody to one day start throwing their books at him, something silly."

"Why?"

"He had humiliated me too many times. The guy was a Saddam Hussein. But he had the class by the nuts."

"They all loved him?"

"Yes." A mischievous grin creased his face. "To turn his little darlings against him would have been a win for me."

"Why didn't you go through with it?"

He shook his head. "It was . . . wrong. It was dangerous."

"You showed it to Tyler?"

"Sure."

"He understood how you did it? How you were going to get those kids to do your dirty work?"

"A practical joke."

"What if it wasn't?"

"What?"

"A practical joke. What if it was bigger? Real life. Real danger. Could you program the people playing video games to do something bad if you wanted to?"

"Yes, sure. You could get them to do anything you wanted. It's another form of hypnotism."

"Why did you call it that?"

"Hypnotism?"

"Practice Run."

"I didn't. Tyler gave it that name. I guess to piss on it, to mark it as his."

"And after you shared this game and the subliminal plan with your brother, you were arrested for hacking?"

He tightened the towel around his waist. "This is all just nuts. I don't even know you. I mean, you storm in here telling me I should hate my brother, the only family I have left, that he stole my idea and I'm supposed to believe this shit? And going on the premise for a minute that it is true, why? Why would he want to program anyone? He's not mad at a professor."

"This is his own personal jihad. He's mad at God."

Drew blinked. "God?"

"He hates God, the entire notion of religion. You know that."

Drew looked the other way. Silence.

She got up and moved to a chair closer to him. "Aha, I hit a nerve. You know he hates God, that he has no faith."

"So he's atheist? Lots of people are. I'm not sure I believe there is a God."

"I'm Catholic. I begged him for us to be married by a priest, but he was rigidly against it. Why does Tyler hate religion so deeply?"

Drew glared at her. "Ask him."

"I did."

"What did he tell you?"

"Stuff that matched the manifesto I first found in his laptop. That it's the scourge of humanity."

Drew slumped, unconsciously tapping the ground with his foot. "So? Maybe he's right. What kind of God put me in here? What kind of God gives children leukemia?"

"He wants to eradicate religion."

"Eradicate?"

"That's his goal. I told you, he wants to create an army of young people to reject the entire notion of God for the rest of time."

"He told you this?" Drew exclaimed, not knowing whether he should be shocked or amused.

She shook her head. "He doesn't know that I know. The thing I found, a 'game proposal,' as he called it, was really the plan behind the extra program."

Drew rolled his eyes.

Quinn reached out and grabbed his hands. "Listen

to me. I'm not mad. *He* is. At first, yes, I thought I was crazy, that I was dreaming. I wanted to believe that this was part of his development of a new game, a prototype for a game. But then I started doing research, I started looking for clues."

"Clues?"

She grabbed her briefcase. "Look at these." She had come armed with everything she had saved. All the clippings. "An accident in the rain in Milwaukee where a teenager had driven his father, who'd sold a religious book, and his mother and sister, into the path of an oncoming truck. Willie Chesterfield shooting those two missionaries in Augusta. Tommy Caldwell in the Crystal Cathedral. That shooting of Cardinal Meeks in the St. Louis suburb. The rabbi pulled to his death by that little boy." She pressed them into his hands. "I think these are only the tip of the iceberg. Who knows how many others have happened that I haven't found out about yet?"

Drew looked at each one. "How did you connect these to Tyler?"

"The one thing they all had in common was being addicted to Practice Run."

Drew looked frightened. "You sure?"

"Yes. Positively."

He shook his head. "You can't be serious."

"I can."

"You mean he . . ."

"Yes, he's not only programming kids to turn on religion. He's programming a select group of kids to murder religious leaders."

Chapter Twelve

When their fifteen minutes were up, the warden returned from her office and ordered the guard to take Drew back to his cell. Quinn made a plea for more time with him. Aggie listened, and seeing that Drew was calm and receptive, she agreed that they could meet again after dinner. Aggie invited Quinn to have a bite to eat. "The food they give me is a little better than the stuff Drew gets." Quinn freshened up in Aggie's private bathroom, and just as she was about to emerge, her cell phone rang. "Hello?"

"Honey, it's me."

"Tyler." Her blood ran cold.

"Where are you?"

"Just going down to dinner." It was not a lie.

"How's the hotel?"

"Better than I'd expected." It was not a lie as well. "Where are you?" She heard traffic in the background.

"LaGuardia, just arrived. Hear it's hot there."

"Sure is."

"Joanie left a message on the house phone. She

and Stephanie are in Boston. They're leaving from
there on Sunday."

"I'll be back by then."

"I know. I told her you'd call her to wish her well.
She said she shipped everything from school back to
D.C. Gotta go, I just got a cab. Just wanted to tell you
I love you. Bye."

She said good-bye, hung up, and had dinner with
Aggie Spivak. She told the warden a bit more about
her quest than she had shared earlier, but kept from
her that Tyler was the man behind the madness. She
made it sound like some crazy hacker had infiltrated
the game and their only hope of getting help was
Drew, because he'd created it in the first place.

Drew was waiting in the interview room, seated
at the table with the clippings in front of him, when
the guard let Quinn in. The guard took his position
at the opposite door. Drew was now wearing a
prison jumpsuit. "I don't recognize you with clothes
on," Quinn joked.

He looked calm, but much more serious than he
had earlier. It was as if reality had sunk in. "I read it
all," he said when she approached the table.
"Twice."

"And?"

He cleared his throat. "It's possible."

"Thank you."

"There are two issues. One is the regular game. It
has an embedded program under it, seductively instructing players to start to turn on religion."

"And the other issue is instructing some of them
to kill."

He nodded. "It's the passwords."

She blinked. "What?"

"The kids who kill. They're the most proficient at the game, the best of them."

"Tyler calls them the Front Runners."

He nodded. "They're your killers."

She shook her head. "Mike and Patrick both thought that. But there are over two hundred and forty names in that group of winners, and none of them matched any of the killers."

Drew looked surprised. But it only took him a minute to think it through. "Of course. It would be too easy otherwise."

"What would be?"

He leaned forward. "The kids who get to be Front Runners are proud of it, right?"

"Yes, of course. It's a big deal. There's even a Front Runner Web site."

"But what if a kid was programmed *not* to talk about having made it there."

She froze. "Oh, my God. Yes! That's it. That's what Patrick must have figured out. That's what he was coming to tell me." That had to be it. "He'd gone to the Web site, thought he was wrong, but then realized that they're also programmed *not* to reveal their Front Runner status."

Drew nodded. "Kids who excel, they get to play the master, and if they win against him, they become a Front Runner. I imagine that if they pick the cathedral as the setting for their final round—I remember creating it, but not for the reasons Tyler kept it there—it must signal Tyler that they are the most susceptible, and thus when they win, he gives them a new version of the game . . ."

She finished his sentence. ". . . that programs them to kill and also never to reveal that they made it to Front Runner status." She saw the pieces fit. Then her face became a mask of fear.

He was startled at her change of expression. "What?"

She grabbed her cell phone and punched in a number. The guard looked up, on alert. When a machine answered, she rattled off, "Susan, listen to me, don't—don't, under any circumstances—let Sam or any one of James' friends win at Practice Run. Don't let them play Tyler! That's the danger, that's what does it. Unplug their computers if you have to, erase the hard drives, destroy the damned things. I'll explain more when I can."

Drew stared at her as she put her phone away. "What was that?"

"My godson and all his buddies are addicted to PR."

"I see."

She looked at him with alarm. "Drew, what should we do?"

"What do you mean?"

"How do we stop him?"

He smiled. "We?"

"You're the only one who knows besides Mike and me."

"And the woman you just called."

"Her husband, Patrick, was the first person I went to. He worked with Mike."

"And?"

"He's dead."

Drew blinked. "What happened?"

"Car accident. The automobile's navigational computer instructed him to drive off a bridge in a rainstorm, where he couldn't see."

Drew's eyes widened. "Computer?"

Quinn nodded. "Which was controlled by a human being who put a little transmitter chip under the fender. You figure it out." She closed her eyes for a moment. "The man was like family—his wife is my partner, my dearest friend. That's when I got scared."

"Jesus."

Quinn said, "I feared that something bad happened to Mike Furnari too, when I suddenly heard he was pulled from the case. It was just so odd. Then, thank God, the warden called and said she'd heard from him, so I know he's all right."

Drew looked curious. "You said earlier that Tyler didn't marry you for love. What for, then?"

Admitting the truth was hard for her. "I think my reach. The organization I work for donates computers to kids all over the country, all over the world. I never could have a second child after Joanie was born. It was my way of having more kids, I guess. I think I was part of the plot to extend Practice Run's reach. I feel like an accessory. I'm as responsible as he is."

"You're not. You know that." His voice sounded almost tender.

She could see he had a heart. "Drew, you have to help us stop him."

"How?"

"That's why I came. That's why Mike is coming to

see you as well. You're the only person who can do it."

"Why do you say that?"

"Because of what you just told me. Because you're the person who started it all."

Drew shrugged. "I'm trapped here," he reminded her. "I can't help anyone."

"You could create a virus, something to destroy the game, erase the programming—you dreamed it up, you should be able to provide the antidote."

"I'd need a game player, plus a computer," he reminded her. "I can't even look at the code without them, and I need Internet access too." He looked hungry, like an addict needing a fix. "That's the real punishment of this hell. I can't go near a keyboard."

She took a deep breath. "I'll talk to the warden. Mike will too. She knows we need your help and that this is urgent."

"The warden knows about this?" he asked, surprised.

"Some," she answered. "I don't know how much Mike wants me to tell her."

"He'd better hurry up."

She nodded gravely.

He touched the file of clippings. "If Tyler is really behind these articles, if he's really out to kill religious authority figures, there's going to be plenty of others."

"We have to find out who is being targeted."

He disagreed. "It's possible that no one is specifically targeted. I rather think he has chosen the best game players to become assassins because they are so smart, and, by that time, so susceptible. You have to find out who *they* are."

"How do I do that?"

He told her what he needed to do to help. "The file of the assassins is stored somewhere. The passwords are there, along with the real names of the kids who are possible killers. The ones who have been programmed not to reveal they made it to Front Runner status. Those names could be proof to law enforcement. You'll find all these kids there," he said, pointing to the clippings, "and also the names of the ones who haven't yet killed."

She realized he was right. "But where? The laptop I found the initial notes in?"

"No. That's too risky for him. I don't know where the password registrations are, but they don't exist only in his mind."

"Drew, could he be doing this alone?"

"No way. It's too big, too involved. There have to be others."

"I have to talk to Mike, learn what he found out in Kansas City. He was going to check out Brandon Di-Forio."

Drew's eyes lit with recognition. "Brandon is involved in this?"

"You remember him?"

"He lived next door to us."

She felt her mouth gaping. "Tyler said they met in college."

Drew shook his head. "That's a lie. Concardi, Di-Forio, we lived in an Italian neighborhood. He was Ty's best friend growing up in Wisconsin. Used to tease me mercilessly. But with Tyler he was always kind of adoring. You know, Ty's Sancho Panza."

She shook her head. "Sancho Panza wasn't evil."

"My mom thought Brandon was the cat's meow. I think she cared for him more than she did for me."

"Where's your mother now?"

"I honestly don't know." He could not mask the pain in his voice.

"Don't you speak to her?"

"She stopped talking to me when I was arrested. Tyler said she felt too much shame. Especially after the pride he'd brought her. But I don't think he's in touch with her either. At least that's what he said."

"He said she's an alcoholic. And she married several times, didn't she?"

"She married anybody who would drink with her."

"I'm sorry. I can imagine how much that hurt."

"Get me a computer, Quinn. You're right—I know how I could reverse it. But I can't do it in my head. Just like Tyler can't store the names and passwords there. You've got to get into his files and programs."

"I'll try."

Aggie put her head in the door. "Concardi, it's time."

Drew stood up, and Quinn did as well. "I'll be in touch. And I'll be back. Mike will too. And the other agent working on this, I suppose. We need you, Drew. You know that now."

The warden walked Quinn to her car, asking what she could do to help her.

"It's his help that I need. Badly."

"How?"

"He needs a computer."

Aggie shook her head. "You know I can't do that."

"Lives may depend on what I want him to do."

"I'm sorry. I can bend rules, but I can't break them."

Quinn tried to think of another way to convince her. "Can Mike Furnari make that happen?"

"Sure. The FBI can do anything. But hell, I haven't heard from him in about two weeks."

Quinn felt punched in the stomach. "What?"

"When he called, he said he wanted me to give you access to Drew."

Quinn felt her blood running cold. "You mean you didn't hear from Mike just before you called me and said I could come out here?"

"I just told you that."

"Oh, my God." She bit her lip. "Warden, when did he call? Exactly."

"I was just about to leave for vacation. Sorry I put it off." The woman remembered the date on her plane ticket.

Quinn shuddered. "That was Parents' Weekend. We were in Virginia." She turned white.

"You're trembling. What's wrong?"

"I mentioned another agent. His name is David Dahbura. Have you heard from him?"

"Nope."

Quinn felt her heartbeat pounding. "What else did Mike say in that conversation? Did he tell you that he was coming to see Drew himself?"

"Yes. But he was going to Kansas City first. I recall that for certain."

Quinn closed her eyes. "Dear God," she whispered. "No one has heard from Mike Furnari since he left for Kansas City."

"I think," the warden advised, "that you should talk to the other agent you just mentioned and find out what is really going on."

Chapter Thirteen

At Dulles, Quinn tossed her rolling suitcase into the rear hatch of Susan Horgan's new station wagon—she'd bought a Subaru, to please James—and jumped into the front. "Hi."

Susan was more than curious. "What was that call about last night? Your message sounded hysterical."

"I was scared for my godson and his friends."

"You look white."

"I understand it all now."

Susan said, "Tell me."

"First, Drew Concardi didn't figure out what Tyler was doing. He was the brains behind the whole thing to begin with."

"How so?"

"He's the one who created the program, not Tyler. Even Practice Run was originally his."

"It was?"

"Two, Mike Furnari is still missing. No one has heard from him since he left for Kansas City. That's when he called the warden, not a few days ago."

"Oh no."

"The most important thing is I think I know what Patrick was going to tell me. Remember he said he had gone to the Front Runners Web site and then thought he was wrong? Patrick must have realized the Front Runners who were killing were programmed not to tell anyone they made it into the elite circle."

Susan understood now. "So that extra version of the game James says they get directly from Tyler—that's what puts them over the edge?"

"Yes. All the kids who killed got passwords but were brainwashed into telling no one."

Susan shivered. "Thank God you didn't give James one when he asked."

"I couldn't have. Only Tyler can do that. That's where he takes control, that's where he's hands-on. He must determine, in that one-on-one playing, if a kid is capable of a suicide mission."

Susan thought for a moment as she eased into beltway traffic. "Can't they track down the ones left and deprogram them?"

"How do we find them? And who knows how many there are? Who knows how many there might be that we don't yet know about?"

Susan bit her tongue. "He can't be doing this alone. He's got to have help. But who else would be so demented?"

"The DiForios, for sure. And Veronica Ashton. And who knows who else? People who hate God can be just as rabid as those zealots who kill in the name of God."

"Like the antiabortionists." Susan changed lanes. "Damn trucks. What are you going to do?"

Quinn opened a bottle of water that was standing in the cup holder and took a swig. "Get the names of the Front Runners who have been programmed to kill in the future."

"What can I do?"

Quinn reached over and touched Susan's hand, which was resting on the console shift lever. "I'm putting you in enough danger telling you all this. You just run the office and let me concentrate on getting him."

"I have a vested interest, remember," Susan said soberly.

Quinn looked at her. She saw her eyes well with tears. She gripped her friend's hand tightly. "We'll stop him."

"Without Mike?" Susan shook her head.

"We need to find a way to get into the offices in Rockville."

"Why not let the FBI do it? What about the other agent who called you?"

Quinn looked apprehensive. "I never had a good feeling about him. I don't trust him."

"You never said his name."

"Dahbura. I think it's Middle Eastern. David Dahbura."

"He was Patrick and Mike's boss."

Quinn felt hope. "Do you know him?"

Susan shook her head. "I never met him. Only heard the name."

"I wish I felt better about him."

Susan nodded. "Me too. Patrick disliked him intensely." Then she realized something: Here was her chance to avenge her husband's death. "We need to check out Rockville."

Quinn's eyes lit with the same realization. "Tyler's in New York all week. Zzzyx, here we come."

"Hey, I have an idea . . ."

Susan and Quinn walked into the Zzzyx Games building that afternoon, bubbling with phony enthusiasm for Susan's ruse: throwing a surprise party for Tyler's thirty-seventh birthday. Veronica Ashton treated the idea with disdain. "Thirty-seven? What's the big deal about turning thirty-seven? Forty is the big one."

Quinn howled. "You think so? Wait till *you* get there!" She knew Veronica had to be pushing fifty, so Quinn had just kissed her big fat ass, gaining brownie points to help put the robot at ease.

Susan said, "Ronnie, he'll just love it."

Quinn and Susan cased the place as they continued to chatter with Veronica. The woman finally seemed swayed, promising not to tell Tyler about the party, offering her help in any way she could. While Quinn kept Ronnie busy with questions, Susan wandered off, as planned, to figure out how Quinn could best get back there to locate the full list of Front Runners when Ronnie wasn't around.

But Quinn had an additional agenda, a more personal one, that she was pursuing. "How about photographs?" she asked Veronica. "Where can I get pictures of Tyler as a kid, when he was a little boy? I'd like to create a video show for everyone."

"Well," Ronnie said proudly, "I've worked for him now for almost twelve years, so I have some."

"Pictures of him growing up," Quinn suggested.

Ronnie shrugged. "I suppose his mother would have some."

Bingo. Quinn pressed. "But they don't speak. Tyler and his mother."

"I know that," Veronica replied, trying to indicate that *she* knew Tyler better, "but Betty might still have photos."

Quinn asked, "Where is Betty?"

Veronica smirked. "For being married to the man, you sure don't know much about him."

"That's probably an understatement."

"What do you mean by that?" Ronnie snapped, her radar engaging.

Quinn quickly back stepped. "I mean, well, you know Ty. He doesn't open up much."

That did the trick. "Game guys," Ronnie said with a shrug. "Geeks of another color. His mother lives in Chicago. In a home. She's not well."

"Do you know where it is?"

Ronnie nodded. "We send checks regularly."

Quinn seemed very concerned. "Maybe, just maybe, there's a chance at reconciliation. Forgiveness. It would be a shame for his mother to die without some kind of closure."

Ronnie understood that right away. "My ma and I, we had a rough time, mainly because I divorced the son-in-law *she* should have married. There were a few years we didn't speak. People would say, 'Mrs. Rossi is hurting,' I'd hear 'Mrs. Rossi is so lonely,' and I tried to deny missing her. But one day I just said that's enough, and called her."

"Are you close now?"

"She's a pain in the butt, but yeah, we are." Ronnie flipped on one of the computer screens on her desk, and after a few keystrokes the address of the nursing home where Tyler's mother lived lit up the screen.

"Thanks, Ronnie," Quinn said, "but remember, don't tell Tyler. I want the party to be the biggest surprise ever." *And*, she thought, *maybe we can have him arrested as the icing on the cake.*

When they finally left, Susan said, "What the hell was all that about the mother?"

"My own personal quest. So do you have a plan?"

"Yup. We've got to get into Tyler's personal office when Veronica's not around. There are a lot of locked filing cabinets in there. The problem is it's all glass— everyone can see in. We should probably go at night, when there are fewer employees in the building. I snatched a copy of the work schedule."

"Good," Quinn said. "You plot it out. I'll be back in a day or two."

"Where are you going now?"

"Chicago."

"Chicago?"

The nursing home was a tawdry place on Devon Avenue, on Chicago's North Side, situated amidst sari stores and pawn shops. The area had once been host to a thriving Jewish community—blue six-pointed stars could be detected under hastily painted signs for new businesses—but now the area was almost all Indian. The rotund black receptionist at the desk was astonished to hear Quinn was there to see

Mrs. Bryant. "That woman ain't had nobody visit in the whole year she be here."

"She has now."

When Quinn walked into Betty Bryant's dismal, dark room, she was greeted by bent miniblinds, torn carpeting, and the distinct smell of alcohol. Not medicinal alcohol like a hospital, but booze. It was emanating from the woman's mouth, for she was singing in bed, giving a fairly decent impression of Liza Minnelli belting "Cabaret." Quinn respectfully waited until she was done, and then applauded.

"Who the dickens are you?"

Quinn told her. "I'm married to Tyler."

"Well, Jesus."

How apt, considering, Quinn thought. "I figured it was time to meet you."

Betty pulled open the drawer of the scuffed metal cabinet next to the bed. "Drink?"

Quinn saw two bottles lying in it. "I'd better not."

"Oh, come on, let your hair down. Benny brings 'em to me. He's the night nurse. Dim-witted, but kind. Sit down."

Quinn thought she'd rather stand. "Mrs. Bryant, I know you're not well."

"Who says? Heartache is what it is. Missing my boys." She ran her hand through her stringy gray hair, pulling it off her forehead. Quinn could see the echo of both Tyler and Drew in her—the lips, the strong nose, the slightly dimpled chin. "But I got no one to blame but me. I'm a drunk." She flipped her hands upside down as if to show all her cards. "What's there to say?"

"Tyler told me he wishes you could make peace,"

she lied. "Drew is in pain because you're so ashamed of what he did. Isn't there any hope to bring your family back together?"

The woman looked shocked. "Ashamed of my Andrew? I'm proud of him! Screw the Pentagon. I never believed those charges."

"Proud of him?" That didn't compute for Quinn.

"I've been writing him ever since it happened," the woman said passionately, "but he's never answered. He was my youngest, he's my favorite."

But that's not what Drew had told Quinn. "Where have you been writing him?"

"To the post office box for prisoners."

Quinn blinked. "Where's that?"

"Washington. That's how you write people in federal jails."

Quinn understood. "Tyler told you that?"

"Yes."

"Is the post office box address actually in Maryland?"

"That's right."

Quinn had figured it out. Tyler had been intercepting her letters to Drew.

"Why does Drew hate me?" the woman suddenly cried. "Can't he forgive me? The boys were right. Tyler said, 'No more benders, Ma.' I embarrassed Drew again and again. Shamed him. Now I'm a lonely old lady." The woman looked down in discouragement. "Honey, you got kids?"

Quinn nodded and showed her a photo of Joanie from her wallet.

"She's pretty. Like her mom."

"Thanks. She just left to hitchhike across Europe. I hate it."

"Yes, but it's her life now." Betty shrugged, weary. "Honey, you try to be a good mom, the best you know, but sometimes we make mistakes, our own problems get in the way. Some of us aren't cut out to be *Good Housekeeping* mothers. Yet we love our children."

Quinn thought she was going to cry. She didn't know if she could handle that. "Betty, I came to also ask if you have any photographs of the boys growing up." She added her story about the phony surprise party, urging that she come.

"Oh no," Betty said, "I'd ruin it. Tyler told me he never wanted to see me again. I don't imagine my popping out of a cake at his shindig, even if I sang 'Happy Birthday,' would go over very well."

Quinn had to laugh.

"But I got photos. That's what keeps you going: the memories. Help me up."

Quinn did so, offering her arm. Once on her feet, Betty steadied herself, reached into the drawer to fortify herself with a belt of cheap whiskey, and then opened the cabinet doors under the drawer. Inside were six or seven bulging photo albums, which occupied them for the next half hour.

Quinn saw the album of their life in Kenosha, Wisconsin—a happy time, by all appearances. Betty pointed out names Quinn didn't know—"That was Tim Morrissey's birthday party, that's Sharon Pascucci, Tyler's first love, Jack Principe, Anthony Ventura, it was a big Wop town, and Terry Wilson, a sweetheart!"—and one Quinn did know—"That's my dear Brandon." Indeed, here was the proof of what Drew had told Quinn, that Brandon and Tyler had grown up together. "And that's Brandon's sister, Sally DiForio, poor thing."

"Why do you say poor thing?"

"She died on one of those planes on 9/11."

Which explains her part in this, Quinn thought to herself.

Betty flipped through further, then stopped at several photos of both Tyler and Drew with a young, handsome priest, playing baseball, fishing, on some kind of camping trip. Betty sighed at the happy memories. "Father John, he was real good to me and the boys. Better than any of the crackpots I wed. Christ, wish I coulda married *him*."

"Is he still there? In Kenosha?"

Betty had no idea. "We moved around a lot. I did factory work, went where the jobs were. Chrysler, Coopers, Bell Telephone, Campbell's Soup." She looked at the pictures with the priest again. "I suppose Father J could still be up there. He took over the parish after the old monsignor died. What was his name? Dutko, I think."

"What was Father John's last name?" Quinn asked.

"Nosko. That's Slovak. He gave me that." She pointed to the wall behind Quinn's head. There hung an ornate crucifix, with a dusty dried palm frond wedged behind it. "You know, I don't know how Tyler would have turned out without Father J. He needed a dad so badly then, and that's what John was for him. Better than a father, actually. Bless him."

Quinn took the woman's hand. "Betty, there's

something I want you to know. Drew never got your letters. And he loves you very much."

"How do you know that?" Betty asked.

"I just saw him. In Arizona. I know he was telling me the truth."

Betty looked flushed with a fleeting moment of happiness. "He's okay? Tell me how he's doing?"

Quinn smiled and nodded. "He's doing very well. And I want to tell you another thing. I know Drew's very intelligent, but you're right: He didn't use his skills to do something so wrong."

Betty was grateful to hear it. Then she gave Quinn a big, sad smile. "My boys—brilliant, both of 'em. I married rats, but they had to have some kind of good genes hiding underneath."

"I'll return the pictures I'm borrowing as soon as I copy them."

"You sure you don't want a drink before you go?"

Quinn winked. "I'm a vodka girl myself."

Betty grinned. "Hell, I knew I liked you!"

Saint Anthony's Parish had seen better days, Quinn surmised. The school next to the church looked like it had been closed for a long time, and so did the convent across the parking lot. She recognized the buildings from several photographs of the boys playing games on the asphalt, kids at recess with nuns and the youthful Father John, and Tyler's eighth-grade graduation photo taken on the church steps.

The church itself was magnificent, Quinn thought as she blessed herself, genuflected, and knelt for a few minutes in prayer. She prayed for Betty, for Betty and Drew to be reunited, and for herself and her quest. When she looked up at the altar, she saw a young priest in tennis shoes carrying some papers to the pulpit. For a second she thought it was Father Nosko, but quickly realized that time hadn't stood still. He was too young. It was likely the current assistant pastor, perhaps placing his sermon there for the next day's mass. She approached him. "Excuse me, Father?"

"Yes?"

"Is the pastor here?"

"He's in the rectory. Just behind the church."

"Thank you. Is his name John Nosko?"

The young man blinked. "What?"

"I wondered if Father John became pastor here. You see, I only know about—"

The man seemed suddenly closed, nervous. "You'll have to talk to Father Hornacek about that. He's the pastor now. Thank you."

Quinn went to the rectory door, where a tall, affable, balding man with a warm smile welcomed her. "Oh, hey, I thought it was my pizza."

She blinked. "What?"

"I just ordered a cheese and sausage from Carl's."

She started laughing. "I'm Quinn Roberts Bryant, and I'm afraid I don't have anything to eat."

He offered his hand. "I'm Father Joe, and all I have to offer is pizza. When it gets here. Come on in. What can I do for you?"

Quinn immediately felt comfortable with this good-natured man. When she asked about Father Nosko, she saw the same guarded look come over him that the younger priest had shown earlier. "John

Nosko," Father Joe said, "was pastor here for some time after Monsignor Dutko. This was my family parish, and I took over a few years back when Nosko left. I'm not crazy about parish work, but I'm not getting younger, and I do feel at home."

"Where did Father Nosko go?"

The priest bowed his head. "Prison."

He really didn't have to say any more. Quinn had already suspected what Tyler's wonderful father figure had done. She just needed confirmation.

"He pleaded guilty to sexually molesting twenty boys."

"And Tyler Bryant was one of them."

He wasn't sure. "I certainly know who your famous husband is, but I'm not sure that was one of the names. You'd have to look in the record."

"Whether it's in the record or not, whether he was one of the twenty or he was number twenty-one, I'm still sure."

"How can you be so positive?"

She took a deep breath. "Father, why else would someone hate God so deeply?"

Kona, Hawaii

When the Reverend Joseph Perry and his wife, Gail, arrived at Kona Village, they thought they had died and gone to heaven. Situated in an inlet, down a road that was lined on both sides with hardened lava, it was an oasis of green appearing almost as a mirage after the flat, dead land of the lava flow. Indeed, the lava parted near the water, leaving a pie slice of sand

and jungle untouched where, years later, someone
built a modern luxury resort.

But not a resort in the Marriott or even Four Sea-
sons vein. Kona Village had no televisions, no computers, no telephones. Rustic huts on stilts rose from
the jungle floor, with only screens to offer privacy.
Delicious meals were provided in the dining room. A
pool and a sandy beach featured daily water-sports
activities, among other exercise classes and various
crafts.

A bright-eyed, skinny boy standing in baggy
trunks said, "Aloha. I'm Ryan. I'm here to help you
with anything you need on the beach. Parasailing,
hiking, drinks, lunch—you name it."

"Well, thank you, Ryan," the minister said. "We're
looking forward to getting some sun."

"Arrive last night?" the boy asked.

"Late last night," the man's wife muttered as she
began applying suntan lotion to her legs. "Butch,"
she suddenly said, sounding alarmed, "you gave me
the number four."

The man grabbed it from her hand. "Sorry." He
dug into the beach bag to find her her usual number
32. "You'll be fine."

"She's right to be cautious," young Ryan said.
"Sun's hotter here. Where you from?"

"Vancouver."

Ryan was pleasantly surprised. "I'm from
Toronto."

Gail lifted her dark glasses and said, "Imagine
that. But you can't be more than fourteen. What are
you doing so far from home?"

Ryan grinned. "My dad's the chef here."

"Hey, I'll bet you're the guy to know," Joe Perry said. "Tell him to put his two best pieces of salmon aside for us tonight."

"Have the ono," the boy recommended. "I helped catch it myself."

They both smiled, and the boy left.

He returned about an hour later to warn them to keep reapplying lotion, and brought them two bottles of icy water. "So what kind of work do you do, Butch?"

"Actually," the minister said, "it's really Joe. Joseph Perry. This is my wife, Gail."

"Hi," Ryan said as Gail opened her eyes for a squinting second.

"Hi."

Joe said, "She's always called me Butch 'cause there are too many Joes in our family. I'm a Lutheran minister."

The boy just stared. He said nothing at all in response.

Joe, feeling slightly uncomfortable, tried to lighten the strained silence. "But we honor all faiths. As long as you believe in God, I don't care what you call yourself."

"My dad makes me go to a Christian Bible church."

"Do you like it?"

"No. Not lately." The boy jumped up from his kneeling position in the sand. "Boat's coming in," he announced. "Gotta tie it up. See ya later." He ran off.

"Nice kid," Joe commented, "but he seemed rather nervous talking about religion."

"Honey," Gail warned her husband, "don't start preaching, huh?"

He lay back on the towel on the chair in the sand, stretched his arms up to rest behind his head, feeling the rays continuing to fry his white skin. "You're right. Oh, this is great."

"Be careful. Number 4 isn't enough," she warned.

"Baste me now and then," he snickered, "because I'm in heaven."

By dinner time, he could barely walk. Gail—with her number thirty-two protection—had a nice brown glow about her, which complemented her blond hair perfectly. Joe, however, was in such agony that he could not even don a shirt for dinner. The ono, as young Ryan had promised, was delicious, and Ryan's father, the chef, took pity on the couple and gave them a salve that he said would really help.

Back in their hut, Gail carefully smeared the salve over her husband's shoulders. "Probably something he got out of the deep fryer," she said.

"Smells like cocoa butter. Maybe it's a homemade Hawaiian remedy."

"Or old Crisco."

He had to sleep on his stomach, for his back was in worse shape than his front. He had a tough time falling asleep, despite the jet lag and the pain pills and the heavy dinner. He tried to read, but it was impossible to hold a book under his chin. The light was attracting a plethora of insects to the screens anyhow, so he turned it out.

A minute later, he was sure he heard someone walking outside. He thought it was other guests. But the footsteps seemed to stop just outside their door.

There was a long stretch of silence—interrupted by the sounds of creatures of the night—and then he heard someone pull open their screen door.

"Ryan!" a man called out.

"What?" Joe was sure it was the boy's voice answering.

"What are you doing there?" The man seemed to be trying to speak in a whisper.

"Nothing."

"Get over here."

"Dad . . ."

The voices were impossible to hear after that.

Joe lay there for the longest time, wondering if he had been right—had the boy been about to enter their hut?—or was it his imagination and the boy was actually entering, perhaps, the hut he shared with his father? Noises carried here remarkably well because there was no sound of the city to interfere.

The next morning, young Ryan greeted the Perrys at breakfast. "No beach today, I bet," the boy sang.

"That's right," Joe said, still burning.

"Take the helicopter ride over the volcano," Ryan urged. "It's awesome. I can set it up for you." They agreed. Ryan took down the time they wanted to leave, and at the end of breakfast, he told them it was all set.

At noon, they boarded a shuttle bus for the airport, where they would board the helicopter. Two other couples went along. Just as the bus was about to leave, Ryan came running up. "Wait, here's some snacks for the trip." He heaved a wicker basket onto the bus and then boarded himself, telling the driver he was going to tag along.

The basket was filled with chips, fruit, sodas, Snapple, and water, and as the shuttle chugged along, everyone commented on what a nice boy he was, how cute he was, how helpful. Only Joe Perry had reservations, still unsettled by what he thought he heard the night before.

When the shuttle stopped near the airport and everyone stood up, Ryan said, "Wait, take some water, at least. The chopper ride is long." With that, he dug into the basket, but his hands reached beneath the bags of pretzels and macadamia nuts, under the sodas and other refreshments. His hands reached down to, they would later determine, a powerful bomb, which he detonated with one finger as his eyes locked with Joe Perry's in their final moment together on earth.

Ryan Thompson was sixteen years old.

Chapter Fourteen

Quinn heard the special report on the car radio just as she was nearing O'Hare Airport. She almost ran off the road as the details emerged. The reporter said the authorities were mystified as to Ryan Thompson's motive. But Quinn knew. He couldn't help it. He hadn't even known, rationally, what he was doing. He had been programmed. But how could she tell anyone? Who would believe her? And if she did share it with someone, as she had with Patrick and Mike Furnari, would she be condemning them to death?

Susan picked her up at the airport, shaken by the news as well. They both wondered—feared—who would be next. And how could they stop him? Quinn was sure now that she knew the underlying pathology behind Tyler's sick manifesto. "My instincts were right," she explained to Susan. "Tyler wasn't brought up atheist, he was raised Roman Catholic, like I was. It turns out the priest who was a 'second dad' to Tyler is in prison for sexually abusing boys."

"Right out of the headlines."

Quinn nodded. "Just like violence in the name of God."

Susan seemed excited. "So this is what you needed. You have motive now. You can tell someone. And if Dahbura doesn't help you, any magazine would jump at this story. Or one of the cable shows."

"I can't prove anything," Quinn said with enormous frustration. "There is no real evidence. We can't establish for a fact that the game has a subliminal program in it, can't demonstrate the technical wizardry that's making kids reject religion, can't prove that Tyler even killed Patrick. And we don't know what happened to Mike Furnari. In other words, we don't have anything."

"We will," Susan said with confidence, "after we make our visit to Zzzyx. I think I know how we can pull it off."

Later, when they were sure Veronica would have gone home for the day, they went to the Zzzyx building in Rockville. Yet she was there, looking like she had no plans to leave. "Ronnie, hi," Quinn said, smiling. "Working late?"

"This is my life."

Susan kept a straight face. "How lucky for Tyler."

"What are you doing back?" Veronica asked.

Quinn said, "I'm gonna use one of the computers in back to scan the photos and create some blowups for the party."

"You have to do that here?"

"The Foundation for Education has less money then Zzzyx," Susan interjected, "so our machines won't cut it. Hey, got some coffee?"

Ronnie rolled her eyes, but she didn't tell her to get it herself. "I'll make a fresh pot."

Quinn took her time and looked around. As Susan had predicted, almost two hundred employees were still working, mostly manning the phones for tech support. Luckily, the creative division was Tyler's private domain. Quinn had to get into his glass-walled private office. So she chose a seat at a computer terminal near it, while Susan tried to drive Ronnie so crazy with chatter that the woman would give up and go home.

That process took nearly an hour. Ronnie finally grabbed her briefcase, ready to depart.

"Why don't you two come back tomorrow?" she suggested.

Quinn pretended she had no idea time had flown. "I've got lots more to do."

Susan said, "Oh, hey, we can lock up for you."

"No one ever locks up," Ronnie said sarcastically. "We have tech support on-line twenty-four hours—you should know that. There's people here around the clock."

"So no problem," Quinn added.

Ronnie shrugged. "I guess not. Bye."

"Bye."

Susan gave her a big smile. "Bye, honey, and thanks."

When Veronica left, Quinn and Susan assessed the situation. More than half the staff had left, and around seven it seemed that another shift was over; more employees left. Indeed, by ten o'clock, while eating Quizno's subs that Susan had gone out to get, Quinn saw that tech support was the only area of the complex that was still buzzing. It was time to make her move.

Susan would cover for Quinn, rapping on the glass of Tyler's office if anyone looked suspicious. Susan took a position outside the door, going through a box of photos that Ronnie had given them, pictures of Tyler that she thought they might want to use for the party. Quinn went inside. Getting in was easy because she'd copied the key off his car key chain. She didn't have any plan to attempt to break into his computer; she had set her sights on the paper files and printed documents. The filing cabinets opened easily. But the walls were glass, and she constantly kept looking out to see if anyone besides Susan was watching her.

Around eleven, after poring through what seemed like hundreds of pages of technical gobbledygook, she found something. A thick file labeled FRONT RUN-NERS. But the contents disappointed her. It was a proposal to create such an elite group of game players, put together back in early 2001. No screen names and certainly no real names.

Shortly before twelve, Quinn hit pay dirt. In a box that contained loose PR CDs was a floppy disc simply labeled FR. Wrapped around it was a note, secured by a rubber band. In a distinctive print that she knew was not Tyler's, someone had penned HERE'S THE UP-TO-DATE LIST WITH CORRESPONDING NAMES. It was signed *B*.

Who the hell was *B*? Sure, Brandon.

Quinn thought fast. She needed a computer—one hooked to a printer—to read the disc.

She turned off the private office lights and

emerged. Susan had a sea of photos spread over a desk. She looked up to read Quinn's face, knowing that she had succeeded. "What did you get?" she asked Quinn.

"I need a computer," Quinn whispered, again looking around to see that no one was listening. "And a printer." There were several computers that were never shut down, but none of them had a printer anywhere nearby. She figured they must be connected to a network, and thus shared the same printer. She hesitated taking that chance, for when she looked in the room where the copying machines were humming and saw the three state-of-the-art laser printers there, someone from tech support was standing, waiting for a document to spill forth.

"Use the one in his office," Susan said.

Quinn nodded. She had no choice.

Quinn returned to Tyler's office and focused on the printer set on a steel cabinet. It gave her an idea. It was a state-of-the-art HP all-in-one, combining text printer, photo printer, scanner, copier, fax, and answering machine. Problem was, this printer was a prototype for a model that wasn't yet for sale, with programming capabilities to numb the mind. It had a floppy and a CD drive—just like a computer did— and photo memory card slots so that you could bypass your computer and simply work through the printer. She wanted to do that. It would look less suspect if the snoopy Veronica Ashton returned and wondered why she was sitting at Tyler's computer. Yet Quinn couldn't find the manual and had to take a stab at it without help.

The buttons were not easy to figure out. She managed to turn on the printer, but getting it to read the disc was impossible. No matter how hard she tried, she couldn't accomplish it. She had no choice but to go through the computer. She turned to Tyler's seventeen-inch G4 and powered it up. She saw a man walk by Susan, and held her breath for a moment, but he didn't even look into Tyler's office. Quinn inserted the disc, clicked on the icon, and watched the screen light up with names. Some of them she recognized:

Front Runners	Screen Name	Password
Loretta Seianas	WowSteph	PR18
Herman Goldstein	Goldplate	PR17
Willie Chesterfield	LuvXbox	PR16
Tommy Caldwell	LordsWorker	PR15
Mary Doyle	Irishstew	PR14
Billy Martinson	Packersfan	PR13
Christina Proctor	Booklover	PR12
Kathleen Murphy	Heaven2me	PR11
Gary Weidner	Penpal	PR10
Ismael Krani	PharohII	PR09
Philippe Minogue	Vivalaphil	PR08
Michael Money	Play8forfun	PR07
Kevin Mahon	Hotbrokerboy	PR06
Ryan Thompson	Riotson15	PR05
Evelyn Coelho	PompanoGal	PR04
Sam Sammons	Britboy177	PR03
_____	_____	PR02
_____	_____	PR01

Quinn's breathing quickened. Most of the names had been in the news. These were the murderers. The passwords gave Tyler access to their very subconscious, allowing him to direct them toward their own deaths. She went down the list, checking off the ones she did not know. Gary, Michael, Kevin, Evelyn, Sam, and two blanks.

Wait a minute. *Sam* Sammons. Was James Horgan's pal's name Sam? Could that be his last name? It petrified her. Seven of them, seven more possible killers. She grabbed a pen and started to scribble the list onto a pad, which made no sense at all. Why not just print it?

She hit the print button. But it wouldn't print. So she got up and pressed a button on the console of the printer.

And nearly jumped out of her skin. For suddenly Tyler himself said, "I'm here." She jumped up from the chair, whirled around toward the door, sure that she would find him standing behind her. The voice continued: "But I can't take this call. Make this a practice run for our next conversation. Leave me a message, please . . ." Click. Beep.

She fell back into the chair. She had somehow activated Tyler's message in the HP's answering device. Once her breathing had returned to normal, she tried another button, and this time it worked. The screen printed.

She circled five names when the paper came out:
Sam Sammons
Evelyn Coelho
Michael Money
Kevin Mahon
Gary Weidner
Quinn was so intent on the names that she only

became aware that someone else was in the room when she felt a slight change of temperature. Standing over the desk was her own nightmare, a very heated Veronica Ashton. "What are you doing?" she snapped.

Quinn was in a jam. She looked outside and saw Susan standing, looking just as panicked as she returned from the ladies' room. Quinn tried to play naive. As she spoke, she quickly pretended she was typing, but her keystrokes were, in fact, a fast and furious attempt at concealing what was on the screen. "Just a note to my loving husband for when he next looks at this screen. I'll be done in a minute. What are *you* doing back here at this hour?"

"I often come back to work at night."

"When do you get your beauty sleep?"

"Is that supposed to be funny?"

Quinn smiled, which, considering the circumstances, she thought quite an accomplishment. "Just making conversation. I honestly have no interest in your personal life." Like hell, she thought. This woman had to be an accomplice. Quinn wondered how many of the employees were as well. The thought chilled her. She wrote Tyler a quick note and stood up. How in the hell was she going to get the disc out of the drive?

She wasn't. Not with the watchdog standing there. She flashed a look to Susan, who immediately hurried in with an armful of photos. Susan took them straight to Ronnie. "Do you think you can identify some of the people in these pictures for us?"

As Ronnie's attention turned to Susan, Quinn managed to fold the sheet of paper that had come from the printer and slide it into her pocket. The disc was tougher because Veronica had set the photos down on Tyler's desk. To withdraw it, Quinn would have to reach around Ronnie's rear end. So she indicated what she needed to Susan behind Ronnie's back.

Susan got it. And managed to drop a bunch of photos to the floor. "Oh, man, I'm such a klutz." Because she dumped them at Ronnie's feet, the woman bent forward, not to help pick them up, but to be sure not to stand on any of them.

Which gave Quinn just enough time to pull the disc from the drive.

The minute they left the building, Quinn asked Susan what Sam's last name was.

"Lasman."

"Not Sammons? Thank God for that." Then she told her why and showed her the list.

In the office the next morning, Susan and Quinn searched the Internet for the screen names belonging to the five Front Runners' names. They couldn't find any of them. Quinn said to Susan, "I'm a wreck. I don't know what to do."

"How about calling Dahbura? You don't have much choice."

Quinn nodded. "You're right." She picked up the phone. But she didn't have to dial. Almost on cue, he walked in the door.

He introduced himself, producing his badge as he entered the office. What took her aback was that he was movie-star good-looking. Tall, slim, ruggedly dark with a Middle Eastern swarthy appeal, he had a five o'clock shadow and black, unruly hair. He looked smart and dangerous. After greeting them, he focused on Susan. "I knew Patrick," he acknowledged. "A good man. I'm very sorry."

"Where is Mike?" Quinn asked, not even giving Susan time to respond. "What's happened to him?"

"I'm going to be perfectly frank. Mike has been missing for too long."

"They killed him too?" Susan gasped.

David shook his head. But he did not tell them the line he'd given his superiors, knowing Quinn and Susan would never believe it. Instead he played along. "We certainly hope not, but we don't know. We know you have been right all along, Mrs. Bryant. Someone created a program that is prompting teens to murder religious figures. We can't as yet break the code, but we are on it."

"Kansas City," Quinn cried. "The DiForios, did you—?"

"Because we believe Agent Furnari was last seen in that city, we swept the DiForio home and thoroughly interrogated them. The place was clean. No reason to hold them. But since we believe they may have played an integral part in this plot, we are continuing to watch them."

Susan looked relieved. "So, you're finally getting to the bottom of this."

"Mike was certainly on to something. There are a plethora of Web sites that are stridently against religion, not the least of which is the one run by the DiForios and their talk show. We think there is a connection between the game and a creeping antireligious feeling among young people the world over."

Quinn blinked. "You mean it's not just the Front Runners?"

He seemed reluctant to admit too much. "Let's just say that there are subtle signs that young people around the globe are being affected. Teens are skipping classes in religion. Attendance at Sunday school is down in many areas. Kids refuse, for no reason, to attend church with their families. A groundswell effort by students to stop saying 'under God' in the Pledge of Allegiance has been noted. The Front Runners may be programmed to kill, but this is what the regular Practice Run is doing to the rest."

Susan suddenly remembered something. "I read somewhere that many bar mitzvahs have been canceled because teenage boys suddenly refused to go through with the ritual. It mystified their parents. I didn't connect it to the game at the time."

Dahbura nodded. "A Bible class lost almost a third of its registration. A girl in Minnesota summed it up in *Newsweek* by saying, 'Religion just isn't cool.'"

Susan was impressed. "You guys sound on top of this."

He looked confident. "We are."

"The game is creating a general unrest about religion with all the kids who play it?" Quinn asked.

"To the degree that the player is susceptible. Like how people differ in how easily they can be hypnotized. But it's happening."

Quinn said, "And then the ones most susceptible get to be Front Runners."

Dahbura thought that was too simple. "Most susceptible, but also the smartest. They are the most adept at playing a difficult game. The winners."

Sadly, Quinn said, "No, losers."

Susan blurted out, "When are you going to arrest him?"

"Who?"

"Tyler," Quinn said emphatically.

"Tyler?" he asked. "We're not positive it's him as yet."

Quinn couldn't believe it. "Who else could it be?"

He seemed surprised at her outburst. "An employee? One of his technicians?"

"He stole the hidden program," Quinn said with frustration, "from his brother. Drew Concardi created it as a school prank. Tyler swiped the technology and used it for his crazy, evil scheme while he had his brother put in prison."

He looked like he distrusted this theory. "What we don't understand is how specific kids become killers."

She snapped, "Why didn't you talk to me before this?" She then explained how Front Runner status was achieved. And handed him the list of names. "These are the kids who killed. They're programmed not to talk about the fact that they're Front Runners, so these names do not appear on the Web sites listing the kids who have that status. These five"—she pointed to the names at the bottom of her list—"are the ones who will do it next. You have to stop them."

He seemed very impressed. "This is more than the Bureau has been able to dig up." He thought for a moment. "There are only two I don't recognize."

"What?" Quinn was startled.

He shook his head. "Michael Money and Kevin Mahon struck over a year ago. They killed two Christian Brothers who were leading a group of school-boys on a camping trip just outside Indianapolis."

She blinked. She had not uncovered that one.

"Lured them out of a tent, drowned them, shot themselves."

She gasped. "Of course it would connect. It had to have been one of the first incidents. I didn't know about that one."

Dahbura said, "And Gary Weidner too. Not far away. Ohio. Another priest, I think it was. A stabbing."

She shook her head to rid it of the horror. "So there are only two we don't know about. Evelyn and Sam."

David Dahbura shrugged. "But who knows how many others there might be that we don't yet know about?"

She thought about it but disagreed. "I think you're wrong. Look at the list."

"Yes?"

"There may be over two hundred and fifty Front Runners total, but the ones who have been programmed to kill isn't that large. Only eighteen of them. With the blanks for PR02 and PR01, and Evelyn Coelho and Sam Sammons, there might be only four more assassins." He looked at the list. He put an X through her circles around Evelyn Coelho's and Sam Sammons' names.

"It's possible." But he looked skeptical. "I guess we don't know if anyone has been assigned the final two numbers."

"Let's hope not."

He seemed pumped by her new information. "Listen, I want to get on this right away. In the meantime, don't tip off Tyler. He may have a false sense of security after removing Agent Furnari from his trail, and we need to keep it that way. I want you to pretend everything is fine."

She groaned. "I'm so good at acting these days, I could stand in for Meryl Streep."

"I'll be in touch with you in a few days. I'm flying to Kansas City to pay a visit to the DiForios myself. You just do what Tyler wants, pretend you've given up." He shook his head. "I find all this so astonishing. I mean, the public persona of Tyler Bryant is so appealing. He's the role model for half the kids in the world—the cool guy who understands them."

"He said in an interview," Susan reminded them, "that all he ever wanted to do was captivate kids. We just didn't know how."

"He obviously isn't what he appears to be," Quinn said.

He gave them a strange grin. "Well, are any of us, really?"

Chapter Fifteen

Quinn took the shuttle to LaGuardia for an afternoon meeting with officials from the New York Public Library. She had just returned to the Columbus Circle apartment and flicked on the TV when Tyler's face appeared. He and Ken Kutaragi, the famous Sony game maverick, were on a cable show discussing the influence of violence in computer games. The host asked Tyler the usual questions. Do games today step over the line? Are they actually good for kids? Even though Practice Run promotes literacy, isn't it too violent? Tyler had all the right answers. He was compelling, funny, seemingly morally centered, and a great advocate of games that "enlighten as well as entertain." Quinn felt like she was going to throw up.

Just then her daughter called. While Quinn was happy to hear Joan's voice, and glad that she was enjoying her adventure in Europe, she had trouble concentrating because her mind was on the TV screen. "Mom, what's wrong with you?" Joanie finally asked.

"What do you mean?"

"Something's different. For a long time now. You seem so edgy, like you're scared of something. I don't know how to explain it—it's just weird. For you."

"I'm involved in something," Quinn fessed up. "Something that I can't really talk about. But it's important and it's secret."

"Government stuff? Computers?"

"That's part of it. A big part."

Joan seemed curious. "So you a CIA agent now? All those computers you're sending to the Middle East have bugs in them?"

Quinn thought, *If you only knew.* "You've seen the new James Bond film, I take it?" She laughed for good measure.

"Is Tyler there? I hear his voice."

"He's on TV, actually."

"The publicity is heating up for Practice Run Five. There are billboards all over Germany already. It's gonna be huge."

Quinn froze. She'd been spending all her time thinking about the current game, about what it did. What about the new version that was coming soon? What kind of leap did it take? Would all kids be turned into killers? The thought frightened her. She had not really even talked to Tyler about it, though she knew it was taking up most of his time. She said, "It's being released here at Easter. There too?"

"Yes," Joanie said.

Not if I can do anything about it, Quinn thought. She pressed a button on the remote, turning off the TV. And changed the subject. "Honey, maybe we can be together for Easter. It's not that far off."

"Sure, Mom. I'd love that. Why don't you come

here? In fact, why don't you come soon? You'd love Steph's family."

"I'm too involved in this project to do anything else right now. But let's aim for Easter, honey. By Easter this whole thing should be finished." *Please*, she thought, *if there is a God*.

"Love you, Mom. Bye."

"A prayer for Steph's mom. Bye, baby."

Seeing Tyler's performance and talking with Joan left Quinn feeling queasy. She had to get out of New York, had to get away from Tyler. She just couldn't face him coming to the apartment tonight. She decided to head for Grand Central to catch the Acela back to Washington. On Forty-second Street, her cell phone rang. It was Tyler. "Didja see the broadcast?"

"Yes," she said warmly, "you were great, as usual."

"Where are you?"

"Just entering Grand Central. Have to go back. Something came up."

"Hey," he said in a disappointed tone, "I thought we'd go to Vice Versa for dinner."

Quinn tried to beg off. "I need to be back in D.C. in the morning."

"Come on, have an early dinner and stay the night with me. I'll take you to the first shuttle out in the morning."

She thought about what Agent Dahbura had said, and she realized she wasn't playing this correctly. "You're right, sweetheart," she cooed. She figured she would grin and bear it one more night. "I'll go down in the morning. How soon can you be at the restaurant?"

"Within the hour."

"Okay," she said. "I'll walk over. See you at the bar."

Quinn arrived at Vice Versa fifteen minutes later. Daniele and Franco were happy to see her, held a table for the two of them, and stood talking to her as she sat at the bar. She tried her best to be herself, but they both sensed something was bothering her. When pressed, she admitted they were right. "But I can't talk about it."

Franco seemed to think it was personal. "Everything all right with Tyler?"

She nodded, but she knew she wasn't convincing.

"What?" Daniele asked, putting an arm around her shoulder. "If he's not being good to you, he's banned from this street forever!"

She laughed at this joke. "It's bigger than a relationship problem. Just wish me luck, guys, 'cause I really need it."

"Anything we can do to help?" Franco asked.

She could not answer because her cell phone started ringing. By the time she dug it out of her purse, it had stopped. The phone had picked up the caller ID. It was Susan. Quinn was about to dial her when Susan called again. "Quinn, thank God! Where are you now?"

"What do you mean, where am I? You know I'm in New York."

"I mean, where in New York? Is Tyler with you?"

"No. But he will be. I'm waiting for him to join me for dinner. I'll be back in the morning."

"No," Susan said bluntly. "Get out of there. Now. Come back here tonight."

Quinn hadn't heard Susan sound so intense since she blew up at James about playing the game. "What's wrong?"

"You know the photos that I took from Veronica?"

Quinn blinked. "What about them?"

"There's one I'm looking at now. It's one of Tyler and another man coming down the steps of what looks to me like the exterior of the Justice Department."

"And?"

"I recognize this guy," Susan said. "And you will too."

"How? I don't understand."

"I'm going to read you the caption under the picture. 'Game Mogul Tyler Bryant Leaving the Justice Department with Agent David Dahbura of the Federal Bureau of Investigation After Bryant's Brother's Pre-trial Hearing.'"

Quinn's heart moved up to her throat. "It's *him*? Dahbura with Tyler? They're friends?"

"Dahbura has his arm over your husband's shoulder." Susan took a breath. "Get out of there, Quinn. They're in cahoots. Dahbura is in on it. That was a fishing expedition he was on with us the other day. To see how much you really know. Quinn, run."

Quinn jumped to her feet. "Yes," she managed to say. "Yes, you're right, I'll—"

She didn't get far. Approaching her was the familiar figure of her husband. As he bent forward to kiss her, she gasped, "Tyler!"

"You were expecting someone else?" he said, grinning. "Ah, that Michael guy must still be in your life." He pecked her on the cheek. "Is that him on the phone?" he asked, seeing it clutched in her hand.

She put the Nokia back to her ear. "Susan?"

"I heard him," Susan said nervously. "I know he's there. Quinn, for God's sake, get the hell out of there!"

"I'll catch a late train tonight in that case," Quinn said, trying to sound disappointed that she couldn't spend the night with her husband. "Don't worry, we'll figure something out tomorrow." She pressed the red button.

"Figure what out?" Tyler asked.

"Oh, work stuff, you know." Quinn put her arms around him. "I've missed you."

He looked slightly surprised. "Didn't think you remembered my name. Hungry?"

Franco stepped up. "Your table is ready." He motioned to the couple's favorite waiter. "Peter, two martinis."

"Lead the way," Tyler told him, and took Quinn's hand as they headed toward the dining room.

Quinn threw Daniele a look that tried to say *help me*, but only confused her. As they walked through the restaurant, they appeared to be the happiest couple on earth.

It was a sham on Tyler's part as well, Quinn realized as soon as they were seated. "Where were you going when you almost ran into me up front?" he asked her, unfolding his napkin.

"What?"

"You jumped up. You grabbed your bag. You looked like you were about to head out." He sounded distrustful, ready to accuse her of something.

She fidgeted. "Susan upset me."

"Ah. So you were going to leave?"

"No."

"Quinn, you don't lie very well."

"What?"

Though they were seated across from one another at an intimate table, the distance between them couldn't have been larger. In the silence that ensued, Quinn realized suddenly that he knew. Ronnie must have told him she'd found Quinn on his computer. She also knew that the visit from David Dahbura could have been a way to lead her into this trap tonight. But was it a trap? If Tyler was on to her, if he was going to hurt her, why would he choose this place to do it?

She tried to prepare herself for what he was about to say, but the way he continued the conversation confounded her. "There is a very old film," he said after the martinis arrived. "It's called *Sorry, Wrong Number*."

She remembered. "Barbara Stanwyck. Black and white."

"Yes. Do you recall the story?"

She tried to think. "She's an invalid, confined to her bed. I think she spends the entire film on the telephone."

"What's the source of her terror?" Tyler asked.

Quinn was attempting to picture it. "She learns that someone is going to kill her."

He smiled and took another sip of his martini. "Yes. And who is it she learns is going to kill her?"

Quinn's lips quivered as the answer came to her. "Her husband."

"Her husband," he repeated, then smiled. "Let's not screw around any longer, baby, shall we? You've figured it out. I know that. You now know that I know. So the cards are on the table."

She had not prepared for this moment, had somehow thought it would never come. But suddenly everything had changed. She mustered her courage and said, "I'm going to stop you."

"How?" he said with a dismissive gesture. "No one will believe you."

"Patrick believed me!"

He grinned again. "And met his fate."

"Fate? Is that what happened to Mike Furnari too?"

"Ah, the flirtation with 'Michael' that you lied about."

"You're calling *me* a liar?"

He gave her a warning, his voice menacing. "Don't tempt fate, Quinn."

"You think this is inevitable?"

"I call it God's will." He snickered. "*Allah akbar.*"

She wanted to pick up her knife and plunge it through his eye. She felt a white-hot barrage of hatred for him. "Death was not Patrick's *fate*. God had nothing to do with it. You killed him."

"An unfortunate, untimely accident. And in such a nice car."

She squirmed. "You bastard."

"So, Quinn, what are you going to do? Who else

do you want to plunge into a river?" He laughed suddenly. "It just occurred to me, that's how your boyfriend Mike ended up as well."

"What?"

"You're like a black widow spider, Quinn. Every guy who gets near your web ends up dead." He sipped his drink. "So tell me, how do you plan to stop me?"

Her words were measured, filled with loathing. "You really think you can create an army willing to kill priests and ministers and rabbis for you?"

"The army comes later. First, the Front Runners pave the way."

"By murdering?"

"*Eradicate* is the word I'd use."

"You're sick!"

"Don't raise your voice. People will think you're crazy."

"They'll think *I'm* crazy?" She looked around, suddenly realizing he was right. She had gotten loud and other diners were staring at her. She softened her tone, but the intensity was just as lethal. "Listen to me. By taking innocent kids with you in this demented quest to reject God, you're no better than the suicide bombers who act in the *name* of God." She found her hands clutching the tabletop. "Yes, you got a few of them to step over the line, got some of them to become killers. But to convert millions of young people to your godless dream, I mean, how can you honestly think this will work?"

He grinned and leaned across the table. Then he whispered, "It worked for me in Columbine, didn't it?"

It left her breathless. She groped for words. "Columbine? Colorado? The high school?"

He smiled. "What do you think those two boys were doing out in the garage every night for months before? Just what their parents told the media—playing video games."

"You programmed them to do what they did?"

He shrugged. "Maybe I did, maybe not." His eyes flickered.

She could not tell if he was putting her on or not. Was he being facetious? Or was he serious? She gathered herself and tried to rise above her fear. "No way," she said. "You're bluffing." The thought that he would take credit for one of the most awful episodes of violence in recent memory was stomach turning. "That wasn't about religion."

"Maybe it was just to see if it would work." He gave her another grin. "Maybe it was my practice run."

"My God," she whispered. "You're sicker than I thought."

He seemed to enjoy the horrified look on her face. "Quinn, Quinn, I don't know what I'm going to do with you."

Fear made her stiffen, but gave her energy to fight back as well. "What do you mean?"

"How is our marriage going to work when we don't—how to put it?—see eye to eye on this?"

"No one could possibly condone what you're doing! It's madness."

Softly, he replied, "There are many who have already praised me. It's a movement, Quinn. It's not vocal yet—it's underground, but it's building. By the time the army is ready, people will come forth in support of the forces."

She gasped. "Other insane bastards like your pal Dahbura? And the demented DiForios?"

"I'm hungry," he said abruptly. He had become bored. Franco happened to be passing. "Can you send Peter over, Franco?"

"Absolutely, my friend. And another round?"

"Please," Tyler responded.

Quinn started to get out of her chair.

Tyler grabbed her hand. "Where do you think you're going?"

"The bathroom."

"You can't escape me, Quinn. This is bigger than your objections or your moral outrage. No one will believe you, you already know that. There is no one who will help you. *You* will appear to be the one who is mad." He loosened his grip on her arm. "Soon, darling, the big guys will start dropping."

"Who?"

He winked, proud of himself. "There are bigger fish swimming in the religious sea."

"Bigger?"

"Then utter chaos. And a decisive change."

"You're crazy."

"Go ahead," he said, nodding toward the front of the elegant restaurant, where the bathrooms were located. "And hurry back, because we have a lot more to discuss." He pulled her bag from her hand. "No cell phone, darling. And don't try to run, because I'm watching, and you are wearing heels. I'll be faster. But perhaps not fast enough to save you from falling in front of a moving cab." He grinned again. "Or a speeding 745i."

She rushed toward the bathrooms, trying to keep her head together, trying to focus, not letting the emotions bursting inside her mar her clarity. She hurried toward the coat check room, where she knew he could not see her. She had to get away from this man. But how? She didn't doubt for a moment that he would shove her in front of a truck barreling up Eighth Avenue.

She saw that neither of the two bathrooms was open. But the door handle was just starting to turn on the one closest to her. She rushed to it, yanked it open, shocking the unsuspecting exiting occupant, shoved him back inside and locked it again. To her astonishment—and relief—she found that she was facing Daniele. "My God," he said when he saw her terrified face. "What is it?"

"You've got to help me!" she cried, grasping his hands.

When she returned to the table, Tyler told her that he'd ordered for her as well as himself. "The strangled priest pasta, your favorite. No pun intended."

She said she was not hungry.

He didn't care. "I want you to understand. I may convert you yet."

She blinked. "You think I could condone assassination? Murder? The kids who are doing your dirty work aren't committing suicide, you're *killing* them. In cold blood, just as you killed Patrick. And Mike Furnari. He is dead, isn't he?"

"Every war has its casualties."

"War? Are you completely demented? It's your personal war, started when some damned priest put his finger up your ass."

Her statement had more effect than a bullet might have had. It shut him down. He went blank. Astonishment was written in his eyes, and his face was white with dismay.

She had the upper hand now. "You know what, Tyler? I'm really sorry that happened to you. I really feel bad for what you had to suffer, the shame and the self-loathing and the loss of your faith. Guess what, though? You were lucky. Some people commit suicide because of it." She thought twice. "If only we could have been so blessed."

As Peter brought salads, the atmosphere at the table seemed icier than the chilled plates on which the food rested. Tyler didn't move. Neither did Quinn. "Fresh black pepper?" Getting no answer, Peter knew better than to ask again. He gave up and walked away.

"I know all about good old Father J. I've seen your mother. And your brother. I know the secrets. I know how sick you are. I could help you, Tyler, if only you'd let me."

It was as if she'd smacked him in the face with a brick. He looked like he was suddenly going to be sick.

She stood up.

"Down," he managed to growl.

She grabbed her salad plate. "You ordered wrong. I hate blue cheese—you know that." She held the plate high and looked around. Daniele, who happened to be near the kitchen door, spied her and waved as if to signal her. "I'm going to get one with vinaigrette," she told Tyler as she walked toward Daniele.

"I thought you weren't hungry." Tyler got up, distrusting her move. "The waiter will bring you one. Sit down."

"Oh, cool off. Where do you think I'm going to go?"

Tyler watched her walk over to Daniele and apparently ask him to take back the salad. He appeared to be assuring her they would replace it with one to her liking.

At that moment Franco approached looking very concerned, asking Tyler what was happening. Why was he standing there? Tyler sat back down. "Quinn wanted a different salad and—"

She was gone. In the instant he'd taken his eyes off her, she'd disappeared.

"Where is she?" Tyler shouted. He jumped to his feet again. "Where's Daniele? Where'd they go?"

Franco said, "I have no idea. They were both right there."

Tyler jumped up from his chair, making a move in that direction, but Franco moved at the same moment, which knocked Tyler into a pillar. "Oh, I'm so sorry," Franco said, grabbing Tyler before he fell into another table. "Forgive me."

"Get away from me!" Tyler told him, forcing his way through the tables of shocked diners to the entrance to the kitchen.

But Franco followed, managing to grab his arm just as Tyler reached the doors. "You can't go in there."

"Leave me alone!" Tyler burst through the doors, only to run smack into Stefano, the chef, dressed all in white, wearing his toque. Stefano happily embraced Tyler, holding him tight, so he couldn't move. "Ciao, Tyler," Stefano said slowly, thanking him for coming, telling him how good it was to see him again. "You liked your dinner so much you came to the kitchen for the recipe? Magnifico." Stefano was starting to speak Italian now, with no plan to let Tyler go.

"Get your hands off me!" Tyler demanded, trying to extricate himself from the man's arms. "You're all in on this!"

Over Tyler's shoulder, Stefano looked at Franco, who nodded that he was doing very well.

Tyler was right. It had all been planned.

By the time Tyler had extricated himself from the chef's strong grasp, Daniele had helped Quinn down the stairs, through the basement kitchen (astonishing most of the help), and out the service entrance to the street. Peter was waiting there with her briefcase and purse, which he'd retrieved from the table when Tyler started toward the kitchen. They put her in a cab and wished her well.

Quinn was on the run.

Chapter Sixteen

"Susan? It's Quinn."

"Oh, my God, I've been so worried."

"I'm okay. I got away. Don't ask questions, just get James into the car and get out of there."

"What?"

"Honey, he knows, he's on to me, and I'm afraid for you. He's crazy. I can't put you in more danger."

"Yes, you can. Explain. Where are you now? What happened?"

Quinn related how she had escaped. When she told Susan she was in a cab, Susan suggested going to the Port Authority Bus Terminal to get on the next bus out of there, no matter where it was going. "I'll pick you up, whatever the destination. Just call and let me know."

"I can't ask you to do that."

"Listen," Susan barked, "you're not asking, I'm demanding. I'm going to wake James and take him over to Sam's house. I'll tell the Lasmans that something has come up. They'll be cool with it. He's safe there."

Quinn shivered. The cab driver was eyeing her curiously in the rearview mirror. She guessed she must look terrified. She tried to force a smile and brushed her hair back. "Okay, I'm going to jump on the next Greyhound. I'll call from the bus once we're on our way."

"It's going to be okay. We're going to find a way to stop him."

"Stop him and how many kids we don't yet know about?"

"Go. I'm waking James right now . . ."

The bus pulled into the bleak Baltimore station at 4:00 A.M. Susan was waiting for her at the gate. "To think I gave up a perfectly good career in television to come work for you," Susan said as a relieved Quinn got into her car. "I feared the doors would open and you wouldn't step off."

"My friends at the restaurant saved my life," Quinn said gratefully. "Tyler has no idea where I am."

"Keep it that way." Susan put the car into gear. "I went to your house. Remembered where the key was, got you some clothes, packed a bag in the trunk. I didn't think you were going to stick around and wait for him to come looking. I broke open that piggy bank you kept in your undies drawer." She handed Quinn a thick envelope. "The one you were saving for Joanie's wedding one day."

"How much was in there?"

"About four, five thousand."

Quinn nodded. "Thank God. I can't use credit cards."

"No, you can't. Be careful of everything, no matter where you are. He will be trying to track you."

Quinn looked clueless. "Where should I go? It's all I could think about, riding for three hours. Arizona is the only bet. I have to see Drew."

"Isn't that dangerous?"

Quinn almost laughed. "A federal prison might be the safest place I could go."

"Will Tyler suspect that?"

Quinn wondered. "I don't think so. I don't imagine he'd surmise that I'd go to Drew for help, at least not at first."

"Just remember, you told Dahbura a lot. What about Joanie?"

Quinn slumped in the seat, finally buckling her belt. "I'm so afraid for her. I talked to her yesterday. She wants me to join her for Easter, but that's too far off."

"That's when his new game is released."

"Yes, and who knows what that version will do?" Quinn bit a fingernail. "I have to stop that game from coming out."

"I think Joanie's safe over there."

Quinn didn't know. "All sorts of scenarios popped into my mind—that he'd kidnap her, use her to stop me, something like that."

Susan played devil's advocate. "He's a very public figure, and the last thing he wants is for this to get out. Kidnaping isn't his thing. He's going to be a lot more subtle."

"I'd say he's the king of subtle."

They took the beltway around the District of Columbia, then headed to Dulles, where Quinn could get the first morning nonstop flight to Phoenix. Quinn wrestled with telling her daughter everything, but the fear that Tyler could use Joan as a pawn to get Quinn to stop trying to expose him won out. "I feel like I've put her in danger."

Susan thought about it. "I have an idea," she finally said. "Patrick and I accumulated a lot of frequent flyer miles on those trips to Ireland. Foundation stuff is slow right now. I can run our business from any laptop, so why not from Dingle?"

Quinn didn't understand. "What's that got to do with Joan?"

"I'll be closer to her this way. I'll get her and that girlfriend to come spend some time in Ireland." Susan didn't give Quinn time to interrupt. "Listen, I don't want you to worry about Joan. When she's safe there with me and James, I'll explain to her what's really happened."

"I should do it myself."

Susan advised against it. "What, on a call to Europe? We're not even sure where she is."

"I can reach her through Stephanie's family."

"So can I. If you alarm her now, she might be resistant. Remember, she adores Tyler."

"She does."

"I won't let anything happen to her, honey, trust me."

Quinn shivered.

Susan reassured her. "Don't worry about her, don't worry about me. Worry about yourself. You've got to outsmart him."

"I think I know how to."

"There's some coffee in the thermos." Susan

lifted it from the cup holder between them. "It might help."

"You should have heard him," Quinn said softly, reaching for the aluminum container. "He actually grinned, seemed proud of what he's done. It was like it was all some kind of . . ."

"Game?"

They drove in silence the rest of the way to the airport.

The guard at the gate of the prison complex remembered her this time. "Go right on in, Mrs. Bryant," he said with a smile. "Warden said she was expecting you. Busy day here today."

Quinn drove past the barriers and quickly parked in front of Aggie Spivak's office.

The warden didn't seem surprised when Quinn rushed in. "He's gone, Quinn."

"Gone? Who?"

"Drew Concardi. Less than an hour ago. The FBI took him away."

Quinn's knees started to give out. "The FBI?"

Aggie shook her head. "It mystified me, but the papers were in order, top secret government stuff. I had no choice."

"No!" Quinn felt her stomach turning over. "Oh, God, no!" That's why the guard had said it had been a busy day.

"But it's the FBI."

"Agent Dahbura?" Quinn asked. "David Dahbura?"

Aggie nodded, but she didn't have to. Quinn knew the moment she had mentioned the Federal

Bureau of Investigation. "He didn't take Drew away to do top-secret government stuff, Warden. He took Drew away to kill him."

That night Quinn was roused from a fitful sleep by the ringing of her cell phone. She jerked awake, sat up rigid. Who was calling at this hour? She saw it was Susan. It was morning already on the East Coast. "What?" she answered.

"Are you at the prison?"

"A hotel. I'm afraid Drew is dead."

"Dead? I just talked to him."

Quinn jumped out of bed. "What?"

"I was making coffee when the phone rang. I thought it was Aer Lingus confirming our flights, but it was the office line. I had the calls forwarded here. It was a guy, out of breath, agitated, babbling, asking where you were."

"Where is he? We thought they took him away to kill him."

"He said he's in trouble, sounded scared to death."

"Susan, where *is* he?"

"Phone booth in Sedona, he said. He'll be nearby to hear the ring."

"How long ago was this?"

"Two minutes at most."

"Give me the number." Susan did. "I'll call you back." Quinn hung up and dialed the phone booth. It rang six times. No answer. Seven. Eight. Nine. She would give it to twenty. No, fifty. She prayed as she counted the rings.

On the eighteenth, he answered. "Quinn?" he whispered.

She was overwhelmed with joy at hearing his voice. "You're okay. Thank God you're okay!"

"I got away."

"How?"

"I'll explain later. Where are you? Your partner said you were on your way to the prison."

"I'm in Scottsdale. In a hotel."

Hope filled his voice. "Can you come?"

"Just tell me where to find you."

Quinn wound her way up the hill toward a chapel that seemed to look out over all God's wonders. Sedona, Arizona, with its red rocks and green pines and amazing beauty, had always been a place Quinn wanted to visit, although not quite in this way. Drew had told her the chapel was a big tourist attraction. He didn't know the name of it, but she would certainly find it. He was hiding in plain sight. Indeed, when she walked up to the structure, she almost didn't see him amidst the group of morning tourists admiring the view and the serenity of the place. As they planned, she did not do anything to acknowledge his presence. She set the rental car keys down on a section of rock wall. And she walked back to the car.

A minute later, Drew appeared where she had put them. Lifting them, he read the key tag: Mazda. Blue. Plate 304TML. Budget FastBreak. Two minutes later, he was behind the wheel of the blue Mazda, driving himself and his passenger down the hill. He said nothing as they sped through town. At a stoplight, he nodded toward a black Chevy Suburban parked in the lot in front of a motel. She knew it belonged to the FBI. A mile away, he turned into a secluded parking spot along the side of the road, nestled between towering pines, put the transmission in park—and lost it. He reached out to Quinn, hugged her so tightly that he shook, and then suddenly kissed her passionately. What shocked her most was that he then burst into tears.

She held him in her arms, cradling his head, running her fingers through his hair, letting him cry it out. She tried to put herself in his shoes. Locked up for years, lonely, frustrated, then suddenly freed by men purporting to be helping you, only to find out they're bad guys too. But was he free? Were either of them? "Drew," she said, comforting him, "let's get far away from here. We'll talk. I want to know everything that happened. But I want you to know that I'm so glad you're alive."

He managed a smile. "Me too." He put the car in gear and tore off.

On the highway heading north, Drew told her what had happened. When Dahbura reminded him that he was familiar with Drew's case, Drew remembered him from his trial. He also recalled that the man was a friend of Tyler's, and the man forthrightly, it seemed, said it was still a shock to have learned of Tyler's scheme. Dahbura told him they were taking him to a lab where Quinn would join them, a place where he would be safe but at the same time he could work with them to stop his brother. The two agents, to gain his trust, took off his handcuffs, ate with him in a Wendy's along the way, assuring him that he'd never be going back to prison.

When they arrived at what seemed no more than a shack up near Prescott, Drew suddenly felt afraid. He tried to tell himself that he was wrong, that the small building was a disguise for a high-tech laboratory in which he'd work. The driver turned off the engine, and because they'd been drinking big Cokes from Wendy's, he said he had to piss. While he went around to the other side of the Suburban, Dahbura walked behind Drew to the door of the structure. When Dahbura pushed the door open, he stood to the side, as if to usher Drew in, but even in the darkness Drew could sense nothing inside but bare walls. From the corner of his eye, he saw Dahbura's hand pulling out a gun. In a frenzied rush, he kicked the door closed on the agent's arm.

"I think I nearly amputated it. He went down, collapsed in pain. I grabbed the gun, stepped over him, ran out, and held it in the face of the other guy. He put his arms up, still taking a leak. I told him to turn around. He did. I hit him on the head. And I ran into the woods."

"Why didn't you take the Suburban?" Quinn asked.

"They'd have cops stop me in a minute," he explained. "It would have been suicidal. I hiked for miles and then came to a road. I hitched a ride outside a country bar that was still open. Some guys saw me get into the truck that picked me up. That's how I think they followed me."

"Someone identified the truck and guessed it was headed for Sedona?"

He nodded. "The driver dropped me off in town. I didn't know what to do or who to call. I was about to walk across the street to the motel you saw to get some sleep when the Suburban appeared."

"Did they see you?"

He shook his head. "The truck driver gave me an old jacket he said he didn't use anymore."

Quinn looked at it. "Lovely."

"I think it helped disguise me. Hell, I was in their headlights for a second. Then I ran. Hid. Finally fell asleep behind a Dumpster. When I woke, I tried finding you in D.C."

"Thank God for Susan."

He drove another few miles. "Quinn, where are we going?"

She shook her head. "I'm not sure. Flagstaff is the next city."

He thought about that. "We should drive a while, put some miles between us and them. We could go through the Navajo Indian reservation. It takes up the whole northeast corner of the state."

"How do you know that?"

He said dryly, "I read a lot of books on the Southwest while locked up in that cell."

"Sounds like a good idea."

He nodded. "People seldom go through Navajo country."

On the way to Flagstaff, they discussed the problem that Drew had no identification. That meant they could not use airports or anything where he'd have to prove his ID. In Flagstaff, they grabbed doughnuts and coffee at a drive-through, stopped in a barber shop to have Drew's hair cut, then found him a pair of reading glasses that helped disguise him even more. Then they went to Wal-Mart and bought him some clothes.

At a hardware store, Drew bought a screwdriver and removed the license plates from her rented car. Drew knew that once Dahbura learned that Quinn had been at the Gallup Correctional Institute, her plates would be on the surveillance tape. He switched them with plates from a rotting American Motors Javelin. When he finished and they started driving through the Navajo lands, Drew reached to the bottom of the windshield and started scraping with his fingernail at a sticker there. "What are you doing?" Quinn asked. He told her the decal, though simply numbers and a bar code, said *rental car* to anyone who was looking for one. She handed him the screwdriver, and he scraped it off in seconds.

They stopped only once to eat, trying to avoid people, trying not to be seen. They had no idea if they were being followed, but they knew they were being hunted. Tyler and Dahbura were not about to let them simply run off. There was too much to lose. Drew was a very real threat to Tyler's plan. He created the game on which it depended, and he could destroy it.

"How?" Quinn asked him in the car.

"It's rattling around in my brain," he told her. "It'll gel. Give me time."

She pressed no further. But a thought came to her. "They will know the car as well from the cameras at the prison."

He'd thought about that. "We'll rent a different car in a bigger city."

"Where will that be?"

He shrugged. They drove through towns like Tuba City, Cow Springs, Kayenta, and finally stopped just south of the Utah border in a place called Mexico Water, where they checked in to a worn Comfort Inn. To be safe, they had to share a room. But that presented a problem—who would sleep where? "Take the bed," Drew told Quinn as he grabbed the extra pillow and blanket from the closet.

"Where are you going to sleep?" she asked.

"The floor."

She wouldn't let him do it. She grabbed his hand and pulled him up. "No way. You haven't slept on a decent mattress in years."

He grinned. "What makes you think this one is decent?"

She sat on it. It was. "And you need rest more than I do."

"Listen," he said softly, "I overstepped my bounds when I kissed you in the car. I can't ask to share your bed."

She laughed. And pointed to the side of the bed where he was standing. He obeyed and flopped down. "Besides," she added, "the bed's bigger than some New York apartments. And don't worry about what happened in the car, I know how . . ." She realized that she was suddenly talking to someone in a coma. He was out like a light, fully clothed. She wondered if she should at least take his shirt off for him, but decided that removing his shoes was intimate enough.

She changed to sweats and a tee, closed the window drapes as tightly as she could to block the morning sun, then slipped under the covers without disturbing him. She lay there for the longest time, feeling numb and scared but safe and determined at the same time. Drew twitched, his right leg kicked out, then he curled up without knowing that one hand was resting on her stomach. She wrapped her fingers around his. And suddenly the strangest feeling enveloped her. She felt powerfully drawn to him.

She had felt it that day she stood facing him at the pool, but she could not admit it to herself. Even though she loathed Tyler, she was married to him, and she took those vows seriously. And the guilt that came with acknowledging a powerful attraction to another man was made even worse because he was her husband's younger brother. She could not bring herself to even admit that she had liked the kiss he'd given her.

She turned her head to see the rise and fall of his breathing. Her hand held his gently, and she rubbed her fingers against his skin ever so slowly. She imagined his hands felt rough because of the work he'd had to do in prison, certainly not from tapping out computer code. Would he be able to change things? Could he stop Tyler? She brought his hand up to her lips and kissed it gently, then rested both their hands between them, still holding on.

But no matter how she tried, she could not sleep. She finally got up and stood at the window, behind the drapes. Occasionally, cars would pass on the highway. With each one, she worried more and more. What if one of them turned out to be a big black Suburban? What if it turned into the Comfort Inn parking lot? Were Dahbura or even Tyler close behind? Would they find them? How long could they run?

And where were they running to?

Chapter Seventeen

Drew woke before Quinn, who finally dozed off, as the sun was coming up. He'd slept only six hours, but it had been the deepest sleep of his life. He didn't remember getting into bed, but there he was, curled up next to her. Waking to the warmth of another body, a woman's hair gently touching his chin, her hand resting only inches from his thigh, was unnerving. He held his breath as he realized it was best that she was sleeping or he'd never be able to get from the bed to the bathroom without revealing a morning woody. That she was so beautiful made his retreat all the more frustrating.

As he showered, he couldn't get her out of his mind. He hardly knew her, had hated her because she was his brother's wife, and now they were running from danger together, thrown into a situation that had brought them to the same bed in a remote hotel. He dried his body with one of the too-small towels and looked in the mirror. He looked okay; not too scrambled. He'd been three years without a woman. Three years without even seeing a woman other than the warden. And now he had slept next to one of the most attractive women he'd ever known. It was enough to make a guy crazy.

As he shaved, he heard the TV go on. He walked in, his bottom half wrapped in a towel, and asked, "Anything about us?"

She shook her head. "Good morning."

"Hungry?"

She nodded. "There's a free breakfast downstairs."

He stuck his finger in his mouth as if he were going to gag. "It'll be like that exquisite prison cuisine I remember. I need real food."

"I like your style," she said, and then went to use the bathroom as he donned jeans and a sweatshirt that they had bought for him in Flagstaff.

In a busy diner nearby, Drew said, "I should feel free. But I don't. I have this sensation of wanting to hide."

"We are hiding," she reminded him.

"I mean I want to disappear. I've felt it before. It's like I'm sinking, going on remote. You'll have to pull me back if I go too far."

"I'll be your anchor," she promised, "if you'll be mine." She laughed. "God knows you have the muscles for it."

"All the muscles in the world don't make you feel any more powerful," he said gloomily, and she didn't know how to answer.

A waitress came over and saved them.

They stuffed themselves with steak and eggs, hash brown potatoes, and coffee. Then he ordered a piece of blueberry pie. "Sorry for coming apart like that yesterday."

"Sorry? Come on. Everyone needs a good cry now and then."

He looked embarrassed. "I don't really even know you."

She reached across the table and touched his hand. "It made me feel closer to you, that you trusted me enough to just let it out." She realized that had made her feel closer to him than all the time with Tyler. "You have the qualities that Tyler said he has but doesn't. He wants to be perceived as sensitive, caring, genuine. But he's none of those things."

"He was. He used to be." Drew looked wistful. The waitress set down a big slice of pie and refreshed their coffee. "Maybe he still wants to be but doesn't know how."

She blinked. "You're defending him?"

"He's still my brother," Drew said flatly.

She needed to know something. "Drew, something happened to Tyler when he was a boy. Do you know about it?"

He looked edgy, suddenly nervous. The waitress was setting down the check on their table when Quinn broached the subject, so as a distraction Drew grabbed it and automatically reached into his pocket. "What am I doing? I don't have any money. I haven't even seen a wallet in three years."

She pulled the check from his fingers, opened her purse, and handed him a couple of twenties. "Just to make you feel real again."

"Thanks." He handled the money as if he'd never seen paper bills before. "This is so strange."

Quinn stood up. He did the same, then sharply grabbed her arm. "Out there," he hissed, his voice brittle.

Out the window, a big black SUV was backing into a space, several cars down from theirs. "Is it them?"

"Dunno." He was frozen. Trying to think. "There's got to be a way out through the kitchen."

"I'm good at that," she couldn't help but say.

"Pay the bill," he said, suddenly taking control, almost whispering. "Keep your back to the guy— he's getting out of the car now—and just leave. He'll be looking for me, or for the two of us, or . . . hell, I don't know. Go to the car and pick me up in back." He dashed into the kitchen, almost knocking a tray of scrambled eggs out of a waitress' arms.

Quinn paid the check just as the man entered the diner. The hostess and cashier were one in the same, so Quinn fiddled with the small jar of toothpicks to delay. "Just sit anywhere you like, my friend," the woman chirped, "and Lois'll bring you coffee." Quinn kept her back to the big man, who, she could ascertain, was looking at every customer in the place. She quietly slipped out the front doors.

She started the car, her heart in her throat, and pulled out of the space. She was about to round the corner of the diner when someone smacked his fist against the passenger door. Startled, she jerked on the brake—and Drew jumped in. "Drive," he ordered.

She hit the gas and they spun away. "He didn't see me. I don't think he had a clue."

Suddenly, a gunshot rang out. It ricocheted with a whine off the back of the car. "He had a clue!" she shouted, and jammed her foot down on the accelerator, flooring it.

"Not so fast," Drew cautioned as they careened onto the road.

"He'll follow us!"

"Not with two flat tires," Drew said mischievously.

"Tyler," Veronica Ashton said, interrupting him in his office.

"Damn it, Ronnie, I'm working." He was staring at computer code for the new version of the game. "You know the deadline."

"Sorry," she said, "but I knew you'd want to take this. It's David."

His eyes snapped from the screen to her face as one hand reached out for the phone. "I'm here." He kept his eyes on Veronica as he listened patiently, but his face turned red with rage. "Escaped?" he gasped. "How?"

Veronica sat in another chair. "Drew?" she surmised.

Tyler nodded to her. "Where did he go? He didn't just disappear!" He listened some more and then growled. "I don't care about your goddamned arm." Then he looked shocked. "Quinn?"

Veronica looked startled. "She's with Drew?"

Tyler nodded. "They got away? *Got away?*"

His assistant wheeled the chair she was sitting in

over to his, taking his free hand, trying to soothe him, but he yanked it away, springing to his feet. "You listen to me, you son of a bitch. Find them. I don't care what it takes. Stop my wife and my brother." He ran his fingers nervously through his hair, pounded his fist on top of the HP printer Quinn had tried to use. "They're the only threat we have, David. Get somebody less inept to help you. And do it fast. We have little time left." Then he turned off the phone and in blind fury hurled it against the wall.

"I don't believe it," Veronica said, getting up to retrieve the handset from the floor. "They're together?"

"He says he's tracking them. I don't want them tracked. I want them stopped."

"I want to know something. How did David get Drew out of Dave Gallup to begin with? I mean, what did he tell the Bureau the reason was?"

"David's position in computer fraud covers a lot. He said since Drew was the best hacker he knew, he wanted to use him to break into suspected terrorist Web sites."

"And he was going to say Drew was shot trying to escape?"

Tyler nodded and sat back down in front of his computer. "There's something about Dahbura that has always worried me. The arrogance, maybe. He's self-assured, but sometimes he thinks he's . . . he's . . ." He struggled for the right word.

Veronica offered one. "God?"

Tyler smiled.

"There is one attribute he has, however," Veronica reminded him, getting up to leave, "that we can't forget."

"What's that?"

"He believes in the cause."

They ditched the rental car as soon as they got to Durango, renting a model completely different from the one they'd had. But they felt no safer in Colorado than they had in Utah or Arizona. They stopped at a Sprint store, where Quinn paid cash for new cell phone service. A number no one would know unless she gave it to them. They debated about stopping for the night. "Dunno," Drew voiced. "I could go a few more hours if I had something to eat."

"How about that?" Quinn said, pointing to a Pizza Hut. "As long as you agree to anchovies."

"That's a bet."

Inside, wolfing down a large pie with extra anchovies, Drew seemed to squirm, and she asked what was up. "I hate these jeans," he snarled. They were part of the new outfit they'd bought him in the Flagstaff Wal-Mart. "They're too tight."

She wanted to tell him they looked pretty sexy, but she thought it not appropriate. On his body, she figured, almost anything would look sexy. "You're so different from Tyler."

"I think we were once very much alike."

It was the opening she needed. "And something changed him?"

He nodded reluctantly. But he wouldn't let her ask another question. He said, "You know, you were telling me about your visit to the DiForios earlier.

Brandon was *my* pal. He is five years older than I am, five years younger than Tyler. We hung out together. He had this kind of hero worship for Ty that I guess he still has today. And Ty sensed that he had a little slave in Brandon, which I think made him feel important. Maybe Brandon resented me for being Ty's brother because that's what he wanted to be."

"Why?"

Drew wiped his fingers with a napkin. "He had a sister, a really happy family, but talk about tragedy. His dad died in a freak accident at work one afternoon when a pipe fell from the ceiling and killed him. The same year, his mother was told that she had inoperable cancer. She suffered miserably and died a year later. He kept saying, 'How could God let this happen?'"

Quinn understood. "Which put him in Tyler's camp about believing God is the root of all evil."

Drew nodded. "I don't know whatever happened to Sally, his sister. She went to live with one set of grandparents—in Scranton, I think it was—while Brandon stayed with the DiForio relatives who lived near us. Tyler and Brandon became real tight after that. I'd say he was the only real friend Ty ever had."

"I know what happened to Sally."

Drew looked astonished. "You do? How? What?"

"She's dead now too. She was on the plane that crashed into the Pentagon on September Eleventh."

Drew could not believe it. "Sally DiForio died that day? No one ever told me." He sat in silence for a moment as the pieces fit together in his brain.

"Which put Brandon over the edge, right? It was the nail in the coffin for whatever reluctance he might have to go along with Tyler's plan."

She nodded. "At least, that's what I assume." She finished her drink. "It's amazing how one wounded person will attract others just like him."

"Yeah," he said, "but how does a person get others to agree with such a sick idea? It's like a cult. Unless you're first brainwashed by a game."

She disagreed. "Veronica Ashton, Ty's assistant, is in love with him. God knows why Brandon's wife seems to share his demented view on religion—she might be sicker than he is. Dahbura probably sees some kind of power for himself in it. Look at the people who followed Jim Jones. Or Hitler, for that matter."

"They didn't stop Jim or Adolf until it was too late."

She agreed. "But we won't let that happen here." She got up and he followed. She paid the bill, let Drew hold the door open for her, and stepped out into the crisp mountain air.

A pickup truck was delivering a bound chunk of evening papers as they were getting into the car. "Get one," she said, handing him a dollar. Drew jumped out, hurried back into the diner, and bought the top copy just as the waitress unfastened the binding.

What he saw startled him. He hurried out, back to the car, got in, and said, "Get the hell out of here! Now!"

"What happened?"

"Drive, Quinn!"

She raced onto the highway. About half a mile down the road, as he sat there reading the newspaper intently, she cried, "What was that all about? What's in the paper?"

He held it up. His photograph was prominent on the front page. The headline next to it read: PRISON ESCAPE MYSTIFIES AUTHORITIES. The article began, *Drew Concardi, an inmate at Arizona's Dave Gallup Correctional Institute, is missing, and authorities are baffled at how he might have escaped . . .*

The manhunt was on.

Chapter Eighteen

In another crappy motel, Quinn emerged from her shower to see Drew sitting on the floor in his boxers, looking almost like a contortionist. "What are you doing?"

"Foot massage. I learned it from a book. Oil helps, but Dahbura didn't give me time to pack my toiletries when he was dragging me to 'freedom.' Here, let me show you."

She did, but first she found a bottle of body oil in her bag. He rubbed the scented liquid in his hands, then took hold of her foot, starting at the ankle, working his way down, wiggling his fingers to stimulate but rubbing with the palms of his hands to caress at the same time. She gave a moan of pure pleasure and let herself lie back on the floor. She hadn't had a massage in a very long time. This was good.

When he finished and she sat up, she could only say, "You promise to do that every night and I'll buy you all the jeans you like. Or cargo pants—they're looser."

"You might have a deal, lady." And he smiled.

Later, in the twin beds, she turned to him before clicking off the light. "You said you and Tyler were once very much alike."

"Yes."

"What changed him so?"

There was no answer. She sat up. This time they had to talk about it. "It was Father John, wasn't it?"

He looked shocked. He sat up, pulling his knees to his chest. It took him a while to answer. "You know about that?"

"I saw Betty."

"*Mom* knows?"

Quinn shook her head. "No. Or if she does, she doesn't want to know. I went to Kenosha and talked to a priest who is now the pastor at Saint Anthony's. I learned that John Nosko is in prison, and I learned why."

Drew winced.

Quinn said, "I can't imagine what it's like to be numbed into feeling there is no God. What it must feel like to lose your faith completely, where everyone around you still believes but you can't . . . can't find that place in your soul any longer where the spirit exists."

He couldn't look at her. "Yes."

She had to ask it. "Did it happen to you too?"

Drew bit his lip, as if it was too disturbing to recall. Finally, he said, "I came close. He wanted me to join them."

"Who did?"

He almost spat the name. "Father John." He suddenly jumped up, awash in painful memories. "I didn't know what was going on, but I saw that Tyler was changing. He didn't want to play ball, he didn't want to work on the tree house—all the things we loved. He withdrew, wanted to be alone all the time. I had been more the loner type, so it was odd. He'd been so—what's the word?—gregarious."

"This is when the priest stepped into your father's shoes?"

He stood at the window, rubbing his fingers over the shut blinds. "Yes. Dad left, couldn't take my mom anymore. Father John was kinda like our dad when Tyler was in high school." He seemed to want to stop himself.

"Yes?" she urged.

"I found them together. I was about six at the time."

"What happened?"

"John would show up. We called him Father J. Mom adored him. He'd even bowled with my dad before he split. Catholic, Italian, Slovak—we were like one big family."

"Were you and Tyler close then?"

"Tyler was my hero, you know? Like he was Brandon's. But I never connected his moods to Father John."

"How did you find out?"

Drew pried the blinds open with his fingers and looked out the window. He couldn't face her and answer. "I walked in on it."

"Where?"

"Our tree house. It was out back, in a big tree behind the garage. You couldn't see it from the house. Father J had helped us finish it." He almost laughed in an ironic way. "I guess now I know why."

"That's where he molested Tyler?"

Drew nodded. "This one time, I came home from school with my report card with an A in some class. I wanted to tell Ty. Mom said he was out in the fort. That's what we called it. I'm sure she didn't know that Father J was there too. I wanted to surprise Ty, so I snuck up. When I put my head up through the hatch, I saw them."

"They were having sex?"

He seemed to groan. "John was lying back on the mattress we'd dragged up there, telling Tyler how good it felt, what he was doing to him."

"My God."

"I didn't really understand it. I mean, I was only six years old. I'd never seen sex before." He qualified his statement. "But I knew this was wrong, a grown-up and a kid."

"What did you do?"

"I froze. John saw me. Tyler didn't. He had his back to me. Instead of trying to hide what they were doing, the priest smirked. I'll never forget it. I think my watching turned him on even more. He kinda winked and curled his finger over Ty's shoulder, beckoning for me to come in, to come closer."

"Tyler didn't see that either?"

"No. The priest kept Ty's head cupped in his hand."

"What happened?"

"I just stood there. John kept telling Tyler he was doing good, being a good boy, stuff like that. But he was looking right into my eyes. I don't know what I was thinking. I was scared, I was shocked, maybe a little titillated too, which made me feel very guilty.

When he figured I wasn't going to move, he cried out and pulled Ty's hair and thrashed up and down, all the time keeping his eyes glued to mine." He looked Quinn in the eye. "It was pretty sick stuff."

"What did you do?"

"I kept the secret. Probably tried to tell myself it was just a game, or maybe I hadn't seen it at all. Denial, I guess. Like Mom."

"So Tyler never knew that you knew?"

"He found out another time. I was weeding the garden and I heard an argument in the fort. Tyler was saying he was going away to college, and Father John was mad. He wanted him to stay in Wisconsin. He kept saying he couldn't leave him, they had been together all those years, stuff like that. Like it was a love affair. Then it got loud, a real fight. I could hear Ty sobbing, saying he didn't want to keep their secret anymore, that he didn't want to do this any longer, he didn't like it, it wasn't right. I heard Tyler cry out, then his voice got muffled. I knew John was hurting him. I was so upset that I ran to the garage to get a shovel. I was going to go up there and smash it over the priest's head, but Mom came out and I covered for them, led her away from the tree."

Drew took a breath. "That night, when I went into the bathroom that we shared upstairs, I saw Tyler's shorts on the floor. There was a lot of blood on them. In his room, Tyler was crying in bed. He lied about why, so I told him that I knew, told him what I'd seen. He broke down, said it had gone on for years, ever since he could remember. He said Father John had often urged him to 'get your brother to come play with us,' but he had resisted. He had protected me.

He said he felt like a fraud when he served Mass—we were both altar boys—and hated the Church, hated priests, hated religion. He developed a coldness from that day that hasn't left."

"Which he disguises well." She wondered something else. "You think that was a turning point in his relationship with you?"

Drew thought about it. "I think maybe he felt guilty about my knowing. Maybe it changed how he thought about me. Maybe it got all twisted in his head and he wanted to punish me for knowing, for reminding him every time he looked at me of what had happened to him."

"He couldn't live with the shame," Quinn said.

Drew returned to his bed and sat down, facing away from her. "I don't think it ever happened again after that night we talked. Mom kept wondering why he was mad at Father J. When Ty went off to college in California, he seemed to want nothing to do with his past. That's why, I thought, he seldom talked about having a brother, even as he was becoming famous. I became kind of a rebel, lurking in the shadows of him starting Zzzyx."

"The thing that gets me," Quinn said, "is when you hear the abuse victims on television or read about them, they all say they long for the faith that was robbed from them. They can no longer believe in God, no longer worship no matter how hard they try. Their anger is as deep as their damage."

"Talking about it gives me the creeps." Drew put his feet under the covers, and closed his eyes. "But you know something? Ty isn't entirely wrong."

"About what?" she asked.

"About the fact that God has been an excuse for murder since the beginning of time. Let's get some sleep."

"Yes," Quinn said in the darkness. "We have to decide in the morning where we are going to go. I have friends near Colorado Springs. Tyler doesn't know them. Maybe there you could start working on the program to stop him."

"I need equipment. Not just one laptop. Real hardware."

"Matt and Becky may have it."

"Good night." His voice was gentle, almost warm. Not as edgy and angry as he often sounded.

"Drew," she said softly, "I'm very glad you weren't hurt as a child. I'm very thankful for that."

"Get some rest," he whispered, and that was the last word.

When the morning sun hit the blinds, Quinn felt her face burning. A beam of reflected sunlight was shining into her eyes like a laser. She got up to see if she could adjust the blinds. It was only seven, and she had no intention of rising this early. Drew was dead to the world, curled into a tight ball on his right side.

She rubbed her eyes and yanked the cord, which brought the entire set of metal blinds, cornice and all, crashing down. The screws holding it to the plaster above the window pulled away. Drew was startled awake, reaching under the bed where he'd put the gun the night before. "It's okay," Quinn assured him. "Go back to sleep. It's only me."

"Huh?" He realized what had happened and

started laughing. "Some wake-up call they give you in this joint."

"Better than no hot water, like in the first room." The desk clerk moved them after they discovered they'd have to shower in ice water. She looked at the pile of twisted metal at her feet. "What can we put over the window to keep the sun out?"

He shrugged. "Maybe it's God telling us it's time we split this joint." He put down the gun, stood up, and stretched, then started toward the bathroom.

But Quinn stopped him. "Drew, look. Down there."

He took a few steps toward the window and peered out with his hand shielding the eastern sun. The black Suburban was parked across two parking spaces, and two men were just emerging from the motel office, followed by a girl they did not recognize, who held a ring of keys in her hand. "It's him," Quinn said, sure that one of them was the same man who had shot at them when they fled the Arizona diner, the same guy who had accompanied Dahbura in securing his release from Dave Gallup.

Drew sucked in his breath. "I think the other one is the pisser."

"Time," Quinn said softly, "to hit the road."

"Get your stuff—fast!" Drew ordered as he grabbed his shirt from the nearby chair and slid on his jeans. Then he picked up the gun again. But when he looked out the window, he was startled. "They're not coming up here—they're going toward . . . oh my God, she doesn't know they moved us."

"They think we're still in 104?" Quinn slipped on clothes, tossed all their bathroom stuff into her suitcase, pushed everything else she could think of into it, zipped it.

Drew strained to see what was happening. "I think so. Come on," he said, unlocking the door. "The stairs on the right lead down to the car. We might be able to make it." He picked up the car keys from the desk, slid into his untied sneakers, and followed her out. She was already pulling the suitcase down the stairs.

When they hit the ground floor, they heard the girl shout, "What are you doing?" And then a loud crash—the door being knocked in—and then muffled cries. "Come on," Drew said. "We got maybe half a minute before they figure it out . . ."

They were in the car and rolling in less time than the men could have learned what room they were really in. Quinn and Drew didn't say a word for three miles. When he finally pulled over just to relieve the tension, they both threw their heads back and gasped for breath. Then Drew smashed his fists against the steering wheel, shouting, "How the hell did they find us?"

She could think of only one thing. "My Palm. I sent Susan a message. I'll bet somehow he's tracing electronic stuff."

"How? GPS?"

She looked at him as if he were stupid. "It's Tyler, remember?"

"Did you ditch it?"

She nodded. "Left it there."

"Thank God we changed cell phones."

She agreed. Then he turned to her. And started to laugh.

"What?" she asked.

"Where's your blouse?"

She looked down and realized she was sitting there in her pants and bra, nothing else. She had completely forgotten. She laughed right along with him.

"Stop," he begged as the laughter didn't stop, as it fed upon itself, "because I had to pee when I got up and I swear I'm going to wet my new jeans."

"No!" she squealed.

He looked around for a tree, a billboard, but there was nothing.

"Do it against the car. I've got to put a top on. I won't look."

He jumped out and did.

She pulled a shirt from her suitcase in the backseat and kept her promise; she didn't look.

When he got back in, he was sober again. No more laughter. "They're after us. They're tailing us. But we can't run forever."

She thought about it. "When we get to Becky and Matt's, we can hide. We'll be safe there, and we can use their computers."

He nodded. "We need someplace to think this through, to make a plan."

"Someplace," she added, "that's safe."

He started the car and drove like he was possessed.

They pulled into Colorado Springs at sundown. In the shadow of Pike's Peak, they drove through the Garden of the Gods. "Joanie and I were here about six years ago," she explained, "when Becky's second child was just born. Isn't it enchanting?"

Drew looked at the incredible rock formations with wonder. "I thought Sedona was something, what I saw of it, but this is way cool."

"The color is amazing."

"Is it always this red and pink and orange? Or is it the setting sun?"

"I think God took his Crayola box and just colored it this way." That gave her a thought. "Drew, would you mind if we stopped at a church?"

"A church?"

She nodded. "I haven't been since . . . well, since that day in your childhood parish."

The church took some finding, but Quinn remembered roughly where it was. Manitou Springs was the next town up the hill, and the parish was Our Lady of Perpetual Help. It was getting dark when Quinn entered the church—Drew had decided to wait by the car—so she lit a candle and held it in her hand as she knelt in the last pew. "Dear Lord, I'm sorry I've missed a few Sunday masses, but as you know, I've been busy. Please, God, guide us and give us courage. Please watch over Joanie, and Susan and James, and everyone I love. Amen." She got up, set the candle in one of the holders on a metal rack in front of a statue of Mary, and hurried out into the dusk. Drew started the car.

"I hope I wrote the directions down correctly," she said, pulling them out of her pocket. She'd talked to Becky's mother from a pay phone the previous day. It turned out Becky and Matt and the kids had left for their place in the Yucatán, would be back in a week. Her mother assured Quinn that she and her friend were welcome, but that she had to promise to stay till they got back. Quinn said she'd try.

"Okay," she now told Drew, "we stay on Twenty-Four and go through Woodland Hills. Good restaurant here, Becky's mom said, called Zaks." She looked at the signs. "Becky's in Divide, which I think is right on the Continental Divide. The view they have is the Collegiate mountain range and . . ."

"How about telling me where to turn rather than sounding like the tourist bureau?"

"Next road, left."

After a winding road up a steep mountain with a fair amount of snow still on the ground, and taking three wrong forks in the road, they reached the house. "Matt built it himself," Quinn told Drew as she reached above the door frame for the key.

Inside, a light was on in the living room and one above the stove. Plants were green and shiny, the place seemed comfortable, with kids' clothes and books and toys all over the place. But it was cold. Quinn turned on the gas under the teakettle while Drew built a fire in the woodstove. Then he headed straight for the computer table in the family room.

It was an amazing moment when he pressed his fingers to the keys for the first time since he'd been arrested. He shuddered, both with excitement and with trepidation. Touching a keyboard again was like getting his soul restored. He felt a surge of energy that made him feel whole for the first time in years.

"What are you going to do?" she asked as the kettle started to whistle.

He had just slipped a copy of Practice Run they'd

bought at a Target into the CD-ROM drive. "I have to start somewhere."

"On that?" She saw it was a fairly new Dell machine, but she worried that he would require state-of-the-art equipment.

He stared at the screen as if possessed. "It's okay. Got an Intel Celeron processor. It'll run the game."

The screen opened with the usual music and flashes of color . . . LET THIS BE YOUR PRACTICE RUN . . . LET THE GAMES BEGIN . . . Then something changed. The screen turned to black and white and was covered with computer code, which only Drew could understand.

She made a pot of Earl Grey and used the other computer to check E-mail, reading only what was vital. Nothing from Joanie. Good. But there was a letter from Tyler. She opened it. YOU CAN RUN BUT YOU CAN'T HIDE! "Drew, look at this."

He was so engrossed in what he was doing that he didn't hear her. Well, so what if he didn't read it? She erased the letter and powered down the laptop. She poured herself more tea as well as a cup for Drew. She gave him a few more minutes, then she touched his shoulder gently.

"Huh?"

"Tea?"

"Oh," he said, as if coming back to reality, but then he slipped back, lost in another world.

Quinn's biggest concern since Sedona had been the strain on Drew. She saw moments when he would zone out, when he would walk off alone at a rest stop and stay in that state. At times he could barely eat, and sometimes he would not talk. But each time, remembering that their survival depended on staying one step ahead, he snapped out of it. Sometimes he seemed completely remote, so distant that she feared he wouldn't even remember her name. Other times he was vibrant, raw, sexy, and compelling. She found him to be one of the most fascinating people she had ever been with.

But he was a wanted man. Every TV and radio station was still running the story. Aggie Spivak had refuted the "prison break" notion in a public statement, which Quinn and Drew heard on NPR in the car. Later the same day, David Dahbura of the Federal Bureau of Investigation called her statement "nonsense."

When Drew finally pulled himself away from the computer, he told her that he was sure that the best bet for stopping Tyler would be not to try to destroy the games out there—an impossible task, since there were millions of copies—but rather to create a new one that changed everything without anyone ever knowing.

"You mean never tell anyone?"

"The panic it might cause could be avoided if we did it quietly."

"But how to get it into all the computers?" she asked. "How do you get a virus to eat up every copy of the game that's out there and replace it with a new game?"

"You're not listening. Not a virus. Not a destroyer. What we need to do is a new patch."

She blinked. "An upgrade? To the game itself?"

He nodded confidently. "There is no way to deprogram these kids by choice or by force. The only way to do it is to make them think they're still play-ing it."

She got it. "Stop the programming the same way they were programmed."

"The new one is coming on Easter Sunday." They'd seen billboards advertising it on the road. "That isn't far off."

She told him, "There are already over fifty million preorders. Easter Sunday. Ironic, huh?"

He nodded. "If we could find a way to replace his program with ours and put it into those boxes, we could end this thing quietly, and forever." He got up from the computer table and joined her on the sofa. "But we can't do it from here."

"Why?"

"I think it's unsafe staying in one place too long. They'll go through your Palm Pilot, find the ad-dresses of everyone you know. And this equipment isn't going to cut it for me."

"What do you need?"

He thought about it. "Tyler's Rockville office would probably do." He laughed, but then bright-ened with a new thought. "Hey, that gives me an idea."

"I'm listening."

"You told me about the DiForio house. About the room Brandon said was his Internet radio studio."

"Right. A real lab."

"I'll bet you that's where the game was perfected. And where the upgrade that's on its way to the world was created. It's the kind of workplace I need."

She blinked with surprise. "You're saying we should go there?"

He nodded. "Kansas City."

"It's too dangerous."

"This isn't?"

She argued. "Mike Furnari was murdered when he went nosing around the DiForio house!"

"Hey, they found us twice. They're bound to find us here too. Kansas City is the only place I can think of where we might gain an advantage. The DiForio place was ground zero for the plan. It's contrarian thinking. Enter the lair of the wolf, where they'd never think you'd go."

She swallowed hard. "I guess you're right. We have to stop running and start working to stop him. Still, we can't just knock on the door and tell Brandon and Candy we want to borrow their computer room."

"The heat's on," he snapped. "I can't believe they'll still be there."

"You think the equipment is?"

He shrugged. "It's worth a chance. We can't do anything here. And we have a race against time."

She nodded. "Other kids have been programmed to kill. And all hell breaks loose on Easter."

"We can't let it be Tyler's resurrection too," he reminded her.

She tried to make a joke of it. "Kansas City, here we come."

But neither one of them could really laugh.

Chapter Nineteen

The Flamingo—Inn Amongst the Flowers was Fort Lauderdale's premier gay boutique hotel. The owners, one of whom had been a director at the deluxe Ritz-Carlton Hotel in Paris, created a haven of style, taste, and service within walking distance of restaurants, shopping, and the beach. Focusing on restful surroundings, with furniture in the airy British West Indies style, the inn was elegant, user friendly, but never pompous. But the beautiful property had another attraction: discretion. Here a guest could be as private and confidential as he wished.

Two men had made a reservation in the name of R. Thomas. They had overnighted cash to guarantee the room. This was unusual but not unheard-of. When Mr. Thomas and his partner arrived, Bernardo, one of the owners, was at the desk. He welcomed them warmly, assured them he'd saved them the Grand English Suite, with a spacious bedroom complete with four-poster bed, and a separate, beautifully furnished sitting room, as they had requested. When asking for the partner's name for the hotel's records and in case there were phone calls, Bernardo was told that the partner did not wish to have his name recorded at all. Indeed, Bernardo hardly got a look at the man, who preferred to wait outside under one of the yellow umbrellas beside the pool. His face quickly turned toward the fountain when he saw Bernardo looking, so he only got a glimpse of what he looked like.

Mr. Thomas asked, "How about an Internet connection?"

"Wireless throughout," Bernardo answered, "but if your laptop isn't equipped—"

"It is," Thomas assured him.

Bernardo gave Mr. Thomas his keys and watched as the two men ascended the stairs across the courtyard. Then he went into the lobby's adjacent sitting room, warmed by yellow walls and a blend of antiques and white stuffed sofas and chairs. Sitting in one of those chairs was Alan, the other owner. "The mystery guests who FedExed the cash arrived."

"Ah," Alan said, slightly curious. "What are they like?"

Bernardo shrugged. "I only met Thomas. He wouldn't give the other man's name. They're both about forty. Thomas is very handsome, maybe Middle Eastern. I thought maybe he's Spanish, like me, but I was afraid it would be too personal a question."

"You didn't see the other gentleman at all?" Alan inquired.

"Well, I caught a glimpse of him." Bernardo looked puzzled.

"And?"

"He looks familiar. I think it's someone famous who doesn't want to be recognized."

Alan finished his tea. "Fine. Then he won't be."

Bernardo looked out to the pool area. "Maybe a movie star," he said to himself.

Upstairs, in the Grand English suite, David Dahbura, who had just registered as R. Thomas, opened his laptop. "Nice joint."

Behind him, hanging clothes in the closet, the other man seethed. "Why a gay place? You didn't tell me that."

"You're the one who demanded we go to Lauderdale. You want to play Nero watching his gladiators die? You go where I choose."

"But why would you pick this place?"

"Hello! Look around you—it's gorgeous."

"David, come on, you're pissing me off."

"What could be more discreet? The last thing you want, with your wife running around loose out there, is for someone to see you in a place that connects to one of the assassinations. This would be the last place anyone would look."

Tyler shook his head and tossed his underwear into a drawer. "I suppose you're right," he said. But it was clear he wasn't happy about it at all.

"And I promise not to ask you to kiss me in public," David joked.

Tyler slammed the drawer shut. He changed the subject. "What's with that warden out in Arizona shooting off her fat mouth? What's going to happen?"

David looked unconcerned. "Nothing. The Bureau only approved me pulling Drew out of there because I needed him on a top-secret assignment on terror.

Meaning homeland security. Meaning they think he's joined the other side." He laughed. "Considering his past, who would argue?"

"So the prison-break story is the official one, no matter what that woman says?"

David smiled. "It sure helps the Bureau. Hell, every police department in the country is looking for your brother."

Tyler nodded. "Let's hope some trigger-happy cop somewhere does what you couldn't."

Far out on the Dingle Peninsula, in the west of Ireland, a rental car made its way down the left side of the dirt-and-gravel road, stopping for cows and sheep that were using the pathway to graze. "Are we there yet?" James asked his mother.

Susan barely responded. Something was happening to her that she hadn't counted on. Grief was overwhelming her. The beautiful stone cottage they were approaching had been a special haven for her and Patrick. They had discovered it on their honeymoon and had returned every year of their marriage. Memories infused everything Susan was now seeing—the fields where they had picnics, the rocks near the water where they used to sit at sunset and drink beer, the farmhouse down the road where Tom and Jane Garvey, the owners of the working farm containing the cottage, threw a wonderful potluck supper and dance for one of their anniversaries, the ancient tree under which they'd laughed themselves silly while waiting out a torrential downpour. It was all she could do to keep her composure in front of her son. *Patrick is here,* she felt. *He's here, he's with us, he will al-*

ways be. There was comfort in the thought. She parked and turned off the engine.

James opened the trunk and grabbed their bags, but tripped on a stone and almost went flying. One of the suitcases whacked Susan in the knee, and she jumped around on one foot as she saw stars. And then they burst into laughter. "That's an ancient ogam stone you tripped on, I'll have you know," she told her son.

"A who?"

"Ogam. Their alphabet predates the Gaelic alphabet in history. It's from the Celtic period before the Romans, Normans, and Saxons invaded."

"Think the Roman invaders tripped over them too?"

Susan put her injured leg back on the ground. "Hope so."

The cottage was situated on a majestic headland with fields rising behind it, while the grassland below sloped down to the bay. Fog rapidly moved in off the water, putting on a magnificent and mysterious show. The sun hid, then peeked out, turning full force only to be shrouded in swirling mist moments later. Most days it rained. The Irish called the showers "a fine soft day," and Susan had come to find comfort in the cleansing rains, which never lasted long. She hoped this trip would be a cleansing experience for all involved.

"What are we gonna do, Mom?" James asked after he'd moved his clothes from his suitcase to the chest in his little upstairs bedroom.

"Later we're going to the Garveys' for dinner. Before that, we're going to go down and sit on a blanket with some tea and watch the sun set into the ocean."

"Can I play on the computer first?"

She shrugged. Against her better judgment, she said yes. But she would monitor him. She could not trust that he would obey her ban on Practice Run. When James hightailed it into the room off the kitchen that had once been a pantry and the Horgans now used as an office, Susan put in a call to Stephanie Korodi's parents in Hamburg. Stephanie herself answered on the first ring. After explaining who it was, she got Joan Roberts on the phone. "Joanie, darling, how are you?"

"Oh, Auntie Susan, hi. What a surprise! But why are you calling?"

"Nothing to be alarmed about. Good news, actually. I'm in Ireland."

"Really?" Joanie sounded thrilled.

"And your mom is coming in a few days."

"She didn't tell me. In fact, I haven't heard from her forever."

"She's busy—more busy than she's ever been. She needs a rest, believe me."

"Well, she'll get one there, from what I've heard."

"Ever been to Ireland?" Susan asked, knowing quite well that she had not.

"No. But Stephanie and I just got back from Lyon. It was wonderful."

"Can you come up?"

"There?"

"Yes. Your mom is off on a whirlwind trip right now, and she'll be arriving next week sometime. If you could be here to surprise her, it would be great."

Joanie considered it. Susan heard her asking Stephanie if she wanted to visit Ireland. "It could be fun. I'd love to see my mom."

"She needs to see you too, honey." Susan tried not to sound alarmed as she asked the next question. "You haven't heard from Tyler, have you?"

"Nope."

"He might be trying to find your mother."

Joanie was puzzled. "What do you mean?"

"Baby, she couldn't tell him where she was going."

"Why?"

Susan had not really planned getting deeply into the subject. "Well, what she's doing is kind of a secret. A government thing."

Joanie groaned. "She told me. It's always like weird stuff with the Saudis and computers in Bombay. So what else is new?"

"This is a mission of real importance. Honey, if you speak to him, please don't let Tyler know that Quinn is coming here."

The odd request made Joanie very worried. "Susan, I think I should speak to my mom. I've tried her, but she never answers her cell."

"I'll have her call you, honey. I promise."

"This is all kinda strange."

"That's an understatement. Listen, you got a fax there? I'll send you directions, draw a map. Dingle is the most beautiful, restful spot on earth. You'll love it."

Reluctant to leave the subject of her mother, Joanie said, "Okay." Stephanie grabbed the phone, rattled off the fax number, then handed it back to Joanie. "Susan, Mom's not in any danger, is she?"

"Why would you think that?"

"You sound like you're covering up something."

"Jet lag, pure and simple."

"Have Mom call me. I'll feel better if I speak to her myself."

"Done. When can you come?"

"I'll check out things here, but pretty soon, I guess. We don't have many pressing engagements on the calendar."

"Come tomorrow. It's a beautiful place."

"Stephanie likes to paint."

"Then it's custom made for her," Susan urged.

"Cool."

"I'll fax in a little while. Let me know when you want me to pick you up at Shannon Airport, okay?"

When she hung up, Susan knew God would forgive her for the lies. Joan would get over the fact that Quinn wasn't going to show up. She would understand once she knew what was really going on. Getting Joan to come there, where Susan could protect her from Tyler's reach, was the only thing that was important now.

She went into the pantry to check on James. Thank God he was in a chat room. But when she sat down next to him to tell him that Joanie might be coming, he winced, and turned the laptop so the screen would be hard to read at her angle. "What don't you want me to see?" she asked immediately.

"Mom, come on. I'm just chatting."

She leaned over. Yes, he was only chatting, but it was a Practice Run chat room. She hit the power button. And ended that.

* * *

"That's the house," Quinn told Drew as she turned off the engine. They were in Lee's Summit, a suburb of Kansas City. She nodded to the end of the cul-de-sac, at the white brick DiForio house. All the windows were dark.

"Doesn't look like anyone's home."

"They could be in the room we want to get into."

"The radio studio?"

She nodded. "It's not dark enough yet. We should wait another hour at least. It's risky enough coming here, but let's not invite suspicion."

He slumped down in the passenger's seat. He'd done most of the driving, so he was grateful that she took over when they neared their destination. She had been here once before, she knew the area. He stretched out his long legs and crossed his arms. But his chance to relax didn't last long. Quinn saw lights go on in the DiForio living room. "Someone's there."

Drew whispered, "Yes." He slowly moved upright. The front drapes were open, but no one moved. In the half hour they waited there, they saw nothing inside. Drew finally said, "It's a timer."

"You think?"

"I'm sure. Click, the living room floor lamp turns on. Nothing else. No sign of life. It'll go off at two in the morning, mark my words."

"Think we should have a look?"

"I think it's as safe as it will ever be."

She pulled the key from the ignition and slid it into her pocket. "Okay, Sherlock, we're about to become sleuths."

From under the seat, Drew lifted the gun he'd

stolen from Dahbura and slid it into one of the pockets in his jacket.

Quinn winced. "Do you have to take that?"

"Yes." His response was firm.

She knew he was right. The people who owned the house would use one on them in a second. Taking a deep breath, she opened the door, stepped out, and started down the sidewalk, trying to look as nonchalant as possible. Drew was right at her side.

They walked past the house arm in arm, looking like a couple out for an evening stroll. The street was deserted but for a teenager who was dropped off by a Toyota Matrix. He soon disappeared into his house. Their hearts leaped together, however, when the garage door in the house they were passing suddenly began to rise. "Keep walking," Drew said. They did, keeping their faces toward one another as a car emerged from the garage and drove off down the street. They passed the DiForio house, straining their heads to get a closer look. "It's empty," Drew assured her.

"Let's go past one more time to be sure." They turned at the end of the cul-de-sac and started back. "There's a woman watching us," Quinn suddenly said.

"Where?" His eyes darted around.

"Next door."

Drew saw her. An older gal, in an apron, looking out her dining room window, a spatula in her hand. "Kiss me," he said.

"What?"

He turned to her, put his hands on her cheeks and pulled her face to his, pressing his lips to hers. She could feel her blood rushing. When he pulled his mouth away, she turned her face from his, embarrassed, afraid the attraction would show.

He felt the same way. It had stirred him, but he could not say so. He tried to cover. "Lovers out for a stroll," he told Quinn. "See?" He gestured toward the house. The woman had gone from the window.

"Probably in disgust."

"Probably in jealousy," he joked. "I can imagine what her husband looks like."

Quinn smiled. Not counting his kissing her the night she rescued him, it was the first time in months that she had been kissed by someone she could trust.

They craned their heads again to see into the DiForio windows, but there was no movement at all. "Okay, baby," Drew said, "time to head up the driveway. If someone sees us, they'll think we're Brandon and Candy."

"I'm not so worried about somebody seeing us. I'm worried about somebody *shooting* us."

"I've got my finger on the trigger in this jacket."

She shuddered. "Information I don't need to know."

The driveway led to the garage, which was separate from the house but connected by a breezeway, and beyond that was a large yard. Drew tried to look into one of the small windows in the roll-up garage door. "It's blacked out."

Quinn was trying to see inside the house, standing on her tiptoes. "Looks deserted."

Drew tried one of the breezeway windows. It slid up easily. He slithered in. Then opened the door for Quinn. "Be quiet," he warned.

"I thought we'd have to pick the door lock."

"Good luck," he responded with a grin. "I could rob a bank's computer of billions, but getting into a Kwikset dead bolt, I'm not so sure." He pulled out the gun. "Let's look around."

She followed him. Enough light was coming in from the living room lamp that they could make their way through the kitchen, which looked normal enough—clutter on the counter, oranges in a basket, dirty dishes in the sink. They went down the hall to the bedrooms, checked the bathrooms; empty. "If they're here, they're in the studio," Quinn said.

They made their way back to the breezeway. Then Quinn nodded toward the steel door. They both saw light coming from under it. "Careful," Quinn cautioned.

Drew firmly placed his left hand on the knob, lifting the gun in his right. But when he yanked it open, the room was as deserted as the rest of the house. In front of them lay a sea of papers, several computers, some still running, microphones, high-tech equipment, and filing cabinets. On the far wall, bathed in a spotlight, was the same advertisement they'd seen on the billboard in Colorado: TIME TO RUN FOR IT. PRACTICE RUN V. ARRIVING APRIL 19TH. It gave them a chill. There was a framed photograph of a smiling darkhaired woman in a United Airlines flight attendant uniform.

"They abandon the place?" Quinn asked.

Drew shook his head as he put the gun away. "They're probably coming back," he said, assessing that nothing looked missing. He was sure this was the lab where the original game and the upcoming upgrade had been created. He proceeded to look through piles of papers with computer code written on them, with hand-marked notes. There was an article on "Hacktivism" ripped from a newspaper. He saw a handbook for SafeWeb. "That's interesting."

"Why?" Quinn asked.

"SafeWeb makes networking hardware. They got some financing from the CIA. They provide free software called Triangle Boy that protects Internet users' identities by routing their browsing through SafeWeb's server."

"Huh?"

"It was popular in Saudi Arabia, the Emirates, and China, but was suspended for lack of money."

"What's the significance?"

"Tyler might have wanted to use it—or something like it—to push his message. Hey, look at this."

"What?" Her eyes widened.

Drew was holding the box for another video game. "Grand Theft Auto—Vice City. Man, I always wanted to play this!"

She rolled her eyes. She started to sift through some papers on a desk near the door. One page was mostly blank but had a name scrawled on it in pencil: Joseph Rangel. Along with the password: PR02. Under it was written: Dalai Lama. She handed it to Drew.

"Wow, we got our name. Front Runner Number Two."

The discovery made her shiver. "His target is the Dalai Lama." She dug to the bottom of pages in a filing cabinet. Again, none of them made sense. Some seemed to be copies of E-mails, some were personal letters to Brandon's children, and some were grocery lists. But there was one that grabbed her attention. She started reading it to herself, then gasped. "Drew, listen to this."

"Yeah?" He was at attention even though his eyes were focused on the screen.

"... and thus the day is coming when God will cease to be. This next Easter Sunday will mark the resurrection of young people everywhere, rising up with strength and power, to repudiate the notion of organized religion forever. Count down to that date. The beginning of chaos, but also of the new order."

Drew looked stunned. "Tyler wrote that?"

"I can't tell." Quinn showed him that the bottom of the printed page had been torn off.

"So the release date of the new game coincides with the day they battle in the streets, huh?" Drew's eyes widened. "Sure, that's it. The new game goes beyond what the others did. The new game starts the revolution." He tapped a few keys and said, "Wait, there's more. An E-mail from Tyler to Brandon, dated a few weeks ago. *You've got to hurry on the new version. To get seventy million copies printed and shipped so they're in the retail outlets at Easter, I need it in Rockville two weeks before. The plants here and in Mexico, Canada, and China are ready to press, the boxes are done, etc. Don't let me down.*"

"So it's finished already?" Quinn asked.

Drew scrolled down. "Here, read this." It was a response from Brandon. *I'm done. I'll keep a copy safe here, just in case. I'm bringing you the master tomorrow. I'll call when I know which flight. Candy is going to go see our daughter. I feel like I can rest for the first time in years.*

"What's the date on it?"

"The day before yesterday."

"That's where he must be," Quinn surmised.

She went back to the sheet with *Dalai Lama* written on it, and what they assumed was the name of the programmed assassin. "Joseph Rangel. He wasn't on the master list."

"It's obviously been updated. He was one of our two blanks."

She shook her head. "But we don't know how to find him."

Drew switched to a different file in the computer. And hit pay dirt. "Look at this!" She hurried over. "Two more names. The Archbishop of Canterbury. And the Reverend Anthony Johnson. Who's that?"

Quinn pulled another chair next to him, sat in it, and looked at the screen. "The head of the Southern Baptist Leadership Council."

"They're on the list. They're going to be killed."

Before she could say another word, she felt the metal rim of a gun pressing against the back of her head. She froze. Drew, his hands still on the keyboard, hadn't realized. He went on talking, rattling off something about Florida and passwords and wondering if they had enough time.

"Just take your hands from the keyboard like the nice boy you always were," a voice from the past ordered Drew.

Drew turned and at once realized what had happened. Brandon was standing over Quinn, having just arrived home, his finger on the trigger. Drew hadn't seen him in many years, but in a way it was just like they were kids again. "Don't hurt her, Brandon," Drew ordered cautiously. He had to get him talking, long enough to give him time to pull the gun from his pocket.

"The prodigal brother returns," Brandon sneered. "You little fuck." Then he laughed. "Here, of all places. That one we never figured. Wish Candy hadn't gone to see our daughter. She'd find this rich."

"It's not going to work," Drew warned him, pushing the wheeled chair back inch by inch as he bought time. "There are too many people on to you. You'll never accomplish it."

"You're too late," Brandon smugly assured him.

"It won't bring Sally back," Quinn said, glancing at the photograph of the flight attendant. "Or your parents."

Brandon pressed the gun against her head so hard that it almost drew blood. "Shut your mouth." He nodded at Drew. "Get up. Put your hands on your head."

Drew obeyed, standing up slowly. "We're going for a little walk," Brandon said, "the three of us. One Tyler will love hearing about later, when I return. Alone."

Quinn, knowing they had little time to live, decided it was her only chance. Brandon's eyes were now on Drew. With a hard kick, she slammed the chair—and herself—into Brandon, knocking him backward. Drew responded quickly, flinging Quinn to the floor. He reached into his pocket for the gun, but he wasn't fast enough.

"Stop right there!" Brandon had recovered, had the gun aimed right at him.

Drew obeyed, with his gun still caught inside his pocket.

"I'll tell your brother you said good-bye," Brandon said, taking aim at Drew's face.

"No!" Quinn screamed from the floor, trying to reach for the gun in Brandon's hand.

A shot rang out, and she screamed again. But Drew did not fall. Brandon did.

Drew had drawn the gun from his pocket by the time he realized it as well. Brandon lay in a heap on the floor, blood gushing from his back. They were speechless.

A voice startled them. "Hello, again." It came from the dark hall outside the studio door. It was a voice Quinn thought she recognized but couldn't place.

Then Mike Furnari stepped into the room.

Chapter Twenty

Quinn and Drew resumed breathing at the same time. Drew put the gun back into his pocket as he realized who'd shot Brandon. Quinn's mouth was agape. "We thought you were dead."

Mike nodded, a wry smile crossing his face. "So does Tyler, and that's good. Dahbura's goons did try to kill me, but this cat has nine lives. Or at least two."

"What happened?" Quinn asked with exuberance.

Mike explained, "The DiForios wouldn't let me into the studio, so after I got a warrant from a judge, I returned here but glimpsed a black Suburban out back too late. The two guys bagged my head and drove me through a rainstorm to a forest, where they pushed me toward a rushing creek."

"Sounds like what Dahbura and another agent were going to do with me," Drew said.

"I doubt the other guy was really an agent," Mike cautioned. "They're just hired killers."

"What happened, Mike?" Quinn asked.

"I found myself falling before they could shoot me—the earth gave way to mud and I was suddenly in the water. Three shots rang out. One missed me, but one went through my shoulder." He indicated with his hand where the bullet had seared through his flesh. "But the final one hit me right in the chest."

Drew and Quinn were both stunned. "How did you survive?" Drew asked.

Mike gave them a grin, reached down inside his undershirt from the neck, and pulled out a medal attached to a chain. It was the shape of a curled flower petal, but it had once been flat. "It's a real irony, considering this is all about religion," Mike said. "Saint Christopher, who got shafted from the Catholic Church years ago, saved me." The bullet had struck the medal instead of his heart.

"But how'd you get away?" Drew inquired.

"The current pulled me downstream. I lost so much blood that I had no strength at all. I grabbed hold of a branch and pulled myself onto a mud bank and lost consciousness."

"But how are you here?" Quinn asked.

"A guy found me the next day, an old-timer. It was right out of the movies." Mike smiled as he described the old coot and the time he spent with the man. "He lives in an old trailer, tells war stories endlessly, and repeats again and again how he is sure his wife will return any day, even though her ashes were in a can on a shelf."

"You didn't go to a hospital?"

Mike shook his head. "I was a medic for an ambulance company before I joined the Bureau. I knew the bullet had done damage, but it wasn't life threatening. Thing is, after about two days I called the only guy at the Bureau who I trust. To learn I was a wanted man."

Quinn blinked. "What?"

"Dahbura did a number on me. Claimed I killed Patrick. And that *I'm* the computer expert who's behind the problem with Practice Run."

"Oh, my God." Quinn was astounded.

"As far as the Bureau is concerned, I've disappeared. And I prefer it that way, for now. The guy I called is the only one who knows the truth. When I read about your so-called escape, Drew, I knew we were both in the same boat."

"When did you come back here?" Drew asked.

"A few days ago. This house has been empty, but I stuck close, waiting for the DiForios to return." Mike rubbed his nose. "I saw you two waiting in the car, and I thought I'd see what you turned up. When I was about to go to the house, he showed up." He looked down at the bloody remains. "I followed him in."

"Good timing, man," Drew said. "You saved my life."

"So what *have* you turned up?"

"There's a copy of the master CD of Tyler's new version in this house somewhere," Drew assured him. "I can change the code on it, rewrite it to erase any sinister programming. Without the next bit of hypnotism, kids who have already been influenced will lose the programming over time. Either that or on Easter Sunday, if the upgrade goes out the way they created it, players will turn into mobs of anti-religion demonstrators and potential killers. At least according to Tyler's plan."

"How about the Front Runners?" Mike asked.

"There are still some left who have been programmed to kill," Quinn assured him.

"You know who? Where?"

"We know about three of them," Quinn told him. "Tyler is going for the big time. The targets are the Reverend Anthony Johnson, the Dalai Lama, the Archbishop of Canterbury."

Mike blinked. "My God."

"And the Pope," Drew said. They both turned to him. He was back on the computer and had just found an addition to the list. "The Pope is the final target. On Easter Sunday."

Unless they stopped it.

Drew helped Mike drag Brandon's body into the garage while Quinn put a blanket where he'd fallen, to hide the blood. Before Mike covered Brandon with a tarp, Drew closed his eyes, feeling real sadness. "I grew up with him. He was like a brother to me and Tyler back then." Mike put a hand on his shoulder and led him back inside.

Over coffee that Quinn made, they talked about what to do next. "We have names. Joe Rangel, Evelyn Coelho, and Sam Sammons. We think Rangel is going to go after the Dalai Lama because his name was on the same page. We don't know about the other two."

Mike asked, "If there are four more targets—the Archbishop of Canterbury, the Dalai Lama, the Southern Baptist leader, and the Pope—why are there only three names for assassins?"

Drew said, stirring in sugar, "We don't know."

"Perhaps no one has yet been programmed to kill the Pope," Quinn said hopefully.

Mike Furnari rubbed his chin. "Who's next?"

"Coelho," Quinn said. "She's got password number four."

"I don't understand," Mike said.

Quinn explained what they were sure of. "Number four is Coelho, three is Sammons, two is Rangel, and the last one's a crapshoot."

"The one who's supposed to kill the Pope."

Quinn shrugged. "Password PR01."

"So we have two objectives," Mike summed up. "Stop these kids and swap Drew's version of the master for theirs, get it to Rockville before it gets pressed and distributed."

Quinn nodded. "Tyler has a safe in the Zzzyx offices. His master copy has to be in there."

"Know the brand?"

She blinked. "Brand?"

"Safe," Mike said. "I've had some experience in these matters." He grinned. "To be an agent, you have to be part criminal. Was it Acme? Sterling?"

"I have no idea."

Mike leveled a finger at Drew. "How soon can you erase the programming if we find the disc?"

"Depends. Fast, I think."

"Okay," Mike said, "you work on the computer and see what else you can find. Quinn and I will tear this place apart looking for the CD."

Drew reminded him, "We only have until morning. That's when his wife will be back."

They started looking, for long, frustrating hours. A little after four o'clock in the morning, Quinn, who had gone to search the living room, found herself staring across the room at a rack of music CDs. And a thought came to her. Tyler's programming of kids was hiding in plain sight, so why not do the same with something you'd want no one else to find? On a whim, she started opening all the jewel cases. Streisand, Beethoven, Pearl Jam, Bowie, Broadway musicals. All the CDs matched their cases. Until she got to an Eminem case. Inside, the CD said nothing. It was silver, with no identifying marks or words stamped on it. She rushed into the studio and handed it to Drew. "Give this a look."

Sure enough, they had what they needed.

They left before the sun came up.

"This is James," the voice said into the phone.

"James, it's Auntie Quinn. Hi."

"Hi! Are you coming too?"

"Coming where? There?"

"Yeah. Mom says that Joanie is on her way."

"Oh, thank God. Honey, put your mom on the phone, okay?"

"Okay."

After a few moments, Quinn heard the rushed voice of her dear partner and friend say, "Oh, I'm so glad to hear you're okay."

"Fine, actually. Susan, Mike is alive."

"Mike Furnari?"

Mike heard her and took the phone from Quinn for a moment. "I'm okay, Susan. Brandon DiForio is dead, though. Plus, David Dahbura's behind it all."

"Patrick's instincts were right. He detested the man."

"I never liked him either. And we're going to get him and Tyler—I promise."

"Mike, I'm thrilled you're okay," she said. "It's so good to hear your voice."

"Here's Quinn again."

"Susan?"

"Quinn, where are you? Kansas City?"

"We just crossed the Mississippi. We're on our way to Florida."

"Florida?"

"We have the name of the girl who is programmed to kill next. We learned she lives in Pompano Beach. Anthony Johnson is there for a week of conferences. We are going to try to stop her, but we have no way of knowing when it's going to happen, and we can't fly."

"Two wanted criminals and a woman on the run," Susan said, trying to interject a little humor. "I'll say you'd better not fly."

"Tell me, what does Joan know?"

"Nothing. I lied that you were joining us for Easter, but once she learns the truth, she'll understand. She and her girlfriend are on their way."

"Maybe I will join you by Easter. We have to defeat Tyler by then. That's the deadline for the new game." Quinn cast an uneasy eye at Drew, who was busily typing in code in the backseat.

"Has Tyler tried to find Joan?"

"She said no."

"I'll still feel better when she's with you."

"Any day now."

"Susan, there's another reason I called you. Remember when we were in the Zzzyx offices? Veronica locked something in a safe."

"Yes."

"Did you happen to notice the make of it? Mike knows it's a long shot, but I thought I'd ask. You have an eye for details."

"Wells Fargo."

Quinn grinned. "You're kidding. How do you know?"

"It said Wells Fargo on it. Only reason I remember it is that I have on-line banking with them. But why do you need to know?"

"To break into it," Quinn told her. "The safe, not the bank. I have to go. Here's a new cell phone number."

Susan wrote it down. "Listen, Quinn, call again when your daughter's arrived."

"Love you," Quinn said, and hung up.

Tyler was hunched over the computer at the Flamingo when David entered the suite with a martini in hand. "I could stay here forever," David gushed. "I don't think I've ever been in a boutique hotel I've loved so much."

Tyler muttered, "Fags everywhere." But he didn't look up from the screen. "I had PR03 on-line earlier."

"I worry about that one."

"Don't. The kid is mine, under the spell. Waiting for the final command."

"How's little Evelyn coming?"

Tyler pulled away from the keyboard and stretched. "I'll talk to her later. Been working on the few glitches left bothering me about the new game. The deadline is upon us."

David sat in a chair with one leg up over the arm. "Nice tan, huh?" He was wearing white linen shorts and light brown sandals, which certainly made his skin seem even darker.

"Screw you, nice tan," Tyler spit back, jealously. "I've been stuck in this room since we got here."

"That's 'cause you're homophobic."

"It's because I'm scared to be recognized in Lauderdale."

"It's both." David sipped his martini. "Why don't you just let the game be pressed, glitches and all?"

Tyler looked shocked. "Are you a total idiot? One of those glitches could ruin everything. It could cause the subliminal orders not to work." He walked to the window and saw a crowd milling about with drinks in their hands. "What's going on down there?"

"Benefit for the Stonewall Library."

"What the hell is that?"

"A library of gay literature and culture. They're raising money for a permanent building. I gave."

"You what?" Tyler was astounded.

"I made a donation. I think it's a good cause."

Tyler muttered, "At least it's not a church group."

"I have bad news." David sounded nervous, which was uncharacteristic. "I needed a drink before I could bring myself to tell you. Brandon's dead."

Tyler's face became a mask as he turned around. "What?"

"Candy found him when she returned from visiting their kid. Shot in the back."

"Who did it?" Tyler gasped.

"Who would you guess?"

Tyler took a deep breath, astonished. He again stared at the elegantly dressed men and women enjoying canapés and cocktails down in the courtyard. "So they went to Kansas City. And they killed Brandon." He honestly couldn't believe it. "I would never have guessed Quinn or even Drew, for that matter, would be able to shoot someone."

Dahbura nodded. "Probably used the gun Drew stole the night we had him in Arizona."

"I thought they were running, that they'd try to get help from authorities who would ultimately arrest them."

"No, they went to Kansas City 'cause they're smart, and your brother is a computer genius." David was spelling it out for him as if he were ten years old. "They went to find the game."

Tyler glared out the window. He visualized Quinn standing down there with the guests, martini in hand, the kind of thing she did so well. "I should have killed her."

David said, "I almost did. Both of them. We were that close. Candy said the house had been ransacked."

In a flash, Tyler knew why. He pointed to the computer. "Did they get Brandon's copy of this master?" he asked with alarm.

"She said she didn't know what Brandon had done with it, where he'd hidden it."

"Wonderful." Tyler thought it through. "What the hell am I so worried about? The programming's set, it's in my safe. All I need to do is fix the bugs." He gestured toward the laptop screen again. "They can't hurt us."

"Don't underestimate them," David warned.

"What? What's he going to do? Destroy every copy once it's in the stores? Create some kind of virus? He can't touch us." Tyler smiled confidently. "You know, for them to witness what's going to happen when the new game comes out, that's gotta be the ultimate horror for both of them, especially my Catholic crusader." He grinned. "It may be a fate worse than death."

David nodded and stood up. He started changing clothes.

"Where you going?"

"I got a date."

"Date? Where'd you meet a girl?"

"Girl? Met a hot guy down by the pool."

Tyler blinked. "Listen, you don't have to play the gay thing behind closed doors."

"Who's playing?"

Tyler blinked again. "You're shitting me."

"You never asked."

Tyler started to laugh. "No, you're right. I never did."

"How do you think I found out about this place?"

Tyler looked amazed. And less than thrilled. "I've been sleeping in the same bed with you."

David looked him up and down. "Baby, don't worry, you're not my type."

"That's not funny."

David was startled. "What's with you? You're the hip Game King! Tyler Bryant, the epitome of cool. Where do you get off being a bigot?" Tyler just stared at him, seething. "Let me tell you something, pal. Get over it. Hear me? We're everywhere." He walked toward the door. "Even in the same bed." He looked at his watch. "Make sure our little Evelyn succeeds tomorrow."

Tyler sat down at the computer and connected. PR04 was already on-line. He typed in a greeting. *Hello, Evelyn, how are you tonight?*

David stood in the open doorway but didn't leave. "Tyler," he said, turning back to him. "I'm sorry about Brandon. I know you loved him."

"Quinn will pay for that. She's got a few big surprises coming."

In a hotel room near Evansville, Indiana, Mike Furnari, working on another laptop that he'd bought that afternoon, tried furiously to find a phone number for Evelyn Coelho in Pompano Beach. They had realized her screen name was PompanoGirl, and he was using his FBI connection to get him unlisted numbers.

They were continuing on to Florida because they'd learned that the Rev. Anthony Johnson was appearing at the Southern Baptist Leadership Council conference starting the next day. "I only hope we can get there in time," Quinn observed, worried.

"And that we can find Evelyn before she does what she's been set in motion to do." Then Mike blinked. On the screen a number for a family named Coelho, Evelyn and Tony, popped up. Mike called, asked for Evelyn, but learned he had gotten the mother of the same name. The woman informed him that the younger Evelyn was in Lauderdale to stay with some girlfriends for the night.

When Quinn heard that, on the speaker phone, she cringed. Lauderdale was where the conference was being held.

Mike took a chance and told the woman what they feared her daughter was going to do. "I know it sounds preposterous, Mrs. Coelho, but we think Evelyn has been programmed to kill someone at a Baptist gathering sometime in the next five days."

"Are you mad?"

"Mrs. Coelho, go to her computer, while we're on the phone—"

"Listen to me, whoever you are," she ordered, cutting him off. "As a responsible parent I feel that computer games are good for kids. There are studies that back me up. They improve visual and mental skills."

"This one does something quite different from that."

"You must be one of those crusaders against the violence and I don't agree. My daughter isn't going to turn into some kind of homicidal maniac because she blows up ships on the high seas on a computer screen."

Mike reacted. His eyes darted to Quinn. "What did you say?"

"I said they're not too violent."

"No," Mike said, "about a ship?"

"That's Practice Run, isn't it? I saw her playing. Blowing up boats."

Quinn shared her astonished look with Mike.

"One of the playing arenas is a marina," she said in fear.

"Tell me more about your daughter, Evelyn," Mike gasped. "Please, something that could help us. Where might she be staying in Lauderdale? Is it near a marina? Near the water? Does she have a cell phone? Do you—"

"Who do you think you are prying into my girl's life? You some kind of pervert? This some kind of prank call?"

"I assure you, Mrs. Coelho, this is very much on the level. I'm an FBI agent."

The woman was flabbergasted. "The FBI is after my daughter?"

"We want to save her life."

"Nonsense. You have the wrong person."

"I think not," Mike told her, and tried to make her understand. When he told her the game worked like a cult leader might, she really took offense.

"My girl doesn't belong to a cult! She's a good, upstanding, God-fearing child."

"Do you know how to use a computer, Mrs. Coelho?"

The woman seemed reluctant to say any more. "Yes," she answered tersely.

"Is her computer there?"

"Yes."

"I want you to get on it. I want you to look in her E-mails, in her files, in her history, tell me if—"

"You're asking me to spy on Evelyn? Listen, I'm going to call the police."

"I'm with the FBI, Mrs. Coelho."

"That's what you said," the woman snapped. "And I don't believe you."

Mike was left listening to the dial tone.

Susan Horgan ran barefoot out to the little car that was creating a dust storm as it bounced into view outside the cottage. "Joanie!" she called, waving as the girl jumped out and hugged her. "I'm so glad you came."

"This is Stephanie," Joan said as the driver stepped out of the vehicle. "My best friend and travel buddy."

"Ah, the other backpacker." Susan warmly took Stephanie's hand. "But some backpacking, huh? I mean, renting a new Mini Cooper?"

Stephanie said, "My family hoarded money all their lives. I aim to spend it for them."

Susan smiled. "Welcome."

After showing them around and getting them settled into two upstairs bedrooms that had spectacular views of the water, Susan made tea and they sat on the back patio, wrapped in heavy sweaters, watching the sun go down. James returned from playing with a friend and gave Joan a big high-five. Later, they ate roasted chicken and crusty potatoes, drank some Harp ale, and topped off the meal with rice pudding, which Susan remembered Joan loved.

After dinner, Susan coaxed James into pounding out a few tunes on the old upright in the corner of the living room. It was so close to the fireplace that, over the years, the heat had charred the front of the cabinet from deep brown to black. But the tone remained glorious. At the end they applauded, and then said good night as James climbed the stairs to his bedroom.

Susan proceeded to take the girls into her confidence. She thought it best to tell them the whole story. Stephanie, who didn't know any of the players, kept asking questions, wanting to know details. Joanie listened almost as if numbed. Her initial reaction—this could not be true, you have to be kidding!—was offset by the pieces falling into place. The lack of phone calls from her mother. Why Quinn had asked several times if she still played Practice Run. The fear she remembered in Quinn's voice. Her fear that something was wrong with their marriage. The reason Susan would take James out of school and hide in Ireland. But that it was safe here. A safe place, a place Tyler would never think of, and that's precisely why Joan and Stephanie were here as well. "I can protect you here," Susan assured them.

"He's been calling," Stephanie suddenly blurted out.

Joan looked at her, surprised at her outburst.

"It's okay, Joan," her girlfriend said. "They need to know."

Susan's fears prickled. "What?"

Joan opened up. "Tyler's called a lot lately. Remember you asked me when you invited us here if I had heard from him?"

"You said you hadn't."

"True. But then, that same day, he called Stephanie's and wanted to know if I had heard from my mom."

"And you said?" Susan questioned.

"I said no, 'cause it was true. But I remembered

what you told me about her doing something secret and so I didn't tell him any of that. I just made like I didn't know anything."

"How did he sound?"

Joanie shrugged. "Pissed off, I guess."

"Quinn was afraid he'd use you to get to her."

"Use me?"

"Hurt you." Just saying it made Susan wince.

Joanie looked distraught. "Is Mom okay?"

Susan explained where Quinn was, and that she now had help—powerful people who believed her—and that she and Tyler's brother were doing everything they could to reverse what the game to that point had done.

"I'm glad I never played it," Stephanie admitted.

"Me too, honey," Susan remarked, "me too." She finished her Powers. "Listen, I want you both to stay with me until this is over. I can't let you leave."

They looked alarmed. "How long will that be?" Joanie asked.

"Easter Sunday," Susan said. "At least that's what we surmise, because that's the day the new game goes on sale."

"I have to tell my family," Stephanie said, "but they won't mind. They kind of look at me as the pain-in-the-ass black sheep, don't know what to make of me."

Susan smiled. "Black sheep can graze here for a long time. I hear that you paint."

"Yes." The girl brightened. "Watercolors."

"It's very conducive here."

Stephanie smiled and said, "I may never leave."

Susan stood up. "I'm ready for bed. Joanie, you okay?"

Joan got up too. "Just a little shell-shocked."

"We all are."

She hugged Susan. "I'm so sorry about Uncle Patrick. I can't believe Tyler did that."

"He's killed a lot of people," Susan whispered, "but we won't let him kill any more."

She kissed Joan on the cheek. "Listen, there are individual space heaters in both your rooms, just in case you need them."

"Thanks," Stephanie said, rising as well. "I'm going up with you. Been a long day."

"Joanie?" Susan asked, wondering if she should turn out the lights.

"Auntie Susan, can I use your computer? I need to check my E-mail."

"Sure, honey," Susan said, leading her to the former pantry. "But get a good night's sleep. We're getting up early and going for a hike together."

"Great. See you then. I won't be long." Joan sat down at the laptop as Susan closed the door.

The Rev. Anthony Johnson, robust and charismatic, opened the Southern Baptist Leadership Council with a prayer the next morning, and then helped himself to a hearty breakfast. He lectured at 9:00 A.M., and by 10:30 A.M. he was back at the hotel to pick up his two oldest kids, Shawnelle and Tony Jr., to do something that wasn't on his schedule: take them deep sea fishing. His father had been an oyster man in New Orleans, and he was somewhat the old salt himself. Nothing pleased him so much as wait-

ing for the bite. He was happy two of his kids loved
it too, and now he had a chance to thrill them.
They'd be going out on a real ocean.

Evelyn Coelho, who was tying a line near the
thirty-foot Ocean Sportfish the Reverend had char-
tered for the day, pricked her ears when the Johnson
family arrived. There was a lot of excitement, a loving good-bye to Ethel, his wife, and the two
youngest children, and then there were waves and
shouts and then the boat was gone. "I get sick on
boats," Evelyn heard Ethel say to someone nearby,
"so my two youngest and I are going to have a nice
afternoon playing *in* the water rather than on it.
Come on, kids, we're going to the beach."

"The wife seems to be leaving," David Dahbura
said to Tyler as he peered through binoculars from a
boat just across the Intracoastal waterway. "Evelyn's
getting into the skiff. She's starting the engine. She's
coming this way."

When Evelyn's boat pulled alongside theirs three
minutes later, Tyler lifted his sunglasses and said,
"Hello."

Her eyes were glassy. She only nodded.

Then he said, "So, you're my marina girl, huh?"

Suddenly she seemed to be infused with energy.
She stiffened, stood up straight, and smiled. "Yes, sir,
ay ay, sir."

"Let's have lunch together, Evelyn. Permission to
board!"

Evelyn tied up her boat alongside theirs, and with
David's help boarded the boat. In a moment, she
was sitting across from Tyler in the little galley

below. "It's nice to meet you, Evelyn. This is the first time I've met one of my soldiers in person."

"It's an honor, sir," she said, almost as if she were talking to a rock star. "I mean, this is awesome."

He took her hand in his. "You know what you have to do, don't you, Evelyn?"

All the excitement disappeared. She nodded like a robot. "Yes, sir. I certainly do."

Out on the water, Tony J., as Anthony Junior was called, truly his mother's son, threw up once he lost sight of the high-rises dotting the Southern Florida coast. But Shawnelle, who had a cast iron stomach, like her father, was charged. Throwing in her line, she challenged the entire fishing boat crew—four strapping guys—to catch something bigger than she would. Indeed, as if God had heard her prayer, she reeled in (with help) a marlin that was almost twice her size. Dad was proud, if a little jealous. At the end of the day, he'd caught what amounted to a minnow next to her prize. "I think it's gonna break a record," the captain said as they headed back a little later than expected, at four in the afternoon.

When they entered the Intracoastal waterway, surrounded by multimillion-dollar mansions and private yachts bigger than houses, Shawnelle spied her mom and the rest of the family waiting for them on the dock. "Hey, Mom," Shawnelle shouted, "guess what I caught?"

Anthony turned to follow her pointed hand. He could hear the squeals of his two smallest children as they approached. He couldn't wait to treat them all to a wonderful seafood dinner, after taking photographs with Shawnelle's prize catch. And then it happened.

The little skiff came out of nowhere. It rounded the corner of the pier, careening directly into the starboard side of the sturdy fishing boat. One of the fishing boat's crew yelled at the top of his lungs to the captain, "Turn, turn!" But the Sportfish didn't have time to avoid the other boat. The captain hardly had time to realize what was suddenly happening. The skiff rammed the side with enough force to knock people overboard.

Horrified onlookers saw the strike—the small boat broke a hole in the starboard side of the fishing vessel—but no one expected the explosion that followed. Ethel was thrown on top of her youngest son, while a man on the dock pulled the little girl to him and held tight to save her from being blown into the water.

Shawnie died instantly, along with her father, for they'd been standing, arms around each other, waving to the rest of the family. Tony J., who was on the port side at the time of impact, was, thankfully, thrown into the water by the collision, and was able, despite being weak from seasickness, to swim away. Two of the crew members on the fishing boat, including the captain, as well as the two men on the skiff, also died.

Tyler watched it all through binoculars. He was beside himself, trembling first with apprehension that something might go wrong, then shaking with delight that he had succeeded.

David started the boat's engines. "No, I want to see it all—everything," Tyler told him. Coast Guard and police boats were arriving, as were ambulances on the dock. People were being pulled from the smoking, debris-laden water. Tyler was loving it.

"They're going to question everyone in a five-mile radius in about fifteen minutes," David warned him. "They're gonna ask who saw what. We are not going to be here to answer those questions." He untied the ropes and went back to the pilot house. "Anyway, we got a date with a certain archbishop."

Tyler smiled as David shoved the throttle forward.

Chapter Twenty-one

The rented van was nearing Nashville when NPR reported the news from Fort Lauderdale. Mike and Quinn were very dismayed. With the little information they had, they'd tried to prevent what happened. The Reverend's security people had not taken their ambiguous warning about a marina seriously, and law enforcement, like Evelyn's mother, thought they were cranks. And being so far away, there was nothing they could do themselves. So they had reversed course, deciding to head instead to D.C.

On the road, Drew finished writing the code for the new patch. The most important thing to accomplish now was to ensure that the new game would stop programming those who played it. They needed to switch Drew's disc for the one in Tyler's safe. They were discussing that very problem—how to get into Tyler's safe—when Mike's cell phone rang. He seemed delighted to hear the person calling.

When Mike hung up, he shared the good news. "That was my buddy, the only guy I trust at the Bureau. He's got a guy who's gonna bug the place."

"The Bureau?" Drew asked, puzzled.

"Zzzyx," Quinn guessed.

"Yes." Mike looked jazzed. "He'll help us get in."

"How about the safe?"

Mike grinned even more. "This afternoon sometime a 'technician' from the Wells Fargo Safe Company will pay a bogus service call to Zzzyx Games, wanting to test the lock they have been having trouble with. He'll even assure them that the report was filed by a Ms. Ashton."

Quinn laughed. "You guys are good."

Drew, who was driving, said, "He going to get the combination?"

Mike winked. "By the time he's done arguing with Tyler's assistant, he'll have everything we need."

"Knowing her, it'll be a long harangue," Quinn said. "Maybe we can get in there tomorrow night."

But when they stopped for gas, everything changed. Drew was drinking a Coke, stretching his legs, when he saw *USA Today* in a dispenser. ARCHBISHOP TO START BOOK TOUR IN NYC, the headline read. He slid a coin in and grabbed one. "Hey, you guys, look at this."

Mike and Quinn read the article and looked at each other. "I alerted Scotland Yard and the London Police. I didn't know he was coming here."

"He's here already," Quinn reminded him.

"And he's speaking tomorrow night." Something Mike had read really gave him the creeps. "At a high school auditorium, no less."

"I think," Drew said, "we are now heading for New York."

"We don't have a choice," Mike agreed. "We don't

want to slip our CD into the safe until the last minute anyway. There'll be less chance for Tyler to see it's been tampered with."

Quinn said grimly, "No, our first responsibility is to save an innocent man's life."

When they got to New York City, Mike went right to bed. He wanted to be rested and alert for the next day. Quinn helped herself to a soda from the minibar, then walked into the bedroom, where Drew was again working on the laptop. She stood behind him, rubbing his shoulders while he faced the screen. "You okay?" He did not answer, did not respond to her touch. He seemed zoned out, and when she looked at his face she saw that he appeared to be drained, sinking. "Drew, you need some rest."

He finally answered. "What time is it?"

"Almost two in the morning. You worked most of the way. Do you want something to drink?"

He slumped in the uncomfortable straight-backed chair. "Man, I wish I could find out more from these."

"What are they?"

"Storage CDs that I grabbed when we left Kansas City. Thought they might be helpful. They're mainly a bunch of notes on different game scenarios."

"Nothing that helps locate Sam Sammons or Joe Rangel?"

"I was hoping even more for a name for PR01." He shrugged, turned to face her.

"Tyler plans to go for the archbishop first, the Dalai Lama next, then the Pope on Easter Sunday. But he didn't count on the fact that we'd be on to him. So I seriously doubt if he's been able to program the final person. Maybe there is no PR01."

"Let's pray that's true," she agreed.

"He thinks that after next Sunday, he won't need specific killers anymore because they'll all be killing."

He stood up, ran his hands through his greasy hair, and shuddered. "I need a shower."

"This classy joint has a great tub. Let me run a bath for you."

He smiled warmly. "Where were you when I was doing time in Arizona? I mean, we're kind of in prison now as well, but man, this is so much more enjoyable."

She winked. She went to the big bathroom to run him a hot bath with lavender bubbles she found, lit two candles and doused the lights, and turned on a classical radio station, which played through the television in the living room.

After about half an hour, she knocked on the door. "You fall asleep in there?"

"Come in," he said.

She entered in a nightgown, ready for bed. He lay back in the tub, just his knees protruding above the water level, which still had remnants of bubble clouds floating on it. His wet chest seemed to shine in the dancing flicker of the candle flame. "Finally relaxing?"

"Mmmm."

She pulled some towels from the stack in the armoire, tossed them on the floor facing him, and sat on them, her back resting against the tile wall. "What are you going to do when this is over?"

He closed his eyes. "I want to see a movie. I want to go to a rock concert. I want to walk barefoot on a beach. I want to kiss a girl."

"You kissed me. In Kansas City, remember? I'm a girl."

He opened his eyes and laughed. "Yes, but that was fake. It didn't count." He settled back in again. "You think I'm going to be free? When this is over?"

"Of course. Mike is sure of it."

He seemed unable to comprehend the idea. "You make plans for the end of your sentencing. Oh, you hope for something to happen before that—appeals, Tyler fixing things, all those pipe dreams. But you don't really count on having a life again until the sentence is done. I'm not sure this is going to work out."

"Lean on me," she said.

He looked at her with an intensity that warmed her inside. "How do I ever thank you?"

"For what? I almost got you killed." She stretched out her legs and crossed them. "At least in jail you were safe."

"You got me my life back. You showed me the truth of what happened. You gave me a goal."

She laughed. "You really do love programming, don't you? I mean, you're like in another world when you're working, zoned out."

"But I'm still human. I'm still just a guy." He moved his hand from the rim of the tub to touch her leg. "I have to tell you, Quinn . . ." He seemed unsure. "I don't know how to say it."

"Say what?" she interjected nervously, feeling the pressure on her knee.

"Thank you. That I'm grateful."

She smiled, reached down, touched his hand, and said, "I feel closer to you right now than anyone on earth, except for my daughter."

He wrapped his fingers around hers and then sat up straight in the tub. Their eyes locked, and he bent forward. She did the same, bringing their faces closer together. Then he lifted himself from his scented pond and leaned forward to kiss her on the cheek. She closed her eyes. He was naked and she didn't want to stare.

But when his lips pressed softly against the side of her cheek, she felt a rush deep inside her that she realized she had never felt with Tyler, not in all the hot and wild bouts of lovemaking. There was something so innocent and so touching about his lingering kiss on her cheek.

He said, "I'm going to sleep on the pull-out in the living room."

She had a fleeting thought of telling him to join her, that the bed was big, that they'd done it before, but there was no excuse to suggest that kind of intimacy. She lifted her arm, ran her fingers through his wet hair, and whispered, "I'll see you in the morning."

In the suite's other bedroom, Quinn got under the covers and turned off the bedside lamp. She knew the feelings she was having, and she knew she had to fight them.

She turned onto her side, mashing the pillow until it cradled her head just right. As she moved her arm under the covers, she saw him silhouetted in the doorway, standing there, wrapped in a towel, immobile, watching her. Her mouth opened in surprise, and slowly she sat up.

Drew was breathing hard. He seemed to want to take another step into the room and yet was trying to force himself to stay where he was. "Quinn," he said softly.

"Drew?" she said, the inflection making his name a question, as if asking whether they wanted the same thing. She sat up farther.

He took a step forward.

And her cell phone rang. She was startled by it, brought her fingers to her lips, then reached for it on the bed stand, fumbling, finally hitting the green button. "Yes?" Who would call this late? Mike was asleep. Then she realized it was her daughter. "Oh, Joanie, hello! I forget what time it is in Ireland." She looked up at Drew.

"Just wanted to say good night again," he said, though she knew that was not at all what he'd come to say.

Once he closed her door, she went back to the call. "Honey, are you okay?"

"Mom," Joanie said, "it's you we're worried about. What's happening?"

"I'm fine."

"When am I going to see you?"

Quinn's heart filled with love. "It won't be long. Once it's over, I'm free to come and be with you all. Believe me, there's nothing I'm looking forward to more."

"Cool. It's a beautiful morning here. Auntie Susan says to tell you that she sent you a ton of E-mails about work."

Quinn groaned. "I can't even read them till this is finished. Tell her just to fudge, mark time."

"Okay. Stephanie is painting. She's a wonderful artist, Mom."

"What are you doing with your time?"

"Writing."

"Writing?" she asked, surprised.

"Been my secret for a long time. Journals at first, but lately I've tried some short stories."

"Well, good for you," Quinn said tentatively.

"Mom, I think maybe I want to go back to school sooner than I thought."

"Got the wanderlust out of your system?"

Joanie laughed. "Don't sound like a mother now, okay?"

"Hey, I'm glad you came to that realization. We can go through life saying we shoulda, woulda, coulda, and it gets you nowhere."

"Mom, I'm praying for you."

"Been to church there, honey?"

"Yes. It's awesome, about a million years old, a little chapel where it's always damp and cool, and the people are so kind. Susan goes even though she's not Catholic. It's very spiritual."

"I can't wait to see it myself. We'll go together and thank God when this is all over."

"Okay, Mom. Love you. Bye."

"Bye, darling."

Quinn woke up the next morning to find Mike and Drew both watching Tyler being interviewed by Matt Lauer on *The Today Show*. The sight of her husband on the TV screen chilled her. "He's going on and on about how the new version is going to 'revolutionize' video games," Mike informed her.

Drew said, "That's for sure."

Quinn sat on the pull-out sofa mattress next to Drew, who was still in boxers and a tee shirt, having just awoke. The sight of Tyler looking ebullient and zestful took her breath away. "I'm rushing to the airport now," Tyler said, "have to get back to Rockville to work out the final bugs. We're holding up production until it's perfect."

Matt Lauer seemed surprised. "You going to get the new CDs pressed and shipped in, what, a week?"

Tyler confidently nodded and pulled on his four-hundred-dollar tie. "We've got factories all over the world geared up to go into twenty-four-hour production. With that, I can be a last-minute kind of guy."

"Wow," Matt said.

"Fucking A," Drew said, giving Mike five. "I told ya!"

Tyler flashed a big grin. "That's what everyone will say once they play the new game. Hey, Matt, thanks." He extended his hand. "My plane's waiting for me."

Mike zapped the TV screen. "Listen, you two, I got up early and called the archbishop's people. I warned them. But I don't think they took me seriously."

"They will tonight," Drew said.

The auditorium at Fiorello LaGuardia High School for the Performing Arts at Lincoln Center was packed. The Archbishop of Canterbury's new book,

Crisis in Religion in the Modern World, had reached the best-seller list in England. Coming to New York for its U.S. release, he was also going to give a series of lectures on the East Coast.

Quinn, Mike, and Drew were trying to stop another murder. They had been trying to locate Sam Sammons, the boy they figured had been programmed to do the dirty work tonight. They had nothing on him; no address or information of any kind. They'd tried to find him through his screen name, but none of the search engines turned up any such listing.

They had no choice but to show up at the lecture and hope that they could somehow prevent the attack. Quinn sat in the first row, on one end, Drew, in baseball cap and bulky sweatshirt to help disguise him, was farther back, and Mike sat at the other end of the third row, figuring the boy who had been programmed to kill the religious leader would position himself somewhere nearby. As the audience applauded the archbishop's entrance onstage, Quinn looked over toward Mike. His eyes were drilling the audience, looking at every male under twenty.

The archbishop turned out to be a jovial, engaging man. He started by saying this very land on which this school was built was at one time part of Hell's Kitchen, which *West Side Story* made famous. He told the story of the first time he'd been to New York City. His parents had taken him to see that show on Broadway, and he'd immediately fallen in love with Carol Lawrence, who played Maria. "I don't know how many original cast albums I wore out over the years just listening to her voice." Recently, in London, he

said, he attended a luncheon on behalf of eradicating
land mines, one of Princess Diana's favorite charities.
"The entertainment was provided by another person
who worked for that charity. I finally got to meet my
idol. Yes, I know this shocks some of you, probably
most of all my wife, but archbishops are human too."

As the audience tittered, Drew, Quinn, and Mike
nervously surveyed the faces. They were on high
alert.

"And today," the archbishop continued, "I had the
great pleasure of having lunch with that wonderful
and talented woman who made me love New York so
much. And she's here tonight. Ladies and gentlemen,
please give a warm welcome to *my* beautiful and talented Maria, who is also my good friend, Miss Carol
Lawrence."

As the radiant Broadway star rose in the middle of
the third row, the audience applauded. The archbishop threw her a kiss. Quinn's heart was in her
throat, however, because applause felt like a cue for
something to happen. Mike was feeling antsy, thinking someone was going to pull a gun or throw a
bomb. The situation was fraught with tension as the
crowd roared. When it died down, Quinn's, Mike's,
and Drew's hearts kept beating fast.

The archbishop spoke for almost two hours. It was
enjoyable for everyone but Quinn, Mike, and Drew.
They sat, tense and worried. But around the time the
archbishop was winding down, they started to relax.
Perhaps, each of them thought, they'd been wrong.

Until the standing ovation at the end. When the
archbishop returned to the stage and had taken a second bow, a girl and a boy walked out from either side

with red roses in their arms. Mike was the first to feel
his throat clench. The security people had told him
that two *girls* were going to present the archbishop
with roses. He leaped to his feet and shouted just as
the girl was handing hers over. Mike's shout couldn't
be heard by anyone because the applause was deafening, so he rushed to the stage. The girl was moving
off, allowing the boy to approach the archbishop.

With a running leap, Mike tackled the boy at the
moment he was putting his bouquet into the archbishop's hands. As Sam Sammons went sprawling,
with Mike on top of him, the applause turned to mur-
murs of shock, and the roses went flying all over the
stage. Along with the grenade whose pin the boy had
just pulled.

Drew bounded onto the stage and grabbed the
archbishop, forcing him to the stage floor. He and
Mike both heard Sam yell "No!" though they didn't
know if it was because he had been thwarted in his
attempt to blow up the man or because of his fear
that he would not die with him, for they knew his
suicide was part of the programming.

The blast was deafening, blowing a hole in the cement wall of the back of the stage, burning the curtain that fronted it, and injuring the two stagehands
who stood at either wing. But Mike and Drew,
though hit by debris, were okay. As were the two
people they had smothered: Sam Sammons and the
archbishop. Two people marked for death who were
far from dead.

The audience became a mob screaming in panic, trying to run from the danger, rushing toward the doors.
All except one. One man in the middle of the audi-

torium moved slower than the others. He seemed to understand there was no reason for the spectators to be fearful. And Quinn saw him. Turning to look at the panic behind her, Quinn froze as she saw Tyler.

He stood frozen as well, but with a different kind of dismay, watching with wide eyes as all around him people trampled one another in their desire to run for an exit. When he turned back to the stage, he saw Quinn standing, with her eyes drilling into him. And at once it came together for him. All at once he realized who had tackled Sam, who had saved the archbishop. A quick glance at the stage confirmed it. His brother, Drew. And Mike Furnari. Mike Furnari, who was obviously far from dead.

Then he realized that Quinn was rushing up the aisle toward him. As he turned and hurried the opposite way, he heard her start screaming for security guards. He didn't look back again as he fled through the doors to the lobby, pushing his way through in a desperate desire to get to the street. But the lobby was wall-to-wall people, and he could barely move.

He glanced over his shoulder to see where she was. She stood in another doorway, her hand on a policeman's shoulder, shouting into the officer's face over the din of the crowd.

By the time Quinn convinced the cop that she knew that a man in the audience had masterminded what had just happened and was getting away, Tyler had crouched down and hidden from sight. When he was close enough to the doors to make a run for it, he burst through, knocking a woman to the ground. Then he ran, like everyone else.

By the time David Dahbura picked him up three

blocks away, he knew that Quinn and his brother and Mike Furnari, having somehow risen from his grave, were now not only on to him, but one step ahead of him.

Tyler shouted at David all the way to the first stoplight. He was furious. At the light, David growled. "Calm down. People are looking at us. They can hear you on the street."

Tyler took a deep breath and hissed, "I thought you killed Furnari."

"I thought I did too," David muttered.

After a long, seething silence, a block later Tyler vowed, "They're not going to stop the final two." Then he turned to face the driver. "I'll kill *you* if they do."

Chapter Twenty-two

They'd not only saved the archbishop but his assailant as well, so Mike remained in New York for another day to interrogate Sam Sammons, the only assassin who had ever survived. Drew warned Mike it would be to no avail. "I think the programing is so deep, so intense, that they don't even consciously know what they're doing. Only after time has passed will that kid start to comprehend what happened."

Drew and Quinn drove the rented van the four hours to Rockville, where they took another two-bedroom suite at a luxury hotel only blocks from the Zzzyx offices. While Drew went to work on the computer to try to learn more about Front Runner PR02, the assassin whose name they knew as Joe Rangel, Quinn called Mike and told him where they were holed up. He promised to be there in the morning. Which would mean, according to what Tyler had said on *The Today Show*, that they would only have one night left to switch discs. That's what they wanted: to make the switch at the last minute.

They ordered Chinese food and opened a bottle of

wine from the minibar. They talked about her having seen Tyler at the high school. "I wish you'd told me," Drew said. "I wish I'd have looked out from the stage. I would have ripped him apart."

"There were so many security people around you on the stage," Quinn explained, "that he would have disappeared if I'd stayed to tell you." She shrugged. "He got away anyhow. It was awful facing him. Awful."

Drew said, "Why did you marry him?"

She stopped eating for a moment. "Why?"

He nodded. "You seem so mismatched. You have a warm heart. His is cold."

She thought about his question. "I didn't know that then. You see, I never thought I'd find love again—ever. I hadn't been happy for a very long time."

"That's right, you were married before. What was he like? Was he like Tyler?"

"You really want to hear?"

"How can I eat wonton soup without getting to know more about you?"

She laughed. She told him that back in college, she met and fell head over heels for Richard Roberts, a jock with a big heart and an unquenchable desire to see the world. They backpacked around the globe their junior year. When money ran out, they took odd jobs, from hustling time shares in Playa del Carmen to chopping sugarcane on Fiji. "I mean, we washed wineglasses in a restaurant in Salerno and painted houses in Melbourne." After a year in China, Quinn started to get homesick and wanted to settle down. She wanted a home of her own. And children.

"We moved to Virginia, near my parents, finished college, married, and got jobs. I worked for my first nonprofit beltway organization. Rich fittingly became a travel agent, spending most of his time on 'familiarization' trips that airlines and resorts offer agents for free. When I found myself pregnant, he said he would stay home, that the wanderlust was over, he wanted all the things I did. But it wasn't true. Joanie wasn't even a year old before he was off on a new career, leading a tour—he'd gotten a position with the classy Maupintour, with better pay than he'd ever made as a travel agent. One trip led to another, which led to hundreds more, and there were times I wasn't sure I was even married."

"What happened?" Drew asked.

"He just didn't come back. I got a letter from Helsinki telling me that when the current tour was finished, he was going directly to do a tour through Russia, and from there he was going to take a group on a sailboat cruise of the Hawaiian islands, and from there . . ."

"When did you divorce?"

"I didn't file for three years. I guess there was some hope that he'd miss us and come back. But I think his peripatetic love for staying on the move won out."

"What happened to him?" Drew asked.

"Who knows?" She smiled wistfully. "And who cares?"

"Do you hate him?"

She shrugged. "Rich wasn't a bad guy—he did nothing evil. He's not like Tyler. He never hurt anyone. He just should never have been a father."

"Or a husband."

"Or a husband."

He was curious. "Did you want more children?"

"Oh, yes," she said with emotion. "But Joanie was a difficult birth. I had toxemia, she came in my seventh month, and barely made it. They told me I couldn't have more."

He nodded. And took her hand. "So when you almost lost her in the accident that killed your parents, it made her even more precious."

"Yes, exactly."

"Did she like being an only child?"

Quinn laughed. "Loved it! Spoiled like crazy." She took a bite of some of her food. "I've dedicated my life to helping kids learn because I couldn't have any more of my own."

He brought his hand up to her chin, turning her head back to face him. "Quinn, the other night . . . I wanted to tell you something."

She swallowed. "In New York? When Joan called?"

He nodded. "And thank God she did, because I was chicken too."

"What?"

He took a deep breath and said what he'd felt for some time but had been unwilling to voice. "I think I love you."

Her heart leaped, but she didn't want to misunderstand him. "I love you too," she said, "I mean, after all we've been through . . ."

"No." He made it very clear that she was not understanding. "It isn't that."

"Drew, it's okay, I understand."

"No, you don't. I came to the bedroom after that because I wanted to be with you. All night."

"Oh," she whispered, feeling completely sober.

His hand moved from her cheek down her neck to her shoulders, and rested there. He brought his other arm around her and pulled her closer to him. "We have only a few more days together," he whispered, "and we'll go back to our lives, whatever mine will be." He kissed her on the mouth, lovingly gentle at first, then with passion. "I don't want to go."

She responded with all the pent-up frustration that had been building since the first moment he stood, near naked and wet, shivering in the hot sun, only inches from her, covered with water at the rim of the pool in Arizona. She closed her fingers around the back of his head, and fell against the crocheted pillows that were piled atop the thick, feathery duvet.

Drew lowered himself to her and kissed her again. As they began to make love, she knew that it would be not only tonight, that this was the beginning of endless nights ahead of them.

They awoke the next morning to find a man standing in the doorway, staring at them with shock and embarrassment on his face. Mike had arrived earlier than Quinn had thought he would. They'd forgotten all about him. As he stared at them curled up together under the comforter, a smile creased his face. "I'll close the door," he said, reaching for the handle.

"No," Quinn said, sitting straight up. "Tell us what happened."

Mike tried to joke to break the ice. He glanced

around. "Nice suite. I mean, you two sure like comfort, don't you?"

Drew said, "Beats a federal pen."

Mike smiled. "Sam Sammons was a dead end. You were right, Drew. He doesn't even know what he did." But Mike could not go on, not talking to them together in bed like that. He politely said, "I'm gonna order up some coffee." And closed their door.

Drew kissed Quinn and they both got up. They had work to do. They dressed quickly, joining Mike in the living room, where a tray with coffee and sweets soon arrived. Mike got right down to business. "The bug we planted told us Tyler is handing over the master copy for production tomorrow. We heard him talking about it this morning."

"So we have to make the switch today."

Mike was more specific. "Tonight."

They rehearsed the entire afternoon, deciding who would do what, in what order, and tried to think of everything that could go wrong so they'd be prepared. Mike's pal, the agent who was bugging Tyler's building, reported at seven o'clock that Tyler was still hunched over his computer and that there had been no sign of Dahbura. "He's hunting for us," Quinn figured.

Mike also told them that the agent was helping locate Joe Rangel.

"How?" Drew asked. "We don't have a screen name for him, don't have a clue where he lives. It's like Sammons all over again."

"We have ways," Mike assured him. "Let him try."

At ten they put on dark clothes and awaited the call. It didn't come until near midnight. Tyler had fin-

ished, locked the master CD in the safe, and packed
it in for the day. He and his assistant just left. The
usual night crew covering the phones were the only
people still in the building.

"How does your contact know all this?" Quinn
asked, impressed.

Mike grinned. "He got himself hired in tech support."

"Man, you dudes are just too good," Drew said.

"Got the CD?" Mike asked.

Drew handed it to Quinn, who slid it inside her
jacket pocket. "Ready," she said.

"Okay, gang, off to the night shift," Mike said, and
they left.

They walked the several blocks to the offices. The
first thing they noticed was the guard standing outside the building's front door. "He's never had one
here before," Quinn assured them.

"He's scared. He's covering his ass." Mike looked
around. "I don't think my guy inside knows he's out
here." Mike told Drew to walk around the perimeter
and check for others. "Remember, we wait until
they're all out of there and then work fast."

She nodded.

Drew returned shortly. "No guards at either of the
two other doors—one in back and one on the side."

"Good. Take your positions," Mike said.

They did. And waited.

At two in the morning, one of the tech support
workers went to the bathroom. On his way back, he
hit the emergency fire alarm, breaking the glass, setting off a siren and evacuation orders from a loud-
speaker. The entire tech support crew hurried out the

front door, the exit nearest them, in minutes. While they evacuated, the FBI plant opened the emergency exit to the back of the complex, where Mike and Drew were waiting. He nodded to them, then joined the other workers out in the front parking lot.

Mike hurried down the hall toward the safe. Drew reached into his pocket and, in front of a smiling picture of his older brother receiving an award, lit a joint, then tossed it into the bottom of a paper shredder near the copying machine. Then he lit another match to make sure the paper ignited. That was so people would not think it was a false alarm. It would look like an employee trying to sneak a joint caused all hell to break loose.

When Drew joined Mike at the safe, Mike was pressing what looked like a garage-door transponder to the front of the safe. Numbers flickered on the little screen of the device. They matched the numbers Mike had already been given. "The combination has not been changed." He entered the numbers, and a click told him he had hit pay dirt.

Drew opened the second exit door just feet from the safe, allowing Quinn to enter. As Mike pulled the heavy door to the safe open and Drew searched inside it for the right CD, Quinn reached into her jacket pocket and pulled out Drew's version of the upcoming Practice Run V. When Drew was sure he had Tyler's master disc, he handed it to Mike, and Quinn handed theirs to Drew. He slipped it into the sleeve with his gloved hands, grinning from ear to ear. She put Tyler and Brandon's version in her pocket. They'd done it.

Quinn opened the door she'd come through, and

they could hear the sirens of fire engines racing toward the building. Mike closed the safe, making sure it was locked. Drew looked down the hall to see the smoke starting to billow. Then his eyes caught Mike's. They shared a satisfied nod.

A few blocks away, they took a wait-and-see position on a stoop. Spotlights lit up the sky over the Zzzyx headquarters. "Right about now they're waking Tyler up, and he's thinking the worst," Drew said.

Mike nodded. "And he'll race over, look in the safe, and feel relieved."

Quinn nodded. "And tomorrow he turns over the master to be pressed and the plants rush into production, churning out millions of copies for the Easter debut."

Drew started to chuckle. "It was almost too easy."

Mike warned him. "Don't say that. We don't know anything for sure. He could outsmart us yet."

"Besides," Quinn said, "this doesn't stop him. It only stops the kids who will buy the new game. We still have two programmed kids to go."

"The Dalai Lama arrives in D.C. today from Frankfurt, on his world tour," Mike reminded them. "And he does his prayer thing at the MCI Center tonight. But the hit could be in Singapore, his next stop."

"Joe Rangel," Drew said, "where are you?"

"Better yet," Quinn voiced, "who are you?"

Drew went through several more discs he'd taken when they left the DiForio house. On one of them he finally uncovered more information on Joe Rangel.

Nothing to lead them directly to the boy, but it did
list his former ISP as ChicagoNet, a local provider. "It
was canceled right after he became a Front Runner,"
Drew said, reading the cryptic notes. "Doesn't list a
new one." He had another thought. After a few keystrokes, he was in a ChicagoNet message area,
searching for anything having to do with the boy. A
photo popped up on the screen. "That's him, I think,"
he said. "He'd posted his photo a long time ago. A
kind of dating thing."

They studied the photo. He looked like a typical
teenager, with a Cubs baseball cap on his head,
standing in a baggy American Eagle tee shirt. He was
good-looking, with short black hair and round
cheeks. From the service provider and the cap, they
deduced that he lived in the Chicago area. First Mike
forwarded the picture to the police with a message
that the boy might be dangerous and might be trying
to attack the Dalai Lama. Then they got a map of the
locales that ChicagoNet served and started calling
every Rangel within the lines.

After a number of strikeouts, Quinn talked to a
woman in Gurnee, Illinois, who said no, her son
Joseph was not available to speak to her. When
Quinn asked if he was a teenager, the woman got
suspicious, but admitted that he was now seventeen.
When Quinn asked if the boy might have any inter-
est in the Dalai Lama, the woman was perplexed.
"How would you know that? Who is this?"

Quinn explained that she worked with the FBI and
that learning Joseph's whereabouts was vitally important to his well-being. The woman admitted that
Joe had dropped out of high school the previous year

to run off to become a Buddhist monk. "We struck oil," Quinn whispered to Mike and Drew.

"First it was the apples and the incense," the upset mother said, sounding happy that someone wanted to listen, "which Frank and I didn't worry much about at the time, but then it was the robes, shaving his head. It was terrible." Mike looked at the photo of the boy and tried to imagine him without any hair. "Finally, he left us a note that we have never understood, about love and beauty and peace and devotion. We raised Joe a good Italian Catholic. We just don't know how this happened." He'd contacted them once from Bangkok, she added, but she had no idea where he currently was.

Mike checked with the INS. Joseph Rangel had returned to the United States from Thailand in December. Mike asked them to monitor him to prevent him getting on a plane to Singapore. Then he took off to see if he could locate Joe by interviewing other monks in the area. In the meantime, Quinn contacted the public relations firm that worked for the Dalai Lama, forwarding the photo and trying to learn if the former Joseph Rangel, with whatever his monk name now was, was anywhere within striking distance of the Dalai Lama. She alerted them to the danger. They took it seriously, perhaps because of the attempt on the Archbishop of Canterbury.

Mike returned late that afternoon, exasperated. "We looked at every Caucasian guy with a shaved head wearing Far Eastern garb in D.C., Virginia, and Maryland. Nothing. And none of them, or any of the monks, had ever seen the person in the picture."

"What time's the rally?" Quinn asked.

"Eight. We've got to be there by seven."

Drew, who'd been quiet, perked up. "You said Caucasian."

"Huh?" Mike responded. "Yeah. The kid's Italian. You saw the picture."

"We sure?"

Mike blinked. He looked at Quinn.

"I mean," Drew explained, "is that photo really him? Internet dating is full of liars."

Mike blinked. "He's just a kid. Why would he do that?"

Drew shrugged, trying to find a reason. "Maybe he didn't like how he looked and thought the baseball cap dude was better."

"Wait a minute," Quinn said, realization dawning on her. "Wait a minute. His mother only said they raised him Italian Catholic. We never showed her this picture. Drew could be right." She grabbed the phone. When she reached Mrs. Rangel again, she put the question bluntly. "What does your son look like?"

"Look like?" The woman paused. "He's got an earring in his nose and runs around in a purple dress."

Quinn picked up the photo they'd printed out. "I mean features. Is he ethnic-looking?"

"Yes, but he's quite handsome," the woman said with a tinge of pride. "Big, round dark eyes—he gets that from me. But he has his father's nose and chin."

"What nationality are you?"

"Tony is Sicilian."

"Yes. And you?"

"I'm Korean."

*   *   *

Backstage at the MCI Center, the Dalai Lama sat on comfortable pillows with twenty-four of his closest followers. They were chatting before beginning a half hour of meditation, to be followed by the rally. As it came time to meditate, the Dalai Lama raised his hands and asked his monks to light the candles.

Several monks took up positions on the pillows. Three young men began to light candles surrounding the altar, and the Dalai Lama took a position near them. He straightened his back, brought his hands together, and began to breathe deeply.

At that moment the door on the far side of the room opened. Few monks looked up because they assumed it was more of the staff who had been serving them. But the faces that appeared—Mike's, Drew's, Quinn's, and those of several security guards—startled several of the robed men. And shocked one.

One of the monks, a boy of mixed blood with distinctive Asian features, did what he had been programmed to do. With the long match that he was using to light candles, he merely moved it to the side of the great spiritual leader and set his robe on fire. Before anyone even realized what he was doing, he had done the same to himself.

The peaceful room filled with pacifists became a free-for-all. But there was only one objective: Save the Dalai Lama. Three monks close to him sprang into action the moment they saw his garment start to burn. One flung his body on the flames, trying to smother them. Another grabbed the thick, large pillow that he'd been perched on and immediately pressed it to the fire. The other grabbed a water pitcher and doused the flames spreading beyond the pillow. As Quinn, Drew, and Mike raced across the room to get to Joe Rangel, two others closer to him tried also to smother his flames, but he erupted as if he had been soaked in gasoline. Later, an autopsy would reveal that he had smeared himself with yak butter, which ensured that the slightest spark would turn him into an inferno, much the way ghee did for funeral pyres. There was no saving the boy who had been programmed to become a monk in order to kill one of the most revered religious figures in the world.

At the back of the vast MCI Center, near the doors, Tyler Bryant stood waiting. Not wanting anyone to recognize him—if they did, he planned to say he had always been a fan of the Dalai Lama because of his interest in peace—he wore a trench coat and dark glasses. He refused to go to his assigned seat, preferring instead to stand behind the last row of seats. He knew he'd want to make a fast exit once they announced that there would be no rally. When it became time for the rally to begin, and yet the revered spiritual leader did not appear, Tyler felt a wave of power roll over him. He stood there, rocking on the balls of his feet, anticipating the announcement that the Dalai Lama was dead.

A different announcement came as the rally was scheduled to start. A man in a suit walked onto the stage. "Ladies and gentlemen, we apologize for keeping you waiting. We have had a tragedy backstage, a fire."

As people began to murmur, Tyler felt a surge of excitement.

"But," the man continued, "please, there is no reason to be alarmed, you are in no danger. The Dalai Lama, with his deep love for humanity, forgives those who wish to harm others, even himself. Now, please, welcome His Holiness, the Dalai Lama of Tibet."

As the Dalai Lama appeared on the MCI stage, smiling benevolently at all who had come, Tyler Bryant cursed under his breath. What the hell had happened?

He turned and hurried for the nearest door. An usher looked at him oddly, for it was a strange time to depart, just as the Dalai Lama was starting to speak. But Tyler had to run. They knew he was here. And now that they had somehow saved the Dalai Lama, they would be after him.

Once outside, Tyler glanced in either direction. Feeling safe, he bolted toward the parking lot a block away where he'd left his car. Halfway there, he had the sensation that someone was following him. When he suddenly stopped and whirled around, he saw that he was being paranoid. There was no one behind him.

He continued along a dark red brick wall on his right, parallel with a line of parked cars on his left. When he reached the area of the lot where he was parked, he cut between two cars, toward the attendants' shack. Out of nowhere, Drew grabbed him by the collar. He'd been following him on the other side of the line of cars, waiting for the moment to strike. "You sick fucking bastard." Drew growled, pushing Tyler up against the side of a Jeep Cherokee.

Tyler looked into his brother's face as he felt his hand clenching his throat. In a lunge he brought his leg up hard, trying to kick Drew in the balls, but Drew deflected the move—he'd learned from fights in prison—and spun Tyler around to smash his body up against the vehicle, twisting his arm behind his back. The violent slam set off the car's alarm.

Drew knew people seldom paid attention to car alarms anymore, but a quick glance toward the attendants' shack told him one of the car parkers was looking in their direction.

"It's over," Drew said to his brother. "You're not going to succeed."

"You're too late," Tyler shouted.

Drew had already punched his cell phone with his other hand. "Mike," he said toward it, still keeping Tyler pinned with his powerful arms, "I've got him. I'm in the lot around the east corner. Get over here and pick us up."

Tyler made a move, ducking down, pulling away, but Drew tackled him, bringing him to the ground.

Then Tyler realized how the situation would seem to others. He screamed, "Help! Help me! Over here!" He knew he had the law on his side. Drew was a wanted man. Getting cops there would be the best thing that could happen. "You were always a fool," he hissed at his brother.

Drew made a fist and slammed Tyler's jaw so hard that his head snapped back. But there was nothing more he could do, for he heard the footsteps of the parking lot attendants rushing toward them. "Get the police, call the cops!" Tyler yelled from his bloody mouth, grasping Drew's shirt tightly, hoping to hold him there.

"Hey, man, chill," one of the two young men told Drew, grabbing his shoulder, trying to pull him away.

The other one started shouting for the police.

Drew jumped up, wrenching his shirt from Tyler's hand. In a whirling move he slammed the guy who was trying to hold him into the Cherokee, cracking his head against the window glass. The attendant collapsed. When Drew eyed the other one, the young man's face was a mask of fear. "Hey, dude, it's okay, man . . ."

Drew took off.

At the corner, he saw the rented van rounding the block and he leaped into the street. Quinn slid open the door even before they'd stopped, and he jumped in. As they drove by, Mike saw two police officers running toward a man who was holding his bloody chin.

Mike gunned it and disappeared into traffic.

Chapter Twenty-three

Mike returned to the Rockville hotel suite at four in the morning, after several hours of trying to track Tyler down, to no avail. He shocked Quinn and Drew, however, when he told them where he had just been. Frustrated and sick of hiding, he'd boldly gone to the Virginia home of Dahbura's superior at the FBI, awakening him in the middle of the night. "I had to risk it. I had to show him I'm very much alive and that I had nothing to do with Patrick Horgan's death."

Quinn hopefully said, "He must have believed you. I mean, you're here."

Mike didn't look so sure. "He's skeptical. But I think I made a good case for myself. The guy has never been a Dahbura fan either."

Drew ordered, "Details."

Mike had explained what Practice Run did to kids when they played it. He told the superior about the uprising that the new game, due to be released in less than one week's time, was supposed to generate. But he assured him that they had stopped that development, thanks to switching the master CD. "I made it clear that the best thing to happen is for the new version of the game to hit the market next Sunday. I also told him Tyler got away, and that the important thing now is to stop an attempt on the life of the Pope. He wasn't very happy when I told him we do not know the identity of the potential assassin. Or really even if there is one."

"Are they issuing a warrant to arrest Tyler?" Quinn asked.

Mike shook his head. "Even though he took me seriously, he wants to investigate on his own. He's bringing Dahbura in for questioning."

"If he can find him," Drew remarked.

Quinn nodded. "He and Tyler won't surface until Easter."

Drew said, "In Rome."

Mike nodded. "Tyler was present at the last two attempts. He won't miss this one."

"That's if he programmed PR01," Quinn reminded them.

"My superior promised he'd alert the Vatican," Mike said. "Just in case."

Quinn looked frustrated. "We can't take the chance that he hasn't been able to program the final assassin. We have to be in Rome to try to stop him."

Mike said, "I'm going on ahead to see what I can do."

"I can't travel by plane," Drew reminded them. "I don't have a passport."

Mike grabbed his phone. In one fast call, he'd ordered one for Drew.

"Who was that?" Drew asked, astonished.

Mike winked. "I have lots of contacts. You'll have it tomorrow."

"I want to stop in Ireland first," Quinn said. "I need to see my daughter."

Mike nodded. "We have a few days yet. Plus, you should remove yourself from the line of fire. You too, Drew. Dahbura is capable of anything."

Drew nodded solemnly. "It's going to be even worse after Easter. When Tyler realizes that the new version does absolutely nothing, he's going to kill us all."

Quinn showed a hard smile. "That's why we have to get Tyler first."

Drew handed Quinn her cell phone from the table. "In the meantime, call your daughter. Tell her we're coming."

In the very private NetJet lounge at BWI, Tyler Bryant listened to Dahbura's frightened rant. "They're on to me. Someone high up in the Bureau listened to Furnari. I got a tip that they're looking for me. I'm going with you."

"Not without leaving two dead bodies behind," Tyler growled.

"Ty, I'm on your plane. All we gotta do is stay low till Easter. We're risking too much here."

"I want them dead," Tyler said flatly. "Can you accomplish that while in Europe?"

Dahbura nodded. "I promise you, the minute we're in the sky. There's a guy I know who can do it."

"Then order it."

"I gotta ask, why the change of heart?"

Tyler shouted in his face. "You fucking moron.

They've stopped the last two attempts. Two of the most powerful religious leaders of our time are breathing because of them. They'll save the Pope too if we don't stop them first."

David nodded his head. "You're right. I just wish you'd have let me take them out sooner."

Tyler laughed. "Sooner? *Sooner?* You were ordered to pull Drew out of that prison and shoot him. But you let him get away. Mike Furnari's dead, you assured me. Like hell. You botched them all."

"Calm down, Tyler."

Tyler grabbed Dahbura by the neck and pressed him to the wall. "Don't you tell me to calm down. Make the call. Now. Tell me it's done or don't get on this plane with me. I swear, David, I'll send you back to the Bureau in a goddamned coffin."

David pulled away, nodded, and shakily pulled out his cell phone.

A messenger delivered Drew's shiny new passport just as they were loading the van for the airport. The flight to Shannon from Dulles was at five. Quinn checked out at the hotel desk, then went back to help Drew with the last of their things.

Down in the hotel's back parking lot, Drew started the van as Quinn set her suitcase inside the back doors. "Did you bring water?" she asked.

"In my bag," he said, jumping out as she rounded the van to the passenger side and opened the door. Drew pulled a bottle from his backpack and handed it to her, then closed the back door. He was about to step into the vehicle again just as Quinn twisted the top of the water bottle outside the passenger door.

Suddenly it exploded in her hand.

"Down!" Drew shouted.

She hit the pavement, crying out in pain as she badly scraped the heels of her palms. She could see Drew under the van, on the other side.

"Where did it come from?" he asked.

She didn't know. "Drew!" she said, frightened to death.

"I've got the gun," he assured her. He reached up to the floor of the van. "It's here, under the seat." His fingers found it.

"What do we do?"

"I'm going to give them something to shoot at. When I do, I want you to jump inside and stay on the floor. Just flatten down, pull the door shut. Hear me?"

"Yes," she assured him.

He reached up and pulled his jacket from the space behind the front seat. Bunching it up, he started to rise, holding it high above his head. A shot rang out the moment it cleared the door, blowing the lining apart. Quinn cried in fear, but then saw that he was all right. "It came from in front of us," he told her, "about two aisles over, probably from another van or SUV."

"A Suburban." She shivered. "What are we going to do?"

He knew he couldn't get off a shot. But there was an alternative. "Drive out of here."

"How?" she asked, astonished.

There was no time to explain. "Crawl into the car," he ordered. "Now."

She did as told, soaking wet from the water that

had splashed all over her. She curled up in a ball on the passenger's-side floor.

"Pull the door closed."

She managed it. "Drew, be careful."

He looked under the cars ahead of him. He could see a man's thick legs, in a kneeling position, a clip at his bent knee. He knew precisely where it was coming from now. If only he could get into the van and back up, they had a chance. But the man had a perfect view of the van's windows. Could Drew drive from the floor, with one hand reaching up and the other on the pedals? Without being able to see?

He crawled inside. "This is the only thing I can think of," he told Quinn.

"What?"

"You'll see." He pulled the door closed. Then he gripped the steering wheel with his right fist, calculating just how long they would have to back up before he had to turn the wheel. "Quinn, put the van in reverse."

"What?"

"The gearshift. Slam it in reverse. Now."

With wide eyes, she did so.

He pressed the accelerator with his knee and the van jerked backward violently. A bullet blew through the windshield just above Quinn's eye level. "My God!" she shouted.

He pressed the gas again and twisted the wheel. The van careened violently to the left. They scraped around the back corner of the vehicle parked next to them. Drew risked a peek. They were out of the parking space—that was all he needed to know. "Quinn, put it in drive."

"Yes," she said, and pulled the gearshift into the D position.

"I hope to hell nobody's out walking." He sank his knee onto the gas pedal again and the van's wheels burned rubber. Two shots rang out, sending window glass flying everywhere. The van scraped the front of another car and both Drew and Quinn jerked forward. He leaned up just in time to see their assailant jump madly to one side to avoid being run over. In another second, they smashed into a black Suburban. Drew instantly slid up into the driver's seat. Wrenching the gearshift into reverse, he backed away from the vehicle. Spinning in a tight turn, he put the van into drive, aiming for an opening that led to the street.

They bounced over the verge of grass and down the curb and hit the street as a hail of bullets sang past them. Pedestrians had taken cover, cars had stopped, and in the rearview mirror Drew could see a burly man in black with a hood obscuring his face, a rifle in his hand.

They turned onto Rockville Pike and roared toward the airport.

Chapter Twenty-four

Joanie ran down the gravel drive, flapping her arms, looking overjoyed. Mother and daughter embraced so tightly that Susan feared she'd have to pry them apart. Hugs were exchanged all around as everyone was introduced to whomever they didn't know. James immediately took to Drew, told him to come see the "secret" creek he had found, so Drew took off before he even got to see the inside of the cottage. "Bring their bags inside," Susan told Joan and Stephanie, "and I'll put up a pot of tea."

"You have room?" Quinn queried.

"We moved into the barn," Joanie explained to her mother, pointing to the structure just down the path.

"It's been converted into another guest house. No one's rented it, so the Garveys let us use it. They're joining us for dinner. You'll love them."

"You've talked about them so often, I feel like I know them."

"Mom," Joanie said as she helped Quinn pull the bags from the trunk of the car, "it's over, isn't it? I mean, you stopped him, didn't you?"

"Almost, honey," Quinn said, kissing her on the forehead. "On Sunday it will hopefully be over."

"Come on," Susan urged, "we'll have tea and some wonderful biscuits I get in town, and then you can tell us the whole story of what happened."

Quinn and Drew related the entire story over dinner in the ancient cottage. They gathered around an oval table that, with the leaves in it, almost filled the room. They brought a couple of extra chairs from the upstairs bedrooms to accommodate everyone, and over bacon-encrusted chicken, squash, a fresh market salad, and peppery French wine, Quinn and Drew took turns telling what happened. Tom Garvey and his wife Jane sat rapt with attention. James was hearing the truth for the first time. He was shocked that Tyler had been the person responsible for the death of his beloved father. He stopped eating for a while until Susan kissed him and promised him that there would be justice, and soon.

When they dug into an apple pie that Jane had baked that afternoon, Drew finished the story with the shoot-out in the parking lot in Rockville. "I was going to leave the gun behind in the hotel. I mean, I couldn't take it into the airport. But something told me to take it in the van."

"But the loose ends," Susan said. "The last person? The Pope?"

Quinn shivered. "We never found a name to attach to the password PR01. We hope no one was ever programmed. But if Mike calls and says Tyler is in Rome, then we can assume he's done it."

"But," Susan said hopefully, "the Pope has massive security."

Quinn nodded. "We'll have to count on that."

When the Garveys had left and James went to the computer for a half hour—"One half hour only, you understand me?" Susan had barked—the rest of them gathered in the living room, relaxing around the remaining embers of the fire. "So, Mom," Joanie said, "you've done all you can. It sounds like it's pretty much under control now."

Quinn didn't seem assured. "You're forgetting one thing."

"What?"

"Tyler," Quinn said. "He won't rest until he gets me. And Drew. Right now he might be trying to track us down."

In a top-floor apartment with peeling walls and a view of the Sistine Chapel out the bathroom window, David Dahbura lay naked with a boy he'd cruised on a motor scooter earlier in the Piazza della Rotunda. They had made eye contact, the kid spun around a few times, gunning the engine in a playful, macho way, and Dahbura had simply jumped on. Once they were careening down a street, David wrapped his arms around the boy's waist, and then let his hands fall lower. Knowing Tyler was out, David took him to the apartment, where they made love for a very long time.

Dahbura was sipping a can of Fanta soda and the boy was smoking a cigarette in bed next to him when Tyler burst into the room. The boy assumed, from the look on Tyler's face, that the men were lovers and

Dahbura had just been caught cheating on the en-
raged boyfriend. The Italian boy, having had some
experience in these matters, simply turned away,
pulling the sheet up over his chest, waiting for the
fight to die down.

Tyler shouted, "You fucking asshole. They're alive.
They got away."

"Come on, Ty, this is hardly the time for a—"

Tyler took three steps toward the bed. And pulled
a gun, equipped with a silencer.

"Ty, hey, man, what are you thinking?"

"I'm thinking that you are completely incompe-
tent. I'm thinking that I was a fool to entrust my
plans to you. I'm thinking that I'm a man of my
word, and I warned you that I'd fucking kill you if
you didn't get rid of Drew and Quinn."

"The guy I hired is the best," Dahbura protested.
"He's a crack shot."

"He got arrested trying to flee. Eyewitnesses saw
him shooting at the van. He said he was hired by
you. And that's going to lead to me."

Dahbura watched the gun, not Tyler's angry face.
It was pointed toward his heart. He slid backward
against the headboard. "Tyler, put the gun down.
Come on, Ty, we can talk about this."

Tyler lunged forward and pressed the gun to Dahbura's forehead. The FBI agent screamed in terror.

The gigolo, realizing this was more than just a
quarrel, turned toward them in sheer terror. At the
sight of the gun so close, he jumped out of bed, his
breathing coming in spurts. He put one hand out as
if to protect himself, but the gesture didn't save him.
Tyler shot him through the chest.

Dahbura gasped as blood burst from the smooth tanned chest. The ochre wall behind the young man erupted with red, and he crumpled to the floor, lifeless. "Tyler," Dahbura whispered in shock, "you're mad. You *are* crazy. Tyler, please . . ."

Tyler pulled the trigger, and the gun fired with a muffled burp. The second bullet created a small hole in Dahbura's forehead, then spattered bits of brain and blood all over the headboard and the wall behind it.

Oblivious to the carnage he had created, Tyler sat down at his laptop and connected, anxious to see if PR01 was on-line yet.

In Dingle, the days of Holy Week passed quickly. Mike called several times to tell Quinn and Drew that there had been no sign of or news about Tyler, but that the Vatican had taken their warnings seriously. He was not sure they needed to come. So they held the decision for the last minute. On Good Friday, it rained when they attended services, and they lit candles later when the electricity went out in the cottage. When it came back on that evening, CNN showed a snippet of the Practice Run V hysteria as kids were already lining up at stores—there were shots of delivery trucks bringing in boxes of the games by the ton.

Another TV story focused on preparations at the Vatican for the celebration of Easter. Drew, Quinn, Susan, and Stephanie played cards near the fireplace, while Joanie checked her E-mail. Long about midnight, Stephanie called to her pal. "Joan, let's get going. I'm tired."

"Sure, okay," the vacant voice said from the little computer pantry.

Susan rolled her eyes. "Man, they all sound the same when they're in front of a screen, don't they? I think computers should be banned from the face of the earth."

Quinn stood up, ready for bed. "You'd be out of a job."

Susan smiled. "Oh yeah, forgot. Good night."

Quinn popped into the pantry and kissed her daughter on the cheek. "See you in the morning, honey."

"Mom, are you going to Rome tomorrow?"

Quinn wasn't sure. "I need to discuss it with Drew tonight. I hope not."

Once the girls had gone across the wet yard to the barn, Quinn and Drew climbed the stairs to their room. She had to steady herself on the rickety wooden planks. "You okay?" Drew asked in alarm.

"Too much Irish whiskey."

He put an arm around her, led her to the bedroom they had been sharing, and sat with her on the edge of the bed. "I love your daughter. And man, James is like my new little bro. You've given me a family, Quinn. For a guy who's been behind bars, that's pretty cool, you know?"

"They adore you." She knew she was going to say her next thought, but she couldn't look at him as she did. She turned toward the rain-spattered window. "As I do." She looked into his eyes. "I have something I need to say to you. I know I said it once, but it was in a different context. I said it almost jokingly."

"Yes?"

"I said I loved you."

"Yes?"

"But I do. I do, Drew."

He wrapped her in his arms. "Quinn, you said you thought you'd never find love again after Rich. You thought you had with Tyler. But I want you to know . . . I'm not very good at saying stuff like this. But I'm trying to tell you that you've found it again here, with me. I will love you forever. I know this. I have never said this to anyone in my life, never felt this way about anyone."

Tears welled up in her eyes. He smiled and pulled her to him, and then he got emotional as well and they ended up laughing and kissing and tumbling and snuggling in the bed. In their joy, they never discussed whether or not they were going to go to Rome for sure in the morning.

On Holy Saturday, a dank and drizzling day, Quinn woke to find she had overslept. When she descended the stairs, she heard voices. In the kitchen, Susan was baking James' favorite Easter cupcakes, a Horgan tradition. Drew was frosting them and adding jelly beans to create little bunny faces. Susan handed her a brimming mug of dark coffee. "The girls up yet?"

"No sign of them." Susan looked out the window. "Oh, their car's not there. They must have gone into town." She pulled another batch of cakes from the old stove with a thick mitt on her hand.

"Joanie didn't even get coffee first?" Quinn asked. "That's a first."

"Where's my buddy?" Drew asked Susan.

She shrugged. "Where do you think?" Obviously,

James was on the computer in the next room. "They're made for each other, huh?" Susan said to Quinn.

Just then James burst into the room. "Morning," Quinn greeted him. He ignored her, which wasn't his style at all. "Mom," he said in a gruff voice, "I don't understand."

"Understand what?" She saw his face turning red with anger. "James, what is it?"

"You won't let *me* play it! You yell at me and scream about it for months, and then you tell all that stuff about him and still it's there."

"What?"

"And I know Drew didn't put it there 'cause he hasn't touched the computer."

"What are you talking about?" Susan asked, bewildered.

James grew more irate. "Being a hypocrite is a bad thing, Mom."

"James! Stop it!"

"No, wait," Quinn said, setting down her coffee, grabbing James' shoulders. "What is there? What are you talking about?"

"Wanna see it?" James snapped. "Wanna see I'm right?" He ran back to the pantry, and they followed. "Look!"

They did. At the computer screen.

Practice Run blared at them in bright bold letters.

Chapter Twenty-five

"Where did it come from?" Susan exclaimed. "James, it can't be on this computer, it just can't!"

"Drew," Quinn questioned in panic, "you didn't install this, did you?"

He was as mystified as they were. "You know I didn't." He peered at the screen more closely, hit a few keys. The hairs on the back of his neck stood up. "It's not the regular game. Look." They saw the image of a basilica, a square that was obviously a virtual version of St. Peter's. "It's a Front Runner game. A Front Runner was playing it."

"My God," Quinn gasped. Sure enough, YOU ARE A FRONT RUNNER was flashing on the screen over the image of St. Peter's. "Joanie!" She headed for the door.

"Wait," Susan yelled, "you can't go out there. It's muddy, you're barefoot. Let me." She dashed outside.

Drew sat at the computer. "I want to see what this is all about," he murmured, starting to dig into the program.

Quinn watched at the window for a few minutes, waiting for Susan to emerge from the barn. Soon, Susan rushed from the barn, and Quinn opened the door, grabbing the piece of paper in her hand before Susan could even explain. She read Joanie's handwriting out loud:

Mom, got up early. Didn't want to wake you. I guess you are not going to Rome. When I told Steph, she said that there's no better city to spend Easter than Rome, so that's where we went. I'll call you in a few days. You guys have fun. Happy Bunny Day! XX J

Quinn crumpled the note in her fist. "Rome. The Pope. It's her."

"No," Susan warned, seeing where Quinn's thoughts were going, "it can't be. Don't even think it. It's too awful."

"What part of this hasn't been awful?" Quinn reminded her.

Drew called them to the pantry. "Hey, come here."

They looked at the screen but saw only computer code. "Tell me," Quinn ordered.

"Well," he said, his fears building, "she's been playing the game, or maybe it was Stephanie."

"Or both," Susan added. "They've both used it this week."

"They could have shared the Front Runner password," Drew exclaimed. "They both could be PR01. They downloaded final instructions."

"When?" Quinn asked. "Can you tell?"

He hit a few keys. The screen flickered, showed him some more numbers and times. "Last night."

"Oh, Jesus," Susan gasped, bringing her hand to her mouth.

Quinn muffled a scream. "No wonder we never had a name. Joan and Stephanie are the final killers."

"And they left for Rome this morning," Susan added.

Drew brought up a travel Web site that the computer had stored in recent memory. "Yup. They booked tickets on RyanAir at 5:00 A.M." He checked his watch. "They're in Italy already."

"A hotel?" Quinn asked, trying to jump ahead.

Drew checked. "No. At least, they didn't book one through this site."

Quinn closed her eyes as the pain and horror flowed through her entire body. "It's my own daughter. Joanie is the last assassin."

They arrived at Fiumicino late that evening. Taking a taxi into the heart of the city, Quinn wished she were anywhere but here. Rome was a city she had visited several times in her life, a city she loved, filled with life and gusto and passion. Now it seemed dark and forbidding and dangerous. Where, in this sea of celebratory humanity, would she find her daughter? And would she find her in time? All day long, Quinn had dialed Joanie's cell phone, Stephanie's as well, but neither of them ever answered.

They'd called Mike before they left the cottage in Dingle, and he'd called them back when they were changing planes in Dublin, assuring them that Joanie's picture had been sent to every police station in Rome. Stephanie's parents, shocked at the news, had faxed one of their daughter as well. Everyone was on the lookout for the two girls. Meanwhile, the Vatican took the threat seriously, but not as seriously as Quinn, Drew, and Mike did. They issued the usual statement that the Vatican looked into all potential threats against the Holy Father and would take this under consideration.

They checked into the Hotel Ponte Sisto, a place Drew had found on-line. It was steps from the Tiber River and Trastevere, putting them within walking distance of St. Peter's. A thought occurred to Quinn in the tiny hotel elevator. "I know when he did it! When she left for Europe. He must have given her her special game as a going-away gift. She had told me she hadn't played it in college, but she was programmed to lie. That's why she quit school in the first place."

They arrived at their floor, moved down the hall to their room. "Stephanie too."

The hotel room was comfortable and cozy, but they didn't even notice. They called Mike, who was staying close by. He told them to meet him on the street for dinner in a small outdoor trattoria.

Quinn couldn't stop talking about her daughter. "When Joanie was seven, she was asleep in the backseat of my parents' car when they were both killed by a drunk driver. It might be what saved her." She gained some strength from the memory and gave them a wan smile. "I didn't lose her then. I won't lose her now."

They slept only fitfully, until the Easter morning sun, beating in through the French doors that opened to a tiny balcony, woke them.

*   *   *

After espresso and rolls in the hotel's breakfast room, they met Mike on the street. He had been out "running the fears off," he told them, dressed in shorts and a tank top. But he assured them he had good news. They looked hopeful, but he shook his head. "It's good news of another sort. David Dahbura is dead."

Quinn blinked. "What?"

Drew said, "There is a God."

"Shot through the head. Police called me, found him along with some Italian boy, also shot to death, in an apartment that David and another man had rented last week."

"Tyler," Drew said.

Mike agreed. "Tyler shot him."

"Because he didn't get us?" Quinn asked.

Mike shrugged. "Now, listen, about today. There is virtually nothing you can do but search the crowd for the girls." He said he was going to be in St. Peter's, at the front of the church, near the Pope, along with other security guards. He was going to be watching for any sudden move, anything suspicious. "Good luck."

Quinn and Drew wished him the same. "Keep in touch by cell," Mike said, and left. When he disappeared into the crowd, they seemed to be the only two miserable people among a population that was giddy with happiness. Everywhere people were wearing bright pastel colors, and dancing was already starting in the piazzas. Yet all of that seemed a blur as she scanned every face on every street in the hopes of discovering her daughter.

The day's High Mass was scheduled for noon. Already, at nine in the morning, St. Peter's Square was filled with people. They could barely move. Priests in flowing cassocks, nuns in robes, children in Easter finery, men in suits, women with fabulous hats, all celebrating Christ's resurrection. But where was Joanie?

"What shall we do?" Drew asked.

"Get in line for the service," she suggested. "If we don't do that now, we won't get in."

"I read in the paper at the hotel that there's a parade after the Mass. The Pope greets people out here."

She looked overwhelmed. "Where will she try it? Inside? Or out here? And how? We have no clue."

"Come on," he said, pulling her hand, "over there. Let's join the queue."

They stood in line for nearly an hour, scanning the faces of every woman who passed. Mike called them to say he was inside the basilica. He was keeping his eyes open. And praying.

Then, suddenly, just as Drew hung up, Quinn grabbed Drew's arm, digging her fingers into him.

"What?" he asked, alarmed.

"There—" She was looking toward the huge marble columns outside the church.

"You saw her?"

"Tyler."

"What?"

She stared in the direction where she'd seen the face. She was frozen, glaring. Then, again, "It's him!"

Drew looked, but couldn't find anyone that looked like his brother.

"He went around that column."

Drew asked the people behind them if they would save their place. They didn't seem to understand English, but some others translated for them, assuring them their place in line was secure. He pulled Quinn with him, toward the columns. "You saw Tyler?"

"I swear, I swear." They pushed their way through a crush of people, mainly families who seemed to be celebrating, wishing each other a happy Easter, and all mentioning "Papa." "He was over here, went around this column."

They rounded it, only to come upon a group of priests smoking cigarettes. Several turned to them as they suddenly stopped, smiling, greeting them. "Sorry," Drew said. He checked. All priests, all in black cassocks. He whispered to Quinn, "You might have been wrong."

"No," she said, "I know what I saw."

"I believe you."

"No, you don't. But that's all right."

They went back to the line. As the surrounding people began to introduce themselves to the Americans and ask why they had come—"Oh, she wanted to be in Roma again on Easter," Drew happily responded—he started hitting the phone numbers for Joanie and Stephanie, again and again, in the hope that one might suddenly answer.

After calling once and hanging up and then calling back again immediately, a stupid trick he hoped might work, Stephanie's phone picked up. She merely said, "I'm all set, don't worry. I'm on the scaffolding. I have a clear shot. If you don't get to take yours, I will. You ready?" She waited for a response.

Drew cupped the phone, grabbed Quinn, and ordered her to whisper yes. "Yes," she said very softly, not knowing why.

"Good. You in the basilica yet?"

He cupped the phone again. "Whisper no," Drew ordered.

"No."

Stephanie, who thought Joan's mother's voice was Joan's, said, "Can you see me, then? Look up."

Drew did. He scanned St. Peter's Square for scaffolding. There was none. What had she meant? Then he found himself looking at a huge metal structure that held TV cameras. Yes, that had to be it. And then he saw her. She wasn't far from them, perhaps forty feet away, up on a perch wearing some kind of press badge. Tyler had thought of everything.

"See me?" the girl asked again.

Drew nodded yes to Quinn, who voiced it into the phone. This time Quinn didn't give the phone back to Drew. She held it to her ear. "Good luck," Stephanie said. "Sing alleluia loud and clear! I love you." She hung up.

"That was Steph!" Quinn gasped, her heart racing. "Drew, why both of them? Why two of them?"

He guessed. "One must be covering the other."

The doors to the basilica were opening. As one, the mass of humanity began moving forward. "Go," Drew said. "Joan is going to be inside somewhere. I know where Stephanie is. I'm going to stop her, but I can't do both."

"Don't get yourself killed," Quinn begged, not willing to let go of his arm.

"Quinn, try Joanie's cell phone. She might think it's Stephanie calling her back. Ring once and call back. It's worth a shot." He kissed her cheek and disappeared into the crowd.

The basilica echoed with chanting, but all Quinn heard was the shuffle of feet as people from all corners of the globe found places for the Easter Sunday High Mass. When she found a spot in a pew closer to the altar than she had expected to get, she dialed her daughter. Despite the fact that people gave her disapproving looks for using her phone in the church, she rang once, as Drew had done when he called Stephanie, and then called back.

"It's me," Joan Roberts whispered.

Quinn braced herself. "It's your mother. Don't hang up, Joanie, please." Quinn held her breath. The connection did not die. "Joanie, I know what you're about to try to do. And I know it's not your fault. Darling, please, don't! Please, tell me where you are. I can still save you from what you aren't capable of pulling back from."

"I'm in Rome, Mom."

"I'm in St. Peter's as well. I'm right next to you."

Alarm. "What?"

"Honey, you'll never succeed. It's hopeless. Only you are going to die," Quinn said, though she didn't really believe it. She feared her daughter would kill the Pope and the Swiss Guard would kill her. "Show me where you are, and I'll help you. Please, baby."

"Crying won't help now," Joanie said coldly. "It's too late."

"No. You know the new game will destroy everything Tyler has started. We told you that Friday night. He's finished, his evil is over, but he's going to let you and Stephanie die for his demented cause. Darling, please, don't do it! Please, Joanie, I love you. Don't do this!"

"Mom—"

That single word was all Quinn needed to hear. She heard her little girl in that moment. In that gasp, she heard the person that no Tyler Bryant and no game or brainwashing or hypnotism could reach. She heard her daughter, not a robot. "Joan, please, you don't want to do this. I know, you've been instructed to do it." Quinn waited for a response. Nothing. But the connection was still open. She went for it, trying to appeal to that place in her daughter's heart where reason and goodness lived. "Joanie, I love you. I love you more than life itself. You can't do this to yourself. You can't do this to the Holy Father. You can't do this to *me*."

The phone went dead.

People around Quinn reached out to keep her from collapsing. Although she remained upright, she was overcome with tears.

A bell summoned everyone. Processional music began. Papa, as the Italians lovingly called the Holy Father, would be making his entrance. The choir rose above the organ singing, "Alleluia, alleluia!"

And Quinn remembered what she'd heard Stephanie say. *Sing Alleluia loud and clear!*

Stephanie Korodi heard the announcement alerting the media that the service was beginning. It would be followed by a procession in the square, with a blessing of all the gathered faithful by the Pope.

"You're with the German network?" a long-haired technician asked her.

She first answered in German, but realizing that he had no clue as to what she was saying, she said, "Reporter."

The thirty-something guy flashed a grin. "Hire them young there, huh? I'm from Toronto."

She smiled demurely. She knew he was trying to hit on her. "Catholic?"

"Nope. You?"

"No. But I like all this."

"Pomp and circumstance, yeah," the guy said. "Want to go for a drink later? Always wanted to see Germany. Through your eyes."

"Perhaps," she said with a sexy wink.

The outside speakers were blaring the organ music and voices of the choir singing inside the basilica. "Alleluia," the boy joked. Then he turned to someone else who had just reached the platform on the scaffolding. "Hey, dude, what's up?" he said, shielding his eyes from the sun.

"Stephanie?"

She whirled about. She knew that voice.

"Stephanie, it's no use. We're on to you." Drew stood with his arms out to her. "Just come on down with me and everything will be all right."

"Man," the technician from Toronto said to Drew, "you got a press badge? You supposed to be up here?"

"Fuck off," Drew told him. "Stephanie, it's over."

Her eyes defiantly flashed back at his.

"Steph, come down with me."

"Man, what's going on here?" the technician said. "I think you should explain what the hell you're—"

Stephanie fell to her knees. She reached under the dark blue bunting covering the railing and felt the rifle, just where she had been told it would be waiting. She gave it a yank and the velcro gave way easily.

As she started to lift it to her shoulder, Drew lunged on top of her. He grabbed her, slamming her against the scaffolding so hard that the gun slipped from her hands and dropped to the ground far below. It struck a cop on his shoulder, knocking him to the ground, and then bounced and landed on top of some flowers that had fallen from a bouquet.

Drew tried to wrestle Stephanie into submission. She kept saying, "No, no, no!" biting him, kicking, squirming. The Canadian technician, having seen the gun, came to Drew's aid, subduing her before they all fell off the scaffolding. In moments, the authorities had rushed up the rungs of the scaffolding and slapped cuffs on her. They took her away in a police van, to the ignorance of most of the people gathered in the square.

Drew called Mike inside St. Peter's to tell him what happened. Then he shoved his way past police, security people, Swiss Guard, and assorted others who told him there was no more room in the basilica. He had to get to Quinn. Half the team of PR01 assassins had been stopped.

But there was one more to go.

Chapter Twenty-six

The procession into the basilica was endless. Nuns and priests of every age, shape, and color, monks in brown robes, from Europe and Africa and South America, hundreds of young Italian altar boys, the College of Cardinals in crimson, monsignors, bishops, and a choir made up of voices from all over the world. At the end, the Pope passed. Quinn expected him to be carried on a throne, but when she saw him she realized *not this pope*; that was in the old days. He walked along, full of vigor, stopping constantly to reach out his hand to the pilgrims who were celebrating with him. Quinn herself got a light touch of his powerful, strong fingers, and felt the ring that everyone so famously kissed.

She saw Mike Furnari standing along with other grim men in suits near the altar. But she searched the choir in vain for her daughter. There were so many girls that it was difficult to scan all the faces. Stephanie had said, "Sing loud." That was Quinn's clue that her daughter would be hiding in the choir.

But as the singers passed, Quinn was sure Joanie wasn't one of them.

The Pope took his place near the altar. Quinn scanned the program someone had handed her when she entered to see what would happen next. A prayer by some cardinal, followed by a soloist, followed by the Pope's celebration of the Mass. Quinn was the only person in the vast cathedral who didn't bow her head during the prayer. Her eyes searched in vain for Joanie.

Suddenly, she felt someone pushing against her, trying to shove her away from the end. "Per favore, no," she started to say, wanting to stay on the end.

It was Drew. She grabbed his hand, made room for him. "Did you find Stephanie?"

He nodded. "It's okay. The police have her." Everyone was making the sign of the cross. The cardinal had finished the prayer and the Pope was blessing everyone. "Joanie?"

"No clue."

The Pope seated himself with the help of two priests who cared for his gleaming white-and-gold robes and turned toward a small podium set up near the organist. Quinn looked in the program. "Some girl from France is going to sing now. I thought Joan was going to be in the choir."

He blinked. "Why?"

"Steph told her to sing loud."

"Everybody sings," Drew reminded her.

"Where is she?" Quinn whispered, looking around. "How do we find her?"

The music started and they turned their attention to a woman who was ascending the stairs to the podium. She carried a violin case. "Francine Voullet," Drew said. "I've seen her on television. She has a beautiful voice, accompanies herself on the violin."

Quinn looked apprehensive.

"I heard people outside saying she was going to per—"

He didn't finish the word. Quinn's fingernails dug suddenly into his hand as they both realized what they were seeing. The girl was not the French singer at all. It was Joan Roberts. She had her head covered with a soft veil, but Quinn and Drew were close enough to know who it really was. She set down the violin case, curtsied to the Pope, and then clicked open the two spring locks on the case. Drew and Quinn knew what was really in there.

"No!" Drew shouted.

Everyone in St. Peter's turned to him.

Quinn shouted, "Joanie! No!"

They started running toward her.

In what seemed like slow motion, Joan Roberts pulled out the rifle, expertly clicked it together, and raised it in her arms. All at once people began screaming. As police came running down the aisles, Quinn and Drew began a mad dash to stop her and to protect her. "Don't shoot!" Mike Furnari cried.

"Don't shoot *her!*" Quinn shouted.

Drew leaped over the small skirted rail around the podium, throwing himself at the girl, grasping for her feet.

He was too late. Joanie had gotten the target in her scope. All the months of programming, the gun practice in Germany shooting cans and bottles and birds, and the download of the final Front Runners programming on Good Friday had finally led to this moment. A shot rang out.

But it was not directed at the altar. It did not go near the Pope. It went in the opposite direction, aimed at a group of monks. One buckled, his face frozen with shock as the bullet blew into his brain. Tyler Bryant, dressed in a brown hooded robe, died instantly.

The Swiss Guard threw themselves on the Holy Father as more shots rang out and Quinn's nightmare became real. She screamed in horror as she saw blood spurt from her daughter's chest, watched her fall on top of Drew. "Joanie!" she screamed, pushing her way toward them. "Joanie! Noooooooooooo!"

The last thing anyone would remember hearing that day was Quinn's grief-stricken voice reverberating throughout the ancient building.

Epilogue

Joanie rushed over the lawn from her dorm toward Quinn and Drew. Quinn opened her arms and her daughter ran into them. "Oh, I'm so glad you came!" Joan kissed Drew and hugged him as well.

"You know," Quinn said, "you don't look bad for a kid who had a collapsed lung and a bullet lodged in her shoulder."

"I'm resilient, like you," Joan quipped. "Honestly, Mom, I'm feeling great."

"How's school?"

"Almost over. I've made up most of my classes. Hey, look at the flowers." She picked one and pointed to a bench. "Come on, sit down. Let's talk."

"You know," Drew said, "it's almost like it didn't happen, like it was all some crazy nightmare. The new game hits the stores running, retailers can't keep up with the demand, kids love it, and nothing sinister happens. It's what we hoped for."

Quinn nodded. "We held our breath while you were in the hospital in Rome, but there was no uprising, no insurrection, no burning of houses of worship, no more killings of religious leaders. No one knows what almost came to pass."

"Well, they might," Joan said.

"What?" Quinn asked.

Joan pulled a folder out of her book bag. "I wrote about it."

"Ah," Drew guessed, "Journalism 101?"

"I did it for class, but I think maybe I'm going to try to sell it to a magazine. See, I think it's important that people know about it—all of it." She handed it to Quinn. "This page is the end. I typed it this morning. You can read it out loud, if you want. I won't be embarrassed."

Quinn, rather liking that Joanie was showing real direction toward a goal for the first time in her life, did so:

"Without that final call from my mother, I would have done it. I would have been a martyr for a cause I had no control over believing in. But the thing that Tyler never counted on was that no one can ever truly program God from our lives. Faith, something to believe in, is as human as breathing. It was my mother's voice that reminded me of that. Even though I was programmed to carry out the ultimate rejection of all things religious, my mother's voice meant faith. She has always had it, believed in it, and counted on it. Her voice touched something inside me, some power deep in my soul that made me turn that gun on the real evil and pull the trigger.

"So I wonder. Was it the power of God that saved me?

"Or was it the power of love?

"Or are they the same thing?"

As Quinn finished, tears were forming in her eyes.

"I'm proud of you, darling," she said, and pressed Joanie's head to hers, whispering, "I love you so much."

Joan pulled away and smiled. "We can't get all maudlin now, it's too great a day. So what are you two up to?"

Drew said, "Since I took over Zzzyx, I've been working on Practice Run VI, which, I'll tell you right now, will reinvent on-line gaming."

Joanie laughed at his phony seriousness. "What about Mike?"

Quinn smiled. "Mike has been promoted to the head of the computer fraud division, taking over David Dahbura's place." Then she laughed. "We go running with him every Saturday."

"How's Aunt Susan?"

"You're not going to believe this," Quinn said, "but she and James are moving to Ireland full time."

Joanie looked startled. "But you work together."

Quinn assured her, "She can do it from there. Besides," she added, taking Drew's hand, "we plan to visit her a lot."

"Really?"

"We're going again in June, as soon as you're out of school. And you're coming with us."

"I am?"

"Yes. Because that's where we're going to be married." Quinn saw the look of delighted surprise on her daughter's face. "And you're going to be my maid of honor."

Joanie gasped. "Again?"

Quinn chuckled. "I promise, darling," she said, moving closer to Drew, "this is for sure the final run."